THE CRUDE KILLER

A Spike Eastman Novel

by

Mick Burkard

Tom —
No Soliciting!
Thanks —
Mick Burkard

DORRANCE
PUBLISHING CO
EST. 1920
PITTSBURGH, PENNSYLVANIA 15238

Dorrance Publishing Co
585 Alpha Drive
Pittsburgh, PA 15238
Visit our website at *www.dorrancebookstore.com*

ISBN: 978-1-6366-1393-2
eISBN: 978-1-6366-1970-5

ACKNOWLEDGMENTS

Thank you to Sandy for everything, support to get the book done, picking up the slack, and providing some of the best ideas for the book. Thanks to my brothers and sister who provided feedback. Special thank you to Tim Flynn for his help.

Much of the research for this work was done using internet sources. The places were mostly imaginary. Spotted Cow is real. You can't get it outside of Wisconsin, but it is worth the trip for many.

The assertions about government, the War on Terror, the threat from Russia and China are the characters' opinions. I fully support Spike's idea that our military and CIA are worthy of our admiration. Thanks to Ty Alexander, Dave Allvin, Hugh Brennan, Bob Holba, Steve Hughes, Jim Gulsvig, George York for your full military career and to Phil Celestini for his FBI service.

For Steve "Cowboy" Hughes,
who inspired me to write. RIP, Cowboy.

PRELUDE

Sheboygan Memorial Hospital
Sheboygan, Wisconsin

Standing in the hall of the hospital and peering through the window to ICU room 314, Spike answers, "Boss, from a macro perspective, the crisis would need to last another two years before it would cause us to make big changes… We've got cash reserves and plenty of inventory to meet our current order volume for another four months.

"Our suppliers are aggressively meeting our requirements; construction activity is continuing albeit at a slower growth rate; and the infrastructure bills in Congress will continue to support several of our key business lines. The biggest threat is macro shifts in commercial real estate, as many large employers are learning that people don't need to congregate in central headquarters buildings. As you know, our restart plan will spur competition between the plants—Jim, I gotta go."

Spike pressed end. He turned to call for a nurse, but Doctor Huebrex and two assistants were running toward him before he could say anything. Doctor Huebrex looked flustered, in contrast to the confident demeanor he'd displayed four days ago and two hours ago. His stethoscope was following him like a cape.

Huebrex yelled, "Code Blue, room 314," as he ripped the door open.

Spike thought back to his mom's life. Bridget Eastman had been the rock for their family of seven. The one who everyone took for granted while she took everyone to their practices and games. While Jack, her husband of sixty-four years, was a good dad who made it to all the games and banquets, it was Bridget who made sure dinner was on the table, the household ran, and the kids made it to all their functions. Bridget was a saint; she was Spike's mom; and she had done so much for so many people. He thought about the time one of his brothers, Fred, was in trouble for public drunkenness and disorderly conduct at nineteen years old and the phone rang at 2 a.m. Jack had wanted to let him spend the night in jail. Bridget said, "Jack, you and I both know we did worse; I'm not going to let Fred sleep in jail to teach him a lesson." She was always the one keeping the family together. And here she was, the victim of a silly, stupid, silent enemy but still pulling us together. Death by drowning in your own immunity fluids.

Spike thought, *How can this happen in the greatest country ever? How?*

Turning back to the glass, Spike saw Doctor Huebrex turn away from Bridget. He looked through the glass with a thousand-yard stare. Suddenly, he shook his head and waved Spike into the room. Spike pulled on his facemask and entered.

Doctor Huebrex shook his head, "Spike, I don't think she'll make it, but try to talk to her. I don't know any medical solutions at this point, but if she continues to fight, she could make it."

Spike thought back to a discussion just two hours before. He remembered recent doctor appointments with her primary care doctor. She had said, "I'm eighty-five, and I'm ready to join your dad." Jack had died three years earlier from a massive heart attack at age eighty-five. One morning, after bringing Bridget her morning coffee in bed at 6:30 a.m, Jack walked back to the kitchen to read the morning paper, which was his habit for the past fifty years. He would start with sports, then local, then national news. He would always finish with the comics and Sudoku. That morning, Jack Eastman never made it to Sudoku. Bridget found him at 7:30, lying next to the table. No chance—Paramedics pronounced him dead at 7:45. Bridget's life as she knew it was over—sixty-four years of love. Over.

Spike looked down at his mom, put his hand into the small access port in her ICU clear plastic tent, touched her hand, and told her he loved her. He said, "Mom, everyone wants you to live, but it is up to you to fight. Do what you think is right. We love you."

This new worldwide virus was weird. Spike's brothers and sister and some of their spouses and children were sitting five miles away at Spike's house. The only sibling who had no dangerous preconditions was Spike, who was the youngest at fifty-one years old and in decent shape. Spike's sister was the most caring and most helpful. She took care of everything...money, visits, emotional support. His brothers were all better at checking in. They called every weekend. Spike felt guilty for not being a great son. Unfortunately, the siblings all had something that left them vulnerable to the disease—diabetes, recovering from cancer, heart issues, asthma.

Finally, she turned her head toward him. She had tears in her eyes but couldn't speak due to the ventilator. She simply nodded, closed her eyes, and quit trying. The ventilator kept trying to pump air into her lungs, but she didn't want it. She wanted to join Jack.

As the tears created a river on Spike's cheeks, his jaw set hard. Dying was okay with Bridget, but it didn't seem right. She'd lived a long and wonderful life, but she wasn't done. Spike was angry. Over the past few weeks, he'd learned some things that made him suspicious of the origins of the pandemic. He needed to learn more, but he wanted to take his frustration out on someone. He reset his jaw and whispered, "Fuck it."

CHAPTER 1

Five Weeks Earlier
Sheboygan Falls, Wisconsin

BEEP—BEEP—BEEP –BEEP

Spike slammed the stop button on the alarm clock. No tech genius, he never really liked using his iPhone to wake him up. That silly, soft alarm begged to be snoozed. But a real alarm clock made you decide. Get up—dumbass!

He rolled his six-foot frame out of bed and dropped to the carpet at 5:01 a.m. Fifty quick pushups, silently, so Shauntel could sleep. No reason to wake her before getting prepared for his day. A hundred steps to the kitchen, a quick piss in the powder room, hit the mudroom for a hundred crunches on the yoga mat followed by twenty pullups on the nifty pullup bar inside the closet door. Finish up with another fifty pushups and some slow leg stretching. Next, he tossed his pajamas in the wash, put on a pair of old sweatpants and a hooded US Air Force Academy sweatshirt to start his day with a six-mile run. The clink-clink of the leash immediately brought the groggy and stretching Ginger, their eight-year-old Golden Retriever, out of the kitchen. She loved these thirty-five minutes of her day more than even eating. It was a glorious ritual, especially in the spring and fall when the early morning temperatures were around freezing. Out the door at 5:15—not a soul stirring in the quiet neighborhood of large, stately homes on the edge of Sheboygan Falls.

Spike Eastman had grown up here. He was an all-American kid who got bored often enough to get into some minor scrapes growing up. Back then, people overlooked some mistakes, and Spike was very thankful for that.

Because he went to a smallish high school, he played four sports. He wasn't a star at any of them but played everything with a hard-nosed, aggressive attitude. His favorite sport was football. He was the captain of the defense for both his junior and senior years mostly because he understood the defense and played linebacker. Then came wrestling season, and the discipline required for that sport was probably the most valuable thing he learned in high school. Track was fun—running the four-hundred-meter race was a cakewalk compared to wrestling. Then baseball. If he could have picked a sport to be good at, it would have been baseball. But, in truth, he wasn't good at all.

School was easy for Spike. He took all the college prep classes and got almost all A's. He was good at the humanities, especially foreign languages—taking both Spanish and German. Since he was ten years old, he read historical biographies and his siblings' high school history books. He was fascinated by the difference between free societies of Western Europe and North America and many of the other parts of the world. Growing up during the Cold War, he had no doubt that he was lucky to be born in the United States. Spike genuinely believed that the United States was the greatest nation that had ever existed.

When he was a sophomore, he walked past the TV and saw the Army-Navy game that his dad was watching. Spike asked, "The army and navy have football teams?"

His dad, Jack, had been an enlisted Air Force crewmember on B-29s during the Korean War. Jack smiled and thought, *I got him hooked.* He said, "Spike, these are two of the most prestigious colleges in the country. West Point is Army's academy in New York, and the Naval Academy is in Annapolis. Air Force's academy is in Colorado Springs. These schools are difficult to get into, but they're great colleges, and their graduates become officers in the military."

Spike sat down to watch the game and said, "Huh."

Two years later, Spike was preparing to enter the United States Air Force Academy. Jack was right; he was hooked by the Army-Navy game. The following Monday, Spike went to the guidance counselor's office and asked what he needed to do to get into a service academy. Since Spike's resume was headed in the right direction, Mr. Wickman said, "Just do what you're doing, and you could add one thing that would be helpful, run for student government." Since Spike knew Mr. Wickman was the faculty advisor for student government, he thought it was a little self-serving to suggest that, but whatever. And some of the prettiest girls were involved.

By the time Spike entered USAFA, he was a chiseled six-footer weighing in at 185 pounds. His long blond hair would be buzzed off on the first day, but his clear blue eyes weren't going anywhere. His natural, easy-going personality might get a bit of a haircut, too. Over the six weeks of Basic Cadet Training, he learned the motto "Cooperate and Graduate." He lived that motto for four years, finishing somewhere in the top 25 percent of his class and enjoying a somewhat normal college life.

While most of his classmates were sweating the small stuff, Spike realized it would be more fun to get enough privileges to get off the academy grounds as often as possible. Cadets called the Academy "the Zoo" because tourists came from all over the United States to watch the cadets march to lunch. Cadets felt like trained animals being watched from the chapel wall. Early in his junior year, on a Saturday night, his life changed forever. Following the Academy football team's game at the University of Wyoming, he and some buddies went to a party at the base commander's house at FE Warren Air Force Base in Cheyenne. The "mixer" was a little more formal than he was used to—sure there were a couple kegs, but they had a taco bar, hors d'oeuvres, and wine. In the line at the taco bar, Spike met Shauntel and fell in love over the course of the next four hours.

Shauntel was a sorority girl at the University of Wyoming in Laramie who was forced to go to the lame party in Cheyenne. Her sorority house mom told her that if she didn't go, she would have to polish all the silverware and coffee and tea sets. Even spending a few hours with a bunch of boring cadets couldn't be as bad as polishing the silver for the nineteen-year-old sophomore. Shauntel's athletic five-and-a-half-foot build was soft in all the right places. She had gorgeous, expressive hazel eyes with a hint of green and soft, long brown hair. While she was clearly intelligent, her true talent was reading others' intentions. Lucky for Spike, his intentions were honorable, because she may have castrated him that night otherwise.

From Spike's point of view, she was hot and offered an alternative to hanging around the Zoo every weekend. Starting three weekends later, Spike and

Shauntel spent as many weekends as they could together. Normally Spike would bring a couple buddies. The visits were always fun, always too short, and more like real college life than a cadet could expect to experience. When Spike graduated a year before Shauntel, the unspoken commitment between Spike and Shauntel was for life.

Spike's disciplined morning routine had started immediately following the terrorist attacks on September 11, 2001. He woke up at 5 a.m. on September 12 and decided he needed to harden himself. He'd been an Air Force intelligence officer stationed at Nellis Air Force Base just outside Las Vegas for a few years. Spike thought it was likely he would be headed to a war zone soon. It didn't take long for the CIA to snatch him from the Air Force. For the next eight years, Spike was deployed more than half of the time. And spouses and children couldn't go where he had to go. The sacrifices he and his cohorts made weren't understood by the people they were intending to protect. But Spike knew it wasn't because they were ungrateful. They just didn't know what it was like to be absent for months at a time. Shauntel was raising two kids in Las Vegas singlehandedly. Not how they pictured it, but her strength and emotional toughness brought them through it almost unscathed.

Ten years ago, Spike and Shauntel moved to Wisconsin to join Maurer Company after Spike left the CIA. They found a nice three-acre lot in a neighborhood just ten minutes from work. Commuting wasn't even a word in this quintessential small Midwestern county. After living in Suburban Las Vegas for several years and driving the kids to Catholic schools half way across the city, the idea of building a sprawling home on a large lot and an extra four-car detached garage seemed too good to be true, especially in the slower paced rural setting. Shauntel customized a plan with an attentive architect, and a year later, they had built their paradise. Four bedrooms on the main level with an office and monstrous mudroom with six closets and a pocket door leading to the laundry. One of Shauntel's many innovative designs.

They had plenty of space to entertain and finish raising their two children. The kids deserved it with a missing father for most of their lives and moving from Vegas to the sticks in Wisconsin during high school and middle school. They needed a place where they could work through challenges of their disrupted lives in at least some comfort. It worked out well because Shauntel knew how to help them. Shauntel could easily have been a psychiatrist or life coach or campaign manager. She used all of those skills to help her kids through the difficult process of moving at a vulnerable age. Spike acknowledged every day how fortunate he was to have made the move with this family. For the children, Penelope and Lucas, it wasn't easy, but they quickly forgave their mom and dad.

One of the main selling points of the rural neighborhood was a biking trail at the end of the second block. Rolling hills with beautifully manicured lawns for a quarter of a mile, then gorgeous rural woods and open fields. Starting out slow down the hundred-foot driveway with Ginger at his side, Spike began warming up by jogging through the neighborhood. Now he could start to get his heart rate up running the first half at a six-minute mile pace. When Spike hit the turn, he and Ginger were both ready to race home; off came the leash, and Ginger sprinted ahead looking back from time to time to be sure she wasn't alone. Spike slowly gained on her, nearly sprinting for the last two miles. As they entered the neighborhood, Spike put Ginger back onto the leash, and they slowed to a jog. Spike's lungs ached from the sprint and the cool spring air. It was another fabulous start to a day. Picking up the *Wall Street Journal* at the end of the driveway, Spike walked the last hundred feet. As he entered the mudroom, Spike pulled a half gallon jug of water out of the built-in refrigerator. After downing a quarter of it, he poured half into Ginger's water dish. While sipping on the rest of the water, he fed the dog and looked up at the clock—6 a.m... perfect timing.

Now to the shower in the custom bathroom and full walk-in closet Shauntel had designed in the mudroom area to enable Spike's awful morning routine. Stepping out of the shower, Spike heard the coffee maker finish its cycle with a quiet beep.

After a quick run through the front page with a cup of coffee, Spike delivered a thirty-six-ounce jug of coffee to Shauntel's bedside as was his habit for twenty-seven years when he was home. He'd learned at least one thing from his father, in his words, "Honor and serve your wife—she deserves the little things because she handles all the big things."

Spike returned to the kitchen breakfast bar for a second cup of coffee and to dig into three WSJ articles that had caught his eye earlier. A scandal at a large bank drew his interest since he knew some of the executives well enough not to bank with them. Some kind of new epidemic in China near the plant

Maurer Company had built in 1999. A political piece about how the broad economic expansion over the past five years had left almost nobody behind before the COVID-19 economic crisis. Now, the post-COVID recovery was helping Wall Street but working Americans were suffering.

CHAPTER 2

Spike took one last walk down the hall to kiss Shauntel goodbye and wish her a great day. He jumped into his three-year-old black Chevy pickup.

Being the Chief Financial Officer of an eight-billion-dollar global company was challenging. But not nearly as challenging as running CIA operations in some of the most God-forsaken parts of the world. A bad day at Maurer Company was a twenty-basis point jump in costs. A bad day in the war torn, lawless countries meant American operators and soldiers lost their lives. Still, in Spike's mind, solutions in the corporate jungle were similar to solutions in the war zones—listen actively, get people to do their best, learn every day, and get better by debriefing new initiatives like it was a wartime mission. And, most of all, keep your sense of humor. Nobody wants to be around crabby coworkers, even if they're brilliant. Smile a lot and don't sweat the small stuff, tell the company's story, and find people you can count on. It works in every endeavor.

Today, Spike had quarter-end preparations—meetings with accounting, financial planners, and the controllers of three of the seven divisions. Not exciting, but as the company stayed disciplined, profits continued to rise at 8.5 percent per year. Smooth sailing on rough global waters. Tariffs, nationalism, and new populism had to be considered to forecast the year and the near-term future. One large benefit of being widely spread across the globe was bad things in some markets could be offset by good things in other markets.

That thought brought him back to the article about China's epidemic. He sent a quick email to the Seoul-based controller for Asia. Jun Park started his day at 6 a.m. so Spike would give him an hour to get settled, and they would meet at 5 p.m. Wisconsin time via video conference. The years traveling around the world had made Spike sensitive to the world clock. Some people used their smart phone to track what time it was in other parts of the world. It was an automatic translation in Spike's mind.

The day progressed as expected, with solid results that would be fun to share with the CEO and Board of Directors. So far, so good. Solid planning, solid execution, and, most important, solid, honest debriefings—almost like after action reports from his former life—led to getting better every day, every week, every month, every quarter.

At 5 p.m., Spike fired up the video conference line to talk with Jun. Jun was a Korean national who had attended Stanford a few years after Spike had finished his master's there. One of Spike's professors had connected them. A great hire, Jun was hard working, principled, and smart. He understood international finance as well as the intricacies of working with global companies. His ability to predict the next market had already helped to get the company's products into the highest margin projects. Luxury construction in Asian markets was exploding. Jun was worth his weight in gold.

"Good morning, Jun, you look fit."

"I am trying to follow your morning circuit; unfortunately, Seoul's air is not suitable for outdoor running. Some days, I cannot see the tops of the skyscrapers from the street. I had to buy a treadmill. Luckily, our indoor air is well filtered."

Spike challenged, "Next month, when you visit, I'll meet you at the club, and we'll see if you like our outdoor air."

"It is a plan. I am sure I can outrun an old man who lives the good life in the brat and cheese capital of the most obese country in the world." Not allowing a retort, he continued, "Now, about this China thing, we are on day three, and it appears that the Chinese government is considering some pretty draconian measures after COVID-19 was mismanaged. The proposal includes shutting down the entire Jiangsu Province and the municipality of Shanghai. This will close our plant in Jiangsu about forty-five kilometers north of Shanghai. The World Health Organization has downplayed the risk and has been vocal about letting the Chinese handle the epidemic. Many of the so-called experts are saying it is only deadly for people who are old or already sick."

Spike said, "Huh, like our parents and my brother who's a cancer survivor. Nice, I guess they're expendable in China. But they aren't in Korea or America."

Jun Park looked grimly into his laptop's camera and said, "I was thinking the same thing, at least in my half of Korea. Maybe we should call the plant and tell them to shut down tomorrow. It is Friday morning here, and we run shorter production cycles on the weekend anyway. A couple days off might be welcome—but we will need to pay them."

"Okay, do I have this right? About twenty-eight thousand dollars per day in fixed costs plus paying the employees at about sixty-thousand dollars per day? So, for the weekend, we might get a jump of two days on employee safety, and it would cost us less than two hundred thousand dollars."

"I did the math earlier and came up with about $163,560," said Jun.

"About? That sounds pretty precise."

"I built a spreadsheet to model this a couple months ago. With all the wet markets in China, epidemics are predictable." Wet markets were open air markets where live animals and unrefrigerated meat were sold to the public and restaurants. For some deep cultural reason, these were common in China, and since the SARS outbreak in 2003, wet markets were recognized as a public health threat. After the COVID-19 world pandemic, China surprisingly allowed the wet markets to reopen. Jun smiled. "I know you never give me more than an hour to get ready for meetings like this."

"What else did you model, Jun?"

"You don't want to know, Spike."

"Are you kidding? I export your ideas to every other division controller. Why don't you bring me some samples when you visit? Then, at least you'll have some pride left when I run you into the ground." Not wanting to let Jun respond, Spike smiled and said, "Out!" and clicked out of the video conference.

As the CFO, Spike had the authority to close a site. But to be a good teammate, he presented the idea to the CEO and the division head in China. Both quickly agreed that it would be worth $165,000 to close the plant for the weekend. If the Chinese government shut them down for a couple months, other than some logistics issues, the company could handle the disruption. Maurer had almost a year of inventory plus six containers full of product on the Pacific. Some employee goodwill and an early response might save them money in the long run.

Spike thought, *Damn, that was easy*, and headed out the door before six.

On the way home, he left himself a voice message to call his Air Force Academy classmate at the Center for Disease Control in Atlanta. Steve Gulstone was a fabulous data guy. He was a typical Scandinavian kid, built like a Viking with broad shoulders filling out his six-and-a-half-foot body and sporting a nearly white blonde crew cut. His eyes were the deep blue color of a fjord and his square jaw and statuesque features made him extremely popular with the ladies and a great guy to take to Laramie. While Guls was flying for the airlines, he began doing data analysis for small businesses. He was a great pilot, but flying an airliner didn't quench his thirst for more challenging mental work. For fun, he built a model to track the movement of birds around large airports and Air Force bases to try to avoid bird strikes. After another USAFA grad had safely landed a passenger jet on the Hudson River, Guls thought about how to avoid such a debilitating accident. Statistically, it seemed nearly impossible to have both engines taken out by bird strikes. The model included large bird mating rituals, flight patterns and altitudes, and airline and military sortie patterns. Someone at the CDC saw the complex model and wondered about the creator. Since the complexity of bird movements around airfields was more intricate than pandemic movements, the CDC figured Gulstone could lead their data department. Guls took a pay cut to serve his country again, and Spike was proud to know him.

Spike entered through the mudroom, dropping his briefcase on a bench meant for removing his shoes. He put his slip-on Italian loafers in the closet and considered changing into some comfortable clothes but realized he needed to check in with Shauntel first. He found Shauntel in the lower level office. With the walkout design of the lower level, she looked out over the pool and hot tub toward the wooded lot. She had two forty-five-inch monitors and a rack of server equipment.

Shauntel's professional life was satisfying. She had a visceral understanding of consumer and public sentiment. Her one-person consulting company helped large consumer product companies find their customers. Spike watched her fingers flying across the keyboard and knew she was on a roll. No interrupting that locomotive, so he simply grabbed a Spotted Cow beer and started reading emails while monitoring the keystrokes. A few minutes later, he heard a sigh—did the locomotive come into a station, or was she just getting warmed up? Spike popped up from the barstool and swung his head around the door frame. "Hi honey, I'm home." By the look on her face, she still had some steam, so Spike said, "I'll get you that great salad from Firehouse Pizza and grab a pie for me."

Absently, she nodded, "Remember, no onions." He hit the app on his phone to complete the order, which would be ready when he arrived—probably his best use of technology that day.

Instead of taking his truck, he jumped in Shauntel's new Chevy Tahoe. The nice leather seats and sound system felt like luxury compared to his pickup. Plus, she probably needed gas, and that would give him a chance to grab some Copenhagen Long Cut. He swung by Dave's Standard station. To Spike, everything was expensive now—thirty dollars for gas and fifty dollars for dip. It's crazy that the government just made more than the convenience store. He remembered buying five tins of dip and twelve gallons of gas for twenty dollars when he was sixteen. Feeling like an old curmudgeon, he hopped back into the SUV and headed downtown.

The pizza place was busy as usual. Most of the forty tables were full. He waved at a couple old high school buddies. Scott Casper and Brian Morgan were both retired, having had the good fortune of starting a local internet service provider before people even knew what that was. When they were bought out by the big phone company, they invested in a dozen cell towers. Good tech vision led to early retirement and lots of evenings for storytelling. Both had hobby farms and some investment properties. Surprisingly, they were in better shape than they were when they played high school football for the Sheboygan Falls Falcons. Spike paid for his order and three bottles of Spotted Cow and headed over to say hello. The owner noticed the change of heart and put the pizza under the hot lights and the salad in the cooler. One thing about small town restaurants is that they anticipate better than city folks.

Scott smiled when he saw the bottles. "Spike, you've been corrupting us since we were fourteen. Here we sit, drinking water with our salads, and you show up with our favorite vice."

Spike said, "I figured you two farmers need to quench that thirst from working the fields, right?"

After a clink of the bottles, all three took a long pull that drained half their beers. Spike grabbed the closest chair and asked Brian, "Any chance I could get you to train another Golden for me?"

Brian said, "Sure, but it will cost you double this time. You just waste Ginger's talent by running her around like a Greyhound. Breaks my heart that you don't take her hunting, so I'm gonna gouge you."

"Fine, but this time, can you train her not to outrun me?" Spike drained the rest of his beer, said, "I'm going to go romance Shauntel. See ya, boys."

Spike grabbed the order and headed home. As he drove, he remembered the secret drinking spot of his youth across the river from downtown and wondered how many times the police just shook their heads and didn't bother to harass them. Not how it works any more. Sort of a shame that we don't let kids mess up like we used to.

Delivering the pizza and salad to the lower level bar, Spike hollered, "Time to eat." As he laid out some plates and silverware, he heard about a minute of heavy keystrokes followed by the sound of the printer firing up. He put the salad on her plate, snatched a couple napkins from the cupboard, and sat down.

As she grabbed a couple bottles of water from the bar fridge, she smiled and said, "That was fun."

"What, honey?"

"Dottie, from my largest grocery account, wanted to know what people would buy if we had a flu epidemic. They wanted the answer by 5 a.m. tomorrow, so I just finished it tonight. I just printed the invoice I'm going to send them. Pretty good, four hours of work, and I'm billing $12,500."

Spike frowned. "What?! I thought your billing rates were three to five hundred dollars per hour."

"They insisted on fast data, and I told them it was a flat rate deal—fifteen thousand dollars, but I settled for twelve thousand five hundred."

Spike looked at her with a hint of skepticism. "That's a pretty smart company; what are they expecting to happen?"

Shauntel looked unconcerned. "This outbreak in China could come here, and they want to be prepared. If they listen to me, tomorrow morning, they'll place record orders for cleaning products, bleach, hand sanitizer, bottled water, and toilet paper. It is a repeat of COVID-19, and all of those items were hard to find for the first sixty days last year."

"Toilet paper?"

"People hoard the necessities before a big snowstorm. They'll buy toilet paper by the cartful, just like last year. I'm no economics genius like you, but if I were in their shoes, I would jack up the price too. Zero price elasticity when people panic."

"Panic, holy shit. This is the second conversation I have had this evening the new epidemic from China. What did the news channels say today?"

"After a few articles in the influential newspapers this morning, all the news channels and CNBC were warning that this is COVID all over again—the equity markets dropped 4 percent, and gold soared. Based on that panic, I feel rather good about my recommendation to Dottie. About fifty people died in China, and they only discovered it a couple days ago."

"Do they know why it kills faster than COVID?" Spike inquired.

"Nobody knows yet, but the World Health Organization is on the case. They weren't ready to call it an epidemic and downplayed the idea of spread outside of the immediate area—I think Shanghai and the province to the north."

"Remember when we visited Shanghai—wall to wall people. I hope this isn't as contagious as COVID-19."

"Who knows?"

CHAPTER 3

Two weeks later

Spike's morning ritual was evolving. Following his normal morning exercise regime, he began flipping on the news. Online news was often wrong and difficult to rely on. The networks seemed to be the most up to date and had more accurate data. The downside was their automatic liberal bias, but it was worth it because they aired government news conferences. Trusting either the media or politicians wasn't easy for Spike. He'd spent years seeing almost comical misreporting on the things he'd seen firsthand in the war on terror. But watching the Governor of Texas, the Supreme Leader of Iran, the President of the United States, the Chairman of State Affairs of North Korea, and the Premier of China all saying the same things was both convincing and unprecedented.

Less than three weeks had passed since the first cases were diagnosed in China. The most common quote on network TV was "Nobody knows how this will play out." The most trustworthy sources, the World Health Organization internationally and the CDC in the United States, were dumbfounded. The sickness that followed infection was much more serious than people initially thought, but the solution was unknown largely because the professional disease trackers couldn't pinpoint the source beyond the wet market in Shanghai. The epidemic was similar to SARS, MERS, and COVID-19 in that it attacked the respiratory system. Like SARS and COVID-19, it originated near an open wet market in China. But the epidemiologists couldn't find any connections from the local area. One thing was for sure—you don't want to catch this virus.

This virus wasn't just attacking and killing the weak and old. At first, it appeared to be the equivalent to a serious flu or winter cold for healthy people. But, less than two weeks after the discovery in China, William Williams, a well-known athlete and celebrity in his thirties, was in the ICU in Shanghai. Everyone expected his recovery to be reported soon. And then a day later, Williams died. Physically fit, highly engaged on social media, he was an icon of Chinese and American culture. William Williams, Billy Big Shot, a former NBA player, and NCAA National Champion who hit a buzzer beater to win the Elite Eight game that brought the University of San Diego to their first Final Four, just died at age thirty-one. Following a good NBA career, he loved the attention he garnered in China playing for the Shanghai team. Billy had built a brand beyond any NBA star in the US and China had four times as many people. Everybody knew who Billy Big Shot was—and he died of this virus. The virus wasn't even named yet, and it took an icon. The unspoken news that hit America and China was "Holy shit, this can kill anyone."

And the virus struck without discrimination. Rich people, poor people, healthy people, street people—everybody was affected. Other than the fact that the infections spread from human to human, the WHO and CDC couldn't seem to connect the movement. That lack of scientific proof alone was causing worldwide panic. After starting in China, it spread to other Asian countries first. Korea, Japan, Southeast Asia were seeing thousands of new infections daily. Given the world economy and travel between these countries, nobody was surprised. The speed of the infections in the Middle East was significantly ahead of Europe, which seemed to be an anomaly. The US infection rate and speed was more in line with Europe, but the US had quickly built physical barriers. The federal government began shutting down international airports, tracking outbreaks by metropolitan area, and quickly searching for medical clues to help slow the spread. Having learned from COVID-19, the US was able to slow the spread by quickly implementing work from home, requiring masks, and limiting large gatherings. At the same time, many citizens were skeptical due to the panic and infringements on rights during the COVID-19 pandemic had seemed political rather than based on medical facts. The infection rate seemed to be controlled in many areas. The largest metro areas, New York, LA, and Chicago, were winning the battle with fewer than ten thousand infections in these cities. Inexplicably, less dense areas like West Texas, Louisiana along the Gulf Coast, Alaska, North Dakota, and Wyoming were suffering high infection rates and hundreds of deaths per day. Per capita, North Dakota citizens were ten times more likely to be infected than people who lived in the high-density cities like San Francisco or New York.

Internationally, this had become a pandemic, and the World Health Organization finally admitted that a few days ago. Almost half a million people were already infected worldwide in just two weeks after the original announcement. Fatality rates, which wouldn't be easy to capture or understand this early in the outbreak, were reaching 10 percent. Public health professionals who studied pandemics and epidemics hinted that this could lead to 25 percent rates as the pandemic spread. Now, just three days later, the number of cases worldwide had shot up to seven hundred thousand people. That's still minute compared to 7.8 billon people worldwide, but if it continues to explode at this pace, 5 percent of the population may be infected within two months.

After Maurer had closed its plant in China, the entire Jiangsu province and Shanghai had been closed down. The plant closed a few days ahead of the government orders. The daily losses for the company were almost all related to personnel expense. The Chinese government had been willing to fund some of the loss, but Maurer Company had simply declined. Becoming beholden to Beijing wasn't a good long-term strategy.

Spike thought back to his phone conversation with Steve Gulstone two weeks before. Spike had asked, "Guls, what do you think about this outbreak in China?"

Steve hesitated and said, "I don't know for sure, but the models don't seem to match the early results. People are dying faster than previous pandemics, and the idea that this is just another bird flu seems too optimistic for me."

Spike did a quick search on bird flu and found out that the Spanish Flu from the early twentieth century killed about fifty million people worldwide. Considering the world population was 1.6 billion then, today that would be 250 million people dead. The US population was only about fifty million in 1918, and 675,000 people died. These are a dramatic numbers when you consider today's world population is nearly five times larger, and the US is six times larger. Spike realized though extrapolating the numbers that we were talking four million Americans. His buddy had his attention.

He asked, "Guls, are you talking Spanish Flu, SARS, H1N1, or COVID-19? It's a big difference."

"I don't know, but this isn't SARS, MERS, H1N1, or swine flu. I used data from all of these outbreaks plus Spanish Flu and COVID-19. The closest based on early data is the Spanish Flu. Because it wasn't as deadly, COVID-19 isn't a good comparison and we know the counting was skewed based on financial incentives to hospitals to report as many cases and deaths as they could. Unless I'm misreading the data, this is going to be a disaster. It is almost as if someone did this exact same analysis and then reverse-engineered the virus. Built it to hit hard and set it free."

"Why am I not reading this in the paper or seeing it in the news?"

Guls expected his buddy to be skeptical. Spike was always a little nervous about the government. He didn't want to raise a red flag that hadn't been fully vetted, but he trusted Spike's ability to keep things close to the vest. He simply said, "If the public saw my models, all hell would break loose. Shit, maybe I'm wrong, but I think this is exponentially bigger than COVID-19. The analytical problem is multifaceted. We really can't trust China's reporting; the World Health Organization is either incompetent or in denial. I'm just looking at the data as reported in countries we can trust: Japan and South Korea."

"And what are you learning?"

Guls sighed. "We'll see, but this seems big already."

"But too early to tell?"

Guls said, "Call me on my mobile in a couple days. I'll validate this—but you can't tell anyone until it's clearer." Guls laughed. "And go buy some toilet paper; it's gonna be gone in a few days."

Spike thanked him and hung up. For the first time, he was becoming concerned for the company, their workers, and the financials. Should he bring this unconfirmed information to the CEO? Should he start shutting down plants worldwide? He thought about Jun Park's model and decided to call him later that day. It would be Saturday in Korea, but Jun would answer his call. Maybe it was time to run financial models to understand the risk to.

Daylight Savings Time was a wonderful thing. It was still bright and sunny when Spike picked up the phone to call Jun at 6:45 on Friday evening.

Jun would be through his first cup of coffee in Seoul at 8:45 Saturday morning.

Jun answered with his normal energy, "What's going on, Boss?"

Spike was careful not to sound too worried when he said, "Jun, I need some help. I'm glad we shut down the China plant for the past couple weeks, but I'm already thinking it isn't enough." He hesitated but pressed on as he thought about Jun's clear loyalty and devotion. "What would you need to model the costs and implications to revenue for all of our plants to shut down?"

"Whoa, Spike, are you serious? That seems very premature. What I am hearing shouldn't require that kind of response."

"Jun, I'm generally pretty calm in a crisis. You know my government background and being the financial caretaker of a fabulously well-run company really doesn't match the level of stress I was trained to operate in. I'm just telling you that this may be an unprecedented outbreak."

Jun panicked. "Are you telling me that I need to worry about my family?"

"Yes, in fact, before you do anything else, take care of them. Tell your parents and your brother and sisters to shelter in place. Seoul has at least twelve thousand cases already, and fatality rates will lead to at least twelve hundred deaths. That isn't great, but I'm afraid it is the tip of the iceberg."

"Okay. Please email me the latest data from the quarterly unit report that each division builds, I can run my model for the company. I'll get it done by Monday morning your time."

"Thanks Jun. Three more things: First, please make the model so I can move the assumptions by division. Second, don't go into the office to do this. That's more for your safety than anything else. And, please, let's keep this between us for now. There will be enough panic anyway. Oh, and run the model at 60 percent, 80 percent, and 100 percent payroll. I want to be sure I can make a sound recommendation to keep paying our workers. At the same time, if we go under, nobody will get paid."

Realizing how ominous the situation was, Jun asked, "I need a start date for the model, and I won't have a clear view yet of what product is in transit by division, so I'll assume 60 percent of the past month's production, okay?"

"That's a good assumption, and please model two start dates: As early as this Tuesday and this Friday, but I would really like it if you can build so the dates can vary by division. I'm not sure how soon I can run it by the leadership committee. I'm also not sure how fast some of our host nations will react. Some might beat us to the punch, but your models will go a long way to explain our plight. Also, do you need an end date?"

"No, the model runs cumulatively for twelve months, but it would be easy to expand further. I pray we will not need that."

"Me too. I just sent the reports. Go take care of your family. And wear your facemask and gloves. Who knows how contagious this is." Spike thought of Jun's situation and realized he had something more to offer. "Jun, please feel free to use the company pension on Kanghwado. It might be smart to bring your family there. Even though the virus is sparing most metropolitan areas, I'm pretty sure you're better off on the island."

"Thanks Spike. Based on the outlook, I don't think I'll be visiting headquarters any time soon."

"Jun, be safe and help your family." Spike disconnected.

Since his initial call to Steve Gulstone at the CDC, he had stayed in contact via a burner cell phone that Guls had purchased. When Spike received a coded text message about one of the girls Guls had dated in Laramie, he knew it was him. He started to wonder how the CDC was treating him if he needed to hide his communications with old friends. It made more sense when the official statements from the CDC didn't match what Guls was telling him. This was getting serious, but the feds and CDC must have feared panic, riots, and looting from the pandemic. Due to the recent COVID-19 pandemic and rioting due to perceived racial inequities, people were on edge. As they learned that this seemed more deadly but less contagious, Spike speculated that they didn't want to repeat the economic shutdown that precipitated the current recession and difficult recovery. Public health is a challenging career, but two large events during less than a year was feeling a lot like two bird strikes on the same takeoff. Guls' continuing comparison to the Spanish Flu was what caused Spike to enlist Jun today.

He prayed for Guls to be wrong, but his gut was telling him that this virus was going to be a disaster.

CHAPTER 4

A week later

Spike sat in the boardroom adjacent to the CEO's office. The normal group had gathered to discuss first quarter results. They gathered differently—mostly via video conference. First quarter results were not impacted by the newly named Mega-Acute Respiratory Virus (MARV). This name was an attempt to avoid any controversy caused by naming it after the area of origin. MERS, Middle East Respiratory Syndrome, was the last time a region was named in a pandemic. Apparently, that wasn't allowed any longer. The quarter had been great, outstanding productivity and huge growth versus the mostly unaffected matching quarter from the previous year. The only two gathered in the boardroom were Spike and Jim DePacker, the CEO. They had sat twenty feet apart at opposite ends of the mahogany table. Nobody was focused on the first quarter.

Jim had been with Maurer Company for almost forty years. His father had worked for the company before him. After earning a BS and master's in engineering at the University of Wisconsin, Jim started in plant operations and eventually became the global head of production. For about five years in his thirties, he had been an accomplished sales leader. When he returned to operations, some of his time was spent building and designing plants in other countries. His innovations included designing plants with automation in mind. The only hole in his resume was in finance, so he sought out an accomplished

CFO and found Tim Blust. Jim was built like a string bean on a six-foot frame. DePacker's full head of brown hair didn't seem ready to fall out or turn gray even at sixty-four years old. Jim was sometimes stopped for autographs in airports and restaurants because he was Tom Selleck's lookalike, including the prominent mustache. As CEO, he was a good leader, but his innovation and vision were his strongest traits.

For the second time in two years, the world economy had changed in a few weeks. Due to the experience from COVID-19, individuals and state governments were prepared. Social distancing, a term nobody knew two years ago, was well-defined and understood today. People knew what to do, and many people had bought personal protection since COVID-19 died down. Disinfecting wipes and hand sanitizer weren't just for germophobes anymore. So, more quickly than during the last pandemic, people locked down at home. This was okay for some industries. About 35 percent of the American workforce could effectively work from home. Unfortunately, the travel and hospitality, retail, and manufacturing industries, which were hit so terribly just one year before, were now reliving their worst nightmare. Due to the fast reactions, MARV was already under control in almost all the cities. The largest distinction between these two pandemics was the fatality rates. It was still too early to predict the fatality rate, but greater than 5 percent of the cases resulted in death in just three to eight days. Like most epidemics, it was difficult to know how many people went untreated and simply beat the illness on their own. Hospitals had a good handle on treatment, but for some reason, some people didn't respond. No clear pre-existing at-risk conditions had been identified. Scientists and researchers were unable to uncover a link between the fatality rate and some other condition in the fatalities.

Still, governors, mayors, and the federal government were already beginning to look past the pandemic. Some states had already begun lifting restrictions. Even California and New York, where the expectation was another year long lockdown like COVID-19, were expecting to restart more normal activity next week. That wasn't devastating to the economy—similar to a European holiday—four weeks of shutdown. The CDC and WHO were talking about the fast reactions along with the difference in the disease. Steve Gulstone's initial analysis comparing MARV to the Spanish Flu was not valid because MARV wasn't as contagious as initially believed, so the number of cases never approached the initial projections. Still, there was some disconnect trying to trace how MARV moved to some areas. It seemed to be airlifted into places versus spreading through contact of people traveling from other infected areas.

People had begun to get a little optimistic, and the financial markets had mostly rebounded to nearly pre-MARV levels. The big outliers were interest rates, oil and gold commodities, and REITs. It was obvious why interest rates were exceptionally low, as all the central banks were trying to stave off another recession. Oil prices had dipped during the COVID-19 pandemic due to market forces related to supply and demand and made worse by the Saudis and Russians engaging in brinksmanship on their production levels. Crude oil prices never fully rebounded last time. Gold had been overpriced going into the MARV outbreak, but after an initial surge surprisingly fell during the outbreak. Finally, REITs, especially those with large retail and office holdings, dropped precipitously. REITs that weren't related to healthcare had been suffering for more than a few years, got hammered during the COVID-19 pandemic and didn't rebound along with most of the rest of the market.

When Spike joined Maurer, his role was corporate strategy reporting to the CFO. Tim Blust was a seasoned CFO at the time with eight years in the role. Spike happened to sit next to Tim at a bar in Paris while Spike was attending a Terrorism Task Force Forum with several European allies' security services in 2009. Tim was in his early sixties with a round face and pear-shaped body. His shiny bald head had white hair skirting his ears with long sideburns and a mullet well past his collar in the back. His most prominent features were his pronounced, bulbous red nose and bright blue eyes. Tim loved food and whiskey, and it showed. At the time, Spike was thinking about being done with the CIA. Spike overheard Tim mention Oostburg while he was speaking on the phone. Spike got the bartender's attention and ordered Tim a refill along with a beer for himself. When Tim hung up, he said, "Do you read minds?"

Spike laughed and said, "No, but I figured someone from Sheboygan County wouldn't have just one drink."

"How'd you know? I barely have an accent."

"Tonight was the first time I've heard the word 'Oostburg' since I went to their Fireman's Picnic in 1990. They had the biggest beer garden of all the surrounding towns' summer picnics."

Tim's blue eyes lit up like a kid who just saw Santa Claus. "Did you grow up around there?"

"Sheboygan Falls. Went to college in Colorado, spent about ten years in the Air Force. Then, I joined a small engineering consulting firm specializing in Avionics. Our firm works all over the world helping US allies with fighter avionics and weapons systems." The CIA had built the legend so that it made sense how much Spike traveled internationally. In fact, the entire company was fiction, but it would have taken a lot of research to figure that out.

Tim bought it and asked a lot of questions about travel and airplanes. Spike admitted, without sounding like a whiner, that the travel was putting a strain on his personal life. It was a great conversation, but Spike, as normal, diverted the attention back to Tim's role at Maurer and life in Sheboygan County. Tim seemed impressed and told Spike, "When you want to come home, just give me a call. I'll figure out how to hire you." They exchanged business cards, and Tim grabbed the bar tab. He said this was the best meeting he'd had in Paris, grabbed his coat, and headed back to his hotel.

After a few years, Tim decided it would be a good idea to begin passing along the CFO role to Spike. Tim had five grandchildren in local schools. All of them were athletic, played instruments, and wanted to be in plays and choir. Tim and his wife Carol wanted to see every event, and that wasn't possible as the CFO of a large company. Given his lifestyle and health, Spike thought it was a smart decision but didn't share that opinion.

By the time Tim retired six years ago, everything but the controller function reported through Spike. The controller, Todd Grasse, was an accounting nerd who was ten years younger than Spike and not interested in becoming the CFO yet. The transition to CFO was easy for Spike because he could count on Todd to continue to work on the most complex tax and accounting issues. Todd was a little strange. After six years with a large accounting firm doing corporate taxes for some of the largest companies in Chicago, Todd wanted to leave the big city. After growing up in rural Iowa, he'd received a full academic scholarship to Northwestern. He realized that moving up in the big firm was unlikely due to his minor speech impediment, painfully shy demeanor, and lack of personal skills. Great accounting and tax work behind the scenes was how he moved up fast, but to maximize his earning potential, Todd needed to move on. Maurer Company was lucky to get his skills, and his personality traits were easily overlooked because both CFOs were accomplished leaders.

This night, in the boardroom, the company brain trust consisted of Spike and Jim DePacker. They wondered what was next. There were a lot of unpredictable parts to their situation. Unquestionably, their capital position, balance sheet, and high-quality brands would pull them through. Their well-known products, including high quality cabinets, natural material and manufactured flooring and countertops, gold and crystal chandeliers, were used in high-end construction. But some of their brands included low-cost replicates of their designer items, and that market may not rebound as quickly as the commercial construction in the fashionable cities in Asia and the Middle East. Time was money in those construction projects, and as soon as it was safe, work would start again. The difficulty was more centered on the unproductive expense related to MARV. This would shave margins for the year but also build loyalty from the eighty-five hundred employees who made and sold the products. Almost all their competitors and most other manufacturers had simply shut down and depended on furlough support from local governments. Using Jun's model, the executive council agreed, and Jim convinced the board that paying 80 percent for people not to work would be both fair and affordable.

Spike started, "Jim, I have to admit that I'm proud of what we've done."

"Yeah, not exactly how they would teach it in business school. I'm a capitalist, and I have to admit that not paying our employees right now is attractive. But I'm also painfully aware of the difficulty we have attracting talent when unemployment in many of our markets has been so low." During COVID-19, the company didn't pay the employees. It took an extra six weeks to get back to full capacity after they could reopen plants. That lower productivity cost them about the same as it would cost if this current shutdown continued for another three weeks. At that point, they may reconsider, and that was clearly communicated to the employees. Since many areas were set to reopen soon, Spike and Jim were convinced that they had done the right thing even if you only consider the capitalist implications. The human part was really icing on the cake.

"Don't worry too much about the expense side, Jim. Our revenue has stayed strong as the construction projects that are delayed are still ordering items, and with longer delivery times, we'll save some on shipping. In the big picture, if this ends in the next three or four months, this will simply lower our inventory of completed work. We could learn to be more efficient by meeting demand without growing our inventory. We've always been a little fat in that area, and my favorite division controller is working on models to improve our production cycles to meet demand more efficiently."

"Do you think you should move Jun to headquarters for the long-term?"

"Not an option. He has aging parents and needs to stay in Seoul. That doesn't mean we shouldn't move him into the Strategy job that we never filled after I moved on; he can do that from Korea."

"When this is over, we should consider doing that. I'm surprised by how confident he is in his models. When he explains his work to the Leadership Committee, the concepts seem so simple. But he builds these complex models to predict the results of implementing the simple concepts. I think he could be a huge asset to your team."

"While I agree, his concepts are simple in theory, but what I like the most is that he models the fog of war."

"Wait a second, Clausewitz? Models the fog of war?"

"The fog of war exists in every strategic or tactical endeavor. You don't know what you can't predict or see. The missing information can't be filled in unless you add variables to take 'unknown' consequences into account. Jun applies common sense and pragmatic human reactions to the models. That's why the models are so accurate."

"His financial forecasts for the Asia Division are almost never off by more than half a percent. Are you saying he does this by adding unknown factors?" Jim seemed unusually skeptical.

Spike answered, "Yes, and we're all better off for his skills. Placing Jun in a more companywide role will help us in many ways. I'm confident he can do it all from Seoul, but let's revisit this in a few months, okay?"

"It is a plan. You know, it's nice to just talk about business. We need to spend more time together thinking forward over the next few weeks. I think we're going to come out of this way ahead of the COVID-19 downturn. A lot of that has to do with our planning and early actions. Thanks for that, Spike. I'm not sure how Tim Blust found you, but his ability to pick talent was legendary. I'm grateful for a lot of things that have happened in the fifteen years I've been the CEO here. You are on the top of the list.

"When Tim came back from Paris, he said that he had met a CIA operative that would be a great hire for our strategy role. He said you were legendary in the intelligence community. That your cover would make your resume seem fine, but you were better than anything that could be written down. He was thrilled but not very confident he could convince you to come back home. I've always wondered what drove your decision."

"Jim, this is the first time I heard that Tim knew my real identity. Any clue how he knew?"

"Tim has a lot of connections. He looks harmless, but one of his lifelong friends is the Director of the CIA, Elizabeth Oliva. They grew up in the same hometown. Tim dated Elizabeth's older sister. My guess is that Tim called Elizabeth right after you met and asked about you. He is also close with the Chairman of the Joint Chiefs. Many of his weekend trips are to Washington. I wonder if he didn't help with clandestine operations when he traveled for business. I asked him about it once, and he gave me a very veiled response that everyone should do their duty to our country. When he told me this, his normally bright blue eyes seemed to turn gray as steel. His jaw was set, and his nose seemed to turn a brighter red than normal. Tim was a great CFO and is a great American."

"I have to admit that making a difference in the war on terror was satisfying and exhilarating. The only person I called for a job was Tim. The main reason was Shauntel and the kids. They deserved a normal life after I'd been absent for most of the kids' lives. Shauntel wanted me to have a job that didn't include a lot of international travel. I owed her so much, and I wanted to repay them for their sacrifices."

To avoid sounding too sanctimonious, Spike didn't tell Jim the rest of the story. Most people don't realize how much families sacrifice when the husbands and wives commit to serving their country. And many of the places where American intelligence officers and military members end up didn't allow families to accompany them. Divorce rates are exceedingly high, because it is hard to put lives on hold for years at a time. And when military members separate or retire, the suicide rate is the highest of any demographic. Some of that comes from the horrors they experienced, but a less-known factor is that the rest of the world simply doesn't have the culture of accountability or the willingness to sacrifice for one another that the military breeds.

Most jobs simply aren't as satisfying as helping win a battle for our nation's sovereignty and culture.

Spike thought about one of his friends from the academy who hasn't lived in the US except for professional schools and a short stint at CENTCOM headquarters. They'd graduated almost thirty years ago, and he's lived overseas twenty-three of those years. His kids barely know him. Now, he's going to the Pentagon as a two-star general. He's hoping they can stay in the DC area for five years so the kids can have a somewhat normal life during high school. His wife is a gem, and he's one of the lucky ones because she kept it together. Only a very small percentage of our military force has served before this twenty-year war on terror. Spike was proud that the US had been able to maintain an entirely volunteer force. The military and intelligence communities deserve our respect and gratefulness.

Jim asked, "How did Shauntel feel about moving?"

"Her business could be anywhere, and the simpler life of a small, Mid-western community felt right. She was concerned about moving the kids, but Las Vegas isn't the most wholesome environment. Although there is a large Air Force contingency there, it's still Vegas to most people. The amount of cash, drugs, and immorality matches the 'what happens in Vegas, stays in Vegas' marketing campaign. One misstep at the speed of adolescence seemed almost inevitable. In total, she was relieved to leave Las Vegas unscathed. And who wouldn't want me around, right?"

Jim laughed. "Yeah, you're a real prize." Spike just smiled.

It was time to head home. No big celebration for good results, but they were still turning out the lights at 8:30. Spike was happy to bond a bit with Jim. He wasn't the warmest person, but he was easy to work for and easy to be around. On the way home he thought back to how he met Tim Blust and his connection with CIA Director Oliva.

CHAPTER 5

Thirteen years before

Spike had disconnected abruptly from the intel community and never talked to Director Oliva about his decision. He was surprised that she had sent him a note to wish him well. Now he knew why. Elizabeth had run the clandestine service while Spike was an operative. They'd met only once, at Langley, when Spike was honored with a medal and citation that nobody would ever read.

Spike had been embedded with SEAL Team Six in an operation to capture an Al-Qaeda terrorist, Khaled Al-Sabani, who was intricately linked to Osama bin Laden. The Saudi national had traveled to Pakistan. The CIA received a tip from an airline employee who recognized Al-Sabani in Abu Dhabi. Heaven and earth moved to get Six into position in Karachi.

Spike was already in Mazar-e-Sharif working with a German intelligence team searching for Al-Qaeda bomb-making labs. His boss asked if he could get to Karachi by end of day. It was four in the afternoon, so Spike grabbed a commercial flight that got him there before eight. Unfortunately for the terrorist, they landed in Karachi about twenty minutes apart. Spike had worked a few years back to layout Al-Qaeda's command structure, so he had seen pictures of this scumbag. He recognized him as he walked through Karachi's Jinnah International Airport.

Karachi is a huge city with overwhelming poverty. The city had grown exponentially over the past fifty years. When Pakistan gained independence in 1947, there were less than a million people in the city. Now it was about twenty-five million. Khaled could easily disappear in the neighborhoods of Karachi. Spike's boss had arranged for a Karachi station CIA employee to pick him up. Luckily, the CIA person was only in country for a few weeks. She wasn't on the radar yet, and she was Latina. Even better, she wore a dupatta, the loose-fitting headscarf common in Pakistan. Wearing the fashionable colorful garment, she looked like an upper middle-class Karachi professional. Spike told Maria he'd meet her back at the consulate in a few hours. He knew he was lying, but he needed her to give up her personal vehicle. The two of them driving around in Karachi neighborhoods wouldn't fly. She grabbed a cab back to the embassy, and Spike waited for Al-Sabani to get to the airport cab stand. He moved quickly with a large roller bag. Spike felt especially vulnerable. He didn't have any weapons and knew he had to avoid detection. He also hated driving on the wrong side of the road. The Brits had messed up their former colonies with this stupid practice.

As Spike pulled into traffic six cars behind the cab Khaled had been assigned, it occurred to him that he could easily disappear in the city, too, but in a much more final way than Khaled. The most incredible thing happened next. Khaled took the cab directly to an American hotel just off the airport property. Spike checked in immediately after Khaled. His plans had to include another flight in the morning. This was going to be relatively easy. Snatching anyone in a foreign city wasn't risk-free. But his location, alias, and travel plans were all attainable through the sneaky geeks at Langley with a little help from Fort Meade, the headquarters of the National Security Agency. He provided the details he knew to his boss. An hour later, Spike's phone buzzed.

"Yeah," he answered.

Bruce Johnson had been Spike's team lead for two years and his main connection to Langley and the intelligence infrastructure. Bruce's cover was as the CEO of the engineering consulting firm. Most of their conversations left out a lot of details. "Your travel plans have changed. The Afghans need some help on the helicopters the US provided. Looks like the engines need some kind of additional filtering. They have Sikorsky working on it, but they asked for some help. Head to Kabul in the morning. You are booked on the first flight, 8 a.m. The Sikorsky guys will pick you up." What all that meant was that the SEALs would pick him up in civilian attire—filtering—at the airport in Kabul.

"Okay, will I still be able to make it to the conference in LA next week, or will they need more than a few days assistance?" Meaning: snatch him in transit or continue surveillance on Khaled?

"This should be pretty quick. They narrowed it down to just a few choices and really just want your input to cover their asses." This meant that, operationally, Spike was in charge, but the SEALs, as always, had a good mission plan ready.

"I'll figure out my travel plans for LA tomorrow. Thanks, boss."

Unknown to Spike, the SEAL team had bypassed Karachi on his intel. They were setting up in Kabul, and all Spike had to do was get some rest. He headed down to the hotel restaurant to carb up for the next day. He ordered spaghetti with a basket of bread and ice-cold milk. Just like the night before a football game or track meet. He loved it when he could follow pregame routines. As he was finishing the second glass of milk, he looked up and saw Khaled with two Pakistani men at the bar. They seemed to be engaged in hushed but intense conversation. Finally, Khaled handed one of the men a small envelope. If it were thicker, Spike would have assumed it was cash. The Saudis provided most of the terrorist financing in the war on terror, and even a few thousand euro went a long way in Karachi. He realized that it could be operational instructions.

Now he had a decision to make. Still unarmed, should he try to get that envelope? Nobody would even know if he blew it off. But, then again, it could be important. He went out on a limb, palmed the used steak knife from the table next to his, and followed the Pakistanis as they left. This all looked very natural because he was finished and had paid his bill, but he saw Khaled grab his phone as he was exiting the restaurant.

Spike could see the Pakis, and he was relieved to see they weren't answering their phone. He followed the two out to the parking lot. His vehicle was nearer, and he jumped in and took off to the only parking lot exit. He slowed as the Pakis came up behind him. The exit narrowed to two lanes where large monuments hid a metal gate used to secure the property. Spike was amused by the fancy etched granite on the monument that politely thanked guests for their patronage. Spike moved his vehicle to the right blocking the exit while downshifting to make the vehicle appear to be stalling. He turned off the ignition and engaged the parking brake to stop. Leaning forward to pretend to try to restart the engine, he slammed his palm on the dashboard with a dramatic flair and put on his four-way flashers. He popped the hood, hit the stopwatch function on his watch, and hopped out. He shrugged his shoulders as he glanced back at the Pakis in a small, non-descript, silver, late model Nissan. He opened the hood the whole way and heard their car door slam close. The guy who hadn't been handed the note walked around the driver's side of the vehicle.

Spike had noticed that he had been driving and assumed he was the muscle of the team. As he came around the car, he had his right hand in this light cotton suit coat pocket clearly holding a weapon. Spike had maneuvered the steak knife into his left hand hidden by his forearm.

"What is the problem?" the tough guy asked in Urdu—the most common language in Karachi.

While Spike understood a lot of Urdu, he wasn't a natural speaker and couldn't hide his American accent even if he tried. He answered in English, "It just sputtered and stopped." Most Karachi residents understand and speak English. Spike leaned in as if he were checking it out, hoping to draw the shorter, thicker man closer to him. It sort of worked, but the guy had his automatic Berretta M9 out of his pocket along his right leg presenting a do or die moment. Spike decided to try stalling. "May I ask you a favor? Could you jump in and try to start it?"

The Paki hesitated. Since he didn't answer, Spike smiled tossed him the keys on the right side of his body. He reacted without thinking and dropped the gun to catch the keys. Spike acted shocked to see the weapon and stepped back feigning fear and to get a better angle to execute a roundhouse kick. The man missed the keys and immediately started to bend down to get his Berretta. The kick landed perfectly on the side of the shorter man's jaw. He was unconscious before his head and shoulders landed on the engine. Spike was thankful that the engine wasn't hot. That would hurt even worse than a simple broken jaw, and the pain might revive the man more quickly. Spike picked up the gun and keys and decided that grabbing the man's wallet and phone could give him cover. Next, he went around the vehicle and approached the Nissan's passenger door. The slim, almost scrawny, brains of the outfit sat smoking with the window down. Spike had the gun in his right hand and put the gun to the Paki's temple. "Give me your wallet and phone," he demanded.

Whether the Paki was reaching for his wallet or gun didn't really matter because Spike threw a vicious straight left connecting with his chin. Another unconscious Paki, another gun, phone, wallet, and the main objective—the envelope. Spike ran around the car, put it into reverse, and parked it in a dark part of the lot. He looked for cameras and, seeing none, decided he'd pressed his luck enough. He ran to his car, pulled the squat Paki up by the collar, and lifted him with a fireman's carry. He dumped him into a small gulley just outside the parking lot exit along the cinderblock wall. He ran around the front of the car, slamming the hood, hopped into the driver's seat, and took off. He drove directly back to Jinnah International. He called Bruce from the road and left a message that he needed to head to Tokyo. He'd leave the car for Maria on the second level at Jinnah. Tokyo was code for aborting a mission. He didn't have code for the car, so he kept it simple. He parked on the second level of the parking structure far away from the entrance but surrounded by vehicles. He locked the car, put the keys on the right rear tire, hidden from view. He'd placed the phones, steak knife, and two guns in the glovebox. His present for Maria and the Karachi station chief.

He'd considered heading to the consulate, but he figured he should get out of the country before the morons woke up. He was sure he made the right decision as soon as he looked through the wallets in the men's room at the airport. They were from the Pakistan's Inter-Services Intelligence, the intelligence service who moonlighted as terrorist support staff. The ISI often played both sides of the war on terror. Their support of the Taliban in Afghanistan over the past decade had been suspected and often ignored by American foreign policymakers. There were plenty of radical Islamists in Pakistan; they even had their own Pakistani Taliban which was powerful along the Afghan border. The State Department was adamant that the ISI would never support Al-Qaeda, but the evidence Spike was examining in a toilet stall in Jinnah International contradicted that assertion. The evidence Spike found would be discussed and analyzed way above Spike's pay grade. He would need to be debriefed, and that might get him home for a few days. The thought made him smile.

The envelope contained two items: a photo of Maria with a phone number and address scribbled on the back and a hand drawn layout of the US consulate in Karachi. He used his Blackberry to photo the items including the ISI identification. He sent the photos to Bruce. Hopefully the device's encryption worked, because if someone intercepted a couple ISI identifications, it could lead to some uncomfortable questions. He put the ISI IDs in the trash, but he kept the photo and the sketch of the US consulate layout. He put them in the bottom of his left sock so the only way they would be discovered was a full strip search. The picture would be easy to explain; Maria was attractive and only a little younger than Spike. The sketch of an American consulate would be more difficult for an aircraft consultant to explain.

Spike went to the Gulf States Air ticket counter and purchased a one-way ticket to Manama, Bahrain. He figured with the US naval base in country, he could get to Kabul if necessary. He went through security to the gate and waited three hours for his flight. His pregame meal was probably wasted, but he was comfortable knowing he would land after the three-hour flight in Bahrain before 1 a.m. local time. He sent another email to Bruce laying out his plans and asking for assistance to get him to Kabul for the operation.

Bruce's email reply was slightly curt. "Don't you sleep? And can't you find your own rides around the world? I'll get back to you." Spike chuckled. He could see Bruce eating dinner with his wife Maureen at some fancy DC area steak joint. Interruptions in this line of work were normal, and he would be more irritated than Maureen. That was normal, too. Bruce had married his college sweetheart, who happened to be smarter and much more attractive than Bruce. In his weaker moments, Bruce admitted that he'd hit the marriage lottery with Maureen. In Bruce's twenty-six years in the agency, he'd been lucky to be stationed mostly in the Virginia headquarters and DC. He had been a Middle Eastern and South Asian analyst most of his career. His role today required him to appear to be running a far-flung but small aviation engineering consulting firm. He made appearances, lobbied Congress on avionics improvements, and went to conferences. The whole time he was really interfacing with the logistics and analysis teams at Langley for his operatives. Bruce was a big, nicely aging man who was generally very practical and frugal in his real life. But, for his cover for the past two years, he'd begun eating at the nicest restaurants, attending high society events, and getting coiffed at high end clothiers and salons. Bruce was enjoying the good life at the expense of Uncle Sam, and he felt like it was a fair payback for the patriotic life he'd lived. Most of the public wouldn't agree, but that wasn't his concern.

One time when Spike and Bruce were at the firing range practicing their shooting skills, Bruce had said, "I could get used to this, but I wouldn't spend money like this even if I really made six million dollars a year like my cover identity. I get to play the best golf courses, hobnob with important people, and Maureen gets to do it all right alongside of me. I am finally providing the life she deserves."

Spike shook his head and thought of Shauntel. Building her business and raising his family, she really was running the show for Spike. "Bruce, you should keep this gig as long as the agency will keep you. The only problem could be an oversight committee decides you're stealing from the taxpayers and indicts you."

"I thought of that, but I have all the emails showing I'm being directed to do this by Elizabeth Oliva. She's got a much longer career ahead of her than I do, so I'm pretty sure I'll be fine. She'll be the director someday, mark my words. She is brilliant, ruthless, and unflappable. She scares me a little. Besides, Congress steals more from the taxpayers than anyone."

Spike said, "Nobody says they play fair. Congressional leaders' indignant reactions when they hear of waste that they have created shows their ethics."

"Don't get me started on that. We better finish up here so we can go pretend to help Grumman with that new airframe. My presentation was created by a really smart engineer from Wright Patterson AFB. I'm going to look like a genius...again."

"You're unbelievable. I hope this isn't going to your head."

Bruce just grinned. "I got life by the ass. I'm not going to screw this up by suddenly getting an ego."

Spike boarded the Gulf States Boeing 737 jet and quickly settled in. He sat next to the window about mid-cabin with nobody in the adjacent seat. Before they were wheels up, Spike was asleep. Since his time at the Air Force Academy, he could sleep anytime and anywhere—even standing up during his philosophy class as a freshman. When the aircraft began its descent, he awoke feeling nearly fully refreshed. A couple hours of sleep is usually enough. As they landed in Manama, Spike's Blackberry started chirping. He smiled and hoped Bruce had found a way to get him to Kabul in time.

Spike walked through the airport and was met by a Marine major. The major looked very much like a Marine with a flat top haircut and pressed utility uniform. He wore wings over his left pocket and immediately asked about some fictional problem the consultant was here to solve. Spike felt he was being a bit dramatic, but in the Middle East, it is better to be safe than sorry. The major took Spike to the airport USO lounge. They entered and got a quiet table in the corner. It was the middle of the night, and a few military members were hanging around eating trail mix and drinking bottles of water. The major briefed Spike on his next steps. He would leave in an hour on a chartered flight to Kabul, connecting with the SEAL team, and hopefully getting Khaled.

As the major stood to leave, Spike nodded toward his wings and asked, "Are you really an aviator?"

"Uh, no. I'm not even a Marine."

Spike laughed and went searching for some trail mix.

Spike was pleasantly surprised when he boarded the Gulfstream G450 CIA executive jet an hour later. He was alone on the plane, which was stocked with roast beef sandwiches, an assortment of chips and beer, wine and soft drinks. There was even a full bar with some nice liquor. He thought next time he'd take advantage of the luxury. This time, he scarfed down a bag of chips and a sandwich and went back to sleep. He had set his alarm for two hours. He would want to spend the last hour stretching, eating another sandwich, and chugging a couple Cokes. He also needed to review the plan that the SEALs had sent to him via Bruce.

When he landed at Bagram Air Base, he was met at the plane by a couple of civilian looking men in their early to mid-thirties. Spike could immediately tell that these were members of SEAL Team Six. Their alert nature, athletic gait, and serious eyes were telltales. While he'd never met them before, he immediately respected them. Becoming a member of SEAL Team Six was especially difficult, even for the elite forces on all the SEAL teams. These two young men were among the top 0.01 percent of warriors in the world. The only other special operations teams that came close were in the other US military services, Israeli Special Forces, and British Special Air Service. What impressed Spike the most was how unimpressive they looked in their civilian clothes. They both looked fit but not overly thin or muscular; both were average height. They could have been from the Middle East, but they didn't look Afghani—maybe that was too much to ask. Bob Allvin and Dave Holba were

Chief Petty Officers. Spike had a whole new reason to be impressed. As they were heading to the airport, Spike learned that both had master's degrees, both were qualified snipers and medics. It would take them at least an hour to drive the sixty-three kilometers to Karzai International. Allvin was driving after mentioning something about being a better pilot. Spike was starting to think they were pulling his leg with all these qualifications, but he kept quiet. They expected the takedown to happen in ninety minutes. Spike liked their plan to grab Al-Sabani just as he left the airport at the traffic circle. Several of the team members were already in place. Spike would be in one of the two large, black eight-seat Chevy Suburban SUVs that would try to flank Al-Sabani's ride. The contingency if Spike's vehicle didn't make it in time was to have another armored sedan take their place.

From the surveillance the NSA provided, it appeared that Khaled was simply planning to take a taxi, but the planners weren't counting on that. One of the consequences of Spike running his little unauthorized operation against the ISI last night was that they wouldn't have eyes on Khaled during his travels. Langley could track him through the airports by pirating the airport cameras. So, unless Khaled parachuted out of the airliner, they should have a good handle on his movements. Spike and the two SEALs delivering him had already donned their comm equipment in the car. There was little chatter as the waiting game commenced.

The SEALs delivered on getting Spike there on time. Their vehicle was waiting right outside the main terminal just ahead of the taxi stand. They had cleared their position with airport patrols and were allowed to loiter unlike most vehicles. The call came that Khaled was the lone passenger in a burgundy-colored cab that was just leaving the taxi stand. Allvin maneuvered the vehicle in front of the cab. A surveillance drone confirmed they had the right target. As they headed toward the traffic circle, the other Suburban moved to a position a car length behind in the left lane. At least the Afghani's drove on the correct side of the road. As they entered the traffic circle, Allvin slowed a little more than normal, and the second Suburban scooted alongside Khaled's taxi. Allvin braked hard; all three vehicles stopped, and four SEALs came out of concealed positions in the center island. One stood guard while the other three simply ripped the back door of the cab open and grabbed the terrorist. They put a black bag over his head, zip tied his hands, and practically carried him to Spike's vehicle. The SEAL who had stood guard used a large crowbar to open the trunk of the taxi and grabbed that large roller bag Spike had seen in Karachi. Holba opened the driver's side back door as Allvin popped open the rear cargo door.

One of the SEALs who had grabbed Khaled followed him into the vehicle just as Holba was administering a sedative to put Khaled to sleep for a couple hours. The SEAL tossed the roller bag into the back of the Suburban, slammed the hatch, and jumped into the other Suburban. The two operators who helped secure Khaled jumped into the second Suburban as well.

Twenty-eight seconds after Allvin stopped the lead Suburban, they were moving again. Smooth as silk. Special forces operators were excellent teammates, and Spike knew if he had a few hours, he'd love to buy them a beer when they arrived at Bagram. Both the SEALs and CIA had contingent units on the air base. Spike just hoped he didn't have to jump right back onto an airplane when they got there. He sent an encrypted message to Bruce. Two words: What now? Spike knew that Bruce had seen the whole thing from the drone footage and heard the chatter from the comms.

His answer came back rather fast. Get back on the G450. The director wants his plane back.

CHAPTER 6

Two weeks later

Spike was just finishing his first cup of coffee after his normal morning routine when his cell phone vibrated. With a worldwide business, calls before 7 a.m. weren't that unusual. This one was different. Local number, but not a contact. His first thought was somebody telemarketing using the local numbers to make people answer. So, as he normally did, he answered, "Who are you, and what do you want?"

After a hesitant gasp, the caller asked, "Is this Gary Eastman?"

That surprised Spike because nobody called him by his real name. He was Spike to everyone since elementary school. The only places that people knew him as Gary were official records, like his military records. He answered, "Yes, but if you knew me you would call me by my nickname. Who is this?"

"This is the admittance desk at Memorial Hospital. My name is Greta, and Bridget Eastman has just been admitted. It appears she may have MARV, but we have begun tests to be sure."

"Well, it must be pretty serious, or she wouldn't let you call."

"She actually didn't ask me to call you, but Doctor Huebrex said he knew you from some of her appointments and asked me to call. He said, 'You should call her son, Spike; he lives nearby.' I looked up the info on her chart because it seemed too forward to call you Spike. That's how I found Gary."

"Okay, whatever. What's the protocol? Can I come see her?"

"No, not yet. I think Doctor Huebrex was thinking you would call her other children and loved ones."

"Thank you for calling. How will you communicate with me going forward?"

"We'll call this number with updates. You can call either this number, or you can call Doctor Huebrex's office."

"Thanks. I'll start making those calls."

Spike poked END on his phone and made a mental list. Start close, call west. He really wasn't sure what he'd tell them, so he started with his sister who lived in the Milwaukee suburbs about forty-five miles away. She would know what to say. He would have liked to just have her call the other three, but she would need to help by calling the other relatives. She had their numbers in her phone.

Spike headed down the hall to talk with Shauntel. She was almost awake, so he sat on the edge of the bed. As she became alert, she could tell something was wrong. Spike smiled and said, "The hospital called. Mom checked in this morning, and they think she may have MARV."

"If she told them to call, it must be serious."

"That's what I said. Her doctor told the admittance desk to call me. We can't go see her, and from what I've seen on the news, the hospitals aren't likely to let us in soon."

"What're you going to do?" Shauntel asked.

"I'm going to call Renee and my brothers. Not sure what to tell them beyond the fact that she's in the hospital and to keep their phones with them. I'll call Renee first; she can help me script this."

"She will want to take over. She's good at pulling everyone in."

"I'll insist on calling Carl, Joe, and Fred. She'll have plenty of others to call."

"What about Penny and Lucas? Should I call them?"

"Sure, but don't bother them before noon. They just need to know, but they might put it on social media before others are aware. That might be uncomfortable.

"I'll call Renee from the car. I might swing by the hospital on my way just to see the lay of the land." As he leaned over to kiss her goodbye, he said, "I love you, honey."

Shauntel sighed. "I'm starting to think 'normal' is years away." She wiped a tear she was trying to hide from Spike. "I'm sorry about your mom. I love you, Spike."

Spike jumped into the Chevy and drove down the driveway. Just a month ago, the neighborhood was hopping at this time of the morning. School kids heading to the bus, parents headed to work, a pack of stay-at-home moms starting their daily power walk. People everywhere, going about their lives. Now, eerily like last year's COVID-19 outbreak, most people were not going anywhere. Spike could be working from home, too. He just didn't think it would be smart. He had a great set up, but the communications were easier in the office. Plus, it was easier than having the headquarters entirely shut down. Most people, including Jim, the CEO, were working from home. He figured if he got the virus, he would be fine anyway. He never got sick. It was probably because his immune system had been built up through two factors: he always played in the dirt and swam in the dirty river when he was a kid, and he'd traveled to unsanitary locations during his years with the Agency.

As he started accelerating on the country roads, he told his phone to call Renee. She answered after one ring, and asked, "Is it mom?"

"Renee, I swear, you are clairvoyant. How did you know?"

"Spike, you text me 'happy birthday.' You would only call about something serious."

"Well, she checked into Memorial Hospital about an hour ago. They think she has the MARV virus but are testing her now. I asked if I could come, and they said, 'Not yet.' So I'm not sure what we should tell people."

"I think just the facts as you know them. What else did they say?"

"Just that Doctor Huebrex told the front desk to call me. Not a big surprise because Mom would have said to call you."

Renee laughed. "Yeah, but more than likely she would have said not to bother any of us."

"I'm going to call Carl, Joe, and Fred. Maybe we should hold off before calling the cousins, but I don't even have any numbers, so I'm hoping you can handle that when the time comes."

"Okay, but as soon as you get a hold of Fred, text all of us so we can start communicating."

"Good idea. It probably won't be until ten our time. I don't think Fred wants to hear from me before eight in Portland."

"They are all working from home, so it's likely they won't be up too early."

"All right. Thanks, Renee. I'll text when all of us know."

Swinging past the hospital was illuminating. The gates were closed, and a line of cars were being stopped as they entered the parking area. A large sign said, "Critical Personnel Only". What did that mean? He left himself a message to remember to ask when he called back. The hard part for a lot of families was not being able to do anything to help their loved ones, and if one in four die, the results are hard to fathom.

As he turned away from the hospital, Spike called Carl, who lived in Dallas. Carl did training around the world and was doing that from home. It would be hard to know what time zone he was acclimated to right now, so why not try? The phone rang three times and Carl answered, "Spike, what's up, dude?"

Carl was the cool one. He worked in cyberspace after teaching himself about computers. He looked like a sixties throwback with a long beard and ponytail, a little gray and scraggly. He was kind and smart. He won state math championships in high school but got a little sidetracked by marijuana when he went off to a large Big Ten school. He kind of graduated, but the details were a little hazy. He'd had some good jobs over the years, and he'd been married a few times. Later in life, Carl rediscovered the Catholic Church and was very devout after trying about everything else, including Buddhism, Hinduism, and strict non-denominational Christianity. He ended up back to where he started, and he was spiritually fulfilled. Carl also did little without applying the question "What would Jesus do?" It could be a little difficult to talk to such a reasonable, calm person. Spike was happy that Carl was doing well, but they really didn't have a lot in common.

"Well, Carl, Mom's in the hospital. She checked in this morning, and the doctor had the front desk call me. They aren't sure yet, but it may be MARV." Straight to the point and just the facts, as Renee had suggested.

"Oh, no. That's terrible. What now?"

"I don't know yet, but the hospital needed a few hours to diagnose before we really know anything. I plan to follow up this afternoon unless they contact me first. I'll keep you in the loop."

"I'm teaching a group in Italy; they're all learning from home. We can come up, and I can do my work from there." "We" included wife number three. They were all likeable enough, but this one was genuine and a wonderful life partner for Carl. Third time's a charm. She was retired, so she'd probably enjoy the trip more than Carl. It had to be hard listening to Carl teach all day. She thought he was funny, and he was really a ham. But six hours straight?

"I wouldn't make any plans until later today, but you'll probably be able to get a smoking deal on a plane ticket."

"We'd probably bring the RV. In fact, if we leave today, I could teach from Kansas City tomorrow and Sheboygan, Wednesday. It's only a six-hour class, from three a.m. our time to nine."

"How are you talking to me at 7:30?"

"I pretty much put them on hold for a few minutes. I should get back to them. Let me know what's going on."

"Will do, big brother." Spike disconnected. He was almost to work. He'd call Joe and Fred from the office a little later.

Spike went into his office; he didn't see anybody else in the building. A few people would show up during the day for work that couldn't easily be done from home. The building was built early in the company's history shortly after World War II. It was on a six-acre campus with another administrative building and two plants. One of the factories had been retrofitted to make manufactured flooring. Before that, it had made real tile flooring. While real tiles required ovens to fire the ceramic, this new product was formed in huge machines. The construction was significant. They removed almost everything, including the non-support interior walls. Then, Jim DePacker redesigned it to be far more efficient. This plant was running, but it only took twenty people to do the work that would have taken five hundred just ten years ago. Robotics and automation made it so that sixteen of the twenty could actually work from home if they had a decent internet connection. Since Scott Casper and Brian Morgan took care of that thirty years ago, almost everybody was connected in Sheboygan County. The other plant on campus was shut down. It was equally as efficient, but the inventory position versus the demand for the chandeliers and lighting fixtures manufactured in that plant created an opportunity to close down. All Maurer employees in the US were being paid 80 percent of their full wages while sitting idle at home. Many employees came in to do spring cleanup, so they didn't feel like they were getting charity. That was a pleasant surprise for Spike. He didn't know that the work ethic of their parents had been passed along. The others were mostly teaching their kids reading, writing, and arithmetic at home since the schools were closed.

Spike settled in and looked at productivity reports for the entire company. Running at about 20 percent capacity, expenses for inputs to the manufacturing process were way down, but the largest expense, payroll, was only down about 18 percent. That left the company running a little bit in the red. Warehouses were running and shipping, so inventory was being used up slowly. All in all, in a couple months when this passes, it would be a down year, but not devastating.

He worked on his email, just sort of passing time until he could call Joe. Spike looked up, saw it was 9 a.m., and called Joe's cell phone. Joe was in Denver, so he was probably already on a conference call or video conference. Joe's phone went to voicemail, so Spike hung up and texted him, "Joe, call me when you get a minute." The answer came back fast, "K-15 minutes."

When Spike's phone rang, it was Joe. "Hello, brother."

Joe answered, "What can I do for you?" Typical sales guy. He'd actually sold and installed some of the automation Maurer Company used in one of the plants at headquarters and one in Mexico. He wasn't happy that Maurer used someone else on the first plant, but Jim DePacker wanted local folks who would follow his directions to the letter. Spike had little influence as a new strategy guy so he just took the grousing from Joe. He probably thought Spike was calling to take advantage of the downtime to retrofit another plant.

"Joe, Mom is in the hospital; it might be MARV."

"Shit. Well, I guess I'll head over there." Joe made decisions fast.

"Let me get some more info first, but yeah, I think you should."

"I'll drive—its only fifteen hours, and I can push it alone. The kids are doing homeschool crap, and Shirley will have to stay back."

"I'll keep you in the loop."

"Who else knows?"

"Renee and Carl, I'll call Fred a little later. Then once I've told him, I'll send a group text and let Renee take over…as she is wont to do."

"Funny. She is good at this sensitive stuff."

"Talk to you later, bro."

Spike decided it was time to do some research. He went onto a nationally renowned college website that was fantastic at tracking these kinds of things. Johns Hopkins University was in Baltimore, and Spike's son Lucas had received his master's degree there after graduating from the Naval Academy. Johns Hopkins was better known for its medical school, but they had a highly rated master's in finance as well. When Lucas heard about COVID-19, he told Spike to check out the website. It was the authority on many statistical parts of the pandemic from the past year and again fulfilling that role for MARV. Spike compared the number of deaths to the number of hospitalizations. It didn't look good. About one in three people hospitalized died. He next checked statistics for people who had heart disease and emphysema. If you had one of these, your survival rate was about 40 percent. Both, about 10 percent. Spike became pensive, but he figured his Mom was a tough bird. She could beat the odds. Or maybe she didn't have it at all. Time to call Fred.

"Hello, Spike."

"Rat, Mom's in the hospital; it could be MARV."

Spike and Fred looked alike in the face, and they were about the same height, but Fred was wiry, where Spike was a little broader. Fred was a tough bastard. When Fred was in high school, he'd find big kids to fight with just to show them how tough he was. He was fearless, too. He had a very sarcastic bite when he was younger, so he found himself in a lot of fights. Another great thing about the old days was people didn't bring weapons to fights. They would just slug it out. Fred was an incredibly good wrestler, so he had balance and the ability to fight on the ground. Big corn-fed farm kids would try to just overpower him and usually end up on their back with bloody faces. Spike saw it happen a few times and was truly impressed.

"Shit, where would she have picked that up?"

"Huh, I hadn't thought of that. Good question. She's been pretty much housebound for the past four weeks. I think she played cards a couple weeks ago, but the incubation period is way too short for that. I don't know."

"Did anyone visit her lately?"

"No idea, but Renee and I have stayed away since this crap started again. We had her food delivered, and I guess that's the most likely source. We aren't sure she has it yet, but I'll be following up in a couple hours if I don't hear anything first."

"All right. I might bring the whole crew to visit. The kids are all working from their homes anyway. My portfolio took a hit at first, but I had plenty of cash sitting back and made two million dollars in the past two weeks. I think I should bring everyone. It is always nice to leave the left coast. These people are nuts."

Spike was proud of his brother. He'd taken risks and ended up selling his business a few years back for a very nice retirement nest egg. Nobody else in the family had been nearly that successful, and Fred had truly earned it. Sometimes, he gloated about it, but Spike didn't mind. Hell, he'd earned it. Fred's comments about Portland and the other large cities on the West Coast aligned well with Spike's view. From their perspective, the politicians had lost control—sanctuary cities, homelessness issues, outrageous city council resolutions about federal issues, and less concern about their law-abiding citizens than the criminals who targeted them.

"You know, if she does have MARV, you may not be able to visit the hospital. But we'd love to see your family."

Fred was a cancer survivor. He'd beaten lymphoma about six years before. Spike had heard newscasters parroting that cancer survivors were at risk.

"Yeah, maybe the kids and Sarah can visit her."

"I'll find out more soon. When I drove by the hospital this morning, the parking lot was blocked, and they were only letting critical personnel through. Not sure what that means, but I'll ask. I'm gonna send a text to the sibling group so we can coordinate and share updates."

"Okay, Spike. See you soon."

"Bye." Spike sent the text to the group to start communication for travel plans.

Another hour of research. He started with comparisons between the MARV pandemic and COVID-19. Statistically, hospitalizations, death rates, and confirmed cases were much different. He checked into the cancer survivor, heart and lung disease, and diabetes facts. Most of the sites said that if you were weak or old, you were in trouble. They listed the same kinds of things that they had listed for COVID-19. But this was different in a lot of ways. The symptoms of COVID-19 varied significantly by individual; it was harder to know what the end infection rate was. It may have been in the one hundred million range in the US, and many of the sick showed no symptoms. That would have put the fatality rate closer to 0.5 percent. So far, it looked like most people who were infected with MARV needed medical attention, but people were far less likely to get the disease. With stay-at-home orders implemented before a single case of MARV was reported in the US, the two pandemics were nearly impossible to compare. States and large companies with contingency plans that worked well during COVID-19 implemented them immediately where they could still protect revenue. The difficult decisions for private enterprise were when to close retail stores, bars and restaurants, and events.

As he grabbed his phone, Spike realized that he had just spent ninety minutes lost on links through the internet. That's an hour and a half he would never get back, and he scolded himself as he answered, "Hello, this is Spike Eastman."

"Mr. Eastman, this is Jennifer Parent from the hospital. We have your mom's test back, and we can confirm she has MARV."

"Can I come visit?"

"No, not right now, but depending on your health profile, you may be able to visit after twenty-four hours."

"Okay, you can tell me the details of how that works later. But, first, how is she?"

"She is comfortable, hasn't been intubated, and we have specific instructions to take no extraordinary actions to revive her. Are you aware of her wishes with respect to that?" Jennifer asked with trepidation.

"Yes, I understand her living will. I'm more concerned about her emotional status. Have you spoken to her?"

"I'm her nurse, and I'm standing next to her bed. She's in a normal room in the area of the hospital we use for the less urgent cases. She's actually giving me an evil look right now. I think she would rather tell you these things herself."

"Well, hand her the phone."

"Hi, Gary. This whole thing is silly. I got a little light-headed this morning and told Sally, my cleaning lady. She called 911 and sanitized everything in sight. Ten minutes later, they had me loaded into an ambulance, and here I am."

"Well, Mom, first of all, this must be very serious, or you wouldn't be calling me 'Gary,' and second, turns out they were right. You have MARV."

"I heard on the radio that only about three out of four of these tests are right."

"Yeah, but they miss on false negatives, not false positives. If the test says you have it, you have it. I've been reading studies from Mayo and Johns Hopkins, not the kooks you listen to on the radio. So, you have this potentially fatal virus."

"Okay, okay. So I have it. Most people survive. They don't think I need to go to intensive care, so let's not get all dramatic."

"Well, I guess you aren't going to like the fact that I already told all your kids. They are thinking of coming."

"Tell them to save their money," the grumpy old lady squawked.

"Money is fine for these people. They're probably bored at home anyway."

"So now they are going to get drunk sitting vigil for a week. Seems like an excuse to drink to me."

"Your genes are strong, Mom."

"Very funny. Well, keep me in the loop on who comes. I'm still lucid and can change my will." Mom had nothing left to will, but it was always a joke she went to when she was uncomfortable.

"Will do. And is there anything we can bring you when we come?"

"Two things. I'd like to have an old-fashioned, and I forgot my Nicorette."

"I'm not sure about the first one, but I'll try. Nicorette is easy. I'll swing by the drugstore. Those busybodies will tell everyone I'm quitting my Copenhagen habit. It will be all around town by tomorrow morning. I miss the anonymous city, but this too shall pass." Spike had bought his first tin of Copenhagen at the liquor store a block from the drug store when he was twelve. Addicted ever since, it would probably kill him, but when he tried to quit, his personality was unbearable. Even Shauntel preferred his addiction to Spike being an asshole. Now the ladies at the drugstore would tell everyone who darkened their door that he was quitting. The silly small-town stuff was an acceptable tradeoff for the wonderful lifestyle.

"Mom, can you hand the phone back to Nurse Jennifer?"

"Sure, she's lurking anyway." Spike could see his mother giving the nurse the evil eye again and laughed.

"Hi, Gary. Back to the visiting question. You must get tested before you can enter the hospital. We have a tent set up just outside the entrance. After the test, you must stay put for about an hour. During that time, you must fill out a questionnaire to be sure you are healthy enough to come into the hospital. At this point, we are allowing one visitor per patient, but you can rotate every twelve hours."

"What is on the questionnaire? What types of problems are restricted?"

"Right now, we are following similar pre-existing conditions to COVID-19, but that could change as more information emerges."

"Okay, but I don't know what that means. Is there a list of afflictions somewhere?"

"Our website has the questionnaire under the visitor tab. The list is pretty restrictive, but I see you sprinting most mornings on my way to work, so I don't think it will be a problem for you."

"Thanks. I'm more concerned about my brothers and sister."

"We hardly have any cases, but hospitals across the country are getting some pretty bad press about being too cautious. Better safe than sorry."

"Agreed. I hope she doesn't get too grumpy before I get there…for your sake."

"Don't worry, we're used to it."

Spike couldn't think of any more questions, so he just said, "Thanks, Jennifer," and disconnected.

Because he wasn't great at sending texts, Spike spoke a message into his phone for the sibling group. *Mom has MARV. She is fine, and I spoke to her. Visiting is restrictive, one person at a time, twelve-hour shifts starting tomorrow. The hospital has a list of health restrictions on their website. My guess is that none of you can pass muster.*

Asshole. I'm coming anyway, I'll be there tonight was the first response. Spike pictured Joe flying along I-76 on the flatlands of Colorado's eastern plain. He had probably left his house about ten minutes after they had talked. And the idiot would likely sleep in a drunken stupor on Spike's basement couch. The good news was that he's an unbelievably unimposing guest. The bad news is that Spike always drank too much when Joe visited.

Fred's answer was about the same. *Asshole, we'll be there tomorrow. We land in Milwaukee at 11:45 your time. We'll get a car and stay at the American Club. Five of us.*

A minute later, *We'll start driving in an hour. Be there Tuesday night. Spike, I'll bring my RV, so I just need to plug in. It's just the two of us.*

On my way. I already talked to Shauntel. She's setting up one of the guest rooms, but it will just be me. Not sure when the Dale and the kids can come. I'll be there in a half hour.

Spike responded to the group, *That was fast. Looking forward to seeing all of you. Nobody can see her today, so I will get in queue tomorrow morning. It's a process. Thanks.*

Spike knew it would be fun to see everyone but the anxiety level could get pretty high.

CHAPTER 7

Later that week

"This is ridiculous. I'm sitting here ten minutes away from my mother with no chance to see her. I'm so pissed; I think I'm going to just drive home."

"Joe, you're not going to drive home." Spike was making Joe his fourth vodka with diet 7-Up. It was the end of the first bottle in just two days. Spike was sticking with his Spotted Cow beers, but he was already feeling it each morning during his routine.

"Truly bullshit. What the fuck, Spike? This is America. I should have the right to see my dying mother."

"She's not dying yet. They moved her to the ICU today because they have plenty of space. They haven't intubated her yet, so until that happens, I'm confident she'll be fine."

"You don't look confident."

"I haven't been there today. Big Dan says it was precautionary to move her to ICU. He talked to her for over an hour today. If she was in bad shape, they wouldn't have allowed that."

Big Dan was Fred's eldest son. He was a solid, serious kid. Dan didn't exaggerate. Spike was confident in his report from the hospital. Fred's second son was due to relieve Dan any minute. Tim's reports might be vaguer. He wasn't as serious, but he was far more expressive. The plan was for Fred's third child, Alyssa, to go next tomorrow morning, then one of Renee's daughters, Bailey, would take the evening shift, and her other daughter, Kelcey, would take Friday morning. Spike would start it all over on Friday evening. As expected, none of the adults could go. Joe lamented while Fred and Carl accepted their fate. Renee was about as agitated as Joe, but she was holding her emotions to herself, withdrawing from the group.

Spike was not surprised that they each seemed to deal with it differently. Carl was simply praying. Renee seemed most pensive. Joe was angry. Fred was proud of his children being there for their grandmother. Like normal, Shauntel was pragmatic. She had to avoid conversations with Renee and Joe. She would point out too many logic errors in their analysis. Shauntel didn't want confrontation while her mother-in-law was dying. She was sure that was what the family was facing, but she only shared her speculation with Spike.

In just the last two days, the MARV pandemic had changed. In the US, the larger cities were rebounding and returning to work. In New York, they even started opening restaurants, although the rules required outside seating six feet apart or inside seating eight feet apart. Many of the best hole-in-the-wall restaurants were serving three or four tables at a time, but the lines were filling the sidewalks. Separate lines were set up for takeout, but most people wanted to sit with a glass of wine and eat a decent meal. Taking food home was getting old for most urban Americans. People were relieved to be able to restart somewhat normal life after just four weeks of draconian measures. Especially when compared to the COVID lockdown which lasted eight months in most large cities, this was much more bearable. The optimism was coming back, and the impact on the overall economy was not nearly as significant as the COVID-19 pandemic.

Still unexplained was the higher infection rate in many rural areas. Many hotspots were in low population areas that were isolated. The one that stood out most was Sweetwater County in Wyoming. Twenty percent of the population was infected. Some scientists were trying to explain it through genetic differences. Much of the population of the county was from the Southern European Slavic nations. They had moved there to work in coalmines in the early twentieth century. However, Slavic nations in Europe weren't seeing similar infection rates, so the epidemiologists were looking for other clues.

Spike finished his beer and told Joe he needed to get some work done before tomorrow morning. It was kind of an excuse, but he did want to check in with Jun Park about the actual results compared to his models worldwide. With things coming back so quickly in the US, Spike was expecting good news from Jun as he called his cell phone.

"Hi boss, calling a little later than normal today. What can I help with?"

"Jun, please work on comparing actuals versus the models you built. Try to find out which plants are restarting operations and apply the other controller's base case predictions. They know what their local governments will allow, so please just go with their direction with respect to increased production. We'll reserve the right to override them, but I think the best decisions are local decisions."

"Okay, Spike, I should have it to you by the end of my day. I already built the models; I just need to plug in dates and production levels by plant. What if they ask about your guidance?"

"Tell them to predict things based on what they know, as if it were their decision."

"Great, they might feel more connected to the answer if they don't think headquarters will be directive. I'll ask them to get their plant manager's input too."

"I'll talk to you after I review this tomorrow. Please try to keep these models in the middle of the curve. If someone seems too optimistic or pessimistic, use their inputs. It will wash out in total."

"Talk to you tomorrow, Spike. By the way, if it weren't for MARV, I would have crushed you this morning."

"I actually think you might have. I'm dealing with family visitors who have weakened my constitution a bit."

"At the top of your game, I would crush you. You're twenty years older than me."

"Ha, I'm old but very wily. I would have fed you lousy, fatty foods and convinced you to drink too much last night. You would have been sweating before we hit a mile. I'm thinking you probably would have puked at the three-mile mark. Not that I would have known because you would have been so far behind me."

"We'll see. I bet I can get there by July. And now I know your devious plans."

"Might have been a tactical error. By the way, how are your parents and family?"

"They're safe and staying at the pension and seem to think their son is a big executive for some American company. They keep bragging to their friends."

"Perfect. Talk to you tomorrow."

As Spike left his office, he noticed Joe concentrating on his tablet. He was sitting in the family room adjacent to the bar with his head down clearly concerned about something he was reading. Spike wanted to go upstairs and talk with Shauntel, but he decided to see what had Joe so enthralled.

"Joe, there is smoke coming out of your ears. Maybe you shouldn't try to think so hard."

Joe laughed. "The analysis of MARV is weird. If you get it, you might die. It isn't as dependent on your condition going into it as COVID was. In fact, it seems like it strikes people who work outside more than office workers. The analysis I'm looking at is for park police, park rangers, and tour guides for national parks. Ten percent of the workforce at Mount Rushmore and Yellowstone has died. That's weird."

"Huh. Any theories that make sense?"

"No, but it has the conspiracy nutbags going wild. They seem to think it is the federal government trying to reduce expense and privatize the parks. Our government, even if they were that evil, isn't smart enough to pull it off." Joe was cynical, but he had a good grasp of politics. Like all of Spike's siblings, he was conservative, and his position was based solely on logic, patriotism, and core values. He was too hardheaded to have an honest discussion with people who disagreed with him. Living in Denver was not easy for him because his opinions weren't popular. Still, most people in business agreed with his point of view, so his circle of friends rarely disagreed.

"Well, I'm not looking for conspiracy theories. Can you do me a favor?"

"Sure."

"Joe, please keep track of outdoor worker thing. Almost like a project in college. I would like to get to a real answer, because the anomalies of this are starting to become stark when compared to COVID-19. There is some demographic data on the Johns Hopkins website that might help." Spike didn't want to lead the witness too much, but he thought maybe there was a connection to the rural and outdoor worker data he'd learned about in just the last day.

Not surprisingly, Joe answered, "Okay, make me a drink, and I'll be your little research assistant."

Spike considered saying no. Another drink for Joe meant two more beers for Spike. He figured Joe would only be around for another couple days, so he could handle another couple of beers. It was always fun to visit. He said, "Okay, I hope I have another bottle of vodka."

"You have two. I checked."

Spike went behind the bar and made the drink while grabbing a Spotted Cow out of the refrigerator. He set the drink on the bar, took a sip of his beer, and said, "Let me run upstairs and put Shauntel to bed. Be back in ten minutes."

Fifteen minutes later, Spike came back downstairs. Joe had moved back to the bar but was again staring intently at his tablet. Spike said, "Shit, I was hoping you'd be passed out by now and I could get a decent night of sleep."

"No such luck, asswipe."

"How's the research going?"

"Broncos are going to be fantastic this year."

"Really, that's what you're looking at?"

"No, but they are. They'll probably crush the Packers in the Super Bowl. Just like '98. I made so much money, plus a ton of beer every time I came home. Packer fans are so easy."

"Yeah, but they have a cool stadium. You know, it is hell living here when they're good. It has always sucked being a Viking fan. I try to keep a low profile about it." Spike smiled; he was wearing a Viking baseball cap, and the bar was decorated entirely with Viking paraphernalia. Spike flew a Viking flag in the front yard that replaced Old Glory on Sundays during the season. Some of his buddies kidnapped the flag one Sunday early in the season during the Packer-Viking game and replaced it with a Packer flag. Spike's Viking flag came back in an unmarked package the following Tuesday. Spike burned the Packer flag ceremoniously during a barbeque the next Saturday. The back and forth was fun. He was grinning as he thought back.

Joe moved on. "Well, I have learned some more. Cities seem to be rebounding more quickly. And apparently many people are becoming immune to MARV without being exposed. The scientists and epidemiologists think it could be due to herd immunity, but they are skeptical because that generally takes higher infection levels. It simply isn't clear enough yet."

"I have a buddy from the academy who works at the CDC. He's kind of a data geek. When I talked to him about a month ago, he was nervous. He even bought a burner phone so we could communicate. He thought this was going to be horrible compared to COVID-19. I'll ask him some more questions tomorrow. It's funny; he only turns the phone on when he walks on his lunch break. He is really paranoid." Spike smiled.

"I ran across a couple more conspiracy theories. One doesn't sound that farfetched. The theorists think that a terrorist group built this. When we think terrorist group, we always go straight to Islamists. This theory is that the terrorist group is more ecological or animal oriented. They want the world to go back to basics—less international trade, less commerce, less fossil fuel usage, less hunting. So they are putting the world through another pandemic and aiming at outdoorsmen. Ducks Unlimited even sponsored a study to try to get more clear data. It is clear that fatalities are more likely when the patient has highly oxygenated blood and Vitamin D levels. The idea of someone doing this on purpose pisses me off."

"Interesting, I think maybe that explains some of my buddy's trepidation." Spike frowned. "I don't want to scare him off, but maybe I'll ask about the origin not being the Shanghai wet market."

"Let me know what you find out." Joe finished his drink. Since Spike had been so engaged, he still had half his beer left.

"Want another?" Spike asked, already reaching for Joe's glass.

"No, I'm going to keep looking at this."

Spike drained his beer, cleaned up the bar, tossed Joe a bottle of water. "Good night, Joe. See you tomorrow."

Spike headed upstairs and quietly slid into bed. Shauntel was sleeping lightly and rolled over toward Spike. She put her hand on his chest and leaned in to kiss his cheek. Spike liked where this was going and turned into her. Shauntel said, "I've missed you lately. You've got a lot on your mind, but I figured I would wait up and lighten your load."

"I've definitely got a load."

He leaned in closer and noticed that she wasn't wearing her normal boxers and T-shirt pajamas. She was all natural and pulled up Spike's shirt to get him naked. Spike needed no help with that; his shorts and T-shirt were off in three seconds. As Spike and Shauntel began exploring each other, Spike felt incredibly fortunate. His life, his wife, their work, and their family were perfect. As things became more urgent, he felt at peace. They slept in each other's arms both quietly snoring, content and fulfilled.

CHAPTER 8

The next day

After carefully extracting himself from Shauntel, Spike dropped for his first fifty pushups the next morning. He found his shorts on the floor next to the bed and stepped into them on his way out of the bedroom. He hadn't set the alarm, so he was running about fifteen minutes late when Ginger saw him heading to the mudroom. She followed with her tail wagging. Spike needed to hurry through his pre-run workout, or Ginger would get too excited and start growling playfully to get him moving. He was already sweating by the time they hit the driveway passing Carl's RV, so Spike started jogging through the neighborhood.

As he turned at the halfway point, he heard a light honk from a small, blue SUV. He waved automatically. Then he recognized Jennifer, the nurse he'd talked to on Monday. He'd met her while taking his shift with his mom. Jennifer seemed like a typical nurse, helpful, caring, and willing to help with the emotional strain people felt both as patients and loved ones. He thought about the day ahead. This is what addicted him to the morning workout regimen in the first place. Solitary, quiet time while going through the motions of exercising provided the best open-minded thinking. He solved more problems, both work and personal, during his morning runs than the rest of his waking hours combined.

Today, he thought about the family sitting vigil. He probably could get through his work by eleven, call Guls, head home, and spend some time with the family. He decided to text everyone and to prepare a buffet lunch in the lower level bar. Hopefully, Shauntel wouldn't have a bunch of heavy analytic work because the commotion outside her office would be distracting. He decided to ask her if it was a good plan when he delivered the coffee. It was always a lot easier to prepare meals like this together, but he could handle it if she didn't have time. He also hoped she would be there so she could talk to the women. Spike had less in common with Renee, Fred's wife Sarah, and Carl's wife Dorothy. They were all fine people, but they had no interest in Spike's favorite topics—sports, business, and the brothers' shared history. It's hard to reminisce when you had to tell the background of each story. Luckily, Dale, Renee's husband, had arrived yesterday with their daughters. Dale was the most knowledgeable sports fan in the family. The only real problem was that he was a diehard Packer fan.

This morning, he wanted to meet with Jim DePacker about moving forward, and he'd need to be sure he had a good handle on the model Jun had put in his inbox about three hours ago. He had some ideas about ways to make the restart of production faster than last year.

As he jogged into the driveway, he noticed Carl was moving around in the RV. He smelled coffee as he approached, so he tapped lightly on the door. Dorothy answered in her thick white robe with slippers on. Spike always thought of RVs as campers and was surprised to see the more formal sleeping attire. Dorothy smiled and said, "Come on in, we have coffee and a donut if you're interested."

"Coffee would be great. Do you mind if I let Ginger in?"

"Sure, she looks pretty worn out. She may as well lie on the front seat. I let her in every morning after you go to work. She thinks she's the navigator. Hops up there like she owns the joint."

Spike laughed. "She can be pretty forward. You can always shoo her away, though. Ginger always finds things to do."

As Carl came into the sitting area, he pulled his beard out of his hooded Vikings sweatshirt. Spike said, "What happened to your class?"

"They are doing online exercises most of today. I just monitor them on my tablet or phone. If they run into trouble, they can get my attention in this chat box, which chimes when I get a question." His tablet chimed, and he looked down and typed for about ten seconds, waited a while, and smiled. "That was easy."

"I just wanted to check in. You know you're welcome to hang out inside whenever you want. We have plenty of room. I have to admit, your setup is pretty slick, but feel free."

"We know, but we generally like to spend our free time praying and reading. We are easily distracted by other things."

"Whatever you want. I better feed Ginger. See you later."

"Have a blessed day," Dorothy and Carl said in unison.

Ginger was already at the door. Keywords "feed" and "Ginger" worked every time.

As Spike delivered the coffee to Shauntel twenty-five minutes later, he asked, "I'm thinking I could come home early and put out a lunch spread for the family. What do you think?"

"Good idea, I actually shopped for that yesterday. I got a bunch of bread, cheese, meats, and a gallon of soup from the store. I figured we would need to entertain at some point. I might be busy, but I can get started on the setup this morning. What time are you thinking?"

"I'll shoot for getting home around noon and tell them that we can eat at one. Okay?"

"That will work. I have a conference call with a client at ten, but I doubt I will need to do anything more this week. MARV slowed my work a little, but I already completed the analysis most companies are going to want. Just need to refresh the data from the consumer credit agencies."

"Big Brother is watching."

Shauntel laughed. "Hey, it pays the bills."

"All right, see you later. I love you, Shauntel." Spike kissed her on the forehead and headed toward the door. He stopped and added, "Thanks for last night."

"I love you. Bye."

As he pulled into the Maurer parking lot, he leaned forward noticing that about a third of the lot was full. He was a little surprised and noticed activity at both plants. Good news, but he wondered why he didn't know yesterday. Before getting out of the car, Spike texted his siblings to invite them to a late lunch. He decided that 1:30 might be a better plan since activity at the plants might create some extra work. Then he put a reminder to call Guls on his calendar.

When he entered the building, he saw Jim DePacker rushing down the hall. Spike was about five paces behind him and said loudly, "Hey boss, we open?"

Jim looked a little pissed. He grumbled something unintelligible. Spike hustled and caught up. "Jim, what can I do to help?"

"We have the opposite of a wildcat strike. A couple foremen called their teams and brought them in. I'm guessing they were sick of teaching their kids and sheltering in place. I'm going to go over there and find out what they are thinking. Do you want to come?"

"Hell yes, this will be interesting. It might guide us on what I think is becoming a groundswell to get back to work. I have some analysis from Jun in my inbox, but I haven't read it yet."

"Skim over it and meet me in Plant Two when you are ready."

Spike turned to go to his office but yelled over his shoulder. "Do you want to grab a facemask?"

"No, they probably don't have any, and I don't want to look like a wimp."

When Spike lit up his computer, he went straight to Jun's email. As expected, it was thorough. All the other controllers had provided input. In total, it would take about a week to get back to 65 percent productivity, two more weeks to get back to normal. The backorder items could be caught up within one month. Spike wrote down some pertinent notes and was out the door jogging toward Plant Two.

As Spike arrived, the group had gathered on the floor going over their plan for the day, and Jim was up on a catwalk trying to get their attention. Spike waved at one of the foremen and then pointed up at Jim. The foreman looked confused and a little sheepish at first, and then he called over to the other foreman. He yelled loudly, "Bill, looks like we got caught."

Jim replaced the silence that followed with a loud laugh. "You guys both served in the military. Hell, Bob was a Marine. Bill, you were in the navy. Didn't you guys ever hear of a chain of command?"

Bob stammered at first but recovered by saying, "And we both learned that taking the initiative is the most likely way to win the battle. This thing is overblown, just like last year."

Bill joined in, "This is strictly volunteer. Everyone who is here feels better about doing something for taking your money. And the stay-at-home thing is only marginally safer than working. None of us have had any contact; none of our families are sick. Bored, but not sick."

Jim grinned. "I get it. Listen, go ahead and do what you were planning to do. However, I still need to be careful here. You'll get paid for today just like yesterday. I'm a little concerned about the impact on those who didn't come in. They might think they are on the outside." Jim pointed at Bill and Bob. "You two need to make that right."

As the conversation was progressing, Spike took the time to get up on the catwalk behind Jim. As he listened, Spike realized that Jim's perspective was valuable. He knew what the others would be thinking because he'd been in plant operations. Office politics weren't as obvious to him, but plant politics were right up his alley. Jim noticed Spike and said, "Hold on a minute, fellas. I need to speak with the numbers guy." Turning to Spike, Jim asked, "What did Jun give you?"

"Bottom line, most of the plants could open next week. Our total lost revenue will be somewhere between three hundred and five hundred million dollars if we restart in the next couple weeks. We can fill all backorders within a month of restarting operations."

"Let's go back to the office and convene the leadership committee."

Spike said, "I think we learned something here. We might need to be more thoughtful as we ask people to return. Maybe we offer to keep paying people who have reasons to stay home. Less likely we get sued if we have a volunteer force."

"But that needs to be overseen by leadership, legal, and HR. We have to avoid creating classes of commitment. I've read a few horror stories from COVID-19 where employers got sued for unintended discrimination. In the new administration, the Department of Labor will look at the people who restarted and compare their demographics to the workforce. If there is a discrepancy of any protected class, we could get hammered."

"That's the biggest thing I miss about the military. Nobody cared if you belonged to a protected class. It was all about the mission and who could do the job. I remember thinking that all these labor attorneys were a waste. But, you're right, it is simply risk management."

Jim and Spike headed back to their offices. Spike told Jim he would meet him in an hour with some recommendations for restarting global production. Thinking about the military reminded him of one of the other reasons he missed military service. He had an idea, but he needed to think through a couple details.

Spike decided to apply some old-fashioned mission planning to tactically open the plants more efficiently. He thought back to his participation in highly effective missions during his military and CIA years. Special Forces teams continually got better because the worked together repeatedly. They learned from their mistakes, because after every mission, there was a debriefing. The leaders planned extensively, thoroughly explained the mission objectives and mission plan with as much prior knowledge as they could get without delaying the mission, executed the mission, and then, most importantly, debriefed with the entire team to improve. In business, leaders coach sales teams using a similar approach, debriefing sales sessions, and thinking about how to do it better next time. This is how a continuous improvement culture is built. He decided to apply this notion to the current problem at Maurer Company.

He considered one of the effective missions. He remembered it distinctly because of two individuals who stood out. One explained the importance of trust and working together, and the other made fast and final decisions without hesitation. And when he debriefed at the end of the mission, he listened thoroughly to what his team had experienced. He was detailed and cared not just about the results but how decisions were made.

CHAPTER 9

Spike was imbedded with a team of twelve army Special Forces operators in 2003. The planning phase was based on actionable intelligence, including where the target was going to be at a specific time. Sometimes that was the most difficult part. As they pre-briefed the mission, Spike told them how he knew where the target was, what level of opposition to expect and then listened as the leader explained the operational plan. Spike hadn't worked with this team before, so he asked who would deploy where. They looked at him as if he were an idiot. Finally, Captain Hammargren, who led the team, said, "Dude, were interchangeable. Everyone on this team is fully capable of any role. Don't worry about us."

"Wait, you are all snipers? You all know how to blow doors open?"

"Yes, sir!" the team answered in unison.

One of the younger operators, Staff Sergeant Gomez, volunteered, "I trust everyone here with my life, and I know exactly how they will react when something goes wrong. Plans are built for these missions to go off without a hitch. I'm the least experienced person on the team—just under one hundred missions—and exactly none have gone according to plan. But we've completed most every mission perfectly." He looked down and crossed himself. All the other operators looked down in silence. Spike figured there had been some lost teammates.

Spike thanked Gomez for the education, finished his briefing, turned to the captain, and said, "Let's go."

The captain smiled and said, "You're the only wildcard, so you need to be where we expect you to be. Hate to frag a former Air Force weenie."

"Yeah, I'd hate that, too."

This was a mission to capture or kill a Taliban leader named Abdul al-Takfiri, who traveled with a small security force. Abdul's favorite pastime was beheading girls and women who weren't living up to the standards of the Taliban's backward view of Islam. Spike had heard from one of his contacts in a small village in al-Takfiri's territory that two preteens and their mother were his next targets.

The helicopters were bringing in the team at 0400 local. The beheadings were likely going to be just after Fajr, the first Salat, at sunrise, so certainly after 6:30. The team would want to be in place in time to take out or capture al-Takfiri as he headed into the mosque in the center of town. The plan for the beheadings would be very public, directly in front of the mosque. The entire village of 145 people would be required to watch these women pay for their sins. Another day in Afghanistan, morning prayer, a preachy terrorist telling people how to live, and a triple beheading.

Two weeks ago, the children were seen talking to a male villager who was a few years older than the ten- and twelve-year-old girls. Word got to al-Takfiri from some Taliban spies who had been watching the village. Girls over eight were forbidden from contact with males who were not in their family. This kind of punishment was becoming less common because US forces had the Taliban on the run. Spike hoped they could be in position for a simple headshot. There was almost no value to capturing al-Takfiri, who was a simple enforcer. His knowledge of the Taliban hideouts might result in a few drone strikes, but more often, the Taliban hid surrounded by innocent civilians and couldn't be targeted. This scumbag needed to die, and putting the team or civilians at risk would be silly. But the mission plan was to capture al-Takfiri, if possible.

Spike was with the captain and five operators including Gomez, designated Alpha Team. The helicopter landed for three seconds leaving Alpha Team along the road about two kilometers southeast of the village. The only other road out of the village was directly north of the village. Bravo team had six operators led by a master sergeant with fourteen years of service. Drone surveillance showed the village was quiet. Both teams were heading toward the village. Bravo team had split into a group of four who ran along the rutted cart path that passed for a road in the northern part of Afghanistan. Bravo Team One reported in thirty meters outside the village at 0440. The other two operators designated Bravo Team Two would set up as sniper support on a rock formation sixty meters to the northeast of the village. They took the high ground at about two hundred meters above the village and reported "in position" at 0445. Sunrise was at 0633.

Alpha team had a shorter hike. Captain Hammargren, Staff Sergeant Gomez, and Spike were designated Alpha Team One and set up in the hills on the east side of the village because it was the best vantage point to view the mosque and its courtyard. They were in place about twenty-five meters from the edge of the village at 0432. The four other operators reported in at 0455 that they had arrived on the south end of the village, two on each side of the road, designated Alpha Two and Alpha Three. The plan required them to low crawl for the last five hundred meters due to the sentries on the south end of the village. Captain Hammargren winked at Spike. Spike was skeptical that the teams would be in place before 0500.

The village began to stir at 0540, and the drone operator reported no unusual activity. The same woman, stationed at Creech AFB outside Las Vegas, had watched the village the past four nights. Pretty boring duty, but today would be different. The intelligence value of watching was still significant. Three extra vehicles were parked in the village, and the drones spotted the target and security team entering one of the structures. Total enemy force was twelve to fifteen terrorists. The villagers wouldn't take up arms with the Taliban, so twelve army Special Forces operators were plenty.

The drone overhead had sophisticated surveillance equipment with incredibly clear video, infrared capability to track heat signatures as small as a rat, and night vision. More important to Spike, it had two Hellfire missiles on board. Because of the dual mission, the drone was large, but still invisible to the enemy. The drone was designated Blue Eyes. Spike knew the operator's call sign was a bit ironic. The drone operator was Black and a women's track standout at the Air Force Academy.

Ten minutes later, Spike noticed two pickups heading south with a driver, passenger, and a person in the back accompanying a mounted machine gun. The drone operator designated the vehicles Tech One and Tech Two and reported that they had left the target's suspected structure. They seemed to be driving a little reckless for 0550. They were heading south, past the mosque, and looked to be on a mission. As the captain reported this to his four operators south of the village, Spike asked, "Blue Eyes, how far are the Techs from Alpha Team Two and Three's position?"

Everyone heard the machine guns open up on the teams' positions before Blue Eyes could answer. The captain asked the operators for a status report; they calmly answered, "No casualties, but they know exactly where we are."

"Bravo Two, do you have a shot at the gunners?"

"Not great, probably seventy percent chance of center mass shot," the first sniper reported.

"Same" was the answer from the other sniper.

"Take them out."

Two seconds later, "One tango down." Tech One's machine gun went silent. The driver veered off the road, and the passenger jumped out and was climbing into the bed of the pickup when his head exploded.

"Second tango down"; a second later, "Tech One driver down."

Tech Two must have noticed it was a bad idea to stop because it continued directly out of town. Spike realized that al-Takfiri could have been in one of the pickups. "Blue Eyes, don't lose Tech Two."

"I'm tracking but need to fire within two minutes if you want me to destroy it."

"Take it out." No hesitation from Captain Hammargren. Spike loved working with decisive leaders, and this captain fit the bill.

Blue Eyes was carrying Longbow Hellfire missiles, which can track the target without further guidance from the operator. Some of the older Hellfire missiles were designed in the 1990s and often required a laser to paint the target to bring the missile in. When Spike was in the Air Force, he knew some forward air controllers who would hide near a target and point a laser to help guide the Hellfires. That was a dangerous mission, and Spike really respected those airmen. Watching a Hellfire missile was surreal. As it tracked to the target, it almost looked like a shooting star, just at a funny angle. Spike saw the explosion. Blue Eyes reported, "Tech Two destroyed. No likely survivors."

"Alpha Three, go make sure and ID tangos on Tech Two," Captain Hammargren ordered. No use guessing when the team had the resources, and it is always a bad idea to risk having an enemy behind your position.

During the last three minutes, all hell had broken lose, but everyone remained calm. Six dead terrorists, but the main objective was likely hidden in one of the mud structures.

"Blue Eyes, best guess for location of al-Takfiri?" Spike asked.

"Almost positive he's still in the fourth structure on the east side of the road about seventy meters south of Bravo Team One. Structure surrounded by three-foot-high mud and rock fence. Looks like five individuals inside, three taking up defensive positions at the front of the structure. The other two appear to be moving toward the back of the structure."

Captain Hammargren asked, "Blue Eyes, what does the backyard look like?"

"Same three-foot fence, about thirty meters of open space to the back. Looks like six goats starting to move toward the rear. Another four-meter by three-meter structure with no heat signature inside along the north side of the backyard about eight meters east of the main structure. Looks like a few craters and a few two-meter-tall trees with little hope for concealment."

"Bravo Two, cover us. We're moving in toward the back of the structure. Bravo One, move forward and lay down cover fire on the front of the structure. Don't kill all three too fast. I want al-Takfiri to think they are holding you back and try to escape."

Spike thought about Gomez telling him that no operation goes as planned. He grabbed his M4 and followed Captain Hammargren down the hill. Gomez took the rear. They were at the edge of the property fifteen seconds later, apparently undetected. Hammargren signaled to Gomez to enter the property and set up next to the smaller structure. He was in position to hose down the terrorists if they came out one of the holes that may have been covered with glass at some point. The craters Blue Eyes described looked like they were made by mortars, only about two meters in diameter and less than a meter deep. Pretty hard place to hide. As the firefight started in front of the house, two men in black robes came out of the back of the home. Almost impossible to tell either of them was al-Takfiri, but the attire made sense. Spike's vote would have been to kill them both, identify al-Takfiri, and head back to base.

Bravo Team Two reported, "One tango down."

Captain Hammargren whispered, "Two runners out the back window. Go ahead, finish the other two, and head around the structure for support. This is a capture mission."

The noise from the front of the structure stopped about twenty seconds later.

"Main Structure Tangos neutralized. Bravo Two will split, two around north side, two around south side. What are your positions?"

Since Spike was furthest from the two men low crawling fairly quickly through the backyard, he answered, "Operator on north side on the east end of second structure. Alpha One Lead on southwest corner of property behind the fence. Embed on northwest corner behind the fence."

"Roger."

Spike could see shadows on the north side of the main structure. They could use the smaller structure as cover. The two runners each held an AK-74 in front of them as they crawled. Each of them slithered into a mortar crater. There was still loud gunfire to the south, so Alpha Two may have been taking fire from the four or five sentries. Spike was curious why the sentries were still alive. This firefight was five minutes old, and normally, the poorly trained Taliban bullies' life expectancy in a battle with Special Forces was one to three minutes. Maybe Alpha Two was waiting for Alpha Three to flank the sentries after checking on the occupants of Tech Two.

Hammargren whispered, "I need two flashbangs about five feet from those mortar holes."

Spike saw hand signals between the Bravo Two team. Four seconds later, one of the operators whispered, "Flashbangs away, cover." Ears were covered with hands, and eyes were averted. The loud noise was especially disorienting when unexpected, and the bright light took out all natural night vision. As soon as the explosions happened, all six operators and Spike rushed toward the terrorists.

Spike saw one raising his AK-74 toward Hammargren. Before he could bring his M4 to bear, the terrorist's head exploded. Gomez killed him with two perfectly placed rounds in the head. The other terrorist wanted to die, too, but one of the Bravo Two operators from the south side of the building shot him in the knee from behind as he was struggling to get to his feet and aim his rifle. As he fell, his rifle flew out of his hands. Captain Hammargren got to him first. He said, "Bingo, this is our enforcer." He put zip ties on his wrists behind his back, removed the ceremonial sword from his robes, and found a scavenged K-bar knife and .45 caliber ALFA Defender probably scavenged by a dead uncle from a dead Czech soldier during the Soviet invasion. They bagged the weapons while al-Takfiri was screaming in pain. Captain Hammargren grabbed the terrorist by his beard and stuffed a sock into his mouth. He grabbed a black bag out of his belt and covered the terrorist's head.

One of the operators took over pulled up al-Takfiri's robes and cut away the trousers from his knee. He administered morphine to cut the pain and bandaged his wound. Finally, he gave him a sedative to keep him quiet for the next couple hours.

"Alpha Two, Alpha Three, report." The gunfire was lighter but still going.

Frustrated, one of the operators said, "They won't put their heads up. Three down, and we're about to flank them and finish the other two."

"Hurry up, we need to meet at the extraction point in forty minutes."

"Not a problem. We'll be there. Out."

Hammargren thought about Tech One, a reasonably fit fighting vehicle. "Alpha Two, after you take out the sentries, destroy Tech One if uncontested."

It was a ten-minute jaunt to the rallying point just over the hill Spike had just been on. One of the bigger operators put al-Takfiri over his shoulder as they began leaving the village. A minute later, the predawn silence returned.

"Tangos down," reported Alpha Two.

A minute later, two explosions sounded less than a second apart, then, two seconds later, another. Grenade to engine, grenade to the machine gun, secondary explosion of the gas tank. "Tech One destroyed."

As they hit the top of the hill, the four operators of Alpha Two and Three joined them. A few minutes later, Bravo Two joined hefting their much larger sniper rifles. While they stayed separated showing their natural discipline, the team was altogether at the rallying point. No casualties, mission accomplished.

Blue Eyes said, "I have eyes on you and the helicopter. ETA twenty minutes. You should be to the extraction point in five. Great work. Out."

Captain Hammargren replied, "Thanks, Blue Eyes, couldn't have done it without you."

Missions like this created blasts of adrenaline. The following thirty to sixty minutes were dangerous for normal combat soldiers experiencing a large reduction in their capacity to fight or even think straight. Special Forces operators trained hard to power through that adrenaline hangover so they didn't experience the lowered capacity. Ambushes are possible. An enemy force could be coming to rescue al-Takfiri. The team was alert as they moved to the extraction point. Captain Hammargren kept Spike close in the center of the formation. Nobody spoke as they moved quietly through the rough landscape.

The captured Taliban enforcer was quiet as expected and, hopefully, not bleeding out. They loaded up on the helicopters and were back to base by 0730. Spike was right about the intel gained by capturing this scumbag. He was clueless. Spike figured Abdul would spend some time in Guantanamo Bay. And likely be back in ten years to behead more innocent women. In Spike's opinion, they should have killed him.

This mission debrief was focused on three things. How were they detected, why had the enemy not placed sentries on the road north, and how could they have deployed better to neutralize the sentries faster? While the mission was a success, it wasn't even close to according to plan. The expectation was that they would attack just before Fajr. The key to that was being undetected. The sentries, Tech One and Tech Two, would have been non-factors. All the black-clad Taliban combatants would have been the last to enter the mosque. Easy to take them out with eight members of Bravo One, Alpha Two, and Alpha Three.

The first answer was not forthcoming, but Captain Hammargren assumed the sentries saw them coming. It is unusual for Taliban warriors to be that alert, but it was possible one was pissing in the bushes and saw them. The sentries would have radioed the info back to al-Takfiri and set the technicals in motion.

The second answer was tactical. The area to the north was controlled almost entirely by Taliban forces. There were roadblocks just five kilometers north of the Bravo Team's drop zone, and the Taliban probably assumed they were covered from that direction. A simple miscalculation on their part.

The third answer was more complicated. The sentries were also guarding the two young girls and their mother in a small hut next to the road. Unknown to Alpha Two and Three, this structure was serving as their jail. The last two Taliban were hard to kill because they were hiding in the hut. In the end, Alpha Three identified the problem. Instead of trying to shoot them through the windows, they entered through the door and killed them immediately upon entry. They found a state-of-the-art night-vision monocle that had been made in the United States. It must have been scavenged from a US unit. That helped explain the first question. Captain Hammargren asked several questions about why the operators did what they decided to do. Surprisingly, the two girls were relatively unharmed physically with only a few bruises on their faces. The mother had been beaten, and her clothes were in tatters. Based on her catatonic expression, she had probably been raped multiple times. The girls would likely be scared emotionally, and the mother would be shamed forever. This was a horrible place.

At the end of the debriefing, Spike reflected on the horrors of this place. He thought about Penelope and Shauntel. Their lot in this place would be unimaginable to them just because they were females. How could a culture treat half their population as property instead of humans?

Snapping back to present after a few minutes of reminiscing, Spike wrote down a list of key tenets. First, planning can be done centrally, but all the intelligence gathering and decision making would be done locally. Second, individuals would be allowed to be furloughed at 80 percent pay if they did not want to work until they felt it was safe. These individuals could not be fired unless they did something outside the spirit of the rule, like working somewhere else but still taking pay from Maurer. Third, local management would be allowed to decide how to get the work done and would explain their plan to their workers at the beginning of each shift. Fourth, production would focus on backordered items first. Fifth, at the end of each shift, the entire team would gather to discuss results for the day, and everyone could give input on how they could do better. In some cultures, this could be difficult because hierarchies were more pronounced. Spike made a separate list for he and Jim to call the plant managers in Asia to coach them on these debriefings. Finally, the plant with highest production per capita would be rewarded with double pay each week for the next six weeks.

Spike headed down the hall to Jim's office at about 9:45. Jim was laughing at some silly politician on a news channel. He grabbed his remote and turned off the television. "I can't get over how far removed these people are from reality. They live like me, very privileged. But they never talk to real people. They are totally insulated from what really happens in Americans' lives. They blame each other instead of trying to solve a problem for the country."

"I'm not going to defend them. I used to think they acted like that because they genuinely believed their solutions were the best. I don't believe that any longer. Both sides seem to be trying to run the country like dictators. They talk about citizens as if they can't do anything without the government's help. Our forefathers didn't predict that the electorate would be powerless versus the parties," Spike replied.

"That's because they never envisioned that anyone would want to be a career politician. It is too lucrative to be a part of the system. They expected citizens to take on civic duties with a serious mind but go back home after a few years to do the things they enjoyed."

Spike said, "Well, we aren't going to solve that problem right now. Let's talk about reopening." Jim listened intently to the background of why Spike thought these tactics would work. Then Spike laid out the tenets. He noticed Jim's expression change slightly twice. The first tenet about local decision making was difficult because Jim knew plant operations better than any of his plant managers. The fifth tenet about individual input from workers on the floor made him uncomfortable too.

But Jim said, "Sounds good to me."

Spike wasn't about to let him have misgivings without a chance to convince him. "Jim, this is too important for you to have reservations. I was trained to watch my audience as I speak. You have two problems with my plan, and we need to discuss them."

"The damn CIA made you into a human bullshit monitor. Okay, what are my concerns?"

"First, you are uncomfortable allowing for local decision making. I think it is a little ironic that you would say politicians have no idea what is going on in America, but you assume you know better than the local plant managers. Am I missing something?"

"Well, we might not have the best leaders in all of our plants," Jim countered.

"I will grant you that, but if they feel responsible for the decisions and results, they can't blame headquarters for the stupid ideas. That is why I added that they needed to work on backorders first. I believe that they will step up. It happens all the time in the military when suddenly a lieutenant is doing a major's job. They often do better than the major could because they listen more intently to their teams. If the plant managers are the wrong people, we'll know that pretty clearly in six weeks."

"I agree with your logic. We'll see about this batch, and my guess is that you're playing the odds that more will step up than let us down." Jim smiled.

"Exactly. I don't want to predict this out loud, but I think we should rank order which plants we think will do the best. We both make a list. If you're more accurate, Shauntel and I will serve you and Mary Jo dinner at our house. If I win, you two can serve us dinner at your house. Deal?"

Jim smiled even more broadly. He knew production better than Spike; plus, he loved to gamble. "Okay."

"Your other misgiving is that during the debriefing at the end of the day, we ask for input from the floor employees. This is very important for the same reason we need local control. The closer someone is to a task, the better they are at analyzing it. I think you picture a bunch of people standing around idle equipment. Fifteen minutes at the beginning of the day and fifteen minutes at the end of the day is about seven percent of their production time. If that matters, the workers will point it out. Remember, the reward for top productivity is double pay. They won't waste time."

"That part I get," Jim started. "The bigger problem I have is getting some of our weaker plant managers to do the debriefing well. I used sales debriefing effectively during my time in sales. I think it is important and valuable to figure out how to continuously improve."

"But?"

"Can you see this working in Jiangsu? Chairman Mao, I mean, Chen will never listen to the employees. He is as dictatorial as they come. And a real micromanager. The employees will never speak up."

"Then have Wang do it. He spends a lot of his time buffering Chen's style anyway." Spike suggested. "Where else is it a problem other than Jiangsu?"

"I think it would work everywhere else, but how do I tell Chen he's the only plant manager not leading the debriefings?"

"Make it his choice. He might be one of the ones we need to replace anyway. We didn't take the government's money. I know his father is a bigshot commie, but someone else can hire him. His dictator style isn't acceptable today, even in China."

"Okay, but you talk to him and Wang. You can get your point across better than me anyway."

"Jim, I'll do it. I actually think I have a decent chance of convincing him to give it a shot."

"So, how do we implement?" Jim asked.

"I'll prepare a written communication for you to edit and email out. Then we can meet with the leadership committee at four this afternoon to set a timeline. I need to run home in a half hour and feed my brothers and their kids. And, on my way out, I'll run over to the plant and ask Bob and Bill to try the debriefing process at the end of today. We might learn something from our reverse wildcats."

"Sounds good. How's your mom?"

"They moved her to the ICU yesterday, supposedly an abundance of caution."

"Hope she gets better. Mary Jo and I have been praying for her."

"I appreciate it. I'll tell her when I see her tomorrow afternoon. She'll get a kick out of that. You're Baptist, so I doubt she thinks it does much good. She's pretty sure you gotta go through Mary and the Saints to have a chance for your prayers to be answered."

Jim laughed again and waved as Spike left his office.

Spike called Joe, "Hey, can you get away from your day job to make a liquor store run?"

"Sure, what do you need?" Joe asked.

"Make sure we have a couple cases of Spotted Cow and then whatever else I'm low on. Probably use a cooler for beer and water, so get some ice. Maybe a case of water, but I think I have a bunch in the closet next to the bar. Figure it out and go to the liquor store where the grocery store used to be. They have my card number, and the Spotted Cow is always cold, fresh, and cheapest in town."

Joe answered, "Okay. I need you to ask your CDC buddy something. If someone were engineering a virus, could they make it more deadly to people who spend more time outdoors. It seems crazy, but the stats seem to point to rural people and people in open-air jobs are more likely to die. Park employees, yes, but construction, delivery drivers, garbage men, postal workers are all dying at a higher rate than clerks in stores and office workers."

"Well, Guls is a data guy, not a biologist, but he's curious. So, if his data is pushing him there, I'm guessing he's asking questions."

"One other thing, I'm wondering if the CDC is trying to trace the origin for some of the rural places. How is this getting to backwater towns in Texas, Louisiana, and Alaska? Even Montana and Wyoming have more cases than Illinois."

"I'll talk to him in about an hour. Got some shit to get done before then. I'll try to give you a report before everyone shows up for lunch."

Spike hit end on his phone and woke up his computer. He had the tenets typed out, plus the plan from Jun on when to open. He decided to start with Jun's timeline and then added a teaser about the contest in the subject of the email. He knew that if the CEO sent an email, most people would be curious enough to open it. He wanted everyone to know about the double pay as soon as possible. He was looking for ingenuity from the plant floors, and money is a great motivator. He finished the email, sent it, and then printed it along with Jun's report.

As he headed to Plant Two, he remembered that Bob and Bill had military service. They could have been mechanics that had no operational planning or mission experience. It was still worth trying to use the military example with them. As he entered the plant, he saw them up on the catwalk watching the floor. They were looking at chokepoints in the manufacturing process and engaged in what appeared to be an argument. Good, they were thinking about process. Spike joined them on the catwalk. They seemed surprised to see him.

"Bill, Bob, you know this isn't my area of expertise, so tell me if I'm going down a bad path."

They looked at each other and nodded. Bob said, "Shoot."

"Well, when you were in the service, did either of you ever participate in missions that required planning, briefing, executing, and debriefing? You know, for an attack or a covert mission?"

Bill asked, "Spike, were you in the military?"

"Yeah, Air Force. But I was more involved in mission briefings when I was in the CIA. I spent a lot of time in sandland and was embedded with Special Forces a lot. Don't read too much into that. I was usually a long way from the action."

Bob answered immediately, "Well, he was a navy puke, so don't ask him. I was part of about twenty missions clearing Taliban out of villages in Afghanistan."

Bill chimed in. "Don't let him fool you, Spike. He was the guy they brought along to fix the Humvees and unmanned vehicles." Bill acted like he thought Bob was never close to the action. Spike knew better. Marines were trained to be warriors first. Their other roles, like fixing vehicles, were secondary to being trained shooters who experienced combat firsthand.

Bob was somewhat defensive, saying, "But I attended all the briefings and debriefings because they needed my input on how we could better protect the vehicles and troops as we continued kicking the Taliban's ass across northern Afghanistan. So, moron, I know what he's talking about."

Spike laughed and put in a dip of Copenhagen. "Okay, you know how the commander and intel guys would tell you what the plan was and any details they thought might help? I think you guys should do that first thing each morning. But, more important, at the end of each day, I want you to spend fifteen minutes figuring out how you can do things better the next day. The guys on the floor should be included because they will know where the bottlenecks are better than you. Remember the debriefings Bob? They spent a lot of time on what could have been better and listened in detail to the ideas from the troops. They did that because each Marine had eyes on different parts of the mission. They saw things that could make the next village clearing better. And did you notice how well it worked?"

Bill laughed. "Spike, you're going to need to slow down. Remember, he was a Marine."

Bob smiled. "I mostly remember that the intel guys asked a lot of questions about whether what they briefed us was right. At first, I thought it was bullshit because it sounded like they were guessing before the mission. Then as things got better and we continued to move through villages, I realized they were trying to learn what intel they could trust and how the enemy was trying to deceive them. The whole process saved a lot of lives." Spike recognized Bob's suddenly somber expression and realized he was probably thinking about a buddy who didn't make it home.

Bill recognized it too. "Bob, I had no idea you were a badass." He patted Bob on the shoulder. This time, he wasn't kidding. "We actually did some mission planning on the LPD I served on. It was more about exercises, but I get the concept. Still, I think Bob should lead our afternoon debriefs and prepare me to lead the morning planning meetings."

"Okay, don't make it feel too military. Bob will need to draw out ideas. Try it today and let me know how it goes. I'll swing by tomorrow morning sometime." Spike looked at his watch. He felt like he could stand here and talk with these guys all day. The inter-service rivalries were mostly just bluster. When it came down to it, if someone who hadn't served tried to give them a hard time about their service, they would band together and attack. It is a lifelong bond for former military members. Sometimes, Spike and Shauntel would go eat at the VFW fish fry just to rekindle the camaraderie. Military husbands and wives made sacrifices that only other military spouses understood. The shared sacrifice was silently honored in American Legion Halls and VFWs throughout the country. And the war stories, mostly made up, were fun to share. Oftentimes, there were quiet guys with the cold eyes that just smiled and agreed. They were probably the real warriors.

"See you tomorrow, fellas." Spike headed down the catwalk to the exit.

Before he got to the stairs, Bob yelled, "Thanks, Captain."

Although he'd actually made major, he didn't correct him. Instead, Spike turned, went to attention, and saluted the two former enlisted men. They returned the salute, and all three laughed.

CHAPTER 10

Spike called Guls from the car. He moved his car to the next parking lot and shut it off. He didn't want to be distracted and might need to take notes. He'd scribbled the questions he needed to ask for Joe on the notebook he always kept in the car—bioengineering of the virus for outdoor workers and tracking to see how it got to the rural locations.

Guls answered the phone in his normal tone, not as hushed as he had been before. "What's up, Easty?" Maybe some of the paranoia was wearing off, but he was still trying to mask who he was talking to. Nobody ever called Spike "Easty."

"We're trying to figure out how to restart our plants. Other than that, just another beautiful spring day in Wisconsin. How are you?"

"Busy as hell. People think I'm crazy for walking every day, but it's the only reason I'm not crazy. The modeling on MARV is difficult. Too many random outbreaks."

"I was wondering about that. How are these rural areas getting higher infection and fatality rates than large cities?"

"That is a mystery. Public health officials like to figure out what the links are between outbreaks. They search for the carriers who bring a sickness into an area. In this case, the tracking seems to break. It is almost as if MARV is transported to small towns through shipments of some kind. That line of investigation has been fruitless, too."

"It is killing people at a faster clip in lower populated areas, too. Why?"

"Not sure why, but people in larger metropolitan areas appear to have already built up immunities. That hasn't happened before that we have recorded, but it is likely that it actually happens a lot. There are billions of viruses that don't affect us. Dogs don't get sick from humans even if they lick the snot off a flu patient's face."

"Wait, dude, did you just compare dogs to city dwellers?"

"You know what I mean; I'm trying to be illustrative, asshole."

"I have a different question that is probably outside your wheelhouse. Is it possible to bioengineer a virus to attack people who work outdoors?"

"Whoa. I have rather good access to the data, and nobody is saying this was engineered."

"I am thinking bioterrorists or bad state actors like China, North Korea, or Iran. That's just my old job coming out. But forget about the motive or reason. Is it possible to build a virus to attack a generally healthier population of people who work outside?"

"You would have to ask biologists, chemists, and researchers. I just know that I'm around people like that all day, and nobody has mentioned anything about this being bioterrorism. They aren't fully confident that it really came from Shanghai's wet market, and they are having a hard time connecting it to any animal that could have been in the market."

"So I'm curious; are they not saying it because they can't say it to the data guy or because they aren't thinking it?"

"I don't know. They don't seem afraid to chase down all leads. These people really care about public health. They are mostly just trying to solve the problem and make prudent recommendations to policy makers and the public."

"Fair enough."

"Talk to you later. Call me on my normal number just to BS. Also, I have a new cell number. I'll text it to you."

"All right. Talk to you soon."

Spike thought about what he learned. Not much. He started the car and headed home. Time to make lunch and entertain the family. Should be fun if they didn't dwell on their mother's current state. He thought about some stories that would keep the focus on better times. His phone rang, and it was an Atlanta area code.

"Hello."

A computerized voice said, "The virus appears to be engineered to be fatal for people with high blood oxygen and high vitamin D levels. Former employer is looking." Call ended.

It was Guls; he must have used a text to voice app. Spike pulled over and wrote down the exact words. Guls was right to be paranoid. It was a risk to call this number. If people were tracking him, they would know that Spike had talked to him on his known phone and his first burner that he used too long. Spike was worried about him. He should have given Guls some tradecraft lessons. Use a burner no more than one day. He sent a text back to the phone. "Take out the SIM card and destroy. Right now!"

Spike tore six pages out of his notebook. He'd only written on one, but he used a ballpoint and pressed hard, so to be safe, he needed to burn all of this after speaking with Joe. And Joe would need to start using one of Shauntel's more secure internet connections. Or maybe he shouldn't get Joe any deeper into this. He pulled back on the road and sped home at eighty miles an hour. Spike would have a hard time explaining to his former employer what he was up to. And they wouldn't appreciate him bringing others into the fold.

When Spike got home, he headed straight to the lower level bar. Joe was setting up. Trays of food with cellophane over them were set up on a long buffet table. It was sunny outside and likely to hit seventy degrees. Pleasant enough to eat and hang out outside. He went into the storage room and grabbed a ten-foot square tent. He would set it up in five minutes to create a shaded area around the built-in outside bar. He noticed that two of the four-seat ice cream tables by the bar had tablecloths and umbrellas set up. Joe or Shauntel must have been thinking outside would be comfortable. As he hauled the tent outside, he saw he'd guessed wrong. It was Dale who was setting up a third table. Renee was nowhere to be seen.

Spike yelled, "Dale, this thing goes up in about a minute if you help me."

"Be right there." Dale finished the third table and walked the length of the pool to help Spike.

"How you are doing, Dale?"

"I'm fine, but Renee and the girls are emotional wrecks. They are quite sure your mom isn't going to make it," Dale offered.

"Ah, they have the feminine emotional thing. They might even be right with their silly intuition. But what are we going to do, lament the future or live in the now?"

"Spike, they may be right; she may be in the throes of death, but how could we help her? And if she knew we're together, what would she want us to do? Enjoy, right?"

"Yep, it's a delicate balance."

Dale replied, "Your sister can be very demanding. Her views are almost always right. I want to figure out how to soften a difficult blow for her."

"Dale, I love you, but don't be a wimp right now. Strength matters, and even if my sister is in charge of your life, now is the time for pragmatism," Spike said.

"I kind of agree. But I can't push too hard."

"Yes, you can. She needs you to be the honest and loving person you've always been. And she needs you to do that for your kids. So kick your macho side into gear and help her get through this, even if my mom is dying."

Dale hesitated and replied thoughtfully, "Your mom was never a big fan of mine. It would be easy for me to disparage her and not care about her situation. But I have read a lot of history. General MacArthur once replied to a reporter regarding one of his critics, 'He's a good man.' The reporter said, 'Don't you know what he's said about you?' I'll never forget MacArthur's response. 'You didn't ask what he thought about me. You asked about what I thought about him. He's a great leader.' The implication is clear, and I feel the same about your mom. She's been a wonderful mom to some of my favorite people in the world. So, regardless of her opinion of me, I want to honor her. And what I know is she would want us to be together, enjoying each other and looking to the future."

"Dale, you're not my only brother-in-law. Shauntel's brother is a friend of mine. But, I must admit, I couldn't ever ask for a better brother-in-law. I think your view of our family has always been fair. My dad and my brothers have always liked you, and probably loved you. More important, we've all liked being around you. You're a good guy. For some people, losing their last living parent is a rite of passage. It makes you alone in the world in a lot of ways. When your dad died, I think you felt that burden. Renee is about to feel that same thing. Love her through it, help your kids through it. They are probably right; Mom is going to die. Let's enjoy being together and celebrate all the things she did for her kids. She was a good mom." Spike was getting a little emotional, probably more so than Dale was comfortable with. Spike was feeling a little vulnerable, too, but with Dale, everything was open to discussion.

"Yep. I want to make sure her grandchildren understand that, my kids and all of the others."

"Thanks, Dale. Let's have a party and hope she doesn't die when one of the grandchildren are on watch. That would be hard for everyone. If we're lucky, she'll make it through this. But if she doesn't, hopefully they don't have to see it happen. Alyssa is passing duty on to Bailey this afternoon. Kelcey has the overnight shift, then back to me on Friday afternoon."

"I have to admit, I'm hoping she makes it past my girls. Bailey and Kelcey wouldn't provide a clear story for the rest of us." Dale, always looking to serve, said, "Anything else I can do to prepare the lunch?"

"I think we're good, but let's check in with Joe and Shauntel," Spike answered.

They went back into the lower level bar area, looked over the setup, and decided all was well. Spike looked over to Joe and said, "Bartender, do you have a couple of Spotted Cows for the crew?"

Joe smiled and said, "Sure, but any new tidbits from the CDC?"

"Give us a beer and make yourself something. That's something that we need to discuss in the office."

Joe gave Spike a nod, grabbed two beers for Spike and Dale and a bottle of water for himself. As he served the beers, Dale noticed Joe's sober look and unusual choice of beverages and said, "You guys doing some covert shit?"

Spike laughed. "Yeah, Joe's trying to figure out what the fuck is going on in Washington. Good luck to him!"

After a few minutes, Fred's family came downstairs. They hadn't seen Dale this week, so they gathered around him. Spike winked at Joe, and they headed into the office. Shauntel was logging out and said, "I'll take over out there."

Spike gave her a hug on the way out. He whispered, "I need five minutes with Joe. He might opt out, but if not, I'll need you to connect him to your safe network."

Shauntel smiled. "As long as this work stays here, I can do whatever you want."

Spike became uncomfortable. He knew that if he found information that drew him deeper into this investigation, he might need to take his act overseas. He would not deceive Shauntel, but his concern was deeper than that. If he needed to pursue the leads, it could put more than just him in danger. His entire family, especially Joe and Shauntel, could be at risk. He decided to worry about that if it happened. Right now, only he and Guls could be linked to the investigation he'd begun. Jun had provided information that had helped him create theories, but only Guls had provided information that was inaccessible to the public. A couple nutbag theories from Joe's research had led him to ask questions that only Guls' access had helped confirm they were worth pursuing. At this point, Guls and Spike were at risk, but the level of risk was high because they were looking into either deep conspiracies or enemies with a lot of resources. As in most things in his life, Spike decided to aggressively move forward. He would deal with the consequences as they became clear.

Joe and Spike headed into the office. Closing the doors wouldn't add much security and would only draw attention, so Spike left them open. He walked into the large workspace and looked at Joe. Joe could see the urgent and focused look on Spike's face.

Joe said, "Holy shit, we bumped into something big, didn't we?"

Spike acted nonchalant about it, but said, "Maybe. My CDC buddy was pretty clear that we might be on the right track." Spike hesitated, but he decided to be straightforward. "Joe, at this point, you can go back to Denver and be safe and forget all about what we've talked about. Nobody would ever know that your simple searches and guidance moved me to ask questions that led us to an important discovery. I need you to become much more vested right now or quit."

"Slow down, butthead. I'm a grown man, but you're gonna have to give me more than that to make a decision about this. What are the consequences if I go forward?"

"If you decide to help me with this investigation, you will be at risk to be targeted. You and your family. No shit. I don't want to put you at risk, and I can get this help elsewhere or do the research myself. So, I need you to decide right now. Is it worth pursuing some crackpot theories to put yourself, your wife, and kids at risk of assassination? No kidding. This could be life and death."

"Spike, if you are convinced that this is important to pursue, I am with you."

"But what about your wife and kids?"

"Shirley and the kids believe in you as much as I do. They are also patriots. If this work needs to be done and we have to sacrifice, so be it. I'm not going to back down."

Spike answered, "Okay. That's fine. But starting right now, we're going to use Shauntel's secure network to do any further investigation. You can't use our basic WIFI to do the next piece of research."

"Fine. How much danger will Shirley, Jack, and Julie be in?"

"Right now, probably none. The IP address leads everyone back to me at this point. But eventually deeper investigation will connect your tablet back to your IP address in Denver and wherever else you've used that device. If we start hitting close to the truth, the bad guys will dig deeper and figure out who you are."

"So far, all I've looked at is what nutbags think about MARV," Joe said.

"Right, but as we go deeper, and hit closer to the truth, they'll look at who might be digging. The people who would be crazy enough to create a world-wide pandemic don't mind collateral damage. They have no problem killing everyone close to this because they place no value on human life."

"Okay, I'm in," Joe said. "Now, what did you learn from your classmate?"

"Key piece of info is that the CIA is investigating because it looks like MARV may have been bioengineered to kill people with high blood oxygen and vitamin D levels. People who are fit and work outside."

"CIA. I know someone who might have some contacts there." Joe smiled. "Just saying."

"That dude left fast and never looked back. I haven't even talked to my contacts in ten years."

"Well, how can I help? I really don't have hacking skills; I don't really know what I need to look for."

"Well, I have a few lines of investigation that need to be tracked down. Let's go socialize. I'm hungry."

As they came out of the office, they noticed everyone was there and seemed a little disengaged. Not tense, but not really talking much. Spike went over to the sliding glass door and opened it wide. He grinned and said, "Time to eat. Go wash up before you come to my table."

Bridget Eastman had uttered those exact words thousands of times. Everyone chuckled. Spike thought that he only had two other catchy lines left. Shauntel grinned at him and knew Spike had been saving that one. She asked, "Joe, did you get any apple cider beer?"

"Of course, couldn't leave the hostess without a drink. I also have some of those seltzer things that are all the rage with the kids these days. The coolers are full and labeled." He pointed to the end of the buffet.

Shauntel announced, "We've got pasta salad, vegetables, and regular salad with some grilled salmon and chicken. Then we have stuff to make sandwiches. Please eat as much as you can…as usual, we're overstocked."

As people made their way toward the food, Spike and Fred went over to the bar. Joe popped the caps off a couple bottles of Spotted Cow just as they hopped onto the stools. Joe asked Fred what he'd heard about MARV in Portland.

"I don't have a clue because the news just talks about how poorly the federal government handled the COVID-19 crisis. Just another way to criticize the Republicans and President Mitchell. You'd think they would lay off the guy. He didn't get reelected because he got screwed by COVID." Fred didn't want to talk about MARV, so he deftly switched the conversation to politics where the three of them almost always agreed with one another.

Joe was nodding. "The national media is the same, but at least in Denver you have some very outspoken talk radio hosts that fight every day. Fox News is the only alternative, but they blather on too about crooked politicians on the left. They are just as obnoxious as the lefties on MSNBC and CNN. The only difference is that Fox tries to link the discussion to facts and the rule of law. The other networks viewpoint is irrational and far too based in emotion."

Spike joined in. "I don't trust any politicians or the media. I think they are all too interested in keeping the status quo and their own power bases. They know nothing about what it is like to live a normal life outside of Washington, New York, and about a dozen of the largest cities. That's their universe. They serve one another's interests and have no concept of the working person's life or the lives of the men and women serving in the military. It is actually disgraceful. They ride in private jets, limousines, and haven't paid for any of it. We do."

Both Joe and Fred had heard it all before. Spike was cynical, but since they didn't have his experience, they usually just listened. Carl probably noticed that their discussion was getting intense and thought he should intervene. He'd already grabbed a plate of food and sat down next to Fred at the bar. Joe went back to the bar and opened a bottle of red wine and poured Carl a glass.

Carl said, "Thanks, Joe. Boys, I think we ought to eat outside. It's only this nice outside about twelve days a year around here."

"We'll eat at the bar outside. But first, we're going to let the ladies get their plates."

Joe glanced at Carl's plate. He always knew how to make Carl uncomfortable. It was a talent since Carl was so considerate.

Fred said, "At his age, he should always be first in line. Hell, he only has a couple years left." Carl was the oldest at sixty-six years old and had diabetes. He tended to get into line early when the food finally got unveiled, mostly because of habit to keep his blood sugar in line. And he needed to eat before he drank.

"I think another beer will make the line move faster." Spike wanted to move on. Carl sometimes became sullen when Joe picked on him. Spike finished his beer, and Joe had a beer open and in front of him before he set the empty down. "Carl, did your students bother you much after I saw you this morning?"

"No, but I did have about a half hour of wrap up at the end of class. Tomorrow, I start the final test, monitor that they aren't using outside resources, and talk for about fifteen minutes at the end. And I get paid extra because of the time zone. Sometimes, I feel like I'm stealing."

Spike smiled. "They need somebody to teach this stuff, and your skillset is pretty unique. You can geek it up with the best of them, but you have a personality and feel comfortable in front of a crowd. Probably not too many people like that in the world."

Spike glanced over and noticed the food buffet was clear. "Time to eat."

Joe got Fred a beer, topped off Carl's wine, and made himself a vodka. They grabbed some food and headed outside. Dale was alone at the bar, and Tim and Big Dan were heading over. Perfect—seven men around a nine-seat granite topped bar. Should be a fun meal.

Big Dan smiled. "Men's table. Think we should let Tim join?"

"I actually like girls, so I fit better than you, Danny Boy." This had been the discussion since they were young teenagers. Both questioned each other's sexuality. They thought it was funny, but Spike always worried that one of them could be gay and would be miserable for life.

Tim had long flowing hair and a beard. He was handsome in a Greek god sort of way. He was popular with the girls and was a nice kid. Maybe a little soft. Dan was tough, like Fred, but didn't fight because it wasn't acceptable in today's world. Spike always thought that Big Dan was born too late. He fit in better with his dad's generation than his own.

"Uncle Joe, how is Jack doing?" Big Dan asked.

"He's fine, going to graduate this year. He's gonna take a gap year and pursue his gaming career." Both Fred and Carl rolled their eyes. Spike was more disciplined and better informed. Jack was in the top hundred players in the world in some computer game that spectators actually paid to watch. Playing video games for a living seems silly until you realize how to monetize it. There were players who made more than some professional football players. Literally millions. If Jack made it, he could retire in ten years. Spike thought about the hundreds of kids who go play junior hockey after high school. Equally as unlikely to make a living playing a sport, but the eye rolls aren't as common.

"Joe, you always told Tim and me that playing those games was a waste of time. Now, Jack is going to forego college to play video games." Big Dan had a point. Joe was a bit of a hypocrite on the subject.

"You idiots didn't make money doing it at seventeen."

Tim laughed. "You have a point there."

Shauntel walked up and asked if she could get anyone more food or drink. Never one to turn down service, Tim said, "Sure, please get me a beer and maybe one of those fruity drinks for Danny Boy."

Shauntel laughed and touched her ear. A signal for Spike to follow. Spike grabbed his empty plate and empty beer and said, "I'll help; anybody need anything else?"

He grabbed the empty plates in front of Joe and Fred as he walked past. Nobody answered, so he just followed Shauntel in. They went behind the bar, and Spike asked, "What's up?"

"Dorothy is over there talking about how Christ died for us all, and 'Mom' will be going to a better place. Renee and the girls are crying softly. Sarah is trying to steer the conversation away from death. Whenever Dorothy calls your mother 'Mom,' Renee sighs. She's getting close to a boiling point. I think you and Fred need to lighten the discussion."

Spike said, "Got it." He grabbed three Spotted Cows, the bottle of wine, and a water.

He delivered the beers to Fred, Tim, the water to Big Dan and placed the bottle of wine in the middle of the bar in front to Carl. He caught Fred's attention and nodded toward the other end of the pool where the women were gathered.

Fred got up and asked, "How do you keep this pool so clean?"

Spike started to answer as they walked toward the women. Then he whispered, "Emergency, God and death talk needs to be averted before Renee chokes Dorothy to death."

Fred smiled and said, "Let's remind them of the time Mom came to pick me up at the police station. That will remind them to celebrate the woman instead of burying her right now."

"Might work. I'll start."

As they got nearby, Spike loudly said, "I think she should have left you overnight. What was the worst thing that could have happened?"

"Well, I might have had to beat up the forty-year-old drunks whose wives wouldn't come pick them up."

Renee loved this story. And she agreed with me that Fred could have used a night in the drunk tank. She got up; crisis may have been averted. She said, "Oh, the chosen one couldn't be left at the police station overnight. Mom is such a sucker."

"I'll admit that she loves me more than the rest of you, but who could blame her?"

At this, Bailey smiled and said as she was standing up, "As I understand things, you were drunk and got kicked out of two bars that night. Who could blame her?"

Fred felt defeated but wasn't giving up. "Look, I wasn't the youngest like Spike or the only girl like Renee. Somebody had to care about me, and Mom took on that burden. She's a saint."

"Is there a patron saint for the drunk and disorderly?" Renee asked.

"Who do you think Saint Patrick represents, dumbass?" Fred knew his saints.

"Now you're going to disparage a whole country to justify your favorite status?" Spike wondered.

"I'll admit to being stupid and young. And that made me wiser as I grew old."

Renee was smiling and enjoying her brothers. Since Spike hadn't had any of his Spotted Cow yet, he handed it to her and said, "We'll get through this." He put his arm around her, and the four of them all started walking toward the bar.

As they reached the bar, Bailey looked over at Dale and said, "I need to go relieve Alyssa." Bailey looked both sad and proud that she could help.

"Take my car. Alyssa can bring it back. She doesn't have a car there, and then Fred can keep drinking," Dale answered.

"Great, what could go wrong?" asked Renee.

Tim piped up, "Danny Boy can go along to be sure Alyssa doesn't get lost. She's not that hot at directions."

"And I am?" Big Dan clearly didn't want to go.

"You're the only one who isn't drinking." Tim offered. "Besides, you know how to work that phone. Set a pin and you can find your way back, just like 'Jack and the Bean Stalk.'"

"'Hansel and Gretel,' you idiot."

"Dan, go get your sister," Joe said. He got a little tired of the boys bickering. "I'm pretty sure your dad didn't hug you two enough when you were little."

That got a laugh, and Dale tossed Dan the keys.

Spike and Shauntel did another run around the pool to clean up the dishes and take drink orders. As they went inside, Joe joined them. As Joe worked on the drinks, he asked, "How much does Shauntel know about our research?"

Shauntel answered, "I know you need to get a secure connection, and I know Guls has fed Spike some fairly uncomfortable information about the virus and his old buddies being interested. What else is there?"

"Guess that's it. I just don't want the inside circle to expand too much. Carl knows a lot about information security. Should we ask him?"

"He set up my network and firewalls. He does vulnerability audits once a quarter. I have a separate service try to break in too. The network is secure."

"No network is that secure. Think about Jimmy Celestini, honey." Spike reminded her of the story he told her a few years ago about a college kid who hacked the CIA network. "Can you two keep these people happy and try to get them to eat another round in about an hour? I need to run back to work for a couple hours to get us up and running. When I get back, I can join the fun for tonight," Spike said.

Joe said, "They don't have anywhere else to go. Maybe I can get Fred and Dale to plan a bonfire for tonight. We have plenty of beer, food, and spirits."

"Good idea, just keep them away from the gasoline. Forest fires are bad for the neighborhood."

Shauntel was covering the food for round two. Spike went over and gave her a peck on the cheek. She said, "I'm a little nervous about what we might find out. If you get involved, you always take things to the extreme."

Spike laughed. "At this point, we're just trying to figure it out. I think the company will have it covered." Shauntel smiled; they always called the CIA "the company" because she had read it in a novel once and thought it was a mistake. Spike explained that inside the CIA, they called it that all the time. Suddenly, she was an insider. It always made her laugh because it sounded so cheesy. Her smile faded as she realized that if what Joe was doing needed to be secure, maybe it was more than Spike was admitting.

Spike headed back to work. He only had to spend a couple hours in the office because Jim had already convinced most of the leadership committee to move forward.

Spike needed to talk with Chen and Wang in China, so he had to wait until 5 p.m. He'd called them at about 6 a.m. their time. Both came to work early, and they explained that Wang already had morning meetings. The additional end of day debriefing run by Wang could be a natural extension. They were already back to work anyway, so they were confident that they would win all of the weekly contests. They were always confident in their capabilities. Chen didn't seem to mind the plan, but you never knew. He could be flogging Wang right now for all Spike knew.

On his way out, Spike walked by Jim DePacker's office. "Hey Jim, I'm heading back to see my family. Hope it isn't turning into a big pity party. Since I'm the only sibling who can go to the hospital, my nieces and nephews have been pulling hospital duty. I guess it is good for them, but my sister and brothers are getting a little restless."

"When is your next shift?"

"I'll start midafternoon tomorrow. We haven't been too strict on the timing. The overnight shift is a little longer, but the hospital lets visitors rest in empty rooms."

As Spike headed home, he decided to swing by the hospital parking lot. It looked very quiet. During COVID-19, hospitals quit doing non-essential work. Looks like they were doing the same thing, and that was a huge problem for the healthcare industry last year. Many doctors and nurses weren't allowed to do their normal work. Hospital staff still had to do all the cleaning and feeding patients, but most of the buildings were shut down. It looked like that might be happening again. Spike thought they could have figured out a way to separate the infected people from the rest of the patients.

CHAPTER 11

Spike pulled into the garage still thinking about the healthcare industry. He snapped out of it as he put the truck into park. The party should be rocking downstairs. He noticed that Carl's lights were on in his RV. That seemed strange; they should have still been downstairs hanging with the family. He closed the garage door and walked around to the back of the house without heading in. He saw Dale, Fred, and Joe at the bonfire pit with a pretty good blaze. No trees on fire, that was a good sign.

He walked to the cooler, grabbed a Spotted Cow and church key. As he opened his beer he asked, "What's going on?"

Fred answered, "The women pretty much just got tired. Carl got a little drunk, ate another plate of food, grabbed another bottle of wine, and invited Dorothy back to the love bug. That's what they call it. Ick."

"How is Alyssa? Anything new from the hospital?" Spike asked.

Fred answered, "Alyssa looked scared when she got back. She said that maybe the ICU was just a precaution, but they wouldn't have intubated her for no reason. Carl talked to the doctor who said she is worse, but it is hard to tell if she is getting stronger."

Dale piped up, "I hope she makes it past tomorrow afternoon. Neither Bailey nor Kelcey are well equipped for this. Neither has been around death before."

"Maybe I should take over early," Spike offered.

"No, the plan is in place, and your mom will hold out for you to get there. She won't put the girls through that."

Dale smiled and added, "Bridget is tough. She'll figure it out for us."

Joe and Fred both seemed a little put off by the assumption that their mom was going to die. Joe said, "She isn't dead yet. Hell, you two should be motivational speakers."

"Couple of glass half full guys, huh?" Fred joked.

Spike didn't really want to talk about it, and that was an easy problem to solve. "So Joe thinks the Donkeys are going to beat the Packers in the Super Bowl."

Dale piped up immediately, "First, Denver isn't going to be there. Second, if the Packers make it, they'll win. Rodgers wants to pass Favre in Packer Super Bowl wins. He's such a self-centered person; it will be all about him. And he's still good enough to win it."

"Neither one of them will make it." Fred jumped in. "In fact, neither one will win their division next year. KC will win the AFC West, and the Vikes are sure to win the NFC North. To prove it to you, I will bet either of you any amount you want that the team I picked finishes higher in their division than your teams."

"First of all, the Broncos aren't my team. Second, KC's quarterback is a flash in the pan. Third, I agree that the Vikes are better than the Packers."

And on it went for half an hour. Followed by a discussion of pro baseball, pro basketball, and, finally, the fact that the Stanley Cup playoffs are the best because the players seem to care. Nobody argued against NHL hockey being the most exciting playoffs, so the discussion waned. Since it was only 8 p.m. and the mosquitoes were starting to come out, the party moved to the bar. Spike ran upstairs to check on the rest of the family. He found Renee and her girls, Shauntel, Alyssa, and Sarah sitting around the TV watching some housewives' reality show. They were laughing and making fun of the silly spats on the show, which were obviously made for TV. Spike asked where Dan and Tim were.

Shauntel answered, "Probably in the office, they asked for the Wi-Fi password."

"We're just going to hang out by the bar. If you get bored with housewives, you can listen to the same old stories downstairs."

They laughed, and Alyssa said, "Either way, it's pretty predictable."

Spike headed back downstairs. The grown men were already picking on Dan and Tim. Joe had made sure that everyone had a drink. Spike headed behind the bar and grabbed a Spotted Cow. Fifth one today, he'd feel it in the morning. He was getting too old for this. He realized that he had not spent this much time with the family in a long time. Mom brings them together again. She truly was the center of the family. Not sure how often he would see any of them if she passed.

Spike was getting a pensive look on his face when Joe said, "What's going on upstairs?"

"They are watching the housewives of someplace glamorous. Reality TV."

"Did you guys see *Tiger King* last year?" Fred asked.

Everyone had seen it, and they all wondered how they could make money with a viral idea. Spike said, "We are too normal. These things are like a train wreck, you can't help but watch."

Big Dan asked, "Spike, you have an interesting past. Do you ever think about how you could make money from that?"

"Nothing I did would be interesting."

Dale said, "What about that time you parachuted into the Kremlin? Messed up their systems and snuck out?"

"Dale, that was all made up. One, I'm scared of jumping out of a plane. Two, I don't know a bit from a byte. Three, I'm not very sneaky."

"Are you kidding me? I've told that story a hundred times. It was made up?"

"You knew that. I was drunk, telling a silly story because that's what I do."

"I was drunk when I heard it. How was I supposed to know you made it up?" Dale seemed a little pissed.

"Want to hear a real war story?" Spike asked.

"Sure. I won't believe it though."

"Dale, I was embedded with a group of army Special Forces. These guys are real snake eaters. Remember in Rambo when the Colonel says, 'He eats stuff that would make a billy goat puke'? These guys were like that. Improvised weapons, totally self-sufficient in the field. The problem was that we were in Bagdad. Not a lot of need for field survival skills. My hair was long and black. I was dressed in robes, dirty, like a street person. My job was to point out a high value target. I had a nine mil inside my robes, but it would have taken me a while to get it. So, I saw the dude and told the badasses over the radio where he was. They came in, grabbed the dude. On the way out, they were ambushed. It appeared that the bad guys had seen the Special Forces coming and decided to try to tag them on the way out. I ran up and was going to help when one of our guys thought I was on the other team. Luckily, when he turned toward me, I realized that I probably looked like a terrorist. I hid behind a car until the Special Forces guys were done extinguishing the threat and headed back to base. Closest I ever came to being shot at or to shooting someone. That's my war story."

Fred and Joe looked skeptical. They knew some of the people Spike had served with and had heard some real stories. Never fully in context, never fully explained. Spike's buddies made it seem to Fred and Joe that Spike was part of the action. They just assumed Spike was a shooter.

Spike thought back to his time fighting Islamic terrorists. He had been in gunfights; he'd killed the enemy. But, more often, he was helping plan missions, trying to develop leads from interrogations, and identifying the enemy. He participated in a lot of kidnappings of high value targets and often began the interrogation process immediately. He wasn't all that proud of all the techniques he used to break the enemy while interrogating them. Spike did what he was there to do, and he believed his actions were morally correct.

The kidnappings were referred to as renditions in Washington, but the fact was, the US intelligence operatives and Special Forces kidnapped people they thought were connected to the enemy. They were probably right over 98 percent of the time. The interrogation techniques, including waterboarding, sleep deprivation, drugs, disorientation, threats, and beatings, were dubbed "enhanced interrogation." Spike was intellectually honest with himself and called it torture when it got physical, including waterboarding, drugs, and beatings. The truth was that these techniques were seldom used. The psychological part of the process, which included sleep deprivation, loud music, hooding prisoners, stripping their clothing, high wattage lighting, standing in stress positions, wasn't pleasant but hardly rose to the level of torture. The idea was to disorient the prisoner. All these techniques worked, and valuable intelligence was gained.

After several embarrassing incidents related to prisoner treatment, including the infamous Abu Ghraib in Iraq in 2004, the stated US policy was to treat prisoners humanely. The policy was mostly adhered to, but in cases where a prisoner was highly likely to have knowledge that could lead to actionable intelligence, most operators and interrogators were willing to bend or even snap the rules. As the administrations changed in Washington, so did the oversight and likelihood of prosecution for not following policy. The changes in Washington made it seem like there were two enemies, the politicians and the terrorists. To be fair, this shift had begun long before the 2008 election. The American public and the more liberal politicians seemed to believe that if the West were nice to the terrorists, they would stop attacking us. In Europe, they tried that line of thinking, including unchecked immigration and less internal security. The results were twofold. First, there were parts of Paris, London, and Brussels where police weren't welcome. Sharia law was in place, and Western legal ideals were ignored. Second, terrorist attacks were larger and more deadly. Madrid, London, Paris, Brussels, Nice, Manchester were all targeted. Since 9/11, the US had fewer attacks. Some individuals who swore allegiance to Daesh or Al Qaeda had succeeded in killing Americans. Some of the successes in preventing attacks were due to intelligence gathered using interrogation techniques of which the politicians would not have approved. Spike was proud of the role he played in helping to protect Americans and America's interests abroad and at home.

Still, Spike wasn't anywhere near as skilled as the Special Forces teams he served with. His role was mostly support. Many of his missions were still classified, but that wasn't the reason he didn't tell his family about them. He simply didn't think they would understand. So, he had never told any real stories to any of them.

In his mind, he felt the public didn't want to know how the war on terrorism was fought on the front lines. To win, you had to play dirty. And, in the end, his view was that finding and killing terrorists was more important than the civil rights of the enemy. The way Al-Qaeda, Daesh, and the Taliban treated people who didn't acquiesce to their view of Islam was evil, especially the treatment of women. Spike felt like the only way to combat that was through force. Since these groups knew they couldn't fight against the rest of the world in conventional means, they fought dirty. Roadside bombs, homicide bombers, guerrilla tactics were their only chance to disrupt the status quo. They hid their armaments in hospitals and mosques. They put their fellow Muslims in harm's way. Then, they would get pictures of the rubble they created to try to recruit more terrorists. Weakness by the West is consistently capitalized on. The Taliban ran most of Afghanistan; later, Daesh held a large part of Iraqi and Syrian territory. While all of this was happening, America largely ignored the problem. The attacks of September 11, 2001, changed that for a short time. But this enemy doesn't think of a decade as significant. The long view is their view. They will celebrate 9/11 for centuries.

"Earth to Spike, Earth to Spike," Dale was calling out.

Spike snapped out of his trance and realized he'd been thinking about his CIA days for at least ten minutes. "Yeah, Dale, sorry."

"I'm sure you were thinking about all those times you didn't do heroic shit over in Iraq and Afghanistan, right?"

Spike finished putting in a pinch of Copenhagen and said, "Dale, I was thinking about how tough those Special Forces guys were. The sacrifices they made and the training it takes to do what they did. Fred and Joe have met some of them. Badasses, right, fellas?"

Joe said, "They told us you were right there with them. You weren't just some pencil neck hiding behind the lines. They specifically said you participated with them."

Spike laughed. "Of course, they said that. They were just yanking your chain. They would be laughing their asses off right now if they could hear this conversation. Remember Captain Hammargren? He and his team were unbelievably effective. I didn't do squat but follow them around. He even put me in the middle of the group when we moved around so nobody would shoot the 'Air Force weenie.' I think he even told you part of a story where he almost got greased, but one of his guys double-tapped the terrorist before I even realized he was in danger."

"Yeah, they also told us you saved some kid named Gomez when you were supposed to be undercover by killing a guy who was about to wax Gomez and his Humvee with a shoulder launched rocket."

"Hammargren must have had me confused with some other dude. I wouldn't have come out of my role to save one soldier." Spike remembered that operation like it had just happened last night. It was about three months after the first time he'd worked with this Army Special Forces unit to catch al-Takfiri. The mission was in Kabul, and the target was a Taliban commander who was looking to disrupt an election. This was probably Spike's fifteenth mission with this team. When Spike saw the terrorist lining up the Humvee, he swore under his breath, pulled his silenced nine-millimeter, and plugged the tango in the head. Pretty lucky, because he was aiming center mass. The RPG went off, hit a building, and the mission was blown.

"Bullshit!" Fred was having none of Spike's denials.

Spike was looking for a change of subject and tried sports. "The Vikings offensive line will be great this year. Finally, the last few drafts are going to pay off."

Joe said, "Not gonna work, Spike. Why won't you tell us about your time serving our country?"

"Fellas, I love you, but I really don't like to talk about this stuff. I did my duty; there were parts of it that were cool. But gunfights aren't fun, shouldn't be discussed outside of the unit they happen with, and even the winning side seldom comes out unscathed. People die; people come home disabled. And most of those things are still classified. The cool parts, like figuring out where the targets were and connecting the dots of the terrorist organizations, aren't very interesting to people who don't know the players. And talking about that stuff could get me thrown in jail because it is really classified. Let's just say I did the best I could with my limited training." It seemed to work, especially the part about casualties. Hell, the casualties were usually limited on our side to minor injuries, but these guys didn't know that. The deaths were nearly always on the other side.

They started arguing about the Vikings offensive line, and Spike was out of the limelight. It might be a relief to tell the real war stories. Maybe even get it off his chest. The only person he had ever told was Shauntel. She knew almost every story. He was afraid to tell some of them, but she never judged him. She just listened and sometimes reminded him that he did the best he could.

The discussion remained light, several rounds were served, and people started getting tired. Fred and his boys went upstairs and found Sarah so she could drive them back to the hotel. Dale headed upstairs to go to bed and worry more about his girls pulling the deathwatch. That left Joe and Spike to clean up. Joe said, "Spike, I know you were deflecting on the CIA stuff. You were a warrior; that's what Captain Hammargren kept saying when I met him. I'm in sales, and I know bullshit. He was being sincere."

"Joe, I can't prove a negative. I meant it when I said there were casualties. On our side, they were mostly emotional. Our Special Forces guys are precise, trained killers, but there is still collateral damage. Sometimes women and kids who aren't supposed to be there get killed. That's nightmare for life material.

I think talking about it dishonors their service. And acting like I was a commando is just not accurate."

"Okay, I'll drop it."

"Did Shauntel set you up?"

"Yeah, she showed me how to connect"

"Start tomorrow?"

"I don't think I would be any good tonight."

Spike bagged the garbage and recycling bins and headed toward the slider to toss it. "I'll swing by around noon before heading to the hospital. Good night."

"All right, see you tomorrow."

CHAPTER 12

The next day

The alarm sounded more shrill than normal. As expected, the next hour would be a grind due to too many beers. By the time he and Ginger turned back toward home, he was pouring sweat. Ginger was way out ahead, Spike whistled twice to slow her down. He pumped as hard as he could on the last mile to get some pride back. If Ginger could talk, she would have told him to take it easy on the beers next time.

As he headed into the office, Spike called Guls who answered with his normal laidback tone. The conversation was about everything but MARV. Plans for the Academy reunion in three years and the mid-term get together down in Florida sometime this summer. Overall, casual conversation. He did add in a couple dates that didn't really make sense, so Spike wrote them down in his notebook. Maybe he was giving him a phone number to text. Spike assumed it would be a seven-digit number he was looking for, because Guls had made reference to April 4th, the area code for Atlanta. He was reasonably sure he had the number, but his burner phones were still at home. He'd grab a couple when he stopped by home before heading to the hospital.

Spike stopped by Jim DePacker's office to check in and remind him that he needed to leave early today to head over to the hospital. Spike was uncomfortable talking about his mom, but Jim seemed interested, so Spike told him how his nieces were a little nervous about being there last.

"Is this the end?" Jim asked.

"Don't know for sure, but she has declined a lot since I was there Tuesday. At first, they put her into ICU as a precaution, but since then, she's been put on a respirator, and they tried a plasma infusion from a recovered MARV survivor hoping to get the right antibodies into her. We're trying to stay optimistic, but I doubt Doctor Huebrex would do the plasma thing unless he thought she was in danger."

"Why don't you leave now? The restart plan is progressing as expected. Things might really start to get busy next week as we defend our plan to local governments and other outsiders and try to build the competition between plants."

"I have a few things I need to check on. I want to see Bill and Bob after they do their morning meeting. I need to check on inventories to be sure we make the right products first. I'd like to check in with Jun later, but I'll need to do that from the hospital. He probably read my mind; I saw an email from him from overnight, so I might not even need to speak with him. He continues to amaze me."

"All right but get out of here as soon as you can. We can handle things here."

Spike went into his office and got enthralled with Jun's analysis. He'd projected production and compared it to orders, inventory, and shipping schedules. Revenue for the second quarter would be significantly lower than expected, but costs were down, too, and by third quarter in the base case model, production would be in line with demand. Jun also included a projection for selling the lower quality products at a discount to clear inventory faster to increase revenue with lower to no margin. Spike sent a quick email to Jun to let him know he appreciated the thoughtful analysis.

Bob and Bill were standing on the catwalk again when Spike showed up at the plant. He waved at them, and they pointed to the office that overlooked the production floor. They met there; Bob was wearing a Marine Corps T-shirt.

Spike said, "Overkill on the T-shirt?"

"I told him to wear it. These guys respect the military, and Bob was a warrior." Bill was sure it was a good move.

"Any reaction from the troops?"

"Yeah, they made fun of it," Bob said.

Bill countered, "Except, you jarheads don't read your crowd well. They noticed, and they were hanging on your analysis of how we could get things done faster."

Bob said, "Maybe, but the best part about yesterday afternoon was how open they were to say what could be better. So, today, we mostly just asked them how they could do what they thought would be better. They really ran the show both yesterday afternoon and this morning. Bill had some good points about safety issues with a couple of their ideas, so we worked through them and decided to compromise on speed to stay safe. It was fun to see the way they thought about alternative solutions. Spike, we should have done this years ago."

"Two reasons why we haven't done this before. First, Jim designs these production lines to meet a certain demand level. The work we are doing to mess with the processes can't be accomplished without extremely competent leadership and a close eye on safety. Second, the new processes could impact our warrantees for some of the automation software in case we use things differently than designed."

"Big deal. Your brother, Joe, could fix the software sitting in Denver. He's a damn genius," Bill offered.

"Don't tell him that. You'll kill any negotiating power we have today. Besides, his ego is plenty big without hearing it from you." Spike thought about how the briefings must have gone. He added, "Great job getting the floor engaged. Anything we can use at other plants to help them work through this new briefing/debriefing regimen?"

Both Bill and Bob laughed. Bob said, "We figured you'd ask. Not all that thrilled about giving away our secrets. In fact, we flipped a coin to decide whether we should tell you this. We want to win, but we also want the company to make money. So, we overturned the coin flip because we were feeling guilty and decided to tell you."

Bill took over. "There are two things that are universal. First, nobody should mess with hard-set barriers to keep man and machine separate. But there are five- to ten-second delays that could be reset to one second. The delays create bottlenecks in our process, and we think the same thing is likely true in all the plants. Second, the precision of the process is calibrated to have set breaktimes. As we speed things up, we decided to allow the employees to pick their own breaktimes. We considered this a safety issue, too, in case of fatigue if people decided not to take any breaks. So, we hit that hard. Everybody needs to click to break at least three minutes per hour."

"The teams were thrilled with the flexibility. Sometimes a couple minutes one way or another costs fifteen minutes of production. Not everybody sees the downstream impacts of their decisions, so we'll learn more about this in today's debriefing."

Spike was impressed. He wasn't a production expert, so he needed to let Jim know what they were doing. It seemed like minor tweaks to Spike, but he needed to check with Jim to be sure these two nuggets could be shared company wide.

"Thanks, fellas. I am so happy you two are here to lead this. I've always thought more flexibility was better. Sort of the difference between traditional warfighting in World War II versus the guerilla fighting that has dominated our conflicts since Vietnam. Combat teams need flexibility compared to the huge command and control structure required to retake Europe. As people have become a smaller component of the manufacturing process, each person is more important. You guys have a great start. And you are one day ahead, so I think you'll probably have a good chance in the competition. Good work!"

"Thanks, Spike," they said in unison.

Spike headed back to the office. He thought about his siblings and their competence in their selected professions. Carl and Joe could help Maurer with their technical skills. Fred went in a different direction and made a boatload of money. Renee was an accountant and supported Dale's business. He'd opened four sports bars in suburban Milwaukee. She ran the books and worked as a consultant on projects, mostly in banks. She was tireless, and Dale was doing what he always wanted to do. Renee always figured out how to help their mom. She was a great wife, mom, and daughter. He was so proud of his family, but he never told them. Maybe he should, since they were always there for Shauntel and the kids while Spike was running around the world. He grabbed his notebook and jotted down some notes in case he needed to break bad news about mom.

He sent a couple emails and checked with Jim about the recommendations from Bill and Bob. They were fine, and Jim promised to share the best practice with the other plants. Spike drove home and ate quick salad before grabbing a couple of burner phones from the safe in the mudroom. He headed downstairs to see what was happening in the office.

Joe and Shauntel were both feverishly working. Spike grabbed three bottles of water and said, "Anybody thirsty?"

Shauntel looked up and smiled, but Joe kept attacking the keyboard. Spike handed Shauntel a water and stood behind Joe. Joe was clicking away at the keyboard…on a mission. Spike put the bottle of water next to him, and he just grunted. Spike wondered what he was working on but ignored him and asked Shauntel, "Hi gorgeous, what are you working on?"

Shauntel said, "Some of my clients are wondering what is next. I'm not the CDC, but I'm thinking they need to start buying summer stuff for their stores. This year's MARV isn't last year's COVID. We'll be open in a couple weeks in metro areas. And my clientele includes a bunch of large retailers. Buy your summer inventory is my message right now."

Joe looked up and noticed Spike was there. "Yeah, this is really weird. All the blogs are talking about how different this is from last year. The nutbag conspiracy people are saying how this was created to target outdoorsman and, by association, the right to bear arms. 'This is an attack on the Second Amendment. The left is trying to kill gun owners.' It's compelling because the people who are dying, based on their analysis, are disproportionately gun owners and NRA folks."

"Well, the CIA wouldn't care about that…it's domestic."

"The blogs say the government doesn't care about gun owners." Joe seemed convinced.

"Joe, both sides of every argument can prove their point with statistics. I'm sure the nutbags on the left have conspiracy theories, too. We need to look for international issues."

"Is there a way to search for that?" Joe asked.

"I don't know, but start thinking, who wins in the international sphere?"

Spike sat in one of the comfortable office chairs that cost about a grand each. Joe had his desk elevated for standing work. Shauntel preferred to sit and stand for one hour at a time, and she was sitting currently. Spike was between them activating the burner phone. He was careful not to associate to Wi-Fi, but knew that if the NSA wanted to know, they would figure out his approximate location. Guls had given a clear clue to his number, so Spike typed it in and texted, *What's up dude?*

Guls would know it was him if Spike had deciphered the number correctly. The answer came quickly. The text said, *Your people know I'm leaking. U R right about creating specific targets. Don't know who, but it feels like terror or state actors.*

Tell nobody else. New number, one use. I feel three years older, talk Monday. Spike hoped he would understand that his next number was all the same with the last digit three higher than the last phone number. Because they didn't plan to need to correspond this way, they didn't have a protocol, but Guls was perceptive. Hopefully, Guls would get it and destroy his current phone.

The CIA knowing that he was leaking was not good. That means they would know who the recipient of the information was. And if they knew, others might also be tracking Guls. Spike hoped that Guls wasn't interacting with any other curious classmates or friends. The company was unlikely to come in the middle of the night to Sheboygan Falls to bother with Spike. He was a known entity whom Director Oliva knew about. She would need to authorize any domestic missions, and she would call Tim Blust before she made a move, so Spike figured he would have ample warning. Guls and anyone else he was telling weren't as likely to have any warnings. For Guls, it would be the FBI who would come to him. He could be in serious trouble depending on how classified his leaks were. Spike assumed it would be a serious federal offense that would land Guls in prison, but if Spike was the only person he was leaking to, the CIA would just watch and learn. Even with all the cooperation between intelligence and law enforcement since 9/11, the CIA wouldn't bother to share the information with the FBI.

Spike looked over at Joe. He was typing like a madman, so Spike waited for him to finish a thought. Joe hit enter and stepped away from the screens. Spike said, "CIA knows that Guls is talking to me. I'm not sure they actually told him, but he's spooked. I gave him a clue for my next burner number, but he could have missed it. Said we would talk Monday. He also said that he thinks MARV is a targeted virus, and he assumes it is either a terrorist group or state actor. See what you can find, but it might be smart to be a little vague."

"If we are getting closer, why should we be vague?"

"Mostly because if the CIA knows I'm involved, they could be watching our servers."

Shauntel looked up. "They can't just watch us. We're US citizens in flyover country."

"My former clearance gives them an excuse to watch me for life. Any FISA judge would sign off on domestic spying of a former CIA operative. They figure I gave up my rights for life when I joined them."

"Liberty has its limits." Shauntel and Spike had laughed about that phrase for about an hour one night after Spike had been debriefed on a particularly sensitive mission. She thought it was overkill when the CIA threatened him with federal prison if he ever told anyone what he'd done. He'd said back then, "Well, I'm not going to test it. Liberty has its limits." She thought he was being melodramatic and started giggling. By the time they were done, their faces hurt from laughing about it.

This time, Spike didn't think it was so funny. It wasn't just his ass on the line, it was Joe and Shauntel, too. He said again to Joe, "Be really vague. I don't want them to know how far we've progressed before we get a little better view of the situation."

CHAPTER 13

Spike jumped into the pickup and headed to the hospital. The process to get in took forty-five minutes. When he saw Kelcey, she looked drawn and tired. She'd probably not slept much. Spike said, "Hey kid, how are you doing?"

"I'm glad you're here. This has been boring as watching paint dry. The nurses told me she was hanging in there like twelve times but never really told me anything else."

"Well, I'm hoping she hangs in there until she beats the tar out of the MARV. Maybe this is part of the normal recovery?"

"Uncle Spike, I like your attitude, but I wouldn't get my hopes up."

"Listen to you, telling your old uncle to temper his expectations. Looking out for my emotional well-being. No wonder you are going to be a psychiatrist. I'm guessing that your professors at Marquette would be very proud of you. I know I am."

"Thanks. I'm going to head back to your house. Is the party over?"

"Yeah, but if you can convince your mom and Uncle Fred to reconvene, you can start a new one."

Kelcey smiled and said, "I'll get them motivated and take an hour nap while they get organized. See you, Uncle Spike."

"See ya, Kelcey."

Spike headed to the nurses' station to ask about his mom. "Hi Nurse Cynthia, I'm Bridget Eastman's son, Gary. Anything I need to know before I head to her room?"

"I'm glad you are here. She has deteriorated, and I'll send Doctor Huebrex down to see you as soon as he's available. He can tell you more, but I know Bridget has been asking for you."

"Okay, thank you, I guess. This is weird. You have my number, why wouldn't you call if she's deteriorated so badly?"

"You'll have to ask Doctor Huebrex. He's been extremely specific that we weren't supposed to tell the grandchildren anything other than, 'She's hanging in there.'"

Spike grimaced. "She's a stubborn woman, isn't she?"

"She's been pleasant and grateful. But, yes, she isn't an open book, if that's what you are referring to."

"Huh, that is an understatement. She had a heart attack when I was at college, and she told everyone to keep it from me so I wouldn't be distracted. 'His finals are more important than my heart,' she'd told my dad. Dad asked her, 'What if you die?' She said, 'Well, then I guess you'll have to tell him.'"

The nurse commented, "Sounds like a very unselfish person."

"The least self-absorbed person I have ever known," Spike said as he headed down the hall.

When he got to the window, he was surprised to see his mom was in a bubble. She was hooked up to a breathing machine and had an IV in her left arm. The whole setup looked like life support, but Spike knew she had a living will that wouldn't allow extraordinary measures. She seemed to be asleep, but he couldn't tell for sure. He knocked on the window sharply, and she turned her head. She raised her right hand slowly and waved. He smiled , nodded, and she just lay back to rest.

Doctor Huebrex showed up a few minutes later. He said, "Good afternoon, Spike."

"Hi, Doctor. You and my mom been scheming?"

"Yeah, you could definitely call it that. She convinced me that her grandchildren needed to know nothing. Once we intubated her, she didn't want them to come close. So, I told the nurses not to let them in the room, and just to say 'She's holding her own' or 'She's hanging in there.' She wrote this last night and told me to give it to you or any of her other children who came in. I told her that you were it, and she sort of rolled her eyes. Not sure what that meant." He handed Spike the note.

"Well, I'm guessing this cut me out of the will." Spike laughed.

"She told me that she's going to hold out for one of you, but she's not all that interested in fighting the MARV. That's what she calls it—'the MARV.'"

"She was always strong, but she probably doesn't want this much attention. I'll read the note and tell my siblings to gather and read it to them over the phone. It will give them an excuse to be together tonight."

"She told me that was one of the reasons for writing it. She also told me that when you get here, she wants me to take the breathing tube out so she can speak to you. She will probably have five minutes of voice; these tubes do a number on your vocal cords. Plus, she may not survive long without the respirator."

"I think I will read the note first, okay?"

"She insists."

"Okay, Doctor Huebrex. Thanks."

Doctor Huebrex left. Spike went over and sat down. He unfolded the legal-paper-sized note and started reading.

> *Dear kids,*
>
> *You all know I'm dying. I know I'm dying, and here are my requests.*
>
> *Please cremate and bury me next to dad right away but wait until August or September to have a memorial service. By then, people will be able to plan and travel.*
>
> *When you have the memorial service, make it fun. Or else.*
>
> *If any of you cry or feel sorry for yourselves, shame on you. I'm an old lady, and I want to join Jack. Selfishly, you probably want me to live. Get over it.*
>
> *Go home now. Sitting around waiting for me to die when none of you can come see me is dumb.*
>
> *Make sure your kids remember Jack and me as we were five or ten years ago. Not these last days of me dying in a hospital. Whoever thought it was a good idea to have those kids here was an idiot. Sorry Renee and Fred, but your kids are too young to be marred with the memory of me dying in their "care." I didn't let them in the room, and that Doctor Huebrex should get a medal for working with me to keep them at arm's length.*

Spike, when you get here, I want to talk to you. They are going to pull the tube out. Don't worry if it kills me. I want to tell you a few things I have thought of that I don't want to write down.

Mom

That was it. Some simple instructions, a message from the one in charge. Spike texted his siblings and told them she wrote them a note. Since they weren't gathered yet, he took a picture of it and sent it after they'd all replied saying that was a good plan. Joe was first to reply. "Shit, that sounds like a suicide note."

Carl replied after careful thought, "More like a surrender note."

Renee sent, "I want to come see her."

Fred immediately sent, "You can't. She wouldn't want that anyway."

Spike responded, "I'm going to ask Doctor Huebrex to let me in. I would Facetime you all, but she'd probably stop talking immediately. I'll ask her, but don't count on it."

Spike went down to the nurses' station and got Cynthia's attention. "Doctor Huebrex asked that I call for him."

She looked up and answered, "Okay, we'll tell him you're ready. I'll help with the tube."

Spike realized that they all knew what was going on. Only three days ago, she was talking about Nicorette and old fashioned cocktails. Now she was dying. When Doctor Huebrex showed up, he smiled and said, "Let's go talk to your mom." Spike thought about how doctors and nurses dealt with fatalities. He realized that they were more rational because they saw it more often. Doctor Huebrex was totally calm.

They entered the room with Cynthia. She went around the bed and opened the plastic bubble. She was "suited up" in what looked like an anti-radiation suit Spike had worn in chemical warfare training. He thought it might be a little extreme for the circumstances and then thought back to Billy Big Shot and remembered that this isn't COVID-19. As Spike settled into what looked more like a barstool than hospital furniture, he realized it was brought in so he could be at eye level with his mom. Doctor Huebrex moved over to the other side of the bed and began scanning the monitors. He had told Spike he would be paying attention to the oxygen level in her blood, and if it got too low, he and Cynthia would re-intubate her. When the tube came out, Mom immediately reached for water that Cynthia had anticipated. Cynthia said, "Drink slowly, or it will hurt." Bridget sipped, and Spike thought that he should have brought her an old fashioned.

She spoke quietly, but there was a speaker and microphone on the outside of the bubble that Cynthia could control. "Well, Spike, you know this is probably the last time we'll talk. I want you to tell everyone that I'm proud of them, and their dad was too. The next generation is also strong. I'm putting you and your siblings in charge. You, Fred, and Joe should listen to Carl and Renee more. They are usually right and have good instincts."

Bridget didn't notice that Spike was recording her. Spike just nodded and said, "Yes, ma'am."

"Next thing, I wasn't kidding in my note. No self-pity. When you lose your last parent, you are now in charge. Your children are watching you. If you act like a big baby over your mother passing, they will think it is okay to be a victim. Don't teach that behavior."

"Yes, ma'am."

"Next, you probably all feel guilty for not being as close to me as you think you should. That is bullshit. Jack and I didn't raise you kids to take care of us. We raised you to be good citizens and to raise your own families well. We succeeded, so don't turn this into a contest of the most doting child to your parents. By the way, it was Renee, but who's counting?"

Spike chuckled. "Yes, ma'am."

"And you should have a fun memorial service. You can have a funeral with the people who are here now, but do it unannounced on Monday so these people can go home and continue their lives. Don't even tell extended family until after it is over. Later this year, when the MARV is gone, have a party to celebrate both Jack and me. His funeral was a downer, and we don't need a repeat." Because it was unexpected, Jack's funeral was not a celebration as much as mourning. That wasn't on purpose, but everyone felt sorry for Bridget. She was shocked, but it didn't help her to sit around and cry about it.

"Yes, ma'am."

Her voice was getting quieter, and Cynthia compensated by turning up the speaker. Spike looked over at Doctor Huebrex. He made a wrap it up motion. Her oxygen level must have dropped.

Bridget said, "Finally, you have to promise me that you will continue to have Eastman Christmas every two years. The family is spread out, but every two years, you must get together to celebrate our Lord's birth."

Spike had thought about that often. Would they keep getting together at Christmas after Bridget passed? Well, there's your answer. "Yes, ma'am. You hit all your points?"

She nodded.

"We'll do our best to live up to these things. None of us want you to be gone."

"I know that, but old people die. It is part of life."

"Do you want me to get Father Thomas?"

"That old blowhard isn't going to clear the decks for me to get past Saint Pete. He probably diddled with little boys when he was younger. Way too far left. He's a communist, you know?"

"Okay then, no priest."

"I didn't say that. If you could get a priest, I don't know, to give me last rites, I'd be eternally grateful."

Doctor Huebrex nodded to Spike. Spike said, "Mom, they're gonna stick that tube back down your throat."

"Bridget, we need to do this quickly," Cynthia said.

"Mom, we all love you."

"Okay," Bridget replied. She wasn't big on professing love. She figured she'd shown them their whole life, why say it? As soon as she said it, Cynthia had the tube ready to reinsert. It looked like it hurt because Bridget teared up. She wasn't crying from sentiment. Her eyes were watering from pain.

Spike laughed that her last word might have been "Okay" in response to "We love you."

He got up and left so he didn't have to watch the pain she was experiencing. He knew she would appreciate that. He stopped recording as he headed for the door.

Fred called ten minutes later and asked how she was doing. Spike responded, "She's dying, and she's okay with that."

As Doctor Huebrex walked out of the room, Spike asked if he knew any other Catholic priests. The doctor looked at his phone and said, "I'll send you Father Tim's number. He's a good dude and lives about a block away. He'll be here in ten minutes."

"Is he cleared to come in?"

"We might be Nazis about this, but we aren't Bolsheviks."

"Thanks, Doctor. I appreciate you doing this," gesturing toward the room. "Probably not normal medical procedure to put a patient at risk for a talk."

"Actually, based on her living will, I might get in more trouble for re-intubating her than letting her talk to you. Besides, she's a tough negotiator. I don't think she would have made it to your turn to visit had I not agreed to her demands. It gave her a goal and a purpose."

"Thanks again." As the doctor was walking away with his head down, Spike phone buzzed. Father Tim Flynn's contact info. Spike called him.

"Father Tim, how can I help?"

"Hi Father Flynn, this is Gary Eastman. My mom is in Memorial Hospital's ICU, and she's dying of MARV. She's been a Catholic for over fifty years, and she'd like to see a priest. She's intubated, so—"

Father Flynn cut Spike off. "Enough, I'm on my way." Spike heard his car door slam and the car start before Father Flynn hung up. *Doctor Huebrex knows his priests*, Spike thought.

Father Tim Flynn walked into the ICU, and it was pretty obvious he was a priest because he was wearing the black pants, black shirt, and white collar tab. He was a little guy, half a foot shorter than Spike, and thin. He was probably about fifty, had a mop of red hair and a thin face with a pointed chin with blue eyes and a serious look. He had a small Irish accent and Spike thought he was a caricature of a priest. Spike smiled and shook his hand. "Not afraid of MARV, Gary?"

"If holy water doesn't kill MARV, nobody is going to survive, Father Flynn. My mom is in Room 314. The nurses are pretty nice, but they are going to make you wear one of these." Spike pointed at his facemask.

"We'll see. How old is your mom, and what is her Christian name?"

"It's Bridget Anne Eastman. She's eighty-five, and she lost our dad a few years ago. His name was Jack, and she's definitely looking forward to seeing him."

"Well, I better get in there quick then." Father Flynn said with a smile. He really was a good dude. Spike followed a couple feet behind him as he passed the nurses' station. No mask for Father Flynn. Cynthia got up to follow, but she didn't try to stop him.

He went into the room, and she followed. Once inside the room, he spoke quietly to Cynthia and she moved to the other side of the bed. Father Flynn sat on the barstool. Bridget looked over at him and tried to smile. He spoke for a while, and she blinked once. They'd worked out a code. It continued this way for about five minutes. He'd speak; she'd blink, mostly once, sometimes twice. Maybe she was confessing, but I doubt if Nurse Cynthia would be allowed to listen to that. Then, Flynn spoke to Cynthia, and she came out to join Spike. She hit the hand sanitizer dispenser as she closed the door.

Spike asked, "Confession time?"

"I'm not sure; I'm Lutheran."

Spike laughed. She said, "Call me if you need me. And make sure he sanitizes his hands."

"You think he'll listen to me?"

"Doubt it, but then you'll have to decide if you want to shake his hand again."

He looked back in, and he could see that Bridget was getting tired. She was concentrating hard on what Father Flynn was saying. Her cheeks rose, and her eyes smiled several times. Spike was happy that he'd ask Doctor Huebrex for a different priest. By this point, Father Thomas would have pissed Bridget off, and she would be rolling her eyes. After another ten minutes, Father Flynn stood up and began making a sign of the cross. He then walked around the bed, unzipped the bubble, and anointed her with oils. He made another sign of the cross and zipped the bubble shut. He smiled at her compassionately, said something. She smiled again with her eyes and cheeks and blinked once.

Father Flynn walked out and used the hand sanitizer. "Cynthia would freak out if I didn't make a big show of the hand sanitizer."

Spike laughed and said, "What does she know? She's Lutheran."

Father Flynn ignored that and said, "Your mom was grateful to see me. She blinked that she doesn't like her parish priest much."

"That's an understatement. I hope she confessed that one."

"I'll never tell."

Spike laughed again and started walking down the hall with Father Flynn. "If she makes it to tomorrow, I'll come see her around noon."

"Doctor Huebrex doesn't think that's going to happen. She held out so I could be here instead of one of her grandchildren. She made it very clear that she wasn't happy with the shift system we devised. 'Whoever came up with that idea is an idiot.'" They both laughed as Father Flynn turned to say goodbye.

He shook Spike's hand and said, "You're all welcome at my parish on Sunday. Call me if you need any help with arrangements."

"Thanks, Father Flynn. It was a pleasure meeting you."

"Likewise. Please call me Father Tim; that's what everyone calls me. May Christ's peace be with you and your family."

"And with your spirit." It came out automatically, as if he were in Mass. Spike thought, *That's what a priest should be like.* Father Tim turned and left the ICU. Spike realized he was all alone to stand vigil, but he felt strangely peaceful. He'd always been Catholic, and he knew the strength of the Church was in its priests. There might be a parish change in his near future.

Nurse Cynthia had come up behind him. "Incredible man. He is always willing to do the hard things."

"There is plenty of room in the original Christian church for recovering Protestants." Spike said as he headed back toward the room.

"I've actually considered it, but if your church has any sense, they'll move him to Milwaukee to become a bishop soon. Then, I would be stuck with some run-of-the-mill priest and regret my decision." Cynthia stopped at the nurses' station.

"Good point." Spike stopped and asked, "Besides standing there watching her, is there anything I can do to help?"

"No, but I'm sure she'd love it if you prayed some."

"Thanks," Spike said, and he headed down the hall.

He realized he should call Jun. He went past the room a little, put his earbuds in, and commanded his phone to "call Jun." It was about 7 a.m. on Saturday in Seoul. Spike figured Jun would be getting ready for his treadmill run. As the phone rang, he wondered if the pollution from China that covered Korean peninsula had gone away like during COVID-19. He had his answer immediately. He could hear wind in the background as Jun answered. "Hey, boss."

"Jun, running on the streets of Seoul? Good for you."

"Nope, I'm staying with my parents at the pension. Decided to run up to the Bomonsa Temple. It's a little rainy, so I need to find shelter. I call you back in five minutes, okay?"

"Sure, Jun. Or you could finish your run and call me in an hour or so. It isn't urgent."

"Okay, I'll take you up on that. I only have seven miles left. I'll be showered by then."

"Bragging? I thought Koreans were humble people?"

"More than that, we are honest."

Spike laughed and hit the end button. Now he had an hour to check in with the family. He called Shauntel. Everybody was in the lower level bar except Carl and Dorothy. Spike said he would text them, and when they arrived, Shauntel should call him back. Fifteen minutes later, Spike's phone rang.

"Hi honey, can you put me on speaker?"

"Sure," and then Carl spoke up from a distance, "We're all here."

Spike pictured them gathered around the bar, his siblings closest and the nieces and nephews hanging back a little. He said, "Mom's gonna die soon. She has had her last rites, and Doctor Huebrex is pretty sure she's going to give up."

He heard Renee sniffle. It was a distinct sound that he recognized since he was a kid. "Renee, remember her letter. She wants us to be strong."

"Screw that. I'm going to cry when my mom dies. Okay?"

"Okay. I just called to tell you I have a recording of my short conversation with her. I don't know if she knew I was recording it, but she probably figured I was since I had my notebook and didn't take notes. The question is, how are we going to listen to it? Do you want me to play it right now or wait until I get home? Could be past midnight. It's up to you guys."

"We should do this together." Carl added, "Right, Renee?"

"Yeah. Let's make a deal. If it's past midnight, we'll do it in the morning. We'll just hang out until then."

"Okay. You guys set for food? Shauntel can order pizza from Firehouse."

"Quit trying to solve our problems, douchebag," Joe yelled.

Spike and everybody on the other end laughed. He hadn't been called that in a while. "Talk to you later, fam." He hit end.

He settled in and waited for Jun's call. He had pulled another barstool over to the window. He was feeling a little tired when his phone rang. It was Jun, and only fifty minutes later. "Did you shower?"

"Yes, sir. For the record, mostly just to warm up. The rain made it easy to run."

"Under six-minute miles for seven miles?" Spike asked.

"Yeah, I'm in pretty good shape. Looking forward to running with you."

"Me too. It will be close. Jun, I don't want to waste too much of your weekend. Just need to know a couple things. Try to correlate our MARV levels in our different locations. The ones I'm particularly interested in are the marble and granite mines. And then compare that to what is happening in our other locations."

"Okay, that won't take long. Do you mind if I ask why?" Jun wondered.

"I have a theory about MARV. I don't want to skew your analysis toward my theory, so I will leave it at that."

"I'm pretty sure we haven't had any fatalities at Maurer, right?"

Spike answered, "Yes, and I'm praying for that continued outcome. And then, second, how long will it take before Maurer is forced to take drastic actions based on your model you sent yesterday?"

"The first one might take an hour or two, and the second one will take me about twenty minutes. I think I have everything I need; I'll just do it from here. I'll have it to you by tomorrow morning your time."

"No hurry on the first one, but if you can get me the second one, I want to talk to Jim about it tonight. Have a great visit with your family."

Jun responded, "Hope all's well at your place."

"We're fine." Spike didn't want to spend an hour talking about his mom. Thirteen minutes later, Spike's phone vibrated. He opened Jun's model and found what he was looking for. He called Jim DePacker and started to tell him about the data when his mom died.

CHAPTER 14

Spike was home by 8 p.m. He was delayed by some paperwork, a call to Father Tim, and a quick discussion about cremation with Doctor Huebrex. They thought they could have an urn of her ashes by end of day Saturday.

He told the family about the arrangements and asked if anyone wanted to change anything before anything was confirmed. Nobody said anything, so he said, "I guess you all just want to hear Mom's voice, huh?"

Lots of nods, Joe, standing behind the bar as normal, said, "Will you get on with it?"

"Sure, could you hand me a Spotted Cow?" Spike pulled out his phone and connected the Bluetooth to the speakers. The recording ended with "Mom, we all love you." And the clear answer, "Okay."

Everyone smiled. Carl shook his head. "Couldn't even say it on her death-bed. That is a determined woman."

Spike said, "I've listened to this a few times. The instructions are: first, Joe and Fred need to listen to Carl and Renee."

Renee piped up, "And you, you little shit."

"Okay, okay. Second, no self-pity. Third, small funeral. Fourth, celebration of life for both Mom and Dad by the end of this year. Fifth, bi-annual Eastman Christmas. That one was very important to her, and we should honor it. And I think it is worth mentioning and honoring Renee for all she has done for our parents over the years."

"Fred was her favorite," Renee said.

"We have no proof," Fred said. "Sounded a lot like you had won her over. And Carl has good instincts. Shoot, I think I was third, at best."

Staying more serious, Carl said, "As your patriarch now, I insist that Christmas is here in Sheboygan Falls every two years. It is home, sort of, since we all graduated from high school here. So, Shauntel, if you can agree to open your home every two years, we'll come here."

Shauntel generally doesn't like to be backed into a corner, so everyone looked at her with anticipation. She smiled her classy smile, and said, "Of course. It will be our pleasure."

Fred and Joe looked at each other and rolled their eyes. Spike laughed and shifted his eyes back toward Carl. They chuckled. The three younger brothers were well connected, probably because they lived in the same room together for five years. Joe said, "Well, patriarch, what other edicts do you want to proclaim?"

"Wine would be good." And with his best Moses impression, stood tall and added, "Joe, serve me."

"This 'usually right and have good instincts' has gone to your head, big brother," Joe said as he grabbed a bottle of red.

The conversation went on about planning the celebration of life party for Jack and Bridget. Most agreed that August or September would work best. Again, Shauntel agreed to open her home. Spike thought, *This is getting expensive*, but didn't say anything. Then the conversation turned to Jack and Bridget as parents. The consensus was they must have done a good job, because they were all productive and generally happy. Spike and Joe looked at each other and started laughing. Without saying anything, they knew that the other was thinking, "Who are we to judge?"

When that line of discussion died down, they talked about the funeral. Spike said, "Father Tim is available any time after noon on Monday. We just have to get the urn and bring it to the parish office an hour ahead of time. He asked if anyone would want to speak, and I offered Carl. He said anyone else is welcome to speak since it will be so intimate. Think about that, and I can let him know after mass on Sunday. They social distance at mass, and don't do communion or offer the sign of peace. He invited us all and said the church will be pretty wide open."

"Which parish is it?" Carl asked.

"Holy Name on 8th and Huron."

"Okay, as the patriarch, my next proclamation is that we all go to Mass. What time?"

"Proclamations don't include details; we'll figure that out later," Fred said.

"10:30," Spike said.

"Can your kids come home?" Renee asked.

Shauntel said, "Lucas is out to sea, but Penelope can make it."

"Does Lucas know?" Dale asked.

"I sent an email to the chaplain on board his ship," Shauntel said. "Not sure how this works, but if they're near a port in normal times, they would probably let him off to fly home. Pandemic times, who knows?"

CHAPTER 15

The party slowly died. Only Fred, Joe, and Spike were left at the bar. Joe was a little drunk and decided to bring Fred into the mission. Spike wasn't thrilled with his operational security, but Fred was trustworthy. The thing that Joe didn't realize was that it could put Fred in danger if this was what Spike was starting to think it was. Spike's background led him to think jihadist. If that was the case, it was unlikely that they could trace phone activity. The worst-case scenario was that it was a Chinese or Russian plot. Spike found that to be unlikely, but either of them could easily track the electronic traffic. It was also unlikely that they would be trolling for cell and internet activity in Sheboygan Falls, Wisconsin. In an abundance of caution, putting Joe onto the secure network was in case of that worst-case scenario. That and to keep Guls out of federal prison.

Joe said, "Fred, what would you say if I told you that MARV was a deliberate terrorist attack?"

"Riddles. Joe, why do you speak in riddles?" He looked at Spike. "Was this a deliberate terrorist attack?"

Spike looked a little uncomfortable but answered honestly, "We really don't know for sure, but there are a lot of weird and hard to explain issues."

"Who? Who killed Mom?" Fred asked.

"That's the ten-trillion-dollar question. Not just because of Mom and all the other victims, but think about the economic costs. If this is deliberate, and I think it is, then somebody did it. This doesn't feel like a terror plot from jihadists. First, they do touchdown dances. Second, they wouldn't have unleashed this heavily in the Middle East, and the spread isn't following COVID-19's pattern. MARV hit the Middle East pretty hard from what I can get out of the Johns Hopkins website."

Fred read a lot, and he thought about what Spike had said. "Spike, think about who's hurt though. Islamic terrorists don't mind creating unrest and economic hardship in the Middle East because it can lead to instability in those countries that the nutbags think are their lands. Their dream is a single Islamic State from Pakistan to Spain, North Africa, and the Middle East. Sharia Law run out of Mecca, with zero rights for women, beheadings for breaking the law, brutal Middle Ages shit. Why wouldn't they like this?"

"For starters, all of their funding comes from there. Plus, I'd be shocked if they could be this organized without bragging about it. Joe, did you see any indication that jihadists did this in your research?"

Fred looked at Joe. "Research? What the fuck? You guys are really looking into this? Why?"

Joe answered, "Because it ain't right and we're Americans."

Defensively Fred said, "I'm an American, too. My question is more specific than just 'Why are you looking?' It's more about what are you going to do if you find out who's behind it?"

"That is a good question." Spike said, "I don't know yet, but if I can help, I'm willing."

"Is Shauntel willing to have you put yourself in danger?"

"So far, yes. She knows what we are doing. She did comment to me that she's fine as long as it all stays here. I think she is worried that I'm going to get back into the CIA. That would be a step she wouldn't support. Hell, I wouldn't either. I don't want to go back to that job. I like my life as it is."

"But…" Joe asked, and Fred nodded as if Spike was leaving something out.

"But I might be able to help by getting them pointed in the right direction. Right now, it is analysis. I was really more of an intel analyst than a true operative, especially when I was in the Air Force."

"I think Captain Hammargren would disagree with that statement, but I'll let it slide," Fred said.

"That dude totally misled you guys. I just rode along once in a while. They let me carry a weapon, but I don't think they really wanted me to use it unless

I was in danger of getting captured." He pointed his forefinger at his temple and cocked his thumb. "Anyway, I'm not going to go unsanctioned into a foreign country and try to do something about this."

Joe interrupted. "Unless you have to."

"It won't play out like that. We have lots of young guys who are better suited to do that work than an old fart like me." Spike was wondering why they were egging him on to prove he was a trained killer. He was capable of shooting people. He'd been trained in hand-to-hand combat, weapons, and explosives. When he entered a room, he saw weapons where others saw lamps and ashtrays. But Spike knew that his skills were worse than rusty, his physical fitness was good for a fifty-year-old executive but not for an operative, and his support was too limited to be effective

"How can I help?" Fred asked.

"In a real pinch, I might want to borrow your passport and a credit card."

"Huh?"

Spike explained, "We look close enough alike that I may want to use your identity to leave the US. I have other things if I can get to Europe, but I don't have anything here."

"That ends the question about how operational you were." Joe laughed.

"Anybody who did what I did has a few safe deposit boxes set up in foreign hubs. You never knew when you might have to lay low. Can't do that without multiple identities, matching credit cards, cash, and some tools. I really didn't have time to collect that stuff when I quit."

"Tools?" Fred asked, thinking strictly about weapons.

"Simple items to avoid surveillance like hair clippers, dye, sunglasses, colored contacts, and hats. Things that probably worked way better before most of Europe put cameras connected to facial recognition software everywhere. Big Brother is always watching." Spike left out the silenced pistols, knives, and lock picking tools. They didn't need to know. They also didn't need to know that he had several of the identities and cards in his safe upstairs. He didn't want to use them until he had to. The expired ones in the safe boxes were renewed using European underground. To the forgers who made fake passports and identification cards, Spike was anonymous. It was worth the twenty-five thousand dollars it had cost him over the years to keep these identities alive.

Spike's phone vibrated, and he saw an email from Jun Park. They had no cases of MARV in the quarries in Italy or Vermont. To Spike, this gave credence to the idea that the virus wasn't as random as advertised. Fred and Joe were talking about how Spike had set aside stuff in case he had to hide out in Europe. They figured out that he would probably be hiding from the CIA if he needed to have fake IDs and disguises.

"For your information, the CIA probably wouldn't hunt down some low-level intelligence person all across Europe. The disguises were so I could get to an embassy to get out of Europe undetected. I wasn't Jason Bourne." Spike yawned. "I need some sleep. This has been a helluva week."

Fred made a face. "I bet my family is already asleep. I can't drive. Maybe I can crash somewhere."

"There are sleeping bags in the storage room. Figure it out, okay?"

"Yeah, I'm good. I just don't want to sleep near this guy." He pointed at Joe. "He snored when he was twelve. Imagine what it sounds like now."

Joe just smiled. He had been pretty quiet, and that was a bad sign. He was thinking. "Spike, do you think it is possible that a country did this MARV thing?"

"I doubt that it was sanctioned by a state. But that doesn't mean that people in governments weren't involved. There aren't many biological labs where virus research is done that aren't connected to governments."

"That's a clue. Where would I find data on research labs?"

"Pretty hard to find. Governments try to keep that stuff secret. Labs do a lot of animal testing, and animal activists are everywhere. Plus the obvious nutbags who would love to get their hands on the nasty stuff made in those labs. Probably not a thread we can pursue ourselves."

Fred shook his head. "If you can't pursue it, who can help you?"

"Guls," Joe blurted out.

Spike looked like he'd been slapped on the face. "Joe, we can't talk about this, even to Fred."

"Why?"

"Knowing our source puts our source and Fred in a bad position."

"I'm in a bad position?" Joe asked.

"Sort of. Not yet, really. But if it becomes clear that I'm involved, Shauntel will likely be questioned while hooked up to lie detectors. If it comes to that, she could give you up. Then, you'll be pulled in. My advice is to tell them the truth. It will be better for you. That's why the need to know principle is so important. That's why the theoretical discussion is okay, but specifics about sources need to be kept close to the vest."

Joe was getting nervous and answered, "C'mon, you're being melodramatic."

"No, Joe, we call it OPSEC. Operational Security. In fact, that source is compromised because he was lax with his phone conversations. He had burner phones that he thought protected him. Burner phones are single use and can't call known numbers. He got caught because he wasn't careful enough. Who suffers? My family, including you guys, because our source didn't know what he was doing." Spike was starting to get angry, mostly at himself for not helping Guls be more careful. He wasn't going to let that happen again. "We need to be smarter than that. Tomorrow, Joe, go to Walmart and buy fifteen phones with cash. Wear a ballcap, either Packers or Brewers. Use the checkout lane furthest from the door because the camera is only directly at the end of the lane. Don't look directly at the camera and try to cover your face. With MARV, you can probably get away with a surgical mask and not look too suspicious. Give five phones to Fred. I have about twenty-five here. My phone numbers are pretty much sequential. We need to list the phone numbers in order, ten for you and five for Fred. Then we create a keyword over normal communications channels to let the other person know to turn on the next phone on the list. We can think about keywords all day long, but the best are a group of things, like birds. So, duck, goose, turkey, robin, blue jay, whatever. If you accidently say one of those words, just call it off by saying it again."

"Can we talk openly on the one-use burner phone?"

"Don't say words like terrorist or Chinese. Don't refer to individual names on either end. Don't say, 'Fred, it's Joe; Spike is after an Iranian terrorist in Chicago at a research laboratory full of MARV.' Instead call each other dude or man, refer to me as he or the sales guy, refer to Persian rugs, bad guy, Second City, facility, but MARV is okay since everyone is talking about it constantly. If the calls get picked up by NSA or another intelligence agency, they won't figure it out. Still, assume someone is listening all the time.

"Next, if something is an emergency, life and death, or very time sensitive, just say it. Worry about the consequences later. You know why? Because you can't un-die."

Fred and Joe laughed. Spike didn't. "I'm not kidding."

Fred said, "I have to go back to why."

Spike set his jaw. "Two reasons really. Number one, Mom. And, number two, we have an opportunity to make a difference because nobody knows we're trying, except maybe the CIA, and they are on our side."

"You sure about that?" Fred asked.

"Yes, one hundred percent. They might get bad press, but the CIA is on the right side of this issue."

"Maybe they did it by accident, and now they are trying to cover it up." Fred read too many conspiracy novels.

"Not their department. Biological warfare is a military mission."

Joe seemed on board. "Back to my point. Can our source follow the thread about research facilities?"

"Not if the CIA is on to him. I have an idea about how to get better info, but I can't share it yet. OPSEC."

CHAPTER 16

That weekend

After breakfast on Saturday, Spike and Shauntel went for a walk with Ginger. Shauntel said, "Follow the money. Who benefits?" She was rational, and she assigned that quality to everyone else. She was usually right when she came up with these things, so Spike thought about it for a while. Spike had a hard time with that line of thinking because the enemies he had faced were irrational. They believe that the only view of religion is their view and anyone who disagrees is their enemy. They had perverted the Islamic religion to focus on the warrior years of the Profit. Those weren't the only tenets of the religion. There are beautiful, peaceful, and family-oriented portions of Islam that are left out of the teachings of the militant Imams who stir the jihad. Spike needed to cleanse his mind of the war on terror, but it was difficult since his entire military and CIA career was about Islamic terrorism. Spike said, "I'm not sure yet. It is definitely worth thinking about."

When they got home, Spike went to find Joe. He was deep in thought staring at the computer monitor. "Find anything?"

Joe was startled, looked up, and asked, "Why do you always sneak up on me?"

"Much easier to take you out if you don't know I'm here." Spike smiled.

"Well, I don't think I found anything, but this rural thing has me thinking. Who would benefit if rural communities suffered?"

"You sound like Shauntel. I was going to ask you who would benefit internationally from MARV?"

"So far, nobody. But if the pandemic ended today, the major country least impacted is Russia. They say it is because they immediately shut down their border which is true. It's a huge country, but seventy percent of the population is west of the Urals in European Russia. It seems strange that the cities didn't have any serious outbreaks. Moscow and Saint Petersburg only had a handful of cases and no deaths. I don't even know if you can believe their statistics; some of the commentary was that the data wasn't accurate."

"They certainly have the means to do this. They have been working on biological weapons since the 1920s. When I was there, it seemed like such a poor country, but that was almost thirty years ago. And, even then, they tried to show us the best of Moscow. The communists would have never let me in, but habits like trying to fool others into thinking you are rich and powerful didn't die when the Soviet Union fell."

"I forgot you spent a semester there. Maybe the Russian language newspapers could give you a clue that I can't see?"

"They track foreigners who read their newspapers. I don't want to get on their radar. Plus, it has been thirty years since I did any reading or writing in Cyrillic alphabet. Speaking is easier, but reading is not going to come back to me quickly. Especially with technical terms used to describe medical conditions."

"You don't think they would do something like this, do you?" Joe asked.

"They are strange. They have little industry outside of the natural resources they sell around the world. They don't have sophisticated manufacturing industry except for military hardware. They have vast land, but their growing seasons are short, and the land isn't very fertile, so their agriculture can't feed their own population. I wouldn't rule them out entirely, but I would be very surprised if the government is involved. The two most likely governments are Iran and North Korea. See if you can find some way that they benefit."

"Okay. What are you going to do?" Joe asked.

"I'm going to run into the office and see what I missed yesterday afternoon." Spike left, thinking that it might be better to send Joe packing. He was smart and good at the research, but he really didn't know what he was looking for. Being honest with himself, Spike realized he didn't either. The words "wild goose chase" popped into his head.

The family gathered that evening for an Italian buffet in the basement. Renee had brought some old photo albums from Bridget's house, and everyone was reminiscing and enjoyed the evening. Carl took a bottle of wine back to his RV to work on his eulogy. Everyone seemed tired, and the lights were out by 9 p.m.

Sunday morning was bright and brisk. Everyone went to Mass together and enjoyed Father Tim's homily. He was a gifted speaker, sprinkled in humor and entertained with a purpose. He didn't mention Bridget's passing partly because she didn't belong to his parish, but also because Carl had asked him not to let people know about the funeral. After Mass, the family stayed behind and spoke with Father Tim for half an hour. Plans were set; the ashes were delivered. Cremation was forbidden by the Catholic Church for most of its history. But now, as long as the ashes are buried, it is allowed. Bridget and Jack were both cremated and had a nice burial plot in the cemetery in Sheboygan Falls. After the burial on Monday, most of the family was planning to head home. As it turned out, nobody else could travel for the funeral. Penelope and Lucas and Joe's wife Shirley and kids Jack and Julie wouldn't be there.

Sunday night was another version of the past two nights of eating and reminiscing about family vacations, weekend trips to Uncle Bill's cabin in north central Wisconsin, and all the stupid things each of the siblings had done as adolescents. It was relaxing and light. Spike and Shauntel headed to bed around 9 p.m., and everyone else went to bed by ten.

In their bedroom, Shauntel asked Spike, "What do you think will come of your investigation?"

Spike said, "Probably nothing. I'm going to send Joe home tomorrow with a bunch of burner phones. He told Fred too much last night, and I snapped at him. It isn't worth him being involved. I'm also worried about Guls. He could get into deep trouble if the FBI gets involved. I need to leave him out going forward. He's going to text me tomorrow, and I'll respond to drop it." He took off his pants and shirt and put on a T-shirt. He threw his dirty clothes in the hamper in the closet. When he returned, Shauntel was putting on a T-shirt.

She looked at him suspiciously. "You don't give up that easily. How are you going to get information without Guls?"

"You remember Jimmy Celestini?" Spike said as he got into bed.

She looked at him with her head cocked. "The hacker kid from Maurer?"

"Yeah, I might replace Joe with him. He can get what we really need so we aren't grasping for straws."

"That's dangerous. Do you know for sure he did this and wasn't monitored?"

"For sure? No. But he was pretty convincing when he explained it to me. Do you remember when I came home that night and we discussed it? I was so impressed that he didn't do anything with the information. It seemed to me like he wanted to forget he had seen it."

Shauntel stopped brushing her teeth and said, "I remember. He might know something about you being ruthless. He may think he can expose you by getting involved." She turned on the water and continued her nightly routine.

Spike knew she couldn't hear him, so he waited. "It could be that he's setting me up, but I think he has a strong moral compass. I've done a little checking. He's smart, and his dad is a local legend in his hometown. He is responsible, great credit score with no criminal record. He hasn't even had a speeding ticket. But he clearly has the ability to do nefarious things that could make him a lot of money. He doesn't use those skills for personal gain."

"That you know of."

"Well, if he agrees to help us, I will need you to set him up here."

"What do I get out of it besides a new office buddy?" Shauntel asked with a sultry look.

"Oh, okay, I can help you out there." He smiled as she got into bed on his side.

She straddled him and started gyrating her hips. He smiled again, and she started getting serious. Slowly, his smile faded. He pulled her T-shirt off and then his own. She found his waistband and removed his boxers. She guided him inside her, and he gasped. She started moving faster, and he tried to think about football to slow down. It worked, and after she climaxed, Spike rolled on top of her, and he picked up the pace and exploded. They both fell asleep satisfied, holding each other.

CHAPTER 17

The following day

Bridget Eastman's funeral was small and fast. Father Tim let them take Communion, probably against a bunch of rules but not without precaution. He and everyone had to use hand sanitizer. The Body of Christ was offered but not the Blood. Spike was impressed by Father Tim and Carl. They both gave wonderfully thoughtful tributes to Bridget's life, and it helped that both kept it short.

After the burial, they all went back to Shauntel and Spike's house for a quick meal. Spike powered up the burner phone that he hoped Guls would call or text, but he had no texts or missed calls. Joe and Carl both stopped for gas on the way back to the house. Spike was grateful that Joe seemed to be prepping to leave. He wouldn't bother to tell him he was going to be replaced.

When everyone was together, Father Tim blessed the food. They ate while Father Tim seemed to be holding his own version of the Inquisition. He asked specific questions about Bridget and Jack and each of their children. He learned about Carl wandering through spiritual life only to return to the bosom of the Catholic Church. He found out that all the grandchildren were being raised Catholic. He asked about education levels, what everyone did for a living, and seemed to catalog the answers in his mind. He was unabashedly curious.

Spike talked about a family trip to Ireland, and Father Tim talked about growing up in Galway. Spike asked about his history, and he was evasive even though he hadn't allowed them to give partial answers. Almost as if he were hiding something. Spike thought he might revisit that later.

Carl said his goodbyes. He was going to repeat his training sessions and would start tonight in Des Moines from the RV. This time, the students were in London, so the start time would be an hour later.

Joe followed, but before he left, he asked Spike what he needed to do. Spike said, "Just hold off until later in the week. Don't waste a burner. We can talk on Thursday and use the bird keyword if we need to communicate more clandestinely."

Joe said, "I don't know how much I want to do this from my own computer."

Spike laughed and said, "Don't worry about it. We're probably going to give up. I don't want to get Guls in any more hot water."

Joe seemed disappointed but also looked relieved. "Hey, I probably don't need all of these," as he bent over and reached into his bag. He handed Spike a bag with five of the burner phones. "I kept the first five, but you will probably have more use for them than I will." He grabbed his bag and took off.

Dale and Renee were gathering up their family. They had two cars at Spike's house, so they planned to drive over to Bridget's house on the way out of town and grab some heirlooms and important papers. Renee was planning to take care of the will and making sure that social security and Bridget's bank and investment companies were properly notified. That part of a person dying can be painstakingly detailed, and Renee had the right disposition to be sure it was handled properly. As they were leaving, Spike felt his burner phone vibrate. He slipped into the mudroom alone and looked at the phone.

The first text message said, "Nobody came for me. Should be good."

The second said, "Try to figure out why someone would attack worldwide energy production."

Finally, "Let me know you got this."

Spike replied, "Got it. Destroy, we're done. Thanks." He would call Guls next week to be sure he understood, but he really didn't want him involved any further.

Fred's family was set to leave for the airport at 5 p.m.. Their car was packed, so Fred and Father Tim took the opportunity to drink a few of Spike's Spotted Cow beers. Big Dan would drive, and the rest of them figured it was time to relax. Alyssa and Sarah opened a bottle of white wine. Spike grinned.

"What?" asked Alyssa.

Spike deflected, "I was just thinking how much your Grandma would like the idea of a couple adult beverages after her funeral. Everyone else had to leave so fast, I think she'd be happy that we're having a drink."

They sat and talked about Irish traditions related to wakes and drinking. With a grim face, Father Tim said, "The local pubs became funeral homes during the Potato Famine because there weren't enough funeral homes. It really began a tradition that may die soon. The pubs were the center of social life, almost as much as the Church. But many of the pubs are on country roads, and the crackdown on drinking and driving has really hurt their businesses. It is both a blessing and a shame."

"Don't they have Uber?" Alyssa asked.

"Doesn't work in the country. Many pubs have bought vans they use to pick up the patrons and deliver them home. That might save some of them."

Spike remembered the Guinness tasting so much better there. According to locals, it tasted better because it was fresh just based on the number of pours per hour. Nearly everyone in the pubs drank the same brand of beer. Americans were always trying different beers in their bars which led to an explosion of craft beers. If you follow the Guinness model, that doesn't bode well for freshness. Spike noticed that everyone else was lost in their thoughts and realized he needed to speak with Fred.

"Fred, backgammon?" Knowing it is a boring game to watch, Spike figured he could get Fred alone.

Big Dan piped up, "I can play the winner."

"We're playing for C-notes. You sure you want to lose a bunch of money to your favorite uncle?"

"Joe left," Dan deadpanned.

Spike grabbed the board, and they went to a far corner where there was a tall bar table. Nobody followed, so he asked quickly, "Did you think about the passport and credit card?"

"Yeah, I made a note to overnight them to you tomorrow."

"I hope I don't need them, but if I do, I'll send them from Europe when I land."

"Won't you need them to get back?" Fred asked.

"No, I have alternatives figured out. You'll see the charges, so you'll be able to see what country I go to. If I need anything, I will use a burner to call you on your normal phone. It won't be on the list because I will pick them up there. We can use the bird signal if we need to talk, but I will need to call you since you won't know my numbers."

"Okay, makes sense. I really hope you don't go. Let the government do what we pay taxes for."

"There are certain things that they can't do. Not necessarily dangerous things, but most operatives are tracked in foreign countries. Nobody will track me."

Fred just shook his head. "I still don't get the 'why,' but if you think you can help, I won't be able to talk you out of it."

Spike just smiled and rolled double sixes. He moved ahead on the board and probably just won the game.

Fred said, "Be gentle on me here." Fred rolled and moved.

Spike won two out of three, and Fred made a big show of giving him a Benjamin.

After everyone hugged and said goodbye, Fred and his family left. Spike was looking forward to speaking with Father Tim.

CHAPTER 18

That left Spike, Shauntel, and Father Tim. Shauntel started cleaning up and took the leftover food upstairs. Spike went around the bar and grabbed two beers. Father Tim accepted the beer with a smile. They sat at the bar, and Spike looked him in the eyes. Father Tim met his stare and didn't look away.

Spike asked Father Tim, "Where did you go to seminary?"

Father Tim answered, "I finished in 2014 at Sacred Heart Seminary in Hales Corners." He noticed that Spike was doing some math, and added, "I started after moving here from England."

"Oh, I thought the Irish weren't big fans of their former oppressors." Referring to the harsh rule the English had imposed on Ireland for most of the past thousand years.

"I saw both sides of the story. The Catholics were mistreated, no question about that. But the British have provided a lot of aid to the Irish people, too. And the Brits were more interested in helping in the war on terror than the Irish. I joined the Royal Marines and eventually served with the SAS." The SAS is the British Special Air Service, one of the world's most elite Special Forces units. Very much like the famous US Navy SEALs or Army Special Forces, sometimes referred to as Delta Force; SAS has an excruciating selection process and lifetime camaraderie. In between, they spend a lot of time training, deploying to hot spots, and providing the tip of the spear for Her Majesty's foreign policy.

"From elite Special Forces to parish priest. That is an unusual background." Spike put in a dip.

"I studied theology in my undergraduate work while I was still in the service. I liked the philosophical work and learning about how culture is shaped by religion. So when I retired, I went to seminary. I think my grandparents would have been proud. The rest of my family had pretty much disowned me when I joined the Royal Marines. They didn't agree with my view of either the Brits or the worldwide threat of Islamists. I haven't bothered to talk to them to find out if the last twenty years changed their minds."

Father Tim continued, "So I got to see the world, actually, mostly the nasty places. I must have had a lot of Viking blood from their plundering of Ireland because I enjoyed a good raid."

Spike laughed. "So it is true, this so-called war on terror is just another Crusade."

"Given your background, I know you don't think that."

"*My* background?"

"Tim Blust is in my parish. He told me about you. He is the reason I came to Sheboygan County too. He's a great man, and his patronage has helped me a lot since I've been here."

"I agree. He's been a friend and mentor to me. I was wondering why you were willing to share so much once everyone left. You were pretty vague in front of the others."

"Need to know." It no longer felt like Spike was talking to the priest who buried his mother today. It was as if a light was shone on the former commando and the priest had faded away. Father Tim, now Trooper Tim, continued, "By the way, you should stop by and see Tim. He wants to talk with you."

"He knows my number, why didn't he call me?" Spike asked.

"You know why. His OPSEC is the best I've ever seen."

Spike wondered how deeply connected Tim Blust was to the intelligence community. It hadn't occurred to Spike before that he may be actively involved as a contractor. And it seemed like maybe Father Tim was involved as well. Blust might already know about the investigation he was working on. Director Oliva must have called him.

Spike would stop by and see Blust this evening. But, for now, he was curious about how active Father Tim was in the war on terror. "The Navy SEALs talk about their lifelong commitment to their team members. Is SAS the same?"

"Not in the sense that we stay connected. But when one is in need, all come to his aid. Once in a while someone might pass through this part of the US. When that happens, I throw my doors open. As a priest, my vow of poverty makes that a little more difficult. Thankfully, I know Tim. He helps me meet the commitment I've made to my fellow troopers."

"Father Tim, I only recently found out how well-connected Tim is. He didn't share his involvement in the intelligence and military communities with me. So, please don't betray Tim's trust. I think he came to me intentionally. I met him in a bar in Paris. He said 'Oostburg,' and I bought him a drink. We talked, and he seemed to believe my cover story. Looking back on it now, I'm starting to see that he orchestrated the entire thing. I don't understand why he did that, but it seems like the current Director of the CIA was a part of the charade."

Trooper Tim didn't hesitate. "You've got the broad strokes. It was clear to people around you that your days were numbered. You were ready to move on, and they preferred that you stay close. Tim knew he would need a replacement at Maurer, so he asked if he could help. Elizabeth Oliva and Tim were connected from childhood, and she called in a favor. I think it was mostly to be sure you didn't stray too far off the reservation. As time went by, they realized that you were out of their sphere of control, but it is always helpful to keep tabs on former agents. That is as much as I know. And Tim was fine with me telling you all of this because he needs to speak with you and wants everything above board. We are all on the same side—the side of good versus evil. I learned to recognize the difference from my training as a priest. As a Trooper, it isn't as easy to distinguish. Do you understand the juxtaposition?"

"Of course, as an operator, I think the lines get a little blurry. I was just an intel analyst, so I didn't experience the same issues."

Trooper Tim smiled. "You know you are talking to a priest, right?"

"Father, you sound like my brothers. They all believe I was James Bond and Rambo wrapped into one. My operational experience was almost entirely support. I was never the tip of the spear; I was more like the feathers decorating the rear end of the spear."

Trooper Tim laughed. He was easy to talk to, but that didn't make the discussion any less dangerous. "Look, I'm not privy to your history. I just know that serious people think you're a skilled intelligence officer. I'm not into subterfuge. I was asked to take your temperature about how interested you would be in pursuing an off-the-books mission."

"I'm not willing to give up my current life. It is too good. My wife has sacrificed enough. Lucky for me, she stuck with me, raised our kids better than I could have, and now I owe her my loyalty and fealty."

At that point, Father Tim seemed to reappear, transforming back to the priest. "Spike, do you think she would ever stand in the way of you doing the right thing? I'm guessing that was why she did her duty at home to support you doing your duty for America. America is a beacon of good in an extremely dangerous world. Shauntel would be unlikely to hold you back."

"Father, it would be up to me to ask her, I'm not sure I want to put her in the position of deciding."

"I'm not married to a person. My loyalty and fealty are to the church and the Holy Trinity. It wouldn't be fair for me not to put a major decision in their hands. I think in a marriage, the same thing applies."

"Point taken, Father."

Father Tim finished his beer. It was nearing the dinner hour. "I better head home."

Spike stood and started heading for the stairs. They walked together toward the front door. Spike said, "All right, I can drop you if you'd like. I need to head over to a friend's house for a quick discussion."

"Say hello to him for me."

"Will do, it was nice getting to know you, Father Tim."

They shook hands, and as Father Tim was turning, he said, "Likewise. I've looked forward to meeting you for a few years."

Spike realized that he'd been unaware of the forces around him for ten years. He felt naïve. Before he headed to speak with Tim Blust, he thought he better check in with Shauntel. He recounted the discussion with Father Tim and Trooper Tim, leaving out the part about whether he would ask for her approval. She sensed he was leaving something out.

Shauntel started, "Well, what do you think they have in mind?"

"I don't know because I don't know who's behind MARV. I think they know, but I don't want them to tell me. I don't want to be a pawn in their game. I feel like I'm about to be used, and I don't like it."

"I don't either, but the people we are talking about are powerful and know what they are doing."

"But pawns get wasted to save more valuable pieces. I'm not interested in being a sacrifice."

"Really, it comes down to how much you trust Tim Blust. He clearly trusts Father Tim. But he has never told you the depth of his connections to your former life. I think you need to feel him out."

Shauntel, as usual, provided sage advice. Spike jumped into the truck and headed over to Blusts'. They lived along Lake Michigan in one of the older, refurbished mansions on an acre of manicured grounds. It would take Spike about twenty minutes to get there. Spike was surprisingly nervous and put in another dip. He told himself he didn't have to do anything. He didn't need to be swept into some international intrigue. By the time he arrived at Tim's long driveway, his mindset was to listen and learn. He drove down the driveway to a large courtyard hidden from the street that could hold fifteen of his trucks. As he got out of his pickup, Tim poked his head out of the garage.

Tim Blust was dressed in khaki trousers and a blue button-down shirt. He had a cardigan sweater on, and Spike wondered what the hell he could be doing in the garage dressed like that. "I thought I heard a car." Tim motioned for Spike to join him in the garage. As they entered, it became clear that it was more than just a ten-car garage. Along with a classic 1956 Corvette and 1972 Hurst Olds Indy Pace Car muscle cars, there was a late model Ferrari Spider. Parked near the front were a year-old Chevy Suburban and a newer Chevy Impala. Spike had only seen the Suburban and Impala. It reminded him of how little he really knew about Blust. They walked past the vehicles without comment and entered an office that looked like a classic library in a London mansion. A lot of dark wood, walls of books fourteen feet high with a ladder on rollers to get to the upper level. There was a mahogany desk and matching conference table and a dozen leather chairs. Neither had spoken for a few minutes, and it was becoming uncomfortable.

Standing in the middle of the space, Spike broke the ice by asking, "Wasn't there enough space in your ten-thousand-foot mansion to have an office?"

"That's Carol's domain. She wanted a reception hall, not a library. I was relegated to the garage. I think she secretly did it so I wouldn't have room for too many cars."

Not wanting to put off the discussion, Spike said, "Father Tim said you wanted to speak with me."

"Let's sit. Would you like anything to drink?"

"No thanks. I need to get back home to catch up on work. We buried my mom earlier today. Father Tim is a wonderful priest. Your parish is lucky to have him."

"Look, I'm sure you're thinking we are scheming all around you. Nobody is doing that. I needed Father Tim to let you know because I didn't want any trace of us talking. I just wanted to tell you that Director Oliva told me that one of your old classmates is digging a little deeper than he should. She told me you would know what she meant."

"Look, you don't have to bullshit me. I know you are currently involved in CIA work. I don't know what or how, but it appears to me that you've either done very well in the stock market or you have additional revenue streams that weren't reported when you were with Maurer.

"As for my classmate, he's a good friend, and I asked him questions because I was trying to plan the Maurer response to MARV. He found out more than either of us expected. He bought burner phones but didn't know he had to be more careful than that. He called my known number with his burner. No chance that would get past the NSA. I have taken no action based on what he told me. He doesn't need to be hung out to dry."

"Okay, but apparently he told you that Director Oliva is involved."

"Not specifically her, he just said my old employer," Spike said.

"He needs to cease and desist. His career and freedom are at stake."

"I was planning to tell him that tomorrow." Spike didn't want them to try to track down his text exchange from this afternoon, so he didn't want to tell him he communicated with him today. He asked, "Has the NSA shared their evidence with the FBI or CDC?"

"Obviously not the CDC. They don't really talk to them. Maybe they should rethink that with two pandemics in two years. I doubt the FBI knows, or he would have been arrested."

"Let's keep it that way. I can guarantee you and Director Oliva if she's interested that he's done. I'm almost positive that he didn't share with anyone but me. I'm a known and trusted entity. You both know I would never cause problems for our country or you."

Blust said, "That's fine. We could leave him out of it. You might be able to help us."

"Not interested." It was a gamble. Blust's tone sounded a little like a quid pro quo, but Spike didn't really think they would try to manipulate him by arresting Guls. They seemed more principled than that. But desperate times could cause them to act out of character.

"It might be a quick trip."

"Look, Tim, I don't feel comfortable talking about this without understanding a little more about how you are part of this. You have a distinct advantage because you know a lot more about my background. You are clearly not just a retired CFO. I trust you based on the time we worked together. Father Tim told me that it was not a chance meeting when you drew me in with 'Oostburg.' I'm not complaining. I actually love how things turned out for me and Shauntel."

"I can't tell you much. Sort of a Catch-22. If you don't agree to help, I can't tell you what I do or how I'm connected. It is a basic need-to-know conundrum."

"Well, let's both sleep on it. I'll swing by on Tuesday or Wednesday to talk more. Okay?"

"That's fine. This is a little time sensitive, but two days won't matter much."

"Good to see you, Tim. How are Carol and the rest of your family doing?"

"Everyone is doing well. One of the grandkids just got accepted to Stanford. We're proud. Just hope she doesn't turn out to be a liberal egghead. That seems to be what the universities are trying to produce."

"The leftist academics can't win if we teach our children to think. I'm sure your grandchildren will be fine." Spike started to get up and look around again. He noticed that the books seemed old and none had dust jackets. He also noticed a fire repression system. He asked, "Which collection is more valuable, the books or the cars?"

"That's easy, the books."

"This is the best garage I have ever seen. I especially like the sidebar. If you have a Spotted Cow the next time I stop by, I'd probably drink it."

"Okay, it's a deal. You know the way out. See ya, Spike."

"I'd appreciate it if my classmate skates on his mistake."

"I think it will be fine."

When Spike got home, Shauntel was in the office. She asked him to wait to talk about what he'd learned until she got some work done. He needed to get caught up as well. It worked out well.

A couple hours later as they were getting ready for bed. He told her about the meeting, and she said, "I think they will try to blackmail you into working for them. Other than Guls, how are we vulnerable?"

"So far, until we engage Jimmy, it is just Guls." Spike got ready for bed in about a minute. He needed rest after the last few days.

"Why not just get the intel from the source, skip Jimmy and sign up to help them?"

"Two reasons, I don't trust them and don't want to be controlled."

"Did you trust them when you worked for the company?" Shauntel asked.

She knew the answer. Spike trusted them until he didn't. Then he left. Spike said, "Rhetorical, right?"

"You know I just like to say, 'the company.'"

"Good night, sweetheart." Spike smiled. Shauntel was giving him the green light to go forward. He was surprised, but then Spike thought about what Father Tim had said. He once again realized how amazing Shauntel is.

"Good night, honey."

CHAPTER 19

The following day

Spike started his day as normal with the morning routine. Two weeks ago, he had increased his workout to four sets of fifty pushups, forty pullups, and two hundred crunches. He was pushing his speed to closer to five and a half minute miles. He needed to get ready in case he found himself back in the field. During his family's visit, the strength training took longer, and he didn't improve his speed much. Now that the distraction was gone, he could refocus on fitness.

As he delivered the coffee and kissed Shauntel goodbye, he was thinking about what needed to get done. He wanted to check in with Bill and Bob in the plant to see how they were progressing. He needed to get up to speed on the global restart and see if he could begin projecting the timing of getting caught up on the backordered shipments. The financial impact would be significant if the restart went well. Then, he needed to check in with legal and human resources to be sure all was well. He knew that people would want to talk about his mom's passing. That would slow him down, so he tried to think of a way to deflect without seeming like an asshole.

As he pulled into the parking lot, he was happy to see that things looked much closer to normal. More than half the parking lot between the plants was full. He walked into the office and found Todd Grasse, the controller. Todd was dressed in jeans and a golf shirt. While the company's executives weren't expected to wear suits and ties every day, jeans were a little unusual.

Spike said, "Todd, you look like you're going to cut the grass."

Todd smiled. "I was wondering what you would say. I have to help move some furniture today, and I figured it didn't make sense to be the only on in dress pants and a button-down shirt. So, I told everyone that today was Jeans Day."

"Good call. How do April numbers look so far?"

"As expected, not great, but way better than last April."

"If this becomes an annual exercise, we'll probably figure out how to improve profitability without a hiccup. Hell, Jim's probably in his office redesigning our plants for social distancing right now. Maybe we should start to modernize our warehouse operations. Do you have a feel for the current inventory versus the cost of the space? Try to compare that to the same numbers at month-end for the past three years. Maybe we can learn something."

"I'll start working on it later this week. I need to check for some tax advantages that the federal government announced to help manufacturers through this downturn. Last year, they were shooting from the hip. The government wasted some of the stimulus during COVID-19 because they were in such a hurry to get money into the economy. This time, they are being more thoughtful."

"No big hurry on the inventory analysis. Any time before the end of the month will work. Maybe share what you find with Jun Park in Seoul. He has built some interesting models. Between your two huge brains, I'm sure you'll come up with some meaningful recommendations. Let me know what you learn about the tax benefits by the time we meet with the leadership group mid-month."

"Will do." Todd looked uncomfortable but continued, "I heard about your mom. Sorry."

"Thanks, Todd. She was a wonderful mother, and I'm glad she got to rejoin my dad. She was sick of being alone." This was Spike's test balloon. He wanted to see how Todd reacted to a two-sentence reply.

"Hadn't thought of that. Huh, that's a good way to look at it."

Mission accomplished. "Talk to you later, Todd. Be careful moving furniture. You're not here for your brawn."

"I'll probably do more supervising that actual lifting."

Spike laughed and turned toward his office. He was lucky to have Todd around. He was curious and paid close attention to the details.

When he got to his office, he started checking in on the results from the restart. Several of the plants were running at nearly 60 percent capacity. Good start, but the real proof was how fast they could get to 90–100 percent. It was about incremental daily improvement, so the starting point wasn't as important as the velocity of improvement. His phone rang, and he checked the caller ID. Jim DePacker.

"This is Spike; what's up, boss?"

"Swing by my office when you get a chance."

"Okay, I'm on my way."

When Spike got to Jim's office, he thought, *Two birds with one stone*. Janice, the chief counsel, and Thomas, the HR director, were both sitting in front of Jim's desk. The discussion didn't seem overly intense, so Spike relaxed. He said, "Hello Suzanne, Thomas. Nice to see you."

Thomas started, "We are concerned about the fairness of the bonuses for highest productivity." He raised his eyebrows as if he wanted Spike to defend the contest.

"That's why we had you two look at it before Jim sent it out."

"It isn't the concept; it is the baseline we use to compare. They all make different things. How can this possibly be fair?"

"The baseline was their productivity prior to MARV. The comparison is versus their plant's history. Seems fair to me."

Janice jumped in. "The issue is that we may have undue pressure on employees to return to work when they really shouldn't either because they are infected, or they are scared."

"When you say undue pressure, are you talking about local leadership or peer pressure?"

"Both."

"What would you recommend?" Spike knew they wouldn't like that. These roles that manage risk don't like making recommendations. They like playing Monday Morning Quarterback.

"We should rescind the competition," Thomas asserted.

"I don't like that idea, but let's assume we take that approach. Do you think the people who worked yesterday and today in many time zones will be happy about that?"

"Probably not, but we could reasonably be sued for pressuring people back to work. Especially if someone gets sick or worse dies." Thomas was clearly more worried about this than either Jim or Janice.

"When we ran this by you last week, you didn't see this coming?"

"I didn't expect we would get complaints."

"How many complaints, and how did you respond?"

"Actually, just one informal complaint. The employee in question is afraid that he may get sick." Thomas stopped.

"How did you respond?"

"I heard about it from one of the other workers at his plant. So, I haven't responded."

"Did the person who was afraid he might get sick report to work?"

"I don't know for sure about today, but he didn't work yesterday."

"Sounds to me like we have no risk until we have someone who actually works due to 'undue pressure.' I'm not sure why we're discussing this when we don't have an actual complaint and no evidence that what you fear has happened. Am I missing something?"

"No, not really," Thomas answered.

"And you made the decision to tell the CEO and Chief Counsel?"

Thomas was getting extremely uncomfortable. Spike liked the guy, but he needed to have a little better business judgment than to react as if there was an emergency with so little evidence. Spike decided to lower the intensity. No reason to make an enemy. Spike said, "I think we should step back, see how the rest of the week goes, and figure out if there is a reason to rethink our position. When we do that, I would like to be sure we keep the employees who want to work in mind."

Jim started to stand up, his signal that the meeting was adjourned. He'd been silent since Spike came in. He didn't want to have to dress down his HR director, but he was happy to have Spike do it. As Janice and Thomas started for the door, Jim said, "Spike, I have a few other things to discuss."

"Okay." After the others left, Spike said, "Jim, before I came in here, did they try to convince you to stop the competition?"

"No, they just said they wanted to discuss it. I said, 'Let's hold off until Spike comes in.' We discussed the weather mostly."

"The word 'complaints' is what really pissed me off. First, it was hearsay at best, and second, it was one complaint. Sorry I put him in a virtual choke-hold, but that's unbelievable. He signed off on the idea four days ago." Spike took a cleansing breath and continued, "I'm over it. I hope you don't mind that I was so direct."

"That's exactly what we needed. People who panic in a crisis are not executive material in this company. I learned something without having to be the asshole. Thanks."

"No problem. Now, what did we learn yesterday and this morning?"

"All systems go. Total productivity was nearly fifty percent of pre-MARV levels. On Mondays, we usually run at about seventy-five percent. Last year, first day back after COVID-19 was about thirty percent. This is a fast start."

"Good, but I'm counting on daily improvement to quickly get back to normal capacity within a few weeks. That's the metric I am concentrating on."

"Agreed. If we get any real complaints, we'll deal with them. For now, we're doing well."

"I asked Todd to work with Jun to analyze the distribution process. I think we can learn a lot from two years of shutdowns. I asked Todd to look at the past thirty-six months. Could be interesting. Or not?"

Jim said, "Good idea. I'm thinking about how we can create un-closeable plants. More operators in offices, two or three people at large intervals on the actual floor. It isn't a big stretch."

"I told Todd you'd be thinking like that. It's a good goal from a cost point of view as well. Workers, even in Third World countries, are expensive."

"We don't call them that anymore—developing countries, Spike."

"Yeah, whatever. Third World is a compliment for some of those shitholes our competitors are operating in. I know, I've been there. That is why we need to avoid places where the governments are too dictatorial. That is a real risk."

"Thanks for coming in today. I know you've got to be drained."

Spike said, "Not really. The funeral yesterday was great closure. I spent more time with my siblings in the past week than since I went to the Academy. Doctor Huebrex and Father Tim Flynn from Holy Name in Sheboygan made it much easier."

"Father Tim, why do I know that name?" Jim asked.

"He's friends with Tim Blust. Maybe that's the connection. He's a little Irish priest that looks the part and really helped my family."

"Yep, that's it, I met him at Blust's once. He seemed very aware of his surroundings."

"You don't understand how priests convert heathens like you. They listen for an opening and pounce." Spike laughed at his own joke, but in his head, he was thinking that Father Tim might have been in the Trooper Tim role when he met Jim. "Anything else?"

"No, just don't forget to take care of yourself. You served a lot of masters for the past week. Take it easy for the next week. It will help you reflect and recover."

Spike got up to leave and said over his shoulder, "Sage advice. Thanks."

Spike had asked Jun for some analysis for Maurer's outdoor operations around the world. Of course, a detailed answer was waiting in his inbox. Maurer Company had granite and marble operations in England, Italy, the US, and Canada. The overall MARV incidence in these countries varied. But these specific local areas had very few cases and almost no fatalities. That was the exact opposite of what Spike expected. The Vitamin D and blood oxygen levels in these areas should have made them hotspots.

Spike responded to Jun's email.

> *Jun,*
>
> > *Thanks for the quick work.*
> >
> > *I'm surprised. Outdoor workers seem to be getting slammed by MARV. Any ideas why it isn't hitting these locations?*
> >
> > *Another thing, I asked Todd to connect with you on inventory modeling. Please let him take the lead. We can make assumptions on timing because we know when COVID-19 and MARV happened.*
>
> > *Spike*

He felt good about the company's response to the pandemics over the past two years, but learning never stops. Companies that don't innovate and grow end up in trouble. He headed over to visit with Bob and Bill. The plant was buzzing with energy as he entered. He saw Bill and Bob on the catwalk.

Spike joined them and Bob said, "These people are doing a great job making adjustments that are making a difference. We're heading to eighty percent of capacity by the end of the week with only forty-five percent of our team."

"That's great. How lasting is the change?"

"Many of the changes are to accommodate people doing two jobs. If we decided to reduce staff because we can do it better this way, so be it. But I think they can only operate at this speed for so long. A few weeks at the most. Kind of like when you were executing a battle plan. You can't keep that level of adrenaline running forever."

Spike nodded. "Okay, that makes sense."

Bill said, "Spike, sorry about your mom."

Bob was nodding, so Spike said, "Thanks, guys. She was ready to join my dad, and she told us all what she thought before she died. She was a great mom. Don't worry about job cuts. That isn't the point. I'll see you guys later this week."

"See ya, Spike," they said in unison.

Spike headed back to his office. He knew he would want to meet with Jimmy later today. He worked through email and analyzed the restart data he had. He kept thinking about hiring the hacker, so he decided to just get to it.

CHAPTER 20

Three years ago, Spike met Jimmy Celestini, who recently joined Maurer with an MBA from the University of Minnesota's Carlson School of Management. More impressively, he was a math major at Drake University. Jimmy had grown up in the part of northern Minnesota known as the Iron Range. The area had been an economic powerhouse in the first seventy years of the twentieth century. By the time Jimmy was born in the early 1990s, Hibbing, his hometown, was shrinking. The mining jobs were gone, but some manufacturing jobs had come along. Jimmy's father, Bob, had been a high school star and played for the University of Minnesota in the late '70s. The Gopher hockey coach was legendary Herb Brooks. Even though Bob wasn't on the Miracle team that made history at the 1980 Lake Placid Olympics, he knew most of the players. When a large, national manufacturing company opened a plant in Hibbing, they realized hiring a local guy to run the plant was good for business. Rangers, as the locals were known, didn't trust outsiders. Bob was well-qualified, and since he coached youth hockey teams, he was well known and popular. Rangers trusted Bob because he was one of them.

Since his dad ran the plant, Jimmy grew up in a well-to-do family. He wasn't spoiled but had very nice skates and always had the newest composite stick. Jimmy loved hockey and played whenever he could on the outside rinks in Hibbing. Like most Minnesota hockey kids, he had practically memorized the movie that depicted the Miracle on Ice that his dad described with reverence. For his part, Jimmy became a talented defenseman with great vision on the ice. Probably due to his slight size at five feet, nine inches, 165 pounds, he was downright mean on the ice. And due to his intellect, he could always account for all nine skaters. When bigger kids were looking past him due to his size, Jimmy would crush them with a shoulder to the sternum.

This most notable part of his game was non-existent off the ice. Jimmy was incredibly bright, especially in math. When his high school teachers found out he was a beast on the ice, they were shocked. Along with his size, Jimmy's longish black hair, bright blue eyes, and preppy clothes made him look like an angel in school. And his intensely competitive side made him an outstanding student. If someone else got a 99 percent on a test, he would want to ace it. He often tried to spy the other good students' scores when papers were handed back. After a while, he decided it would be easier to just look on the teacher's grading system. Like most things, the data was held on computers, and he knew he could get to the information. So, he started figuring out how to hack into systems. How hard could it be?

Jimmy got good at it. Since he was driven to be the best student, it would have been easy to get other data—tests and papers were held on the same system. But Jimmy had an unbending moral compass. He simply couldn't lie, steal, or cheat. It wasn't in his DNA. Hard work was the only way to improve. His dad had always taught him that teamwork and hard work were the key factors in the Miracle on Ice at Lake Placid.

When Jimmy started getting calls from colleges in Minnesota to play hockey, he only had two questions: Could he go straight to college from high school, and how was the math department? Since none of the coaches who wanted him to play hockey would allow him to skip the customary two years of junior hockey, he never really researched the math departments. Bob, for his part, was indifferent to Jimmy playing college hockey. It had helped him grow into a successful leader and manager, but he wasn't nearly as academically gifted as Jimmy.

When he chose Drake University in Iowa for their math department, Jimmy didn't realize how much he would miss playing hockey. He joined Drake's club team and enjoyed playing. Unfortunately, the hockey wasn't as competitive as Minnesota High School hockey. It was still fun. When not studying or skating, Jimmy spent most of his free time at Drake trying to get into the CIA's database without detection. When he finally did it, he learned about unconstitutional activities that he didn't want to know. It haunted him that he couldn't unlearn what he'd found. He never told anyone what he'd seen—and some of it was frightening.

At a company picnic few months after Jimmy joined Maurer, he overheard that Spike was former CIA, and he acted extremely uncomfortable. Spike Eastman was an operative in one of the Afghanistan missions Jimmy had learned about. It must have been the same guy; how many Spike Eastmans could the CIA have?

What Jimmy remembered was spotty, but something about an interrogation of a Taliban leader who had access to Bin Laden. As Jimmy broke out of his trance from reaching back into his memory, he noticed that Spike was watching him. Since Spike was trained to see anomalies in human interaction, he had noticed Jimmy's behavior. A couple weeks later, Spike called Jimmy in for an informal mentoring discussion.

Jimmy was visibly shaken when Spike asked him some innocuous questions about his past in relation to the intelligence community. Spike finally just said, "You're nervous—even more than a financial analyst should be talking to the CFO of your company. What's up?"

Jimmy was a geek at heart and truly proud of his escapades infiltrating the CIA. It didn't take long, and he matter-of-factly admitted his sins. Clearly, Spike's laidback demeanor and matching distrust of government led to the admission. Somehow, Jimmy just plain trusted the friendly, laidback guy who happened to be the CFO. More than anything, Mr. Eastman reminded him of his dad, Bob. Spike knew all about the lack of transparency to the public and the media. Clearly, he agreed with Jimmy's point of view that the government was not telling the public the truth. The only difference was that Spike supported the deception because the public wasn't really equipped to understand the depth of the enemies' evil the CIA was dealing with throughout the war on terror. Jimmy, inexperienced and naïve, believed that the public had a right to know. In the end, they agreed to disagree on that point.

After all, Spike was more interested in Jimmy's newly discovered skillset than the implications of his less than legal and nefarious past activities. After their discussion three years before, Spike kept the knowledge of Jimmy's expertise as close as an "Eyes Only" top secret dossier. He thought someday he could ask Jimmy for some help. That day may have come.

Spike invited Jimmy to a twenty-minute lunch at 12:10. He ordered a couple salads from the employee cafeteria, chicken Caesar for him and some kind of vegan concoction for Jimmy. He was a weird dude, but if he thought eating vegan was good, that was okay with Spike. The food arrived ahead of Jimmy. Jenny brought the boxes in at noon and said she'd send Jimmy in when he arrived. Jimmy showed up right on time. He was cordial, not knowing what to expect.

Jimmy laughed about the Vegan food. "How did you know I like this stuff?"

Spike said, "I just asked the cafeteria lady to make something you'd like."

"Well, I eat this crap a lot here, but I'm more of a pizza eater than anything. I like a good four-meat pizza or pasta with meat sauce like any other Italian kid from the Range."

"Good, I was concerned about your protein levels." Spike smiled and took a bite of his lunch and leaned forward at his conference table. "Jimmy, what do you think about this virus in China?"

Jimmy smiled and said, "The impact on the company has been serious but not nearly as bad domestically as the COVID-19 virus." Jimmy was thinking the CFO was testing his knowledge of current events and their impact on Maurer Company.

"Well, I have an assignment for you that is probably a little illegal. The news out of China has a lot of other implications. Some of the issues are more related to our country's stability than our company's stability."

"Sir, I need to do some research. I follow the news, mostly from Twitter feeds, and all I know is that China had another outbreak of some a virus related to their weird obsession with eating animals that are alive when they buy them. Nothing wrong with eating animals, but the weird stuff they eat is plain crazy."

Spike said, "Look, Jimmy, I eat lots of animals and four-meat pizza is my favorite. Having said that, I agree it is way outside of our culture to kill and cut up bats for soup. I'll give you one more hint. Push your research sources a little further than Twitter and Facebook. I don't want to know what the news media is saying. I want to know what the World Health Organization, CDC, FBI, and CIA aren't saying." Spike leaned back and said, "If this turns out like I think it might, I need you to do the things that were never on your resume."

Jimmy understood the implication. "I'm not going to be able to do that from my Maurer workstation. There are too many controls that I could but shouldn't work around. The speed of our systems is a huge benefit for what I'd need to do. But working around the controls would allow others to follow my path."

"Okay, Jimmy, I'll act like I know what you're talking about, but I don't. In dumb old guy language, what do you need?"

"I need a set of linked high-speed servers, a very high-speed internet connection, and an eight-thousand-dollar laptop."

"You sound like my wife—she said about the same thing when she was setting up her home office." Spike pulled out a piece of notepaper. He wrote Shauntel's cell number on it and said, "Please collaborate with Shauntel on what you need. Give me ten minutes, and I will let her know to expect your call. She'll talk geek with you and figure out how you can do this from my house. We have two workstations in the basement, but mine is dusty. You can set up there."

"What about my job? I have Maurer work to do, and my boss is kinda particular."

"Jimmy, officially, you'll be on temporary leave, but you can tell coworkers that it is vacation. I'll pay you a thirty percent premium and work out something with HR to make sure you don't actually use your vacation. My guess is that this will take two weeks max. Call my wife and start working on getting set up. She'll get what you need; she's very resourceful. I'll call your 'kinda particular' manager and smooth it over."

Jimmy hesitated. He had a healthy distrust for authority, but Mr. Eastman was a different kind of person. Jimmy believed that he really cared about the world, about people. He knew he was an outstanding executive, but more importantly, he was levelheaded and seeking truth. He thought that maybe he had nothing to lose; then he thought that the 30 percent bump could get him that Corvette he wanted a lot sooner. He thought, *YOLO*.

Jimmy said, "All right, Mr. Eastman, I'll do it."

"Thanks, Jimmy. Two things. First, please keep this to yourself; tell people you are going on vacation if they ask. Second, from now on, please call me Spike. Mr. Eastman makes me feel pretty old."

CHAPTER 21

The following day

When Spike was in the CIA, he was often surrounded by elite CIA operatives, military special operations teams with drones capable of striking and tracking the enemy and the most advanced electronic surveillance being picked apart by teams of CIA analysts. The complexity of the operations required a significant amount of support.

This wasn't really an operation at all. It was just fact-finding and analysis. He also realized that staying small would help them avoid the trackers who watched all the electronic discussions the world over. Those trackers were in the US, China, Russia, and several European countries. Even North Korea and Iran were part of the game of watching for anomalies in the use and dissemination of data. Staying under that radar would save a ton of scrutiny.

Only one big change now that he'd replaced Joe with Jimmy was the level of risk. If Jimmy is detected entering the CIA database, they would all be in deep shit. The simple answer to avoid that risk would be to follow Shauntel's logic and just ask the CIA for the information. But the simple truth was that Spike trusted Jimmy more than the CIA.

Jimmy got set up on Wednesday afternoon. The only new equipment was a better laptop than Spike used. Shauntel had Carl connect to the network environment to create a few new segregations in the servers—Spike glazed over as Shauntel and Jimmy tried to tell him what that meant. It all reminded him of the nerds who explained how the NSA analyzed the millions of messages they intercepted every day. He didn't understand any of the terms or methods and didn't care. He just wanted the analyzed information they gleaned through their gigantic supercomputers.

They could see that he was uninterested. They started making fun of him, so he told them he had something to do. Truth was that he really didn't have anything to do until he went to visit Tim Blust later that afternoon. He was glad when the doorbell rang.

Spike ran upstairs and saw a FedEx guy at the door. He had to sign for whatever it was. As he was walking back into the house, he ripped open the envelope using the cord that ran through the cardboard. Inside was Fred's passport and Visa card. A little note attached said the limit was thirty-five thousand dollars. Spike thought that would be plenty to get him to Paris, Frankfurt, Zurich, or Amsterdam where he had safe deposit boxes. Thinking ahead, he would likely go to Amsterdam first. It was more familiar to him, and he could pass for a Hollander.

He needed to think about how the meeting with Blust would play out. He wanted to know why they wanted him to help. His assumption was so that they could claim no involvement, and they didn't want to use less reliable contractors or share their knowledge with people they couldn't trust. He wanted to keep them hopeful that he would help so that they wouldn't take action against Guls. He also wanted to know more about Tim Blust and Father Tim. He started to consider what skills he had that Father/Trooper Tim didn't. If Spike were in Blust's position, he'd rather use Trooper Tim than Spike for a mission that included wet work or snatching someone. Wet work was company code for assassination. They had so many of these silly euphemisms.

Spike had to assume that the work they would want would be similar to what he'd done before. Helping identify and track the target with no current connection to the US government. The idea that he wasn't connected was pretty thin because most intelligence services would have a dossier on him. They would also likely have photos of him, and he hadn't changed enough to avoid a match if he was in the comparison database. Since the software is capable of matching to multiple databases, it would only be a matter of time before he was identified in almost any country in the Middle East, Europe, or Asia.

Spike looked at his watch and noticed he'd been thinking about this for a long time without any conclusions that didn't include a lot of assumptions. He decided to run over to Blust's home. He sent a quick text to Tim to be sure he was home. The reply was "I'll be here until after dinner. Now would be good."

Spike told Shauntel where he was headed and left. He pulled into Blust's driveway just like last time, and Tim just opened the side entry door to the garage, waved, and went back in.

Spike went through the garage and noticed the Impala was missing. Carol was out. When Spike entered the library, he was surprised to see Father Tim sitting at the conference table. They both had notepads with writing in front of them. Bad tradecraft.

"Father Tim, good to see you." Spike was surprised at how true that was. He felt very connected for knowing the man for less than a week. He thought about that and realized that Father Tim had been honest with him. Blust went over to the sidebar and grabbed a couple Spotted Cows and poured some brown liquor over ice. Spike assumed it was an expensive scotch or whiskey, but he didn't like hard liquor much, so he didn't recognize the bottle. Blust asked, "Glasses?"

In stereo, the answer was "No, thanks."

Blust brought the beers to the conference table. Father Tim grabbed a few leather coasters and slid them to the others. Blust put the beers on the coasters and held his glass up saying, "To liberty."

They tapped bottles with Blust's glass and said, "Cheers."

Blust began, "Spike, we need you to help us. You are uniquely qualified to help our country."

Spike said, "I've been trying to figure out how I'm unique. Can you tell me before I agree to help?"

"Not entirely, but two things that you probably know. First, you are trustworthy. Second, you are not officially connected to the government."

"To the first, thanks. As for the second, not really. Interpol and intelligence services databases worldwide would include me. Ex-military and Ex-CIA, I'm traceable."

"But you could be working for anyone."

"From my perspective, that doesn't matter. With the level of Big Brother facial recognition systems in major cities, I'd be identified in a minute. Once

I'm found, I'll be followed, and that doesn't make me feel safe because I have nobody to turn to if I'm detained."

Blust said, "Did you forget your tradecraft? You can slip anyone who is following you."

"Not really, I'm pretty rusty. Plus, if I slip them, I become a person of interest immediately."

"Okay, let's not get too far ahead of ourselves." Blust was out of answers so he moved on. "Mostly, we just need eyes in a certain city. There is someone we need tracked because we think MARV is a deliberate attack."

"What would my cover be?" Spike figured if he kept asking questions, he might learn more about what they already knew. He thought about Jimmy, and whether he could really get into the database.

"Probably just traveling for Maurer," Blust said.

"Where?"

"Can't answer that unless you agree to sign up."

"Not that I mind, but why is he here?" Spike pointed his beer bottle toward Father Tim.

"Father Tim is likely to be called to Rome next week. He might be someone who could help you if you got into a tight spot."

"Rome?"

"It's not the city you would be working in, but a lot closer than here."

Spike thought, *Middle East or Europe, not North Korea or China.* He asked, "What other support could I count on?"

"Normal stuff, safe houses, weapons if you need them, surveillance equipment. Maybe a few team members." Was Blust running this operation? Why wouldn't it be someone in the company?

Spike asked, "Is there a mole in CIA Ops? Why wouldn't this be handled at Langley?"

Blust looked at him without any noticeable reaction. Spike realized that his old boss was a very cool customer. No reactions to his probing questions. "I don't know of any leaks that would concern Director Oliva."

"Okay, fair enough. Father Tim, you know more about this than me. What do you think my chances of success would be?"

Father Tim looked at Blust. Blust nodded, and Father Tim said, "Based on what I know, I'd say somewhere between seventy and eighty percent."

"Okay, that's not bad. How do we make it more like ninety to one hundred?" Spike put in a pinch of Copenhagen Long Cut.

"That's the trick."

"I'm not in yet, but let's talk tomorrow or Friday. I need to get Shauntel comfortable with the idea. Father Tim, I guess I'm going to test your theory about Shauntel's support and my fealty to her."

"Good luck."

Spike stood to leave. This had turned out better than he thought it would. Looking to Father Tim for the odds was a ploy to get a feeling for what type of operation it would be. If Tim had said he didn't know, that would mean that he wasn't involved in the planning, which meant likely just surveillance. Since he assigned a probability of success, the mission would include either assassination or kidnapping. If Director Oliva had the support of the president and cabinet, she wouldn't be using a bunch of unaffiliated people in Sheboygan County, Wisconsin.

Spike headed straight home. He went straight down to the office and asked Jimmy how much he knew about intercepting phone or email transmissions. Jimmy laughed and said, "I have no way to capture communications. I would need to hack into either the internet company or the phone company. I wouldn't really even know where to begin."

"Well, at some point, we may need to do that so if you get any extra time…" Spike laughed.

Jimmy was getting comfortable with Shauntel and looked over at her and said, "Can you believe this guy? How many federal laws does he want me to break in one day?"

Shauntel said, "He's a little pushy." They both laughed.

Jimmy said, "I made some progress. They've changed some settings since I hacked them five years ago. Also, I was looking more into archived activity. Current operations may be in a different place. Did you ever keep data on current activity on a computer?"

"I didn't, but I'm sure the operations center did. Sometimes when I was debriefed, they would check my answers against what they had recorded during the mission. Sometimes, I would get times mixed up, and I would ask for help. Most of the time, it was simple stuff. You know, like did I shoot the fat guy first and then slit the skinny guy's throat or the other way around?"

Jimmy knew Spike was kidding, but Shauntel scolded him anyway. "He already thinks you're a monster; you don't need to add to it."

"Okay, sorry, Jimmy. But the point is that the operations center keeps pretty close track of the action that is going on around the world. In this case, we are looking for intel that either an allied intelligence agency or the NSA provided. So, it was unlikely to be received by operations. More likely, the information was being analyzed on the intel side of the agency."

"I need more background to figure this out. I don't know squat about how the CIA is organized."

"Basically, there are three divisions plus administration. They call the divisions Directorates. Operations, Intelligence, Science and Technology, and Admin. Operations does the field work, including spying; Intel does the analysis; DS and T gathers info from satellites and other surveillance and keeps track of foreign media. We can concentrate on Intel, because if Operations had found something, they would likely be handling it themselves. If it was DS and T, they would likely pass the info to Intel for deeper analysis.

"Intel is broken down by parts of the world mostly. Layered across the world is terrorism analysis. If you get in, look around for items that are marked TS-SCI. TS is Top Secret and SCI is Sensitive Compartmentalized Information. You will be able to tell if Director Oliva accessed the information because it will be tracked on the 'envelope.' Look for that."

"Spike, I just poked around before. I don't know how efficient it will be to try to find specific info."

"Well, first and foremost, don't get caught. If you think you are setting off alarms, abort. As you find stuff, that you need direction on, tell one of us. Don't text, email, or call either me or Shauntel. Everything is oral. Also, if you write anything down, we'll burn it. Great memorization skills are table stakes in intel work. If you don't have those skills, don't risk it. Write it down. But we have to burn anything you write down at least daily."

Spike continued, "Make sure you two have a plan to make us clean every night. Okay?"

"Okay, but they may still be able to track that someone got in. One of the tricks is to look anonymous. I'm good at that. But if they are on to us in some other way, they may be able to track back to here. If that happens, what is held on this computer or those servers won't really matter. The CIA will know what we got."

Spike looked at Shauntel. She nodded and said, "We have a lot of ways to avoid them knowing where we are and who we are. But, like Jimmy said, if they find us through other resources, connecting the dots between their end-point and our starting point is much easier. Do you have any reason to think the CIA or NSA would be monitoring us?"

"Well, yes, if you include my relationship with our source; they know that he's shared information with me." Jimmy didn't know who Guls was, and there was no reason to let him know so he would be their source in front of Jimmy.

Shauntel nodded. "That's different for two reasons. You've never interacted electronically with the source from any of these servers or our Wi-Fi. And anyone who knows you knows that you don't have any hacking or computer skills."

"Hey, I'm not a total dummy."

"Sorry, Spike, to people who do this kind of work, you are a total dummy." Jimmy smiled.

"Okay, well, do you two geniuses know how to cover our tracks?"

Jimmy said, "Yes."

Shauntel agreed. "Yes. From what Jimmy explained to me, we are able to avoid detection and tracking."

Spike thought he should make sure they were all thinking about the same problem. "Here's what we know: Director Oliva is involved. The CDC is seeing things that make them suspicious that this isn't a natural pandemic. The CIA is using outside resources to try to figure this out. But the outside resources are only very trusted resources. This leads me to believe that the bad guys aren't a foreign government. But they may be tied to a foreign government, like a business in China that is really just an extension of the government. Or it could be sensitive, like the way members of the Saudi Royal family support Al Qaeda and other Wahhabi nutbags."

Spike was on a roll and continued, "We also know that MARV is more fatal for people with two attributes, high Vitamin D levels and higher blood oxygen levels. Normally these attributes are found in people who are generally healthier than the average population. Previous flu pandemics were less threatening for people with these attributes. I also learned today that we should concentrate on Europe and the Middle East."

Shauntel said, "I should be able to figure out based on the economic and social impacts what country or countries are being targeted. I should also be able to figure out which sectors of the economy are recovering and which are not. In the world economy, there will be winners and losers from MARV. If I figure out who loses, maybe we can make some assumptions about who wins."

Spike said, "Okay, is the data you need to do that available from the sources you already use for your consulting company? It would be nice to not expand our data footprint."

"Yes, I should have everything I need. I'll need to link in some data from that Johns Hopkins website, but that isn't a red flag because I've been downloading their data since COVID-19 started. It was the most reliable data I could find last year, and I trust their methods of collecting the data. Especially in North America, Europe, and the Middle East."

Spike said, "Our source gave me a tip. Look at energy production worldwide."

Shauntel smiled. "I'll start there."

Spike went out to the bar and grabbed a bottle of water. He realized that while he was taking it easy from work, he would have time to focus on the investigation. He also realized that he had not followed up with Brian Morgan about the new golden retriever. He called the breeder who said he could pick up the dog anytime in the next couple days. He texted Brian to see if he had capacity. His phone rang a minute later.

"Spike, what's this texting bullshit? You're too old to act like a teenager."

"I figured you would be out plowing a field or something. Besides, I want to support your cell towers."

"Okay, whatever. When do you get the pup?"

"Anytime now. Do you want to start at eight weeks or wait until twelve like we did with Ginger?"

"I can do whatever. I recommend that you potty train her first so she doesn't get used to being a badass farm dog."

"Okay, is a week from now good?"

"Sure. And I was kidding about the higher fee. Scott is always talking about his poodle being a smarter dog, and I ask him about taking it hunting. So, I had to give you shit about not hunting with Ginger."

"I think your services are worth the higher charge, but I'll pay you what you invoice me. Hey, I might want to come out and fire a few rounds on your property later this week or this weekend. Maybe we can have a little competition."

"I can't shoot the handguns like you. But if you want to go rifle or shotgun slugs, I'll bet you a case of beer. Ten rounds, thirty yards. I'm going out on Lake Michigan Saturday, so it will have to be Friday or Sunday."

"Let's make it tomorrow at about four."

Brian said, "Sure, should be done with my chores by then."

"Thanks." Spike made a note to pick up a case of beer for Brian and some extra ammunition. He'd never beat him with a rifle. But Spike was in desperate need of practice. He could practice drawing and firing while moving at Brian's property. Most gun ranges didn't like that.

Spike checked his email and saw that Jun had responded. He said he looked forward to working with Todd on the inventory project. He noticed that the only places where they had significant outdoor labor were areas not hard hit by MARV. Because Jun was curious, he looked a little deeper and found some interesting information about the spread of the pandemic. It seemed to skip a lot of areas that had high levels of world travelers. Places like Las Vegas, Monaco, Paris, and Amsterdam were almost unaffected. Other places, like Dubai, Singapore, Kuala Lumpur, and Calgary, were hard hit. Spike didn't see any relevance until Jun pointed out that these were some of the most important oil- and gas-producing cities in the world. That matched what he had learned from Guls, so Spike thought he should learn more about the industry. He figured Shauntel probably had a lot of that info, so he headed back into the office and asked her.

As he entered, Ginger was the only one who noticed him. The other two were hard at work staring at monitors and working their keyboards. Ginger wagged her tail and Spike couldn't resist her. He went over and pet her while waiting for a break in the click-click of the keyboards. Both Shauntel and Jimmy stopped at once. Jimmy asked, "What's up, Spike?"

"I'm wondering about oil and gas. Shauntel, what do you know so far?"

"Since I don't have any clients in the space, I started with basic research on the industry. Companies are headquartered in large cities usually near production. Aramco is the giant Saudi government-owned company in Dhahran. Gazprom, Sovol, and Rosneft are fifty percent owned by the Kremlin. These government-run and subsidized companies are difficult to track, but their production leads the world. The independent companies that are not controlled by their governments are Exxon, Shell, Chevron, Total, and BP. All have suffered in recent years due to overproduction and some reduced demand. The biggest players who control the industry are closely tied to OPEC. Since the dispute on production between the Saudis and Russians early last year, it has been hard for these companies to recover. Production in the US is down, but the reserves and amount of oil that is available to be harvested at higher prices will eventually be valuable. MARV has been tough on oil companies, but the demand reduction caused by COVID-19 is really the bigger long-term headwind."

"Shauntel, I'm not looking to buy oil stocks. I'm wondering how these individual companies and, by extension, countries are impacted by MARV."

"It appears that the hardest hit companies are in the Middle East, but I need to correlate the JHU data to the oil production areas to create an overlay on a heat map of MARV versus oil and gas production."

Spike asked, "How long will that take?"

"A couple hours."

"Jimmy, anything to report?"

"Not a lot. I did figure out how to get in undetected, but that's about it."

Spike smiled. "That's a big deal, Jimmy."

"Now, I need to find how this is organized. That may take a day."

"Doesn't matter, just stay undetected. Is getting in repeatable, or do you have to find new routes every time?"

"Spike, that is the first intelligent technical question you have asked. The answer is that it depends on how they do things. That is the other thing I'm working on...finding paths day after day."

"Well, good luck." Spike realized he better quit while he was ahead. He turned back to Shauntel. "Let me know when you get the heat map correlated, okay?"

"Will do. Any other ideas?" Shauntel asked.

"No, based on what I've learned from our source and Maurer's international results, I think we need to look at oil and gas and see what Director Oliva has been up to. If we come up empty, we might need to reconsider. I think we should quit for tonight. Are you at good stopping points?"

"Doesn't matter to me," Jimmy said.

Shauntel smiled and said, "Yeah, I can stop."

"Does anyone have notes to burn or stored data to delete?"

"Not yet, what I've done doesn't get stored, and I haven't written anything down," Jimmy said.

Shauntel said, "I'm just doing normal research. Deleting it would be more suspicious than leaving it in my in-process files."

"Great, I got some steaks and asparagus for the grill. You two hungry?"

"Steaks and asparagus, sounds great, but do you have any potatoes and garlic? I can make some mean mashed potatoes." Jimmy was fitting in well.

Shauntel said, "We have russet potatoes; are they okay?"

"That's what I usually use. I brought an overnight bag and a couple changes of clothes. I hope you don't mind, but I think I should bunk here for a few days."

"I'm all for that, Shauntel?"

"Good idea, you can sleep in the bedroom down here. I'll get you started on the potatoes."

CHAPTER 22

The following day

Spike decided to press his workout harder. He doubled the pullups, pushups, and ab crunches again. He also changed up his route to add three extra miles. It added a half hour to his routine and confused Ginger. He felt good about his fitness level. Later today, he would see if he could hit anything with his bullets. It had been six months since he had shot, and he knew it wasn't the same as riding a bike. Practice is what drives accuracy. Good equipment helps, but eyesight and steady hands can't be replaced by fancy weapons.

After delivering coffee and kissing Shauntel goodbye, he heard Jimmy in the shower downstairs. He was a good, hardworking kid, but his comments about the public having a right to know about covert activity would need some attention. He seemed to like figuring things out, and he did keep it to himself for five years that he'd hacked the CIA. Spike made a mental note to check in on his new intel analyst's perspective on what he was doing.

Spike went into the office for the morning. The restart was progressing as expected with productivity levels nearing 80 percent. He went into Jim De-Packer's office and asked about any fallout from HR and Legal.

Jim said, "Nothing so far. They won't bother me with it unless it is real, so I'm thankful for that. I even asked Thomas if he'd heard anything new, and he said, 'No, looks like Spike was right.'"

"Huh, maybe he's learning. How about the restart? Looks like we've made good progress so far."

"Yeah, and I've made some progress on the un-closeable plant."

"We might want to keep that quiet for a while if it is going to mean job losses."

"I don't think we'll see much reduction in manpower; I'm just thinking about separating the people so they can work from home or in isolation at the plant. The production level will go up by twenty percent, that's where the ROI is. In about a month, I'm going to need you to model the financial results. For now, I want you to take it easy."

"I might take off this afternoon. I'm thinking of taking Shauntel to Door County for a long weekend. We need some away time. I'd really like to head to the Bahamas, but I don't know how they are doing with MARV."

"There has to be a beach open somewhere. Just send me an email if you decide to take off. You can track the restart from anywhere. Probably an hour or two a day. Sounds like a vacation to me."

"I agree. Do you ever really check out?" Spike asked.

"I feel funny if I don't look at some of the reports every day."

"Me too. I'll see if Shauntel can make a trip happen."

Spike left Jim's office and went straight out to the plant. Bob and Bill were in Bill's office. "How's it going, fellas?"

Bob answered, "We keep getting better. We could have done this a long time ago. I think the idea of trying new things, especially with an experienced crew is making the teams way more productive. They aren't walking in and turning off their brains like they did when everything was defined for them."

"I expected that with your leadership. I may be out of the office for the next week or so. Good luck finishing this week's competition. If you don't win, you can get still win next week."

Bob said, "If we win, the rest of the company will think we won because of our proximity to headquarters."

Spike said, "Fuck 'em. This deal is fair and square. If you win, you did the best against your own results. See ya, guys." He left the office and headed home.

He made a steak sandwich and headed downstairs to check on the progress. Shauntel and Jimmy were hard at work. He didn't want to disturb them.

When Ginger smelled the steak, she wagged her tail and came over to the door. Spike went back out to the bar with Ginger. He read and cleared out his Maurer email. He spent a couple hours going over the reports he'd sent himself. The reports fit with the progress they were expecting from the restart. He dug into an analysis of return to work by site. It was time to go see Brian and shoot. On the way back, he would get some takeout, so he asked for orders from Shauntel and Jimmy. They settled on pizza and salad from Firehouse.

Spike got his weapons, jumped in the pickup, and stopped at the liquor store for a case of beer. On the way to Brian's, he swung by the gun shop and picked up two hundred rounds of nine-millimeter ammunition and four hundred .223 Remington rounds. He arrived just before four, and Brian was out in the yard playing with his black lab, Pepper. Pepper was a large female, and Spike loved to watch her retrieve. She would practically hand the Frisbee to Brian.

Brian saw Spike unloading his weapons and smiled. Spike knew Brian was thinking about the beer he would win. Brian started his Gator and helped Spike load the gear in the back. Brian's rifle didn't have a magazine in it, and the breach was open. Brian was a safety fanatic, which suited Spike fine. Most outdoorsmen were respectful of their weapons. Spike wasn't a big hunter, but he knew that hunting accidents were almost always caused by carelessness. They headed over to a small clearing with two large loading tables built into large oak trees. It was a great place to shoot.

Spike fired ten rounds with his M4 and said, "I'm ready to compete. Want me to set the targets?"

"Sure, but I should probably take a practice shot to make sure my sights are right." Brian seated his magazine, cycled a round into the chamber, and hit the target in middle of the ten circle. He smiled. "Guess it's okay."

He removed the magazine, reopened the breach, and removed the round from the chamber. He nodded, and Spike went down with two fresh targets and attached them to hay bales at thirty yards. When he came back, they fired two rounds each and alternated until they got to ten. On the fifth shot, Spike lost. He hit the nine circle and knew Brian wouldn't miss. It ended up one hundred to ninety-eight, and Spike admitted that he bought the case of beer on the way.

"Hope it's still cold when you get done. Looks like you brought a lot of ammunition."

"I'm going to do some tactical shooting. Pretend like I'm a badass."

"Let me take a few shots with your M4. How do I set it for three round bursts?"

Spike showed him, then handed him a full twenty-round magazine. Brian tapped the magazine like he'd seen on TV and smiled at Spike. He slammed the magazine home and shot from standing, kneeling, and prone positions. Even shooting three rounds at a time, he never hit outside the nine circle. Brian just knew how to handle a weapon.

They walked back to the picnic table. "Spike, don't worry about the brass. I have a contraption to pick it up. Besides, I can recycle it and make a fortune."

"All right, thanks."

They walked over to the picnic table, and as Spike was putting on his tactical holster for his nine-millimeter Berretta, Brian said, "I'll come back to pick you up. Half hour?"

"That's fine; the beer is in a cooler in the truck."

As Brian drove away, Spike opened another gun case and assembled another Berretta, this time adding an illegal silencer. He didn't want to put Brian in the position of knowing about the illegal hardware. He put that in his elongated shoulder holster. Spike had learned to shoot with both hands almost as effectively. His right was still dominant, but he could score almost as well with his left.

Spike shot from several different positions. He had set up several different targets at different heights. He pictured a gunfight and went through the motions. He moved around, hid behind trees, rolled in the dirt. It was fun and a decent workout. When he finished, he put the silenced weapon away, put up new targets, and started plinking with the normal weapon. He shot ten rounds as fast as he could with each hand in three different firing positions from fifteen feet. This was his test to see if he still had it. Satisfied that he hadn't lost his touch, he started cleaning up. Brian came along a few minutes later, and Spike was happy to see he had a cold one in the Gator for him.

Spike loaded his gear into the back of the Gator, hopped in, and opened the beer with the church key hanging by twine from the shift stick. He said, "I'm still okay with the pistols, but I swear, I'm not as comfortable as I used to be."

"Hell, Spike, you're fifty."

"So are you, Brian, and you just hit eleven straight bullseyes from ninety feet."

"I'm retired and have little else to do."

When they pulled up to Spike's truck, Spike finished his beer and loaded his gear. He wanted to get moving, but they decided to have another beer. They shot the shit about their kids and life. There is nothing like old friends; it was as if they had done this same thing every couple weeks for thirty years. Truth was, Spike had been gone for twenty years, and since returning, they saw each other occasionally, but the comfort of shared locker rooms of their youth made up for that. They finished their beers and said goodbye.

Spike needed to pick up the order at Firehouse so Jimmy and Shauntel could quit working. When he walked in, the place was empty. He didn't realize that they were only taking to-go and delivery orders. He hadn't really been paying attention to the local conditions in response to MARV. The owner, Vince Zuccaro, was at the register wearing a facemask and rubber gloves.

Spike asked, "How is business, Vince?"

"First, do you want a beer, Spike?"

"Is that allowed?"

"Sure, as long as you are waiting for your order." Vince looked down at his screen and said, "You have about five minutes."

"I'll have one."

Vince grabbed a Spotted Cow from the cooler and opened it. "For our business, we learned a lot from COVID-19. I'm not losing money this time. I'm looking forward to reopening so we can make money again. Most of my waitstaff is on unemployment. Some of them are delivering, but they make better money from the government. Feels like a bad trend to me."

"I agree, but odds are pretty good that we won't have to worry about this again for a while." Spike took a long pull on the beer.

Vince frowned. "I think the government is rooting for more pandemics. State and federal government control more of our lives, and politicians like that. I don't really pay attention to them most of the time, but it seems like they are using these pandemics to become bigger and get the working class more dependent on the government. That same working class is starting to notice that politicians and government workers still collect their pay when businesses are forced to close."

Spike nodded. "It will be interesting to see how this plays out over the next couple years."

"Yeah, I guess I'm lucky. My building is paid for, my margins are decent, and I have really good employees." Vince's eyes got wide, and he said, "Oh, hey, I heard about your mom. Where do you think she got it?"

"It doesn't matter, but I'm guessing from some delivery. She was ready to join Jack anyway. You know how it is. Married over fifty years, then one day Dad died. She never really adjusted to life without him."

"Well, I'm sorry she passed. She used to bring her friends here on Wednesdays. She was funny." Vince's high-school-aged son came out of the kitchen with Spike's order. He set it on the counter and said, "Salad and Pizza for Eastman."

Spike finished his beer and grabbed the order. "Thanks, Vince. Nice visiting."

"See you soon, Spike."

CHAPTER 23

As Spike drove into the driveway, he saw Tim Blust's Suburban parked in the driveway. Spike pulled into the garage and headed in through the mudroom. Shauntel and Tim were sitting at the kitchen island, both looking a little uncomfortable. They had bottles of water in front of them. Spike said, "Hi, Tim. To what do we owe the pleasure?"

"I just wanted to be sure Shauntel knows how much we need you."

"That's a chickenshit move, Tim."

Shauntel interrupted, "Tim has been vague about why he needs you. I mentioned that I think I need you more than he does."

"Tim, if you can provide a little more detail on what you want me to sign up for, how you are connected, and why I'm uniquely qualified, I can make a decision based on facts. Right now, I'm leaning toward eating my pizza before it gets cold. And continuing my life as it is."

Tim took a sip of water. "Your mission would be to track an individual. I am a contractor, and I only deal with the director. Your background of covert tracking is your unique qualification."

"That's a start. You are going to have to tell me more. Before I can agree, I need to know where and who the target is. I'd like to know how I get back home and whether it is a kidnapping or assassination, but that can wait until I decide. If the path home seems too risky, I might push back. If you need to go ask permission to give me what I need, please do. I'm hungry."

"Okay, but in the meantime, be careful." He stood up to leave. Shauntel began getting up, but Spike shook his head to keep her seated.

Spike followed Blust toward the front door. "Tim, what does 'be careful' mean?"

"If you decide to help us, I can tell you a lot more." Blust opened the door and walked out. Spike followed him to his Suburban.

"Tim, if I decide not to do this and anyone fucks with me or Shauntel, I will consider you an enemy."

As he got into the driver's seat, Tim smiled. "Two observations: The first is that you know me better than that. I'm not asking you to trust me, but I am a moral man. I will not do anything to threaten you or your family. The second is that you don't need us, but we need you for more reasons than I can share."

Spike didn't smile. He simply said, "Tim, I wish you had brought me into your confidence a long time ago. That would have made all of this easier."

"Enjoy your pizza." Tim shut the door.

When Spike came back into the kitchen, Shauntel asked, "Is he gone?"

Spike nodded but put his finger to his lips with a serious look. He went into the mudroom and almost bumped into Jimmy. He gave Jimmy the same serious shush look. Spike reached into one of the closets and put his thumb to a gun safe bio-reader. He grabbed a device that looked like an old Blackberry phone. He powered it up and went back into the kitchen. He opened his notebook wrote a note, "What rooms had Tim been in?"

Shauntel took the pen and wrote, "Foyer, kitchen."

Spike hit a few buttons on the device and started searching the room while watching the device closely. He continued doing this throughout the kitchen and then walked slowly into the foyer. He came back and said, "Clear."

Shauntel said, "Jimmy, come in here." Shauntel had put the pizza into the oven to keep it warm and was setting placemats, napkins, and plates on the island. Jimmy came out of the shadows in the mudroom area looking confused.

"What was that?" Jimmy asked.

Spike said, "It would have been easy to leave a listening device. I don't trust anyone, but especially people who work with the CIA."

Jimmy laughed. "Me too, but that included you."

Spike looked at him and smiled. "That's why I left." Spike continued, "That was an interesting visit. We were lucky. First, I'm glad we put Jimmy's car in the garage. When I saw the Suburban, I thought maybe they were on to us. Second, there is some compelling reason they want me for this operation. Third, I really am hungry, so I'm glad he didn't stay long."

Jimmy said, "Me too. Do you have any beer?"

"Of course, run downstairs and bring back four Spotted Cows and a bottle of white wine."

When Jimmy was gone, Spike said, "Tim won't come after us unless he's forced to by the CIA. Jimmy needs to be incredibly careful."

"I think he's paranoid enough to cover his tracks. He really has a high level of concentration. He worked straight through the day without any distractions."

Jimmy came up the stairs, his arms full of beers and a bottle of wine. He had eight beers. Spike said, "Did I say eight?" as if he was confused.

Jimmy smiled. "I think my work is done here. I want to celebrate. Everything I did is erased except for a few pages of notes. Director Oliva is trying to get someone to track down Boris Fedderov, a Russian oligarch. They think he unleashed MARV. I got into the CIA file on him. I didn't print it, but I made a few notes." Jimmy pulled out about ten sheets of unlined computer paper. His printing was large, probably almost half an inch high. There were arrows and bullet points in some sections, straight prose in other sections. "Interrupt or ask questions as we go, but I think I have it well organized."

Jimmy began, "Fedderov is from Saint Petersburg but splits his time between there and Moscow when he is in Russia. He's a huge shareholder and chairman of one of the oil-and-gas-producing companies, Sovol. He also has interests in several other energy exploration companies and owns a large aircraft parts manufacturer. In total, he owns at least half of one hundred and twenty different companies. Interestingly, he owns one hundred percent of a chemical company that the CIA thinks is the source of MARV. Another of his fully owned companies is the pharmaceutical company that supplies the annual flu shots that are administered through the Russian Public Health System."

Spike interrupted, "Jimmy, wait, did they say why they think he's their guy?"

"Disruption of the world oil economy. Sounds official, but the reason might be somewhat circumstantial."

"What do you mean?"

"They seem to be biased toward their theory that MARV was economically driven and the oil industry that was the target," Jimmy said.

Spike thought that it was good that he was skeptical. "I wonder why. It makes sense based on what our source told us, but they must have more reasons to think that."

"I guess I'm not done, I'll look tomorrow." Jimmy made a note and then continued. "Fedderov is seventy-five years old, very rich, and travels internationally more than he stays in Russia, especially in the winter. He has homes in the South of France, a fortress in Sicily, and a mansion in London. His company owns several homes in La Jolla and LA, but when he visits the US, he mostly stays in his Houston mansion. His background is KGB from the former Soviet Union. Fedderov is close to the Russian dictator, President Andrei Solokov. He's one of the big winners from the economic changes that happened due to the fall of communism. His net worth is well over seventeen billion dollars.

"The CIA thinks he is acting without the president's knowledge or approval, but they aren't positive. It seems unlikely to them that Fedderov would act without approval from Solokov. They are trying to find some link. As you know from your past, they watch the Russian government and, by extension, the oligarchs very closely. They can't find a link, but they aren't satisfied that there isn't one.

"Fedderov hasn't left Russia since he spent Christmas in the South of France. He doesn't believe in God, but he celebrates Christmas. He generally seems to be enjoying his wealth. His current and fourth wife is a swimsuit model one-third his age; he's rumored to have several mistresses. The CIA has pictures of him in various sexual encounters with women and men, so the rumor seems pretty well-founded. He might be bisexual, but they didn't really elaborately describe the orgy pictures they had of him.

"His main company is Sovol, and it seems to be doing well in the era of cheap oil. Fedderov uses his old KGB and government connections to be sure he gets the first crack at new investments. The CIA thinks he is one of the most favored oligarchs from the corrupt Russian government's perspective. His companies get a lot of work from the Russian government. He supplies parts for aircraft that are sold as part of Russia's second biggest industry, exporting arms. According to his company press releases, Fedderov is staying in Russia because of MARV. The CIA thinks he is afraid to venture outside of

Russia in case anyone has figured out his bioterrorism plot." Jimmy stopped. He chugged half a beer and smiled.

As Jimmy was briefing Spike and Shauntel, Spike was thinking that he would have been a great intel analyst. He recited the info in a coherent manner, answered questions before they were asked, and sounded confident throughout. Spike asked, "Anything else?"

"Depends on what the next step is. They had some information about his personal security protection team, and I took some notes, but it didn't seem very detailed."

"Well, you may as well tell us," Shauntel said.

"Basically, Fedderov has two armed security men that go everywhere, and they called it a two by two by seven team. Not sure what they meant by that."

Spike interjected, "Two bodyguards, two shifts per day, seven days on, seven days off. Total of eight, probably ex-Spetsnaz Special Forces, probably very large individuals who know how to take care of a prima donna executive. Fedderov probably keeps additional security personnel trained for more offensive actions on his payroll as well. He probably has close ties to Russian gangsters who he can call on if he needs them to enforce some of his contracts. Those assumptions need to be checked, but I'm not sure if the CIA keeps track of links like that in his main folder."

"I'll see what I can find." Jimmy made another note and continued, "For transportation, Fedderov has a chauffeur-driven black armored Maybach. When he travels, he brings a full complement of eight bodyguards and a black armored Mercedes SUV in addition to a Maybach. He has vehicles prepositioned at his residences around the world. He has an eight-passenger Learjet XR 60 that he takes between locations in Europe. He also has used Russian military air for cargo if he needs to move vehicles. He sometimes takes a helicopter between his residence and his office in Saint Petersburg and almost always in Moscow. The CIA assessment considered that his most vulnerable mode of transportation. All told, he has eight to ten Maybach armored cars, four or five armored SUVs, two helicopters, and the Learjet. When he travels to the US and other overseas locations, he charters full-sized jets, because in addition to bodyguards and chauffeurs, his personal staff usually joins him. He also includes some executives from his various companies on many trips." Jimmy turned to the last page of his notes. He said, "That's about it."

Spike asked, "What's on that last page?"

"Questions mostly." He finished his first beer and said, "We can talk about that over dinner."

Spike took the cue, got up, and pulled the pizza out of the oven. He put Shauntel's salad on the island in front of her along with silverware and a set of tongs from the utensil drawer. Then he opened the bottle of wine and poured a glass for Shauntel. He opened another bottle of beer for Jimmy and put the other five in the refrigerator. He dished out two slices of pizza for himself and two for Jimmy. He handed Jimmy a fork and knife, knowing the kid from the range wouldn't use them.

Spike said, "Fire the questions whenever you're ready."

"First questions I wrote down are all around what you or we are going to do with this information. Maybe you can make my research easier by telling me your plan."

"I don't know yet, but before I tell you, what do you know about Tim Blust?"

"Just that he used to be the CFO at Maurer, and he is some kind of outside muscle for the CIA."

"Muscle? Have you ever seen him?"

"Okay, maybe not the operational type, but he clearly has a lot of influence, and they use him on missions that can't be sanctioned by the government."

"Wow, how did you find that?"

"One of the strings of information I followed mentioned Maurer years ago. I figured it was you, but it was before your time. I figured out that, given the international travel, it had to be either Jim DePacker or Tim Blust. De-Packer isn't serious enough to do this kind of thing, but I really don't know Blust well, just that he seems secretive when I see him at car shows and company functions."

"Good logic. He is involved, and he's a contractor. But he's at a pretty high level. He's trying to reel me into helping him, but so far, I've been putting him off. How long ago was the Maurer connection?"

"About fifteen years ago. He helped find a North Korean defector in China and brought him back to the US on Maurer's private jet."

"That's pretty cool, but I'm surprised it was that long ago. He had just started at Maurer." Spike seemed distracted, as if making a mental note to check it out. When he resumed, he said, "Back to your questions. If I get involved, I want to keep as small of a footprint as I can."

"When you say involved, what do you mean?" Jimmy said with an intense look but a calm voice.

"Honestly, I don't know. I think I can track this guy down. I speak fluent Russian and spent time in Moscow and Saint Petersburg when I studied there for a semester as a cadet. That was just after the fall of the Soviet Union, and they were acting like they wanted to be friends with the US. It was a typical Russian stunt. Making friends that they figured they could take advantage of later. We won the Cold War, but they always thought we were weak. They picked the bear as a national symbol because they believe they are mighty."

"So you track him down, watch his habits, and unleash the CIA or its surrogates on him?"

"Something like that. The question Shauntel and I had, until tonight, is why not just work for them?" Spike was trying to think through this himself.

"That's what I was thinking, especially now that I know Blust was recruiting you and that he showed up here."

"Now that I know the target and the country, it makes sense that they would recruit me. I am uniquely qualified, and I don't know what their alternatives are. Trying to recruit a Russian speaker is hard, because most Russian speakers are Russian and therefore not trustworthy. Most of the people they would have to use are in our government's service already. No plausible deniability."

"So, join them?"

"No, I think I'll have a better chance on my own."

"Really?" Jimmy finished the first slice, wiped his mouth, and chugged the rest of his second beer.

Spike went to the refrigerator and pulled out another Spotted Cow for each of them. "Yeah, it comes down to one person traveling anonymously versus an electronic footprint that includes communicating back to the handlers back home.

"If I'm alone, I can abort at any time. I can get in and out of places without using their resources. Those resources can be compromised without the CIA's knowledge. They are just too big to trust. Too many people involved in the operation, and too many enemies are tracking them. If three unconnected people can figure this much out in Sheboygan Falls, how many nations know the same things? They are probably tracking Tim Blust in Beijing, Moscow, Tel Aviv, London, Paris, and Berlin. They all have excellent intelligence services."

Shauntel had been quiet. She seemed comfortable with the idea, but she was showing signs of nerves. She said, "I'm sure you have thought through all of the steps in your head, but I don't think Jimmy needs to know your plans."

"You're right, but I'm going to need both of your support when I get there. So, I think broad brush, I go to Europe tomorrow and avoid all contact with any government, including ours. Get to Russia and wait for Fedderov. Pick up his trail and watch him. After assessing his habits, security, and opportunities to snatch him, I make contact with Blust, give him the intel and get back home." Spike smiled, "Everyone gets what they want. I'm not beholden to them; they get their target; they don't get to debrief me. Two weeks from now, we're all back to normal."

Jimmy took another big gulp of beer, "The best-laid plans of mice and men often go awry."

"Okay, Steinbeck, any more questions?"

"Not really. I agree with Shauntel, you should keep me in the dark."

"Well, let's not stop celebrating. You have earned it, Jimmy. There are only a few things you need to follow up on. Before we think about that, are there any notes you want to keep or commit to memory?"

"When I write things down, I remember them. Got me through the boring classes at Drake and at the U of M. But maybe you should look at them while I get another slice and drink some more of your Spotted Cows." Jimmy handed Spike his notes. They were meticulous. There were more details about the vehicles and helicopters. A couple names of the bodyguards and personal staff. Spike grabbed a highlighter and picked out some things he might need to remember. He spent a half hour committing it to memory. In the meantime, Shauntel finished eating her salad and had another glass of wine before cleaning up. Spike didn't notice that he had eaten four slices and drank two beers while Jimmy finished the other six of each. Jimmy went downstairs and grabbed another handful of beers. When Spike finished with Jimmy's notes, he handed them to Shauntel. While Spike and Jimmy had another beer, she read over the notes twice. Both Spike and Shauntel had asked some clarifying questions. Jimmy made a few new notes of things he should try to find out.

Shauntel had her own list of things to research. Spike researched a few flights from Chicago to Amsterdam from one of his burner smartphones. He would buy the ticket at the airline counter at the airport.

Shauntel handed the notes to Spike. He went over to the kitchen sink, opened the window, and ceremoniously lit the pages. Shauntel just sighed and said, "Really, in the kitchen sink?"

"Only garbage disposal we have, boss."

He held the pages two at a time by the corner. He expected the smoke alarm to go off, but it didn't. When he finished the last sheets, he asked, "Jimmy, what did you have under these pages as you wrote?"

"I used the clipboard."

"Any sheets left over?"

"Yes, I folded them in half. I'll go grab them."

As he went downstairs, Shauntel whispered, "He knows enough to get you in trouble if he's interrogated."

"For sure, he knows the target and the cities. That's why I'm going tomorrow afternoon. I can get a flight out of Chicago at five and land in Amsterdam the next morning. Kit up and head to Moscow on Saturday morning."

"Fedderov will be in Saint Petersburg for the weekend."

"Probably doesn't matter, because I need to get my bearings anyway, and I will need to change identities the first night. The NSA monitors all the arrivals into Moscow. They'll realize I'm there and start trying to find me. I'll check into the Metropol in City Centre so I'm close to everything and disappear the first night. But I'll want to stay close, because Sovol's office there is near Red Square." They heard Jimmy coming back upstairs. He took his papers over to the sink. Spike held out his hand and said, "Hold on, Jimmy. Let me show you something first."

Jimmy handed him the papers. Spike went over to a drawer, found a pencil, and moved the barstool away from the island. He laid the three pages down flat on the granite surface. He slowly ran the flat edge of the pencil over the paper. As he got the motion down, he began going faster. When he finished the first page, you could make out some words, not many, but since they had seen the original document, it was easy to figure out that it was the sheet with the questions. He did the same thing to the other sheets. On the last one, which was clearly on top, you could read almost the entire page. The whole exercise took less than five minutes, but it would last forever in Jimmy's mind. Not that these skills mattered very much in finance or the rest of his life, but he was shocked at how clear the notes he'd written were visible on the sheet underneath. You could even make out some of the page he'd written before the page with the questions.

Jimmy said, "If someone took an image of this, they could easily remove the clearest writing and read the former page."

"You got it."

Jimmy took the sheets and went to the sink with the lighter in hand. He had learned well from watching Spike earlier. He burned the three sheets at once. Still no smoke alarm. It was an effective day. Everyone seemed tired, so Spike said to Jimmy, "One more?"

Jimmy laughed. "I guess old people don't remember how to party all night. I think we should have two more. One for getting the big lead and the other to celebrate the next move. We won't be together again for a while." Jimmy seemed like he was getting a little worried about whether Spike would come back at all.

Shauntel said, "You boys can do what you want, but I'm heading to bed."

Spike was reminded of when Lucas would come home on leave, and they would drink until the wee hours of the morning talking about what it was like at the Naval Academy, what Lucas thought about global affairs, and who would win the Stanley Cup. "Okay, at least two. We should go downstairs so we don't keep Shauntel awake."

Jimmy stood and picked up the empty bottles and put them in the recycle bin. Spike thought maybe they should keep this kid around. He wondered if he would be safer here or in his own apartment in Sheboygan. Shauntel could defend the home by herself given the security system and well-placed weapons. Once Spike was identified by the target, his family will be in danger. The connections between Russian organized crime and Fedderov were the biggest concern. Maybe Shauntel should go stay with Penelope in San Diego. Or maybe she could hide out in Vegas with friends or back home in Wyoming. He made a note to talk about it before he left so they had a designated plan. He couldn't be worried about Shauntel's safety while he was tracking Fedderov thousands of miles away.

As they sat down at the bar downstairs, Spike asked Jimmy about hockey. Jimmy said, "I loved playing the game. The tactical part of the game, making one person defend two, finding ways to break out of the defensive zone when the other team is pressing, setting up plays by taking a hit, and drawing the other team out of their defensive pattern."

"As a player, what makes hockey so addictive?"

Jimmy answered, "It is the speed of being on skates and the competition. And you can play forever; my dad plays and coaches even now, and he's sixty."

"Are you going to try to coach?"

"Probably, but not until I have my own kids."

"I wasn't around enough to coach when my kids were young. It's one of the hard parts about doing what I did. It's something I regret, but luckily, Shauntel was Super-Mom, so the kids were fine."

"What did you do in the Air Force?"

"After the Academy, I was a finance officer for a few years. Then, I was allowed to go full time to get an MBA from Stanford. After the MBA, I transferred into intelligence. I was working on supporting a fighter wing when 9/11 happened. Wrong place, wrong time, I got noticed by the CIA. They recruited me, and because I was pretty pissed about the attack, I accepted. Then, as a CIA guy, for some reason, I kept getting attached to warrior teams. SEALs, Army Special Forces, sometimes Marine Recon teams. I learned about their tactics and supported them with intel.

"You know a little about that from your hacking, but the job I was there to do was get actionable information from the captured people as quickly as I could. Back then, we were still using the rendition programs where we would snatch the guys and send them to Eastern Europe and sometimes the Middle East to be interrogated and tortured. If I got the info quickly, we would send them to Guantanamo Bay.

"My job was much easier than you would think. I would tell them their choices, torture or Gitmo. They knew what that meant because some people had come back from both. I seldom had to use any violence to get them to tell me what they knew."

Jimmy looked confused. "Weren't they prisoners of war? We should follow the Geneva Convention, right?"

"That's a loaded question, Jimmy. First, they weren't soldiers. They didn't wear the uniform of any country, which is how the Geneva Convention defined enemy combatants. They used guerrilla tactics and slaughtered civilians who didn't follow their rules. They were from other countries in the Middle East, Egypt, some from Saudi Arabia, a few from Yemen, and a lot from Pakistan."

"Slaughtering civilians is the only part of that which gives me pause. Is it true?"

"Jimmy, the rules you have to follow to meet their standards would make you sick. Girls can't go to school, be alone outside their homes, and are treated like their existence is to serve their husband who probably married them when they were fourteen and against their will. Homosexuals are beheaded or crucified. These are bad people imposing their will on others using terror and murder."

"But when we go there, aren't we doing the same thing?"

"Building schools, infrastructure, and trying to create a civilized society are different goals than subjugating half of the population because they are women. Look, I believe we were there for good."

"Okay, but didn't they think they were doing good too?"

"Yes, and here's why. Think about being eighteen years old, from some country where you grew up in poverty. You were fed, cared for, and taught by the religious leaders in madrassas funded by Wahhabi Saudis. The goal was to build jihadist youths who would take the war to evil Westerners who were ruining the world. They poisoned your mind since you were seven years old. By the time you knew enough to become a target we would want to capture, you were at least twenty-five years old. You'd been living in caves and camps for years, terrorizing local people to keep them in line. The first American you meet is me. I have a fairly good understanding of the Koran and the lies the enemy had been fed by the Imams and then by their fellow terrorists. I usually treated them with dignity, because it surprised them. I often asked what they were fighting for, and their answer was always Allah."

"Why did they tell you anything?"

"Because I was just another human who actually listened to them. I explained those choices between torture and living on an island in the Caribbean with plenty of food, clean water, clean conditions, and your own Koran at your bedside."

"They believed you?"

"Jimmy, think about when you told me about hacking into the CIA database. Why did you tell me that?"

"I trusted you. I'm not sure why, but I did."

"Same."

They'd both finished two more beers. Spike hadn't expected to have a philosophical discussion about his past with Jimmy, but he was glad he did. Jimmy still had questions, and he would need to process a lot of what he'd just heard. Spike went to the refrigerator and opened two more beers.

Jimmy smiled. "I thought you said two more?"

"I want to celebrate, and I want to figure out how you would feel about staying here while I'm gone. I don't know how long it will be, but for sure a week."

"Well, if I go back to work, where I come from won't matter very much."

"You can probably go back Tuesday. I might need some help over the weekend."

"We'll be here," Jimmy said.

"I think you will be safer here, too. Shauntel knows how to defend the home, and you probably haven't noticed, but the home is hardened in ways that aren't obvious. The windows and doors are reinforced, and the walls on the main level are all Kevlar lined. Down here, it is concrete and windows."

"I'm not really worried about being attacked, but staying here is fine with me."

"I agree for now. At some point, this oligarch Fedderov is going to figure out through his contacts in the government who I am. If he finds I'm tracking him, he'll look for leverage. That makes Shauntel, my children and siblings, and maybe even you, targets. They'll want leverage. How quickly they can mobilize is questionable. So, I want to move quickly."

"Sounds good to me. I don't know as much as you do about these things, but I trust you."

Spike finished his beer. He smiled at Jimmy and said, "I'm going to head to bed. I really appreciate what you've done. We'll settle up when I get back, but I don't want you to worry about it. You'll be happy with the compensation."

Jimmy looked at his beer. He still had most of it left. He laughed and said, "Where did your beer go?"

"Jimmy, old guys pick up the pace at the end of the night. Not sure why, but the last one is better than the first. I could slam another in two pulls, but I really need to go to bed."

"Okay, boss. Thanks for trusting me to join you on this affair."

Spike was surprised by the wording. He knew Jimmy chose his words carefully. He thought Jimmy was an unusually sophisticated kid. He was glad they were working on the same side.

CHAPTER 24

The next day

Spike woke up at 5 a.m. and began his routine. He knew he would be flying overnight, so he decided to push his workout hard to help him sleep. Ginger seemed to love the extra work, and Spike thought about the new puppy driving Ginger crazy. Her world would change in a few days when Shauntel brought the new puppy home. They planned to name her Piper, and Ginger and Piper would have to establish their own rules. Ginger would surely be in charge.

Spike headed into the office for a quick visit. He saw more cars than the last few days and thought the recovery was in full force. He wondered how many people had been diagnosed with MARV in Sheboygan County and checked it out on his phone. Only three deaths according to the JHU website. That meant his mom and two others. There had been no new cases in the county in the last four days. The curve was flattened, and people seemed to be willing to work again. The place seemed almost normal. He went directly to Jim DePacker's office.

"Hi Jim, I'm gonna take a week or so off."

Jim smiled. "I'm happy to hear that. Be back by the end of the week after next. I'm heading out of town on vacation the last week of May, and frankly, I don't want to have both of us gone at the same time."

"Where are you going?"

"We're going to the Caymans. Mary Jo found a beach house rental we can use for ten days. We need a break. The house has Wi-Fi, so I'll connect, but I need you here."

Spike nodded. "That's fine. I'm looking forward to disconnecting too. I might only check my email every other day."

"That's fine."

Spike really had nothing else to do at the office, so he did a few small tasks, told his team that he'd be gone for a week or two. He asked Todd Grasse, the controller, to stop by. He put Todd in charge and told him to handle things the best he could. Anything Todd wanted help with should be marked "URGENT" on Spike's email. He told Todd, "Call me in an emergency. Otherwise, I trust your judgment."

Todd grimaced. He said, "Your view of the company is so different from mine. I might not know what is an emergency, but I'll do my best."

"Todd, you have all the skills to handle this. Just don't let the other department heads try to push you around. If someone tries to mess with you, make them tell you what they think the outcome of their plan will be. Use your well-developed business judgment to decide. You'll be fine."

Spike felt a little uncomfortable, because he wasn't telling anyone where he was going. They assumed, and he let them think, that he was going on vacation somewhere warm with a beach. They certainly didn't need to know he was going to run a surveillance operation in Moscow, but he didn't like being less than fully transparent, especially with Jim and Todd.

He grabbed his briefcase and headed home. When he got there, he started getting into mission mode. He packed his carryon roller bag that he'd used when he was in the CIA. He put currency, three passports with matching credit cards, and a few electronic tools into hidden compartments in the bag. He packed casual vacation clothes plus a charcoal blazer, which had a built-in holster. If these items were found, he would face a lot of questions. Shauntel always separated her outfits into gallon-sized re-closable bags. She did it to be organized, and Spike used the idea to help him quickly take what he needed as he packed and repacked as a mission progressed. He dressed in khakis and a blue button-down oxford shirt with a dark blue blazer. When he got to Moscow, he would buy whatever else he needed.

Spike went downstairs to get the answers to some of the open questions Jimmy and Shauntel were working on. He didn't expect to have everything before he left, but he needed to be sure they had some coded words set up for contingencies. They decided references to fruit would mean that Shauntel and Jimmy should leave Sheboygan Falls—berries would be to go to San Diego, citrus would be to go to Wyoming and warn the rest of the family, apples meant to hide out wherever without further communication and warn the rest of the family. Spike thought if he started to feel vulnerable, San Diego would be okay. The second option, Wyoming, was if someone might come, thinking they would be easy to spot in small town Wyoming. The last option was if Spike was likely to be interrogated, it would important to be untraceable. He didn't want to be able to tell anyone where they would be.

In any scenario, Shauntel would have a false ID, passport, and credit cards, and Jimmy would have to just travel with her. Driving was better, but using a rental would be smart, and to be sure they weren't followed, drive somewhere in Jimmy's car, take public transport to the rental facility, then use false identification to pick up the rental. Hats, sunglasses, basic disguises would be helpful. As Jimmy listened, he was shocked at how prepared Spike and Shauntel were for these possibilities. Jimmy started to see that he was naïve and was glad he'd stayed. Spike explained that they had put these things in place when Spike was in the CIA. He didn't want to go into hiding without her, and he had set up false identities for the kids as well. Penelope would know exactly what to do, but the navy wouldn't allow Lucas to just take off to go into hiding. He would be deployed for the next month at least, so it was unlikely they could target him. Penelope was ready to go at any time and would listen closely for the code word from Shauntel. Hopefully, they could meet up.

Feeling satisfied that Jimmy and Shauntel had solid plans to flee, they moved on to the things they had learned today. Jimmy had found out more about the people who protected Fedderov. The most important thing he learned was a former Spetsnaz soldier who had gone on to work in the FSB as an assassin was now on Fedderov's payroll. His name was Vladimir Zmokiniv-ich. Zmokinivich was very dangerous, and Spike memorized his features, size, and how he moved. The CIA had a video of him making a hit using an injection of radiologic poison on the streets of London. He was athletic, smooth, and clearly alert without standing out in the crowd. If Zmokinivich was onto him, Spike needed to be very careful and very defensive.

Shauntel had learned that Fedderov was scheduled to speak at a conference about Russian oil and gas exploration in Moscow on Tuesday. Spike assumed Fedderov would arrive in Moscow on Monday at the latest, but Tuesday was fine. He could pick up surveillance from the conference.

Jimmy also learned more about the reasons the CIA were so convinced that Fedderov was the person who unleashed MARV. The chemical lab had a facility north of Moscow that had six unexplained worker fatalities two years ago. The flu shots his company produced were created in a highly secure environment for the first time since the Soviet days. The published flu shot ingredients were exactly the same as the year before. However, the addition of the COVID-19 vaccine was publicized as the reason the shots weren't available until July. Normally, the distribution process started in May of each year. The ingredients couldn't be the same if COVID-19 was now protected by the flu shot. The CIA tried to get samples of the flu shots, but the shots were more controlled than morphine in the labs, clinics, and hospitals where the flu shots were administered.

Spike's mission just got scope creep. In his mind, he needed to come home with a sample of the flu shot and more information about the chemical lab north of Moscow. He and Shauntel went upstairs to say goodbye. When they got to the kitchen, she seemed more determined than nervous. "Be careful, abort at the first sign of danger."

"Got it. I'll probably get Blust connected on Tuesday, lead his team in, and head home."

She kissed him long and hard. She smiled and said, "I love you. Promise me you'll come home."

"I promise. I love you, Shauntel." He picked up the luggage and went out the door to the garage. He felt nervous, because he hadn't done anything like this for over ten years. He was in good shape physically, but his senses were dulled from inaction. He would need to be more tuned in because it wasn't as natural any longer to notice the details of his surroundings. Luckily, he could still shoot straight, but he hoped he wouldn't be doing any shooting on this trip. As the garage door closed, he pictured pulling into the driveway in ten days to open it again. He thought, *Visualize success.*

CHAPTER 25

Chicago and Amsterdam

Spike parked in long term parking at O'Hare at about 2:15. The flight he was targeting was scheduled for 5:30. When he got to the ticket counter, he pulled out Fred's credentials. The passport was seven years old. TSA was the last passport challenge, but it shouldn't be a problem. Ten years ago, it was almost impossible to get caught, but the X-ray equipment had improved, so Spike was concerned about the extra passports and credit cards in his luggage.

He had experience sneaking in and out of countries, so he didn't look nervous. He passed through security quickly and headed to his gate. He didn't have a clean smartphone so he bought one with Fred's credit card. He had left his phone with Shauntel. She would cover Maurer business as if they were on vacation. He had a burner phone in case Shauntel needed to contact him. The smartphone was mostly to check an anonymous email account that he and Shauntel set up to pass messages. It was an old trick to write a draft message, never send it, and share the accounts. No need to create additional electronic trails.. One new account was set up for each day for the next two weeks.

He checked a couple generic news feeds and the email account. Nothing new. Surprisingly, the media hadn't reported on the obvious fact that MARV was hitting oil-producing areas the world over with the exception of Russia. Looking at maps provided by the World Health Organization, the CDC, and Johns Hopkins University, the trend was obvious due to the color coding on the maps. West Texas, the Gulf Coast, Alaska, Oklahoma, Wyoming, and North Dakota were hot spots on the US map. In the Middle East, Saudi Arabia, Iran, Iraq, Kuwait, and UAE stood out. Even CNBC wasn't noting the oil industry's woes. They probably figured it was natural because the symptoms were the worst for people who performed hard labor outside. Spike wanted to ask Guls how MARV got to these smaller, more isolated towns, but he wouldn't jeopardize Guls any further.

Spike boarded early with business class and settled in for a nine-hour flight. His carry-on luggage was directly above his seat; his thoughts turned to moving about Amsterdam avoiding cameras. One advantage of Amsterdam was the level of freedom that the Dutch tried to flaunt. In several of the other cities, like Paris or London, it would be almost impossible to stay unseen. Since the airports all captured images, and tried to match them to passports, the ruse of using Fred's passport might hold. Fred and Sarah had traveled to Europe six times on this passport. He had also landed in Amsterdam from Detroit five years earlier. Spike had memorized the details. The Eurozone allowed free passage between borders, so it was not tough to memorize the dates of travel.

At 8 p.m., Spike ordered a pair of beers. He downed the beers, used the restroom, and pulled a Seattle Mariners baseball cap out of his carry-on luggage. He pulled the cap down almost over his eyes and laid back to fall asleep. Since he was a cadet, he could sleep just about anywhere in almost any position. He remembered sleeping in the mock prisoner of war training on his ten-inch stool. It was an eight-inch four by four with an eight-inch two by four nailed on top of it. He could balance against the wall and sleep like a baby. Compared to that, the airliner's reclining leather seat was pure luxury.

As the plane began its descent, Spike woke. Five full hours of sleep would carry him through the day. Today was likely to be the last day when his movements wouldn't be tracked. Today was the logistics day and would make or break his success for the next week and what Spike was thinking of as his mission.

Spike deplaned with the crowd. Getting through EU security at Schiphol Airport in Amsterdam should be a breeze. His past transgressions had all been elsewhere, mostly France and Greece. But they hadn't caught him in the act, so he wasn't even sure they knew he'd used a false identity to enter their countries. He assumed they had figured it out after the fact. If the EU was still looking for him, they must have kept a long list, but with today's technology, Spike didn't discount the possibility.

Spike started a conversation with a family of five in front of him when he got in line for passport control. He asked them why they decided to travel during MARV.

The dad answered, "My grandmother and grandfather are in their nineties and it's their anniversary. We thought it was now or never, and we bought the tickets four months ago. It would have been easier to cancel, but my kids need to know that it's important to continue to honor the elders in our family."

Spike said, "When is the last time you saw them?"

"We visited a few years ago, but the kids hardly remember. They came to see us last summer."

"They must be pretty vibrant to take a transatlantic flight during COVID-19."

He looked at him with pride. "We Huebrexes are built to last."

Spike cocked his head and said, "Strange question, but do you know a Doctor Huebrex in Sheboygan, Wisconsin?"

The man smiled. "He's my cousin. Sort of the pride of our family. I probably make three times what he makes, but Jerry's a doctor, so he's the golden boy."

"But you're not bitter…"

The guy laughed. "Right. It does sort of bug me, but what am I gonna do?"

"He treated my mom with MARV, and she passed last week. He is a great guy, but I didn't even know his first name until now. When I get back home, I'm going to send him a gift. Think he'd like tickets to a Packer game?"

"Yeah, get him Bears at Packers tickets. He'll invite me, and I will watch the Packers lose with a big smile."

"Look, I'm a Viking fan. I hate the Packers more than anyone. But I don't really want to see you profit from his pain." Spike looked away and smiled. When he looked back, he said, "Then again, he didn't save my mom…. Okay, it's a deal."

They both laughed. Spike pulled out his notebook and wrote a note to himself to remember to send four tickets to the Bears at Packers game to Doctor Jerry Huebrex. They were approaching the end of the line, and Spike was happy to appear connected to the family. He hoped to connect back with them as they moved through the airport. It would help camouflage his entry to Europe when people were looking for a lone man traveling through the Amsterdam airport in a couple weeks as they tried to figure out who he was and how he got to Moscow.

The Huebrex family was called to passport control. Spike was called a few seconds later. As he walked up, he removed his baseball cap to show his cooperation. He was stamped through with no delays. He connected with the family as they headed toward the baggage claim. The kids asked about Jerry's kids, and Spike said he lives in Portland and only met Doctor Huebrex for a few minutes. Spike asked if they'd checked luggage, and they said they had just two bags. The wife rolled her eyes like it was some kind of big sacrifice to pack for a week with only a hundred pounds of luggage. The husband seemed proud of their frugality. Spike pulled the Mariners cap down a little further over his face. He told the Huebrexes that he'd wait with them if they didn't mind. He realized he didn't know their names, so he asked.

The wife took over. She said, "I'm Jeanine; this is Gregg. We've been married eighteen years. Luke is fifteen, Liz is thirteen, and Abby is twelve. Gregg is such a pain in the ass, I agree with his family about Jerry being the golden boy. But Gregg's a great dad, and we love him."

Spike was getting nervous; he didn't really want to get this intimate. As he reached for his chewing tobacco, he looked over at Gregg who was looking at the dip like he wanted some. Spike motioned as if he were going to toss it to him, and Gregg just grimaced. Jeanine said, "When I was pregnant with Luke, Gregg quit dipping, cold turkey. He said he would start again after Luke finishes college. So far, he stuck with it. He's two-thirds through it, so I'm guessing he'll make it."

Spike looked at Gregg and thought he'd actually like to be there when Luke graduated. He'd probably puke after twenty years without a dip. At a minimum, he'd turn green. He also admired the idea. Maybe he'd get enough tickets to join them at the game at Lambeau next season. It would be fun to spend more time with Gregg. Their luggage came, and Spike offered to help, but Luke and Gregg each took a bag. As they walked through the airport, Spike noted and tried to avoid the surveillance cameras, but he wasn't confident in his tradecraft. The ballcap helped, but with luck, the facial recognition would peg him as Fred Eastman.

Spike headed to the airport hotel shuttle area. The Huebrex family was headed downtown for the day, so they said goodbye and split up when they continued to the cab stand. They wanted to see the city before heading to the grandparents' place on the North Sea the following afternoon. Spike thought it was peculiar how much people shared about their lives and plans with strangers. He even told them about his mom dying under their cousin's care in Sheboygan. He needed to remember how to drive the conversation with questions, to evade his own background.

CHAPTER 26

Amsterdam

When the shuttle arrived at the Hilton, it was about 8 a.m. local time. It was sunny and probably fifty degrees Fahrenheit. He was greeted by a very friendly and large blonde young woman who spoke English and checked him in quickly. He booked the room for two weeks but told her that he would be in and out a lot and may not sleep in the room every night. She glanced at his wedding ring and thought she knew what he was up to, just another pervert coming to Amsterdam for the Red-Light District. That was fine with Spike, allowing assumptions to play out in others' minds is a good way to stay under the radar. She offered bell service, but Spike told her he could handle the one little roller bag. On the way past the restaurant, he bought a large cup of coffee, a fruit and yogurt cup, and a cinnamon roll. Spike didn't bother to check the room for electronic surveillance. He wouldn't be talking to anyone about anything important from here.

Spike stripped down to his boxers and T-shirt and did a quick twenty-five-minute workout. Mostly stretching, push-ups, abs, and some dips on a chair. He felt good and would have enjoyed a couple mile run but didn't want to draw any extra attention. He used the room phone to set a private appointment at the bank downtown. It was a private bank, and Saturday morning appointments were common. Most of Spike's assets with the bank were held in the Zurich branch, but he wanted to access the safe deposit box, not his money.

After shaving and showering, Spike took a taxi to the Zuidas financial district. The streets were quiet, which would help him notice if someone began to pay too much attention to him. He walked around for a few minutes to familiarize himself with the area. It had been over ten years, and a lot of construction had changed the landscape. Beatrixpark was nearby, and that probably hadn't changed much. He'd used that park to make sure he wasn't followed in the past. There were several entrances, so it would be difficult to stay with someone who knew how to detect and avoid surveillance.

Spike met a private banker named Milan on the sidewalk near the main lobby entrance. Milan was medium height and had a touch of Southern Europe in his slim features. He had on a heavy wool suit, stylish, longish dark hair, and a very bored demeanor. He took Spike to the second basement where the vault held safe deposit boxes. There were several customers and very professionally dressed private bankers. Spike fit in wearing khakis and a blue button-down shirt, tieless. The blue blazer topped off the look of a typical executive on a Saturday.

Milan took Spike to a private room and instructed him on how to summon him when he was done. Spike decided to clear out the contents of his box. He forgot that he had several illegal items in addition to the Berretta. He would need to get rid of the switchblade and some heavy-duty painkillers plus destroy the old credit cards and passports. He could use the cash and several disguises to match the passport photos on the passports he had brought from home. Still, the glasses and hats would be helpful along with some scissors, hair clipper, theatrical facial hair, and a wig. He would need to get some spirit gum to adhere the face hair.

Spike summoned Milan, shook his hand, and asked him to replace the box. Milan was still bored and nodded his understanding. It occurred to Spike that while Milan spoke English, he might not like Americans very much. As Spike left the bank, he felt comfortable that he wasn't being watched, but he donned a fedora to try to cover some of his face from surveillance cameras. The sunny weather had warmed the temperature to a pleasant sixty degrees. He headed north on Beethovenstraat toward the Princes Irenestraat entrance to Beatrixpark. The park was green with large trees, as if it had been a park for as long as Amsterdam was settled. As far as Spike knew, it had been. The walking paths were clean, and families were playing on playgrounds. It was a beautiful urban park with sculptures, monuments, ponds, and large expanses of grass. And a nice place to detect surveillance while enjoying a quiet walk.

He needed to get rid of as much of the contraband as he could. Spike dropped the switchblade into Zuider Amstelkanaal as he left the park on Diepenbrockstraat. He walked along the north side of Amstelkanaal back to Beethovenstraat. He walked about a kilometer north and stopped in a Starbucks for coffee. He got rid of the painkillers in the toilet and decided to toss the wig in the trash. As he headed to Starbucks, he had seen an Etos on the opposite side of the street. Etos was a large pharmacy chain in the Netherlands. He was confident he could find pay-as-you-go smartphones and spirit gum there. He also picked up some protein bars, gauze pads, three-in-one oil, and some candy bars. He walked back toward the bank to find a taxi. He found one after a couple blocks and took it back to the hotel.

He spent the next few hours preparing his disguise, cleaning his pistol with the gauze pads and oil with BBC news on the television in the background. Most of Europe, especially this far north of the Mediterranean, was unconcerned with MARV. Many people still wore facemasks, but often they seemed to be more of a fashion statement. He checked the email drafts for the third time today and found that Shauntel had left a message. Tim Blust had called and asked where Spike was. She'd answered that Spike had taken a quick trip to the quarry in Vermont and that he'd be back by Wednesday. Blust didn't seem satisfied with the answer and wondered why Spike wasn't answering his cell phone. Shauntel told him that she didn't know. There were a couple of emails to answer from Maurer, and Shauntel told him what she would say.

Spike deleted her draft and typed a message of his own.

Good work. On the work items, go ahead and answer. Please make sure you use my normal signoff. For Blust, I'm sure they are trying to track me right now, but they won't think of Fred's passport. They will look for some of my old identities, but they don't know about the ones I'm going to use. I'm only using cash for now, so they won't be able to track me before tomorrow. They will likely find me at the Moscow airport. I will be careful, but passport control is impossible, and I assume that they still have access to those cameras. They might try to get people from Moscow's CIA station to find me, but they won't be overly aggressive. Please have Jimmy find me a car dealership, the shadier the better, near Moscow Centre. No big problem yet. If it becomes dicey, I'll just abort.

He left the message in the draft mail and headed down to the restaurant for a late lunch. After a quick sandwich and a beer, Spike decided he should head to an anonymous internet connection.

He took a cab to the Van Gogh Museum. The weather was still pleasant, and he walked around the museums like a normal tourist. Using one of his new burner phones would help establish his tourist intentions in case anyone was watching his digital footprint. He needed to be sure his e-visa was complete to visit Moscow. Russia had relaxed their visa requirements for EU members after tourism to Russia had grown fast over the past few years. But COVID-19 had caused a serious reduction last year since Russia forbade visitors from China, which accounted for nearly a fifth of their visitors. To make up for the shortfall, EU visas had become electronic applications, and the passport Spike would use was issued by the EU in Ireland. Spike applied for his visa online Thursday evening, and he expected to have the electronic visa on his passport account. He didn't want to use the Irish identity in Amsterdam too soon, but he needed to be sure he could board the plane in the morning. Hopefully the Van Gogh Museum Wi-Fi would be anonymous and busy enough to avoid any tracking. As he strolled along the exhibit hall, he connected to the public Wi-Fi. His visa was approved, and his plane was scheduled to leave on time in the morning

Spike left the museum and walked to Vondelpark to see Joost van den Vondel's statue. In the United States, statues of Washington, Jefferson, Grant, and even Lincoln had all been torn down in 2020 by rioters due to modern rules being applied to history. Vondel's statue was safe because he wrote *Lucifer*, a book about the dark side of man and a fallen angel. Being held to today's standards without historical context is tough, even for the first, third, seventh, and sixteenth presidents. Vondel had a meandering park with ponds and paths surrounding his monument. The Dutch seemed much too civilized to deface a beautiful urban park. Spike was feeling melancholy about the future of the greatest country in the history of the world. His understanding of history made him concerned about erasing it from the landscape of America. The less we understand, the more likely we are to repeat the horrors of the past.

In Europe, socialism seems to constantly reappear even though it hasn't made European life better. The consistent pressure by progressives in Europe and the US was driving the West toward unsustainable government spending.

Unquestionably, the biggest outcome produced by the National Socialist Party in Germany, the Marxist experiment of the twentieth century in the Eastern Bloc, and Mao's China was the mass murder of nearly a hundred million Europeans and Asians. In socialist countries, the people in power lived lavishly while the masses suffered. China's movement to more free economic system was refreshing, but the freedom and liberty that Western societies required weren't available in China. It was depressing to think about, so Spike instead decided to concentrate on his mission.

A few days in Russia could go in many directions. He knew that getting to Fedderov was going to be a challenge. As long as he stayed under the radar, it wouldn't be dangerous. The three main goals were straightforward enough. He would provide surveillance and weaknesses of Fedderov's movements. That was first and most important goal. Second, he needed to try to get a sample of the flu shot used in Russia last fall. Finally, and only if it was reasonably accomplished, he would obtain a vial of the virus that became MARV. That would be the smoking gun if anyone ever wanted to go public with the fact that MARV was actually a biological attack by a foreign power. It was doubtful that something like that would be announced, so Spike put that at the bottom of his list. Besides, reverse engineering the flu shot would be enough proof to link Fedderov's companies to MARV. If he were FBI, he would say, "Means, Motive, and Opportunity—Guilty as charged."

Spike was getting used to moving about with his senses alert. It was getting dark. On his way into the park, he had noticed a group of five eighteen- to twenty-year-old men wearing all black clothes with black Vans skateboarding in the park near the monument. As he passed them on his way out, they seemed to be paying close attention to his movements. One of the young toughs was taking a picture of Spike with his cell phone. Spike had kept his face shielded from the photo with his hand and the fedora. It looked like they were planning to mug a single weak person. Spike muttered, "Good luck, boys." Ahead, there were two others with skateboards looking at their phones. Photo received.

Spike noticed that his five admirers were about fifty feet behind him, and he would get to the two in front of him in less than twenty seconds. Spike chuckled to himself and thought, *I won't need my gun for these clowns.* As he approached the two, the group of five was still about twenty feet behind him. Spike rushed the larger young man who happened to be holding his skateboard over his right shoulder. He started to swing the board toward Spike's head. The thug was way too slow, so Spike charged and applied an extremely aggressive knee strike to his testicles. The skateboard went skidding down the path well behind Spike. The thug's partner decided to try to use his skateboard to separate Spike's head from his shoulders. With the first thug whimpering on the grass next to the path, Spike simply ducked out of the path of the skateboard and used the attacker's momentum to line up a roundhouse heel to the attacker's solar plexus. The attacker's feet kept going, and his head hit the pavement pretty hard. He wasn't moaning, but he was breathing. Both attackers were now disabled for a while but hopefully with no permanent damage, just a lesson in picking unpredictable victims.

The pack of five stopped about ten feet away. Spike turned to them and smiled. He put his hands in front of his chest and waved them in with his fingers. Spike yelled in his best German, "Komm mit mir spielen." He knew that the Dutch translation was close, but he wanted to emphasize that he was a foreigner in Amsterdam. They knew that he had asked them to come play with him. Since their two fallen friends didn't seem to like the game, they simply turned and walked away. So much for solidarity with their wounded comrades. They probably didn't want to get their Vans dirty.

Spike looked around for both surveillance cameras and to see if anyone was watching. It seemed like the park had emptied out quickly as the night approached. Spike decided that was enough fun for today and took a taxi back to the Hilton. He went to his room to drop off the pistol and headed down to the restaurant for a steak and a couple beers. While the steak was adequate, he noticed that Amstel was bitter compared to Spotted Cow. He replayed the incident at the park in his mind. Spike congratulated himself for not using his hands to defeat the muggers. It hurts like hell when you punch someone in the bony face. Broken fingers, bloody knuckles draw attention in customs. The thugs were clearly surprised that Spike went on the offensive. The results were guaranteed the moment they decided to try to mug him. The only real question was how many of them would get hurt. He decided cheesecake would go good with Amstel, so he ordered dessert and another beer. On his way out of the restaurant, he swung by and got another beer for the room. The Amstel was starting to taste better.

He checked the email drafts and found Shauntel had read and deleted his draft. She gave him four alternatives for car dealerships in Moscow and ranked them by how sleazy they seemed, and the second worst was in a familiar area. Spike memorized the address but didn't delete the draft so he could go back to it if necessary. He finished the beer and went to bed by ten. Tomorrow would be a busy day.

CHAPTER 27

The next day

Spike woke up at 6 a.m. He had four hours until before his plane left. He did a light workout of fifty pushups and fifty ab crunches just to get his blood flowing. He took a shower, dressed, and packed his bags, tossing his dirty clothes, scissors, and clipper into a paper bag to discard. It was unlikely that he would come back, but just in case, he wiped down his gun and clips and sealed them into a re-closable plastic bag. He tested it in the sink to be sure it didn't leak and put it into the toilet tank. Since he had the room for two weeks, he didn't think anyone would discover it before he was home in Wisconsin. He used the smart phone one more time to check the email drafts. Shauntel and Jimmy were trying to track Fedderov's movements. The message said, "F M MTW for sure. T conf still a go." Translating Shauntel's shorthand, Fedderov would be in Moscow Monday through Wednesday and his speech at the conference on Tuesday was still expected to happen. Spike deleted the draft and typed in the phone numbers for the burner phones he would use today and tomorrow, removed the SIM card from the old phone, and put the parts in his sport coat pocket. Spike went through the room to wipe down his fingerprints. It was an old habit and unlikely to matter, but it was always smart to be too cautious if you have the time. Spike left the room taking his roller bag, small carry on backpack, and paper bag with items to discard.

He had about an hour and a half to get to the airport to have plenty of time to work through security and check his visa. The trip would take him through Belgrade, and being photographed there would be a significant problem because the Russian FSB would know he was coming. There are three main agencies Spike needed to avoid, but the FSB would be the main concern. The FSB is roughly similar to the FBI in the US, but they mainly focus on counterintelligence, counterterrorism, and cyberattacks while the FBI is also concerned with federal law enforcement. The second group to be concerned with was the SVR, which is roughly equivalent to the CIA except they were more aggressive in cyberattacks. They are the ones who could identify him in Amsterdam and Belgrade. The third group was the GRU, which is most like the Defense Intelligence Agency in the US, and the reason he needed to be concerned with them was that they were closely aligned with Fedderov. Getting spotted at Sheremetyevo International Airport in Moscow was expected but giving as little notice ahead of time was critical.

In the lobby restaurant, Spike ordered coffee, orange juice, six strips of bacon, three eggs over easy, and four slices of sour bread toast. He wanted enough protein to carry him through to the evening meal. He wasn't familiar with the Belgrade airport, so he didn't expect to be able to move around freely. It would be easier to lay low if he didn't need to find a restaurant. Spike finished his third cup of dark roast coffee, left thirty euro on the table and headed through the lobby to the exit. He took a taxi to the Red Light District and walked around the block and made sure he wasn't being followed. Along the way, he discarded his bag of clothes in a trashcan and the phone in the canal. Spike dropped the SIM card in a storm sewer along the street. He went into a Starbucks to double-check surveillance and add the mustache and goatee to match his Irish passport in the restroom. Satisfied that it looked right, he ordered a double espresso over ice, tossed the spirit gum in the trash, and headed out.

Spike caught a cab to the airport, and twenty minutes later, he was standing in line to check his roller bag. He knew he would be spotted in Moscow and didn't want to have his bag with him until after passport control. Hopefully, Air Serbia and Aeroflot would get the bag to Sheremetyevo. If not, he would need to figure out a way to travel without the benefit of extra identities. Spike thought back to Jimmy's comment about the best laid plans and decided it was worth traveling lightly between Amsterdam and Moscow. The security at Schiphol was as easy on the way out as it had been on the way in. He went to his gate and waited for boarding. He powered up his second new burner phone to be sure Shauntel and Jimmy didn't leave him a message. He was down to less secure voice and text communications because he didn't want to check the email account until he arrived in Moscow and could get a few new smartphones. Before boarding the plane, he removed the SIM card from the phone. One of the benefits of MARV was that some people in Amsterdam were wearing facemasks. He had packed three tube scarves made of stretchable fabric known in the fishing world as a neck gaiter. He brought three colors, black, royal blue, and gray. He also brought a black balaclava. He put on the black gaiter once he was in the plane. He kept it around his neck, but it would help him stay anonymous in transit.

The airport in Belgrade was modern and very clean. Spike was lucky to land and takeoff at gates with jetways, because almost half of the gates required passengers to board the planes from the tarmac. The two gates happened to be only a hundred feet apart, which was favorable because he had less than an hour layover. Spike sat along the windows with his gaiter up and his head down trying to defeat surveillance. He was confident he was not identified. He replaced the SIM card in the phone because there was a security check at the gate, and he wanted to avoid questions. He was comfortable with the contents of his backpack making it through the check. Spike was happy not to have his roller bag because the security check was very thorough. The Aeroflot staff was surly but efficient, and the plane pulled away from the gate almost five minutes early. The service included water, coffee, peanuts, and vodka. Spike skipped the vodka and ate one of his protein bars.

The flight was three hours, and about two hours in, Spike could feel his adrenaline level increasing. Spike checked his face hair. He had almost forgotten he'd put it on, which was good because he wanted to look natural, but also bad because he needed to be sure it was properly affixed. He had learned years ago that many people with goatees tend to touch them often. His goatee was about an inch and a half long with a reddish tint even though is hair was blonde. That was a common look for people with Irish passports.

His name today was Thomas O'Gara. He was in character now with a slight Dubliner's accent. He was going to Moscow as a tourist and had been to Poland, Italy, and Norway in the past four years since the passport was issued. Before that, Thomas O'Gara had been to Moscow once in 2003. When they landed, Spike pulled up his gaiter, replaced the SIM card, and downloaded a tourist application to the phone. The app had an interactive map and a list of the most important things to see in Moscow. As the deplaned, Spike realized it might be smart to connect with another passenger. He noticed a very plain-looking woman with red hair heading up the jetway to the terminal. She might look like a spouse since she was about his age. He caught up to her as she headed into the women's bathroom. Spike entered the men's room across the hall. He washed his hands for a long time expecting that it would take her longer in the restroom. He then waited just inside the restroom with a view of the women's room. Spike saw the woman exit, and he made eye contact with her and smiled. She smiled back, and he approached and asked if she'd been to Moscow before.

"Yes, but it has been nearly twenty years," she answered.

Spike thought, *Lucky for me she speaks English, but it sounded more British than Irish*. Not a problem; since they weren't traveling together, they wouldn't go through passport control together. The Russians were more suspicious of the British anyway, so she would likely get checked more thoroughly than he would. Spike said, "I was here in 2003 last. I'm looking forward to seeing how it has changed. By the way, my name is Thomas."

"Thomas, it is nice to meet you. I'm Saundra. I'm looking forward to seeing whether things work better, but I'm mostly here for business. I'm attending an oil and gas conference."

"I don't really know that much about oil and gas, but I thought the British imported mostly from Norway because it is so close."

"About two-thirds come from Norway, but we are looking to diversify to be sure we aren't too dependent on one nation. Our concern for the stability of the House of Saud and the Middle East has made us consider production shortages more likely over the next ten years. We want to be ready so building relationships with the Russians will help us over time to be able to take advantage of the broader market," Saundra said.

"So, you think Russia will be more stable than the Middle East?"

"Russia needs oil and gas revenue to pay for their ambitions, but I admit that we're not fully on board with being dependent on them. Our government doesn't dictate how we do business, but they do nudge us in certain directions."

Spike nodded. "It is such a strategic resource, I would expect the government to be concerned with your decisions. I'm Irish, and we import mostly from your country. I guess our concern should be that you're able to import enough so you can export to us."

"It's all very interrelated. The Russians are probably the most erratic supplier for us because they are feeding the continent with so much oil and gas, we are not important to them. The Saudis and many of the other Middle East suppliers are arrogant but predictable. The Americans have higher production costs and use most of their own product internally. We still import almost twenty percent of our oil from the US because they are the most stable and their economy isn't as dependent on oil exports as some of the other large producers. Norway is similarly stable but a little more dependent on the oil industry. As trade partners, we can trust these countries and their companies. We are beginning to see the need to improve our relationship with the Russian suppliers, and they are very tied to the government through ownership and corruption."

They were walking fairly fast, and Saundra was very comfortable in her analysis of the industry. Spike was less comfortable hearing her say the Russian government was corrupt in public. As they neared the passport control lines, they would need to separate because UK citizens couldn't use the EU line any longer. Russian visas for UK passport holders were still paperwork intensive, but for the oil and gas conference, Saundra likely was granted a streamlined process. Before separating, Spike lowered his voice and said, "Saundra, it might be a good idea to not be critical of the Russian government in public. The KGB is gone, but the FSB still monitors subversive speech. Be careful." And then louder, he said, "Saundra, it was a pleasure meeting you. I'm sure the conference will be eventful. Good luck."

Saundra smiled and, while searching her purse for something with her head down, quietly said, "Being in Moscow, I guess I should tone it down." She pulled a business card out of her purse and spoke with her normal volume. "Have a nice trip, Thomas. I'm staying at the Four Seasons near Red Square. Here is my mobile number. Text me if you're nearby."

Spike realized that she thought he was hitting on her. He took the card and said, "Okay, thanks." Then he turned to head toward the EU passport holders' line. It was time to get detected. At a minimum, the CIA would be watching for him. Hopefully, the FSB wouldn't connect his photo to their old database. Recent unrest in Chechnya may have them more concerned about internal terrorism than foreign espionage.

A woman and a man at a makeshift booth took the body temperature of the incoming travelers and asked questions about where they had recently traveled. It was a MARV screening, but Spike knew it was just meant to appear like the Russians were taking this extra precaution. They had been adamant when they closed the borders from China immediately after the outbreak in Jiangsu province that Russia would not be victims of another Chinese pandemic. It didn't appear that anyone actually failed the test in the twenty minutes Spike had been watching.

As he got closer to the front of the line, he noticed cameras above the line and assumed there was a room somewhere nearby where people were trying to identify Chechen terrorists and other persons of interest. These weren't the cameras to which the CIA had access. The cameras that were sure to catch everyone with no chance to avoid were in the actual passport control booths. Hats, masks, gaiters, and headscarves were forbidden when passing through this area.

When Spike got to the front of the line, he smiled and spoke in broken Russian. He tried to act like he wasn't fluent, and it might have worked. The passport control person was named Dmitri. He was an older gentleman with a wrinkled uniform over a large belly and a large black mole on his nose. Dmitri seemed to appreciate the effort to speak Russian. He asked if Thomas O'Gara was a "turist"…lucky, it was about the same word. Spike answered, "Da."

Then, Dmitri changed to English. He asked how long Thomas planned to stay in Moscow, and Spike answered, "Ten days. I'm staying at the Metropol. If I can work it out, I'm hoping to take the train to Saint Petersburg for a few nights and return to Moscow to fly out in ten days."

"Yes, is good plan to see both cities. Using train, no problem. Don't drive without to tell us. We help when tourist get lost."

"Thank you. I will stick to trains."

The fat guy smiled, and the entire booth shook when he stamped Thomas O'Gara's passport and visa. He handed Spike the paperwork and said, "Have nice day."

Spike smiled, gathered up his visa and passport, and said, "Spasibo, do svidaniya."

It was already almost 6 p.m. local time, so Spike knew he was running behind his expected arrival time at the Metropol. He had an hour taxi ride and still needed to clear customs with his roller bag. He pulled his gaiter back up to stay in character and hoped it didn't mess up his goatee and mustache. He headed to bag claim and found his bag almost immediately. It was hard to tell if his roller bag had been tampered with, but he expected that it had been opened. The Customs agent made a big show of looking through Spike's luggage and backpack. He seemed bored but tried to look intimidating and grunted a lot instead of speaking and giving instructions. He spent more time with the backpack, especially interested in two items, electrical ties and a screwdriver set. After about two minutes of messing up Spike's luggage, the agent pushed Spike's open roller bag forward about an inch and nodded. Spike assumed he was cleared, so he closed his bag, zipped his backpack, and headed toward the taxi stand.

He knew he would be tracked to the hotel and he would need to show his passport and visa there. There was no reason to try to evade anyone, but Spike was alert and noticed the faces and body language of the people around him. He cataloged the people he saw and assigned each a threat level, green, yellow, or red. Almost all the people he saw were green or low threat. Still, if he saw the same faces again over the next few days, they would become at least yellow, maybe red.

The ability to stay alert and focused while appearing to be unaware and oblivious of your surroundings was so ingrained in Spike's mind that he forgot he was doing it. Last fall while Shauntel and Spike were out to dinner, he noticed anxious body language of one of the people waiting to be seated at a nice restaurant. He told Shauntel to be ready for action, the guy in the khakis and blue blazer was acting strange. He assumed the thirty-ish man was up to something nefarious. Shauntel laughed and said, "Okay, secret agent man."

Spike kept a casual watch on the peculiar and uncomfortable man as he and his female companion were seated nearby. As usual, Spike was sitting with his back to the wall. Shauntel was used to his obsession with never sitting in the middle of a room, always knowing where the exits were and paying close attention to any weapons within the reach. When they went to out in public, Spike usually carried his Berretta nine-millimeter. While most people wouldn't notice his alert nature because he had been trained to hide it, Shauntel knew.

About ten minutes after they sat down, the young man got down on one knee and proposed to his date. Shauntel almost peed her pants laughing; luckily, the restaurant burst into applause so nobody noticed that she couldn't control herself. It had become a story she couldn't stop telling, especially to the kids. Spike always just smiled and said, "Yep, he had all the signs of someone about to make a horrible decision." That got him in trouble, but at least she would stop laughing at him.

Spike waited for about two minutes in the taxi line. He saw about eighty faces, all green. His driver was big, and the car smelled like smoke and sweat. Spike said, "Metropol, City Centre." The driver nodded, and Spike put his roller bag and backpack in the back seat. The ride took almost an hour in light Sunday evening traffic. Spike was silent, pretending not to speak Russian. The fair was about two thousand rubles, and Spike gave the guy fifty euros easily a 60 percent tip. The guy smiled about that and said, "Spasibo." Spike just nodded and carried his bags through the lobby entrance into the hotel.

The Metropol is a gorgeous hotel with grand spaces and gleaming marble floors. Spike was thinking it would be nice to just relax here with Shauntel for a week and really be a tourist. He realized that it was unlikely that he would ever get to do that after this week. Spike checked in for a week and paid with his Thomas O'Gara credit card. He gave his Irish passport and visa for Russia to the clerk who took it into the back office to make a copy. Spike had always been nervous about that process. People would know a lot about Thomas O'Gara from the passport data, and he figured identity theft was likely following a visit to Moscow. Then Spike laughed at himself and thought, *Hell, I stole it in the first place.*

Spike exchanged five hundred euro for about forty thousand rubles, got his room keycard with instructions about Wi-Fi, a small map of the local attractions, and a brochure on the bar and restaurant in the hotel. On the way to his room, Spike noticed a lean, athletic-looking man in his thirties who he'd seen at the airport. Normal tradecraft would be to go to the third floor on the elevator and take the stairs back down to his room on the second floor. The problem with that was it could tip off the watcher that he was noticed. In this case, Spike thought it might be smarter to keep the tracker he knew than to have a new, unknown person start to track him. So, he went to the second floor on the elevator, and the watcher stayed in the lobby.

Spike opened his roller bag and donned a pair of white cotton gloves. He put his clothes in the drawers and hung up two pairs of pants and two shirts. On the bed, he laid out the charcoal blazer, a blue button-down shirt, and pair of dark blue dress pants. He opened the hidden compartment of his luggage and retrieved his two extra identities. Since he spoke Russian, the identity he planned to depend on was Ukrainian, Oleksander Barabash. His Ukrainian language skills were fairly weak; however, since Soviet times, many Ukrainians spoke Russian and the Russian ego would expect a Ukrainian to bow to Mother Russia and speak Russian. The second benefit of the Ukrainian passport was that he wouldn't need a visa from Ukraine. Most importantly, the only change he needed to make to match his passport picture was to dye his hair to black, make his eyes brown with contacts, and remove the mustache and goatee because the photo was actually his face. It was definitely his best chance to stay under the radar, but he needed to evade his tracker and avoid electronic surveillance to make the change.

He dressed in the dark slacks and blazer. He packed the re-closable bags with his extra identities, three tins of Copenhagen Long Cut, a few pairs of underwear and socks, and three T-shirts into the backpack. The other items he'd had in the backpack included his balaclavas and gaiters, a roll of duct tape, a package of twenty-five eighteen-inch electrical ties, and what looked like a small screwdriver set that were actually lockpicking tools. He placed his dirty clothes in the hotel laundry bag. He messed up the bed to appear he'd slept in the room, turned on the shower, and poured some shampoo and conditioner down the drain. He wet a towel and washcloth and put them on the floor. He took the thick cotton robe out of the closet and threw it in a heap on the chair next to the bed. Before leaving the room, Spike cleaned the surfaces he had touched before putting on the gloves. On his way out, he removed his glove from his left hand and wiped down the door handle with his right hand. As he headed toward the elevator with his backpack and laundry bag, he made sure the surveillance camera saw his face. The Moscow metropolitan area has thirteen million people; it should be easy to get lost in the sea of humanity.

In the lobby, his watcher was loitering near the check-in area. If the guy was FSB, the most likely suspect, he would have checked the passport and visa and found out the room number to be sure Thomas O'Gara wasn't trying to pull a fast one. His room would be searched, and if the audio surveillance in the room needed to be updated, the FSB would place more listening devices. Maybe video, too, but they probably didn't have many rooms prestaged for video. Audio was almost certain, so Big Brother may not have been watching, but he was listening to almost all foreign travelers in Moscow. At this point, the Russians probably wouldn't have identified Spike because he hadn't done anything suspicious. In an hour or so that would change, and the FSB would start trying to dig deeper by isolating his eyes, nose, and mouth and running his photo through more databases. It could lead to his real identity, but by then, he would be hard to trace.

Spike walked casually through the lobby, and on his way out the door, he saw that the watcher was moving toward the exit in his peripheral vision. Spike was surprised by his hyper-alert state after little practice over the past ten years. It felt easy to look clueless while picking up cues all around. He hoped the FSB would only have enough manpower to follow him with one person. His plan may not be as effective with the ability to track multiple escape routes.

There was a Rigla pharmacy less than a half a kilometer away. He walked in, found the hair dye and rubbing alcohol, quickly purchased the items along with two bottles of water and some hand sanitizer. Spike put all the items into his backpack and left heading in the same direction toward the Moskva River. His tracker was across the street, smoking a cigarette and acting uninterested. Spike needed to move fast so the tracker couldn't see him as he turned a corner to dump the laundry bag. Still out of sight, he dropped it into an open stairwell heading to a garden level apartment. He slowed down so the tracker could catch up. Spike needed the tracker to see him make his next move. He headed toward Saint Basil's Cathedral remembering the geography from his visit thirty years before. He would cross the Moskva River to get to one of the nicest hotels in the city. The Café Kranzler Bar in the Hotel Baltschug would fit the bill perfectly.

Spike made sure the watcher could see him as he pulled a water bottle from his backpack about halfway across the river. The watcher wouldn't have been able to see what he'd purchased at Rigla from across the street, and he hoped the water would quench the watcher's curiosity. He stopped and leaned on the railing along the river to watch the river traffic of barges and pleasure craft. The watcher stopped about twenty yards away and looked at the river too. It was about 8:30, and Spike finished the water, put the empty bottle back into his backpack, and moved on. It was dusk, and it would be dark in about forty-five minutes. He walked to the Baltschug and entered the lobby. He spotted a fire exit sign past the elevators to the guest rooms. It would be important to find an exit that the singular watcher couldn't cover.

CHAPTER 28

Moscow

The Hotel Baltschug lobby had a full-service bar that served appetizers. The lobby felt very subdued with about forty people in the bar area. There seemed to be a lot of business travelers and probably some additional FSB agents watching their own foreigners. He noticed some more watchers who seemed less interested in watching than in reading their phones and drinking their cocktails. An occupational hazard for watchers was that they had to blend in, so if they were in a bar, drinking was part of the job. Spike headed to the Kranzler, which had a much more festive atmosphere. It was decorated in typical dark reds with a lot of golden accents in what was probably considered fabulous in the 1960s but was a little worn now. Still, it was a very upscale venue, and the patrons were what Spike had expected. A lot of wealthy-looking older men, and for every man, there were two younger and extremely attractive women. It wasn't a whorehouse, but there was clearly sex for sale.

Spike went to the bar and, in English with his Irish accent, ordered a Nevskoe Classic, a pale lager he had sampled when he was in Moscow in college. He remembered that it was bitter, but thought maybe it would taste better now that his palate had become accustomed to stronger microbrews as the craft beer industry had grown so much in the US over the past fifteen years. The bartender served the beer in a frosted mug, which got him an extra couple hundred rubles tip. As Spike took his first sip, he was disappointed that it still tasted very bitter to him. He made a bit of a face, knowing that several of the prostitutes were watching him to decide whether to offer him their company.

Spike noticed a fabulous blonde young woman beginning to circle. She was about four inches shorter than Spike with long, thin legs, a flat stomach, and large breasts. She had a pretty face with very white, straight teeth. She could have been a runway model, and maybe she was. She was wearing a short black skirt and a low-cut dark gray top which accented both her milk-colored skin and cleavage. Spike guessed that she was around thirty years old. He felt sorry for her because this wasn't going to end as she expected. When she approached, she asked in broken English if he would like to buy her a drink.

Spike looked at this beautiful woman with feigned surprise. He had the look of someone who just won a meat raffle at a country bar. He said, "Sure, what will you have?"

"Wodka."

"Martini?"

"Da, with olive." She smiled seductively.

Spike motioned for the bartender who came over smiling. "Da."

"Vodka martini with olives for my new friend."

The bartender went about making a martini with three shots of Beluga Gold. Spike figured it would run him five thousand rubles. He dropped two olives into the glass with a long plastic toothpick. He handed the woman the drink and said, "Should charge to room?"

Spike said, "I don't have a room; I'm just here for the beer."

"I make you tab, da?"

"Please." Spike smiled and handed him Thomas O'Gara's credit card. Then he turned to his new drinking buddy and said, "I'm Thomas, what is your name?"

She said, "My name is Janet. It is nice to meet you." She put her hand out as if to shake hands, and Spike took it into his hand gently and bent down and kissed the back of her hand. Two thoughts popped into his head: he should have used hand sanitizer, and neither of them were using their real names.

"I'm from Ireland, and I just came to Moscow today. Have you lived here long, Janet?"

"Da, all of life."

"It seems like a beautiful city. I was here in 2003, and I really enjoyed the museums. My wife and I went to the ballet."

"You are married?"

"Widowed, my wife passed away two years ago from breast cancer." Spike looked sad.

"I can help you forget tonight."

"Well, just talking to you makes me feel better. Would you like another martini?"

"Nyet. There is problem; you have no room," Janet said.

"I can get a room, but maybe you should, and I will pay you. I have euros. How much is a room?"

"Depends how long you want to stay and what you want to do in room." Again, she had that seductive smile.

Spike smiled back. "How long does five thousand euros last?"

Her eyes got bigger, and she said, "All night, and tomorrow could be."

Spike gave her five hundred to secure the room and asked the bartender for another beer. He said, "Please go get us a room, two keys, and I will enjoy another Russian beer."

"You did not look happy with first one. Maybe you should try Heineken. No bite."

"Okay, I'll try it."

She walked away toward the lobby. Spike needed it to get darker out, so he took his time with the beer and, when he saw Janet coming back, ordered another and asked if she wanted another martini. She declined, and Spike thought, *Time is money for her.* Spike asked for a key, and she gave it to him. They sat and mostly just looked at each other for about half an hour while he nursed his fourth beer. She was getting impatient. When she had gone to the restroom, he gave the extra key to Dmitri along with five hundred euro. He asked if he would check on him in about an hour. Dmitri thought Spike wanted to share the hooker, which was fine with Spike. Finally, it was time to start his disappearance from surveillance. He said, "Please lead the way."

Janet smiled seductively again. "I like lead the way." She got up and headed toward the lobby. Spike followed a step behind. He needed to be sure he was free of surveillance when he changed his face and hair and, of course, when he tied her up. He knew the room would have cameras because honey traps were encouraged by the FSB and SVR. They would catch married people, usually businessmen and diplomats, show them the video and blackmail them, maybe for money, maybe for disloyalty, if possible, for both.

Spike thought it was fine that his watcher saw him take the prostitute to a room; he would find out that she'd got the room for the night. He might even just leave and report that his target was going to bed, but Spike doubted it would be that easy.

The room was on the fourth floor, and it was about the same as his Metropol room. Very nice, very opulent. Spike wondered where the surveillance was and whether the FSB monitored it real-time or just collected the video intermittently. He assumed worst case and knew he had to leave surreptitiously. "I need to use the bathroom," Spike said, smiling. He went directly in with his backpack. He immediately turned on the water, opened his backpack, put on rubber gloves, and started dyeing his hair. As the dye was setting—the package said two minutes—he removed his goatee and mustache and used the rubbing alcohol to get the rest of the spirit gum off. He removed two zip ties from the backpack and tore off a five-inch length of duct tape and stuck the end on the doorknob. The two minutes had passed so turned off the water and put the finishing cream in his hair. He flushed the toilet and turned the water back on. He rinsed his hair and towel dried it. Some of the black came off on the towel, but he now had black hair with no highlights. He stuffed the alcohol, dye packaging, and towel into the backpack and put his fedora at the top of the backpack, pulled out five thousand euro in a bank strap and put it on the vanity next to the zip ties. He put a balaclava on his head, opened the door slightly, and said, "Janet, could you help me?"

She said, "Da, what is?"

He said, "Viagra."

She laughed, and Spike could hear her approaching the door, and he slipped behind the door. She pushed the door open and came into the bathroom wearing only a silky bra, gartered hose, and thong underwear. As she entered, he grabbed her right wrist with his right hand and put his left hand over her nose and mouth pulling her so her back was to his front. He whispered into her ear, "Tishina," which is Russian for hush. She nodded her head, and he released his left hand slightly.

As he turned her head to see the money, Spike said, "You get paid if you do as I say. I won't hurt you. Okay?"

Janet nodded. Spike used his left hand to duct tape her mouth. Then he grabbed her left wrist and lifted her right wrist behind her back. He held both her wrists with his left hand and grabbed a zip tie from the vanity to secure her hands behind her back. He took the other zip tie and helped her step into the bathtub. He put her back to the safety bar and fished the zip tie through the zip tie that bound her wrists and secured her to the bar. It looked a little uncomfortable, but five thousand euro is a pretty good night. He said, "Someone will come get you in a one hour at the most. Try to relax." He tore two more lengths of duct tape and secured her mouth gently, and then he went out to the room and grabbed her purse and clothes. He put the money in her purse and helped her put on her skirt. He wiped his prints off the faucet, the only thing he had touched before putting the rubber gloves on. He couldn't waste time to put her blouse back on because the room surveillance had likely just seen him wearing a mask.

Spike put the backpack over his left shoulder, turned on the fan, and left the bathroom. As he headed to the door, he removed the rubber glove from his left hand. He used his right hand to open the door. Nobody was in the hall, but he kept the balaclava on and headed to the fire escape on the east end of the building where he'd seen the emergency exit signs. He hoped the ground floor exit to the street wasn't alarmed. There were surveillance cameras in the staircase, so he kept the balaclava on while he took the stairs two at a time until he made it to street level.

Spike exited the stairwell and saw the emergency exit. It didn't appear to have an alarm, but there was a security guard standing next to a desk to the right of the door. The balaclava caught the security guard by surprise, and he started reaching for a radio. Spike was about ten feet away, and he said, "Politsiya!" The security guard seemed confused, and he started to set the radio down. Spike closed the distance and spun to create momentum for a right elbow strike to the guard's jaw. The guard's head snapped sideways, and he was out of commission. Spike caught him before he hit the floor and dragged him behind the desk. He exited and went left down a dark alley. He knew that he would come out near the river. He removed the balaclava as he headed north toward the river and put the fedora on low above his eyes, tilting it forward as best he could. Now was the moment of truth, become anonymous, find shelter and food. Disappear.

Spike was concerned because he didn't expect to have to confront a security guard. He did the best he could to just knock him out and move on, but it would definitely speed up the chase from the FSB. There was a chance that they wouldn't put it all together, and Spike realized he needed to stay calm. No adversary had all the information. He had learned academically about the fog of war at the academy and in real life in Iraq and Afghanistan. It was unlikely that the FSB had connected the hooker in the room upstairs to the unconscious guard on the main floor yet. And even if they had, it was unlikely that they had surveillance of him beyond the building. Right now, he should move on quickly, find a new location, and become Oleksander Barabash of the Ukraine. The rest of his goals were out of reach if he didn't escape now.

Spike jogged to the main road along the Moskva River and headed east. As he walked, he kept his head down, hiding his face from any possible surveillance cameras, pulled his backpack in front of his body, and extracted the incriminating items—the towel and dye package. He tried to see if he was being watched by Big Brother's cameras. He didn't see any, but he was feeling very paranoid and assumed they were there. He stopped along the river about two blocks from the Baltschug and dumped the items into the river. He felt relieved but knew he needed weapons, a new place to sleep before he started hunting Fedderov in the morning.

The time he'd spent in Moscow as a cadet was about to pay off. He met a lot of recent graduates from Ivy League schools in his time here. They were all staying at hostels. They were all communists deep down, and they seemed to like the communal nature of the hostels. He thought they were nuts, but he liked to learn, so he had gone to their places when he had free time. The funny thing was that they all seemed to have wealthy, capitalist parents. One of them, Billy Hale from Yale, stayed at the Makarov Hostel nearby. Billy loved his parents very much but hated that America had won the Cold War. Spike was intrigued by this seemingly incongruous view of the world. Spike knew that all the goofy lefties would assume that he was a closed-minded military person, so he was careful when asking questions about Billy and his friends' beliefs.

He learned that these people had no concept of history or human nature. They thought utopia was built on the back of inertia. The producers would keep providing value whether they were rewarded or not. It was the producer's nature to build value. Spike had read Ayn Rand's *Atlas Shrugged* as a teen. He understood what these Ivy League kids couldn't conceive: Incentive drove work; capitalism drove incentives; capitalism built wealth; and wealth created charity. Communists didn't understand that humans are generous and good and excessive government is evil. At some point, the producers would say, fuck it and withdraw when government became too onerous and controlling. Spike had thought that Ayn Rand's and George Orwell's writing was missed by the leftists. In the middle of a mission, he found himself smiling about the values that had made him who he was. Even if he never returned home, fighting for good to defeat evil was more important than his life.

Billy's Makarov Hostel was only about three hundred meters from the Baltschug. If the hostel was still in operation, Spike would be excited to forget all about the irrational lefties and take refuge in the hostel. Spike was happy with staying close to the scene of the escape because the authorities would expect that he would try to get as far away as he could.

Spike took inventory of what he had left. He had a credit card with a Ukrainian identity, cash of about $120,000 in euro and US dollars, an alternate ID to escape, and a target. He didn't have any weapons, a true plan for what he was going to do when he found and tracked Fedderov, or any exit plan. Over the past day, he'd decided that if he could take out Fedderov himself, he'd do it. This was more than mission scope creep. Tracking wasn't enough and he wanted to see the man dead after learning more about him. It felt liberating to decide he would go it alone if possible.

Spike whispered to himself, "What the fuck, I'm free; I'm clear of Russian surveillance; and I know Fedderov is a criminal. I got life by the ass right now." He hoped that the cash would help him more than anything, but he didn't know who he could contact to convert that cash into resources to make Fedderov pay. He assumed he would need to get assistance from either the Russian Mafiya or some terrorist group who would align with him. Clearly, he would need support to get that alignment. He hoped that Shauntel and Jimmy could connect him. If not, he would need to connect with Tim Blust to get help.

Spike showed up at Makarov within ten minutes of exiting the Baltschug. He was confident that the FSB would not have traced him. They wouldn't know that it was the Irishman Thomas O'Gara who'd knocked out the security guard. They wouldn't be trying to track and identify Thomas O'Gara yet. Eventually, they would connect Thomas O'Gara to Gary Eastman, former

CIA Agent and US Air Force officer. But that would take time. Spike thought, *The longer it takes, the better.*

Spike gave the hostel operator two hundred euro and, in Russian, asked if he could stay for a month. The guy measured up the clean-cut, black-haired old guy as some kind of lost soul. He saw plenty of weird people coming to see Moscow, home of Soviet communism. He assumed that Spike was Russian and didn't ask for a passport. The hostel operator just said, "Da, sixty thousand ruble, eight hundred euro."

Spike knew he was getting screwed on the exchange and on the advertised nightly price, but he really didn't care, so he handed over another six hundred euro, and said, "Spasibo." The operator smiled knowing he'd just earned an extra twenty-five thousand rubles from the idiot standing in front of him. Spike was happy to be that idiot as long as he didn't have to show any identification. The Russian pointed to the staircase to the left, Spike said "Spasibo" again, and headed up the lobby stairs to the second floor. The building had this center staircase and stairwells on both ends.

When Spike entered the room he was assigned, he counted four beds and only one other occupant. The person in the top bunk on the right side of the room was a man, but Spike really didn't care. The room had a large window that was big enough to jump to street level, but it would be about fifteen feet down. Not perfect, but it wouldn't kill him if he needed to exit fast. It was about 11 p.m. local time. He knew he needed sleep, and he couldn't be sure when he would have another chance, so he hopped onto the top bunk on the left side of the room with his backpack along the wall and the straps wrapped around his left wrist. He went to sleep immediately.

CHAPTER 29

Moscow
The next day

He woke up at about 4:45 when the room's other two occupants showed up. The two men were in their early twenties and looked a little drunk. They were being courteous to their roommates by whispering. They were speaking in Americanized English, and it sounded like they'd had a great time in Moscow. It was light outside, and the sheets over the window didn't darken the room much. Spike didn't let them know that he was awake. When they fell asleep about thirty minutes later, Spike decided to sleep another hour and then leave to scope out the conference area where he would find Fedderov. He began his mental list of things to do today. He needed to find transportation to move around Moscow without using public transportation, because train stations always had surveillance. He needed to connect with people who would sell him weapons. Sleep was a priority, so he quit thinking about his to-do list, set his internal alarm clock for an hour, and fell back to sleep.

Spike woke again at 6:30 and took his backpack to the community bathroom. There were two shower heads, two sinks, and two toilets all in a wide-open space. He was alone, so he set his backpack in one of the sinks, used the toilet, stripped down to his underwear and T-shirt. He did pushups, ab crunches, and squats for about fifteen minutes. He shaved, put in brown contact lenses, and took a long, cold shower. He didn't have soap or shampoo, but he really didn't need it. He put on a clean pair of underwear, gray T-shirt, and black socks. He was wearing the dark blue pants, blue button-down oxford cloth shirt, and charcoal blazer. His shoes were heavy leather-souled black mock toe dress shoes. His clothing matched the business environment as if he were attending a conference or had a business meeting. He would blend in well in Central Moscow.

Spike left the hostel from the back staircase with his backpack and his fedora angled over his eyes with the gaiter over his nose and mouth. He headed back west along the Vodootvodny Canal. The canal splits off from the Moskva River for about four kilometers where it rejoins the river. The river and canal are just south of the Kremlin and flow west to east in that part of the city. He walked north toward Red Square, crossed the river. He walked through Red Square, turned right on Maroseyka Street to walk to the conference center called Gostenyy Dvor. There were conference rooms, a large open area under a glass roof, and some shops inside. Once the conference began later that morning, he might need credentials to enter the building. The setting seemed less formal than Spike expected. The VIP entrance would be from the parking area behind the building. He walked through the exhibit hall and out the rear entrance. The parking area would be heavily guarded later in the day. He headed north to the Rigla. He purchased three smart phones, water, and food. He used most of his rubles so went into a money exchange a couple stores way from Rigla and exchanged five hundred more euro.

He headed west and went into a Starbucks next to the Four Seasons Hotel. He kept alert to be sure he didn't bump into Saundra from the airport. She would call him Thomas, and his name was Oleksander today. He bought a double espresso and a second double espresso over ice. He tossed his dirty clothes into the trash in the restroom of the Starbucks.

Oleksander Barabash of Ukraine was still not active electronically, and he hadn't shown the passport to anyone. It was 8:30 a.m., and he had to walk about half an hour to get a car. The used car dealer Jimmy had found that seemed shady was near the Tretyakov Gallery. Spike remembered the area. He headed south, past the conference center, past the Kremlin, past St. Basil's, across the river, past the Hotel Baltschug, across the canal, and continued south. At 9 a.m., he arrived at his destination as it was opening for the day.

He found a salesman who looked like a used car salesman the world over.

Boris was around thirty-five years old, about the same size as Spike, in decent shape, very well groomed with short, stylish hair and manicured fingernails. Boris wore a pinky ring and a counterfeit Rolex watch. Boris wasn't wearing a surgical mask, but Spike kept his gaiter up. Spike spoke in Russian and asked about newer model Vestas. He was hoping to get a sport version. The salesman said, "I have exactly what you are looking for," and smiled with the fake smile of a transacting salesman. Boris walked away to get the keys, and when he came back three minutes later, he motioned to the parking lot. Spike followed and the walked to a 2018 dark blue Vesta Sport. Perfect. It reminded Spike of a Toyota Corolla. He knew that the Russian auto industry has improved over the past ten years, and the Vesta Sport had been reviewed by industry observers on par with many American and Korean vehicles. Spike asked the price, and Boris said, "Four hundred and fifty thousand rubles."

Spike said, "I'll give you five thousand euro, six thousand if I can drive away right now with no paperwork."

Boris smiled. "I don't like paperwork either. Who should I say is the new owner?"

"Put your own name. I'll give it to you in a year or so and you can sell it."

"Why am I so fortunate today?"

Spike said, "Because my wife can't know that I have a car. She'll just get it in the divorce anyway. I'd rather you have it than her."

"Yes, but if you use it for illegal activity, my name is on the line," Boris reasoned.

"How much would it cost to get you to agree?"

"Eight thousand euro. Do you need anything else?"

"Nyet, that is very expensive, that is all I need."

"Give me the money, and I will get the vehicle ready for you in fifteen minutes."

Spike withdrew ten thousand euro from his backpack, counted out two thousand, and handed Boris the balance. "I need to use your Wi-Fi; is there a password?"

Boris smiled. "Da, is on sign in waiting room." He led Spike into the building, pointed to the waiting room, and headed into an office with the general manager.

Spike pulled out one of the smartphones, started it up, and connected to Wi-Fi. He went into the draft email and found three new drafts. The first one was mundane communication about work at Maurer. Spike answered the questions quickly. The second one was the locations of the chemical lab that had made MARV and the facility that made the flu shots. The last one was not surprising but still alarming. Tim Blust had called and asked what Spike was doing in Moscow, and who was Thomas O'Gara? Then he called back and asked why he'd gone underground. Shauntel had feigned ignorance, but Blust didn't believe her. He threatened to hook her up to a lie detector. While she didn't know anything about Spike's whereabouts or identities, she did know what his overall mission was. Blust told her to give Spike a number to call in Moscow for assistance. Spike memorized the number and put a new draft in the box. He told Shauntel to tell Blust that he was going to track a target and hand him off to Blust as soon as he could, at the latest, by the end of the week. That should put him off for a while. Spike used the restroom to unload his coffee and went back to the waiting area.

Boris approached with two sets of keys dangling from a generic keyring and a document that he handed to Spike first. He showed Spike where he needed to sign and fill in his name. Spike was reticent to sign anything, so Boris explained that it was similar to a rental agreement and Boris wouldn't have a copy. The point was that Spike could use it as a registration if he needed to show it to the police. The form was filled out, but the name had been left off. Spike could write in whatever he wanted, and Boris didn't want to see it.

Spike smiled. "Spasibo, you've done this before?"

"Nyet, but Igor has, usually for the Mafiya. He asked if you could go to his office, maybe he could help you with other things." Boris acted like he didn't understand what those other things were.

Spike needed to decide how much he could trust these people. They could be connected to either the Mafiya or the FSB. His mind was going toward "don't trust a Russian," but he didn't have many other resources. He thought he would listen to Igor. As he entered the boss's office, he lowered his fedora over his eyes and had the gaiter covering the rest of his face. He just said, "Da."

After about a minute of silence, the boss introduced himself as Igor Igoravich. Spike didn't offer a name.

Igor was trying to intimidate Spike with the silence and what seemed like a false name. He hesitated again and asked, "Is there anything else you might need?"

"What are you thinking?" Spike asked.

Igor said, "Makarov pistol, AK-47, RPG?"

"You sell those here?"

"Nyet. I have friends."

"I won't talk with anyone else. You are the only person I will meet. Da?"

"Da." Igor nodded.

"I need a Berretta or Makarov nine-millimeter with silencer, one hundred rounds, three magazines. That part is easy. And I'll give you two thousand euro for that."

"Da, that is easy. Twenty-five hundred euro."

"Da, twenty-five hundred. But then it has to be a Berretta."

Igor was writing this down which seemed like a bad idea. It isn't that complicated. He looked up, and said, "Da, Berretta nine-millimeter, silencer, one hundred rounds, three magazines. Twenty-five hundred."

Spike felt as if he were at a diner in a small town. He thought, *Well, what the hell, it might be better to break the law with one person than spread the risk by engaging more criminals*, and said, "Can you really get RPGs?"

"Da."

"I'll take three disposable Rocket Propelled Grenade launchers, RPG-22 preferably. The market for these is less than one thousand euro each. I would give you ten thousand euro for these. But I don't want to talk to anyone but you, Igor."

He went back to writing. Igor said, "Da, three RPG-22, ten thousand."

"What time should I come back?"

"Not here. I will call my friends." Igor stood up and was going to leave to make the call. Spike stood and blocked the door, saying, "Ostavaysya zdes'," which roughly translated to "stay here" and pointed to the floor. Igor nodded and made the call from the office. Spike could only hear one end, but Igor was making the order and arranging to pick it up. Igor was careful not to say where he was going to meet the arms dealer. He simply referred to the place as "your warehouse."

"How long will it take?" Spike asked.

"Two hours I will bring to you," Igor said.

Spike wrote his phone number on a one-hundred-euro note and handed it to Igor. "I'll be at the Tretyakov. Text me when you arrive, and I will meet you at the corner of Malyy and Bol'shoy by the old Church of Saint Nicholas. You can follow me to a place that seems safe to me. Da?"

"Da."

"What kind of car will you be driving?"

"Black Mercedes SUV. It is parked right outside of front door." Igor pointed vaguely at the front of the building.

"Don't fuck with me."

"Da." Igor smiled; Spike didn't.

Spike got up and left the office. He waved at Boris, exited, studied the Mercedes, and walked to his new Vesta. As he started the car, he thought, *What a dealership*. He smiled because he had the thought in Russian, not English.

Spike removed the SIM card from his phone and drove the car around the area to be sure he wasn't being followed. He wasn't planning on entering the museum. It was full of Russian art that he remembered was wonderful. But there would be cameras, so he would stay on the perimeter. He drove around the Tretyakov Gallery and the other buildings that had become part of the art center. It was a quiet area with a lot of foot traffic and large buses with tourists. He was happy he selected that area to meet to procure the weapons. He drove the nearby streets and found a good place to make the exchange. He parked about a block away and counted out the euro. He put the money in five twenty-five hundred bundles separated by rubber bands. He wanted to be able to keep his eyes on Igor when they met. He'd learned long ago in Afghanistan to be careful when dealing with criminals.

Spike remembered his dealings with one particular Northern Alliance warlord. The warlord's main business was drug trafficking, and he hated the Taliban, because they were trying to use his money to finance their crazy plans. He joined up with the Americans because the enemy of my enemy is my friend. But when Spike went to see him, he always made sure the warlord knew he had a couple snipers covering him. Once, he had a drone fly low enough to be spotted. That kept the warlord honest. Still, Spike couldn't shake the idea of being ransomed for one hundred thousand dollars to offset some of the warlord's losses.

Spike thought today would be a good day to have a sniper nearby. He would need to be cautious and abort if he felt anxious. He would have to trust his senses to be aware of threats. He used the key fob to open the trunk of the Vesta and pulled open the spare tire compartment to get the tire iron. He smiled at the idea of bringing a tire iron to defend himself from people selling him RPGs. Ridiculous. He was as comfortable with his plan as he was going to get.

Spike looked down at the dashboard and realized he needed to disable the navigation software in the Vesta. He didn't know how, but he read the owner's manual to figure out what fuse controlled it. Things weren't this technical back when he was in the field. The internet of things had changed the world in ten years. He needed to remember that whenever he became confident that his tradecraft was coming back. It took him ten minutes to figure out how to disable the navigation system, but he realized it was a good use of his time.

He had an hour to kill so he decided to take a tour in the car to get used to moving between the areas he would need to go. He drove toward the Kremlin. The traffic was horrible. It took fifteen minutes to drive what had taken him thirty minutes to walk. He drove around the area in front of the hostel and the Hotel Baltschug. He crossed the river into central Moscow and noticed that the weather was beautiful. It was sunny and about sixty degrees. People were walking along the sidewalks and in the parks wearing short-sleeved shirts. Spike drove past the Metropol, past Lubyanka, the former home of the KGB, which reminded him that he was in a land of peril and looped around the central part of Moscow. The Vesta handled well and had enough power for city driving, but it didn't feel like it would be fast enough to outrun someone chasing him. He hadn't driven in Moscow when he visited when he was younger, and he was surprised by how well traffic seemed to flow in this part of the city. It was still slow, but cars didn't seem to be darting between lanes and cutting others off. This may have been because it didn't look like many tourists were driving or maybe because the pedestrians weren't aggressive like other European cities where he had driven. They seemed to understand that cars could crush them.

Spike headed back toward the Tretyakov. He arrived fifteen minutes before the two hours was up and found a parking spot just west of the corner where they were going to meet. He assumed that Igor would come from the north on Malyy or from behind his position because Bol'shoy was a one way heading east. Spike alternated his watch between the side mirrors and the T intersection where Malyy ended at Bol'shoy. He replaced the SIM card, ate a protein bar, and sipped a couple mouthfuls of water. He could be waiting for a while since Russians weren't known for punctuality and didn't want to have to take a piss any time soon. Spike was paying close attention to the sidewalk on the right side of his car to be sure no large men were approaching on foot. At the appointed time, Spike's phone vibrated, and he received a text that said, "Pyatnadtstat minut."

Spike replied, "Da." Fifteen minutes.

He removed the SIM card again and pulled into traffic. He wasn't sure who he was dealing with, and it would be easy for either the Mafiya or FSB to track him. He drove around the block, which took about eight minutes, and parked so that he was heading south on Malyy about twenty-five meters before the T. He waited until twenty minutes had passed since the last text and re-placed the SIM card. The phone buzzed immediately after booting up.

Igor texted, "Parked on Bol'shoy, just west of intersection with Malyy."

Spike responded, "Watch intersection, follow me."

Spike removed the SIM card again, pulled his gaiter up, and pulled out when traffic was clear. He slowly approached Bol'shoy. Igor was parked in the same spot Spike had been. He appeared to be alone, but the windows were tinted, and it was impossible to be sure. Spike made sure Igor pulled out to follow and sped up. He drove as fast as he could without drawing attention and headed south toward the area that he'd scouted earlier. In Spike's mind, this entire exchanged was about speed. He wanted to maneuver so that Igor would have to park in front of him. At a stop light three blocks before the street he had selected for the exchange, Spike replaced the SIM card. He en-tered the street he had picked. As he pulled to the side of the road, he dialed Igor's number.

"Da," Igor answered.

"Pull in front of me, open the back."

"That is where the weapons are. You could steal."

"I have five bundles of twenty-five hundred euro. After you open the rear cargo door, I will come to the passenger-side window and give you three bun-dles. I will grab the weapons and leave the other two bundles in the back cargo area. Da?"

"Do you trust me?"

"Nyet." Spike said, "But I cannot have your friends angry with me. I will not cheat you." Spike pressed end, removed the SIM card for the last time, and grabbed the money and the tire iron.

The cargo hatch opened. Spike checked the mirrors and looked around like a fighter pilot in a dogfight. When he got out of his car, he had the money in his left hand, tire iron in his right, and he left his door open wide. He took the route behind his vehicle and looked around the area for threats. Seeing none, he approached the right side of Igor's SUV about eight feet away. He turned toward the front passenger door and tossed three bundles of money into the front seat from about three feet way. Then he ran to the back, hoisted a large heavy duffle bag over his left shoulder, and opened his own trunk with the key fob. He went back, unzipped the bag; it looked like what he expected, but he wouldn't be sure with just a quick visual inspection. He slammed the trunk and walked around his vehicle on the left side and tossed the last two bundles into the cargo area of the Mercedes. The cargo door began closing, and Igor leaned out of his vehicle said, "If you need anything else, you have my number." He drove away quickly, and Spike ran to his open door, got in, and made a U-turn to expand the distance from Igor as fast as he could. He headed west and got onto Yakimanskiy Proyezd, a six-lane highway, to head north toward the city center. As he approached the canal, he noticed a black Mercedes sedan coming up fast from behind him. It slowed as it fell in a few cars behind him.

As he approached the river, he changed lanes quickly and exited while still on the island between the river and the canal. The sedan couldn't make it through traffic to make the same exit, and it continued on. Spike had to assume that the Mercedes driver was able to alert others who might quickly pick up the chase. He maneuvered to get back onto the highway heading south, away from the city center, hoping that they would expect him to head into traffic. He headed south, and it occurred to him that they had a tracking device either on the car or, more likely, in the duffel bag with the weapons. He pulled off the road and parked between a large cargo van and a pickup truck. He opened the trunk from inside the car and rummaged through his backpack for his handheld device that could help him find anything emitting an electronic signal. He'd had the device since his CIA days, and it was disguised as a Blackberry phone. He turned it on and got out of the car, went around to the trunk, and found a signal from the bag. He removed weapons one at a time until he found the tracking device was sewn into the canvas at the bottom of the duffel bag. He removed the bag and put it into the pickup truck's bed. He went back checking for more tracking devices as he went around the passenger side of the vehicle. He passed the device over the items in the trunk and was satisfied he'd found the only device. He got back into the car and headed for the north-bound lanes on Yakimanskiy again. As he entered the highway, he was confident that he'd be clear for a while.

CHAPTER 30

Moscow

Fedderov's speech would be the next day, so Spike needed to look around the area to be sure he could track him. Spike parked north of the city center in a parking lot just off Lubyanka Street. He pulled out of the parking lot and headed west toward Neglinnaya Street, just north of the Metropol. Spike stopped at the Rigla again to get water and a protein bar but mostly to see if he was being followed. He hadn't seen anyone watching him, so he walked to the northeast corner of the Gostenyy Dvor where Fedderov's security team and vehicles would wait for him during his speech. He kept an eye on the parking area as he walked down Rybnyy Street and continued to check to be sure he wasn't being followed. He walked around the conference center and headed toward Sovol's headquarters building two blocks to the east. Almost all Central Moscow real estate was officially government buildings, but some of the favored industries had offices in the government administrative buildings. Sovol's building had a large square in front of it for parking and the helipad. Spike walked around the block and saw the helicopter, a black Maybach, and a black Mercedes SUV. From the photos Jimmy had found, Spike recognized one of the bodyguards hanging around the Maybach. He entered the adjacent building and saw that it had security, so he just continued through the lobby to another exit.

Spike walked back past the Gostenyy Dvor and headed over to his car. He drove to the street in front of Sovol's offices and found a parking spot where he could keep his eyes on the helicopter. He walked around the block and entered several of the office buildings which had armed security guards. One building, a two-story shopping mixed use with a small grocery store, a couple clothing stores, and gift shops, had no security guards in the lobby. The building was on the opposite corner of the intersection in front of Sovol's helipad. Spike walked past all the shops and went upstairs using the back staircase. The second floor was mostly offices that appeared to be a local chamber of commerce quasi-government enterprise. It was hard to tell because the name of the office sounded official, but the people inside looked disorganized, and as Spike walked around, several people entered and exited. It looked like they were delivering packages. On his way toward the front stairs, Spike stopped in the last office. As he entered, Spike estimated that the square room was about twenty feet on each side. He thought it would have the best view of the street that ran in front of Sovol's square. The office had a counter all the way across the room cutting it in half. The counter had ten columns of three openings about ten inches wide by three inches high starting just under the countertop. The openings were marked with numbers from one to thirty, almost like mail slots. Behind the counter, which was about four feet high, there were two rows of four desks with people sitting at six of them seemingly doing data entry work. The corner office had windows that were open on this nice Spring day even though it seemed much warmer in the office than outside. The door to the office announced that it closed at 4 p.m. Monday through Friday, and no late submissions were allowed afterhours.

A young man walked into the office and put an inch-thick file with a rubber band around it into the slot marked twenty-four. As he turned back toward the door, Spike got his attention and said, "Prostite, why twenty-four?"

The young Russian had blue eyes and close-cropped brown hair. He was wearing a cheap suit, white shirt with a dark blue tie, and rubber-soled dress shoes. He looked worn out, and his attire reminded Spike of a Mormon missionary. He answered, "My sector is twenty-four."

"What are you reporting?"

"Sales to tourists for clothing, gifts, and accessories from the stores in my sector."

"Oh, for tax exemptions?"

"No, this is our marketing agency. We track all the results for Central Moscow tourist sales. That way, we know what to stock, how to improve sales, how to serve customers better." The young missionary seemed immensely proud of the work he was doing.

Spike smiled. "Spasibo, do svidaniya." Spike walked out of the office. He went the rest of the way down the hall to the front staircase, went back downstairs, and entered the grocery store. He bought a couple bottles of water, a premade roast beef sandwich, and an apple. He exited the building. Fedderov would likely pass by this building. He went outside to wait for Fedderov to leave his headquarters. He walked across the street and past Sovol's building to a church square adjacent to the headquarters. He ate the sandwich and drank a bottle of water while looking at his phone. This was the first time he had used this phone. He went directly to the email drafts. The first one laid out the conference schedule. Fedderov's speech was supposed to end by this time tomorrow, so he would likely come back to headquarters following his speech. The second one said that Blust needed to talk with him and Shauntel thought it was a good idea. Spike had a phone he could use for that, but he wouldn't actually call him. Spike wrote his own draft saying he would text Blust and requesting any new intel about Fedderov's schedule tomorrow.

He removed the SIM card from the phone and took another phone out of the packaging. He turned the phone on and sent a short text to Blust. He just typed, "O'Gara here."

A minute later came a reply. "Do you need anything?"

"Not yet. Do you have vaccine or MARV?"

"No, yes."

"Anything else before I destroy this phone?"

"Airport acquaintance is Bond. Fed the number."

Spike assumed he meant that Saundra, the British oil conference attendee, was MI-6, British Foreign Intelligence. Again, Blust was a step ahead of Spike. Spike thought he was the coy one who initiated contact. The phone number Shauntel had given him was for an FBI agent. Probably the only Russian speaker they could find who was under the radar for the FSB. The implication was that Spike could contact either of them for support. He removed the SIM card and put it in the bag with his sandwich wrapper and empty water bottle.

He needed to move in case they had traced his location in the three minutes it took to text back and forth.

Spike headed back toward his Vesta and tossed the bag into a trashcan on the side of the church. As he started to cross the street, he dropped the phone into the storm sewer. He was down to the phone he had used to read and leave the draft email. It was probably not being traced, but he needed to get more phones and try to find a dose of the vaccine that included the MARV antigen. He assumed it was too early to get flu shots for this year, but he thought he would give it a try. He headed across the street and circled around the car. His head was on a swivel, but someone watching him would never know. He headed around the block, stopping twice to look at his phone and make sure he wasn't being followed. The phone was powered down, but someone watching him would assume he was reading an email or looking for walking directions. He was relieved to see that about a third of the tourists he saw were wearing some kind of facemask. His gaiter was starting to smell bad from the Copenhagen but it was worth it.

Spike was on the opposite side, almost two hundred meters from his vehicle, when he heard the helicopter engines begin to wind. He knew that it was unlikely that Fedderov was already in the helicopter. People like him didn't get into any transport to wait for a pilot to go through their pre-flight checklist. He wasn't worried that he would miss seeing the flightpath. He was more concerned that the pilots would alter the flightpath each day. If the CIA could figure out that the helicopter was Fedderov's most vulnerable time, his bodyguards would know the same thing. As Spike approached the intersection in front of Sovol's headquarters, he saw two bodyguards ushering what looked like Fedderov to the helicopter. Thirty seconds later, the helicopter lifted off, going vertical for about four hundred meters. Smart move. Spike's RPG had an effective range of about 150 meters. He would need to be almost directly under the chopper to get a quality shot likely to take it down. Spike realized he probably wasted ten thousand euro.

He hopped into the Vesta and headed east toward a clinic he had gone to when he was a cadet to help one of his fellow students get a shot for gonorrhea. His friend was a student from Oxford who was afraid that the whole world would know his affliction. Spike spoke Russian better and was more likely be able to communicate the need for discretion. Spike was quite sure the Russian government kept track of foreigners with embarrassing problems, but he went along and did his best.

The clinic was nearby, and when he entered, he kept his gaiter up. He went to the reception desk and asked if he could get a flu shot. She asked for his name and he said, "Igor Igoravich." The woman behind the counter pointed to the waiting area and said, "Sadat tam."

"Spasibo." As directed, Spike headed over to some beat up plastic chairs that looked like they had been there for many years. Several had brown stains on the seats, and he tried to pick one that looked a little cleaner than the rest. He put his backpack down and used a napkin to cover the seat. He smeared hand sanitizer on a separate napkin and wiped down the chair handles. He walked over to a garbage can, threw the wet napkin away, and walked back to his seat. Before sitting down, he seemed to be inspecting the area, put another glob of hand sanitizer on his hands and rubbed it in. Spike sat down without leaning back on the plastic upper part of the chair. He noticed that the woman behind the counter and the four other patients looked at him as if he were crazy. After five minutes of waiting, very still, he made a big production out of sanitizing his hands again. By then three of the four other patients had been called back to be seen.

He cleaned his hands once more before they called him back. Hopefully, he had established that he was a little bit of a germophobe, and like most clinics, the word had traveled back to the nurses who took care of the patients. They went back into what looked more like an emergency room than a normal clinic in the states with individual private exam rooms. There were just curtains between the patients here. The nurse asked him to sit down, and Spike looked at the chair and said, "Nyet, I can stand, da?"

The nurse looked like she'd been doing this for a while and told him that it was fine. She sat at a little desk that was on rollers. She said, "Flu shot?"

Spike said, "Da."

"They aren't ready yet."

"I didn't get the one last year because I was traveling to Central Africa. I got home in December, and it seemed too late, so I didn't bother. When MARV started, I was encouraged that we didn't have a large outbreak in Moscow. But, lately, I have become a little paranoid about germs, and I need to get a flu shot."

"It is unlikely to help you much this time of year, but I can administer one from last year if you would like."

"Da."

The nurse smiled at him to try to make him comfortable. He put some more hand sanitizer on and didn't touch anything. She said, "It will take a few minutes to get the immunization."

Spike waited about ten minutes, and the nurse returned. She had a small vial with a permeable rubber top and a needle. Spike looked very nervous. He said, "I was hoping it would be one of those air gun shots. I hate needles."

The nurse smiled. "I am very good at this. You will not feel a thing. Remove your coat and shirt. I will give the shot in your shoulder where it doesn't hurt at all."

Spike began undressing. He made a show of being uncomfortable putting his clothes anywhere, so he held them in his left hand. The vial looked full, and the needle would probably only use 20 percent of the vaccine. He needed the vial, so he would need to cause enough of a disturbance to distract the nurse but not draw in other medical personnel or security.

The nurse put the needle through the vial membrane at the top and drew the plunger back slowly. Spike was staring at the needle, and the nurse noticed and turned away to hide the needle with her body. She finished filling the syringe and set the vial on the small rolling desk. With her back still to Spike, he could tell she was clearing any bubbles from the syringe. She turned back but kept the needle out of sight. This nurse knew what she was doing. Spike spread his feet wide and looked away. As she came closer, he flinched. The nurse put her left hand on the top of Spike's shoulder and started rubbing. She smoothly brought the needle up, and Spike felt the prick. He tensed and looked at his upper arm just as she was finishing and applying a cotton ball with medical tape. Spike swayed back and to the front with his eyes wide open. He swayed back again and allowed his body to fall forward as if he were unconscious. He angled his shoulder so it would topple the rolling desk. Some papers and the vial slid off the table. Spike caught his fall with his left arm and spilled his sports coat and shirt in the direction of the vial. He immediately came up to his hands and knees and shook his head vigorously. The nurse had watched the whole thing but, with the needle in her hand, couldn't really break his fall. Spike looked up at her apologetically and said, "Prosti."

She smiled. "You are fine, da?"

"Da." Spike got to his feet and picked up his shirt and slipping the vial into his pants pocket. He noticed that it was cold. He put his shirt on, picked up his coat, and searched for the sanitizer. He found it and squirted it onto his hands. He rubbed his hands together. He put his sports coat back on and smiled at the nurse. "You are a very good nurse. Usually I pass out for much longer. Spasibo." Spike started to leave. He realized that open nature of the room would help him. If she realized the vial was missing, she would look around to see if it rolled into another stall. As he exited the hospital, he grabbed his phone and dialed the FBI agent's phone. The agent answered, "Volga."

"Great name. This is O'Gara. Imagine there's no heaven. Thirty minutes. I'm wearing a black gaiter."

He hoped Volga was old enough to know John Lennon's song and understood that Spike wanted to meet him at Lenin's Tomb. He removed his SIM card and put it with his phone in his right suit pocket. He left the parking lot and headed south toward the Moscow River. Spike parked the Vesta just south of Saint Basil's Cathedral. With nobody around and no cameras in sight, he took a chance. He went into the trunk, and put the Berretta, the three clips, silencer, and box of ammunition into his backpack. He didn't want to load the clips in broad daylight, so he headed into the cathedral. There was a tour group ahead of him, so he followed along with them for a while but stayed back. The natural light is extremely low inside the Cathedral, and it was easy for Spike to slip away from the group. He sat in a pew away from the crowd and put his hands into the backpack. He could load a clip by touch and completed the task of assembling the weapon in about two minutes. He slipped the Berretta into the holster in the left side of his sport coat. He felt safer already. He went to a row of candles, lit one for Bridget, and prayed for a minute. He put ten euro in the offering slot, got up, and headed toward Lenin's Tomb.

He walked toward Red Square paying awfully close attention to his surroundings and the faces in the crowd. In central Moscow, the FSB could easily mobilize an army to apprehend him if they knew what was happening. As he was walking toward the mausoleum, Spike noticed a very clean-cut man in a suit watching him. The guy looked away but put his thumb to his nose like Paul Newman in *The Sting*. Spike shook his head and thought, *This is amateur hour.* They both headed toward the middle of the square.

The guy said, "Eastman?"

Not good, but verification was quickly accomplished. Spike had the vial in his right palm, shook Volga's hand, and, in Russian, said. "Nice to meet you." And then quietly in English, "Get this to the embassy fast. It needs to stay cold."

Spike pulled out his phone and showed it to Volga as if he were asking for directions. They chatted about the weather in Russian. As they strolled, Volga tried to get more information from Spike about what he was doing and asked if Spike needed any support.

"Nyet, I have what I need. I will call you if I run into trouble."

They strolled together across Red Square toward the shopping mall and restaurants on the east side of the square. As they neared the entrance to the shopping mall, Volga peeled off heading north. Volga's Russian was superb, and he was about fifty years old. As Spike walked around for a few minutes to be sure he wasn't being followed, he wondered where the feds had found Volga. He went into the Bosco Café, ordered a glass of water, a double espresso, and a sweet roll to go. He dropped his cell phone into the trash container in the restroom. Spike went outside and sat at one of the tables facing Red Square. He drank most of the water, ate part of the sweet roll, and slurped up the espresso. He dropped the SIM card into the water and put the wrapper from the sweet roll on top of it. He tossed the trash in a receptacle on the way out of the seating area.

CHAPTER 31

Moscow

With half the mission accomplished, Spike considered getting out of Moscow while he was ahead. He could brief Blust on a good plan to kill or kidnap Fedderov and let real knuckle draggers take care of the rest. Then he thought about his mother and the other innocent people Fedderov had killed for his own economic gain. He wanted to take care of this himself. The evidence against Fedderov was in the bag.

Spike walked back to the Rigla and purchased three smartphones and two bottles of water. It was almost 5 p.m., and he'd had a long day. He felt secure with no digital footprint for Oleksander Barabash, nobody tracking him, a pandemic giving him an excuse to cover his face, and only one more thing to accomplish. He had weapons that he hadn't had to expose. So far, this couldn't have been better. He headed back toward the Vesta and realized he could pay to leave the car where it was overnight. He used a previously unused prepaid Visa card and deposited fifteen hundred rubles in the automated parking attendant. It was about a two-kilometer walk back to the hostel, and this was a good a place as anywhere to leave the vehicle. Along the way, Spike stopped in the park just north of the river.

He used one of the phones to check email drafts. Nothing new about Fedderov's schedule for Tuesday, but Shauntel said he had a meeting Wednesday morning in Saint Petersburg, so it was likely he would leave soon after his speech. Then Spike sent a text to Blust, "Did you get the flu shot? Has anyone noticed me?"

Blust replied about a minute later. "Got it. Not that we can tell."

Spike replied, "Out," and removed the SIM card and walked back toward the hostel.

He crossed the Moscow River, stopping to watch a barge go by and check to see if anyone was following him and to drop the phone and SIM card into the river. He passed the Hotel Baltschug on the other side of the street and continued across the Vodootvodny Canal to a Nordic restaurant called Bjorn. He was seated along the back wall so he could keep an eye on the entrance. Spike noticed the restrooms were down a short hall that also led to the kitchen and an exit to the back alley just inside the kitchen. Spike's waiter, a Russian named Sven who looked like a Viking, gave him a menu and welcomed him to the restaurant with Nordic stoicism. Spike noticed almost all the employees were large and blonde with Nordic features, but they spoke native Russian. The service seemed good, and the restaurant was clean and decorated with a masculine touch that looked like the north woods with caribou and bear taxidermy, brick and rough lumber furniture. He asked for a menu and ordered a familiar Belgian beer called Limburgse Witte. When Sven returned with his beer, Spike ordered lamb, which was served with mushrooms and potatoes.

He would need a hearty meal to prepare for what would be a very demanding day. He knew exactly where the target would be for a few hours. Thinking about tomorrow, he was concerned about the assessment that the helicopter was a vulnerable target. He'd witnessed the tactical takeoff and the RPG-22 wasn't built to hit a fast-moving aerial target. He should probably shift his plan to hit the limousine instead. No matter how he did it, it would be loud, and he would need an escape plan. The plan to shoot from the marketing agency seemed solid until he saw the helicopter ascend to four hundred meters in three seconds. Following the shot, he could disappear in the chaos. From the street, firing at a limousine would have a lot more variables. And, either way, he would be killing a lot more people than Fedderov. That had weighed on Spike's conscience all along. Time for a new plan altogether. When the lamb arrived, it was steaming hot, and the waiter nodded toward Spike's beer.

Spike said, "Da, spasibo." He finished the first beer and took in the sweet aroma of the lamb. He cut a piece of the very tender meat, added mushrooms and mashed potatoes to the fork, and tasted his best bite of food since he'd left home. The meal was fabulous. He finished faster than he should have; he had time to burn. So, he ordered dessert and a third beer. He left fifty euro on the table and walked back across the canal to the Makarov Hostel. It was dark out, and Spike felt a little tired, which was partly due to the three beers.

He walked past the hostel entrance on the opposite side of the street along the canal. He didn't notice anyone who appeared out of place, but he stood and looked at the canal for a while to be sure. After ten minutes, he strolled toward the entrance and went in. He saw the same guy who sold him the room, and when their eyes met, the guy looked down and away too quickly. He should have met Spike's eyes and nodded. It can be a small reaction that tells the story. Spike wasn't sure how, but this guy had turned on him. He had his gun in his sports coat holster, but he had only the one magazine loaded with seventeen rounds plus the one in the chamber. Spike glanced around the lobby for targets but didn't see any obvious enemies. The smart thing to do was turn around and find another place to stay. Instead, he went to the stairs as if he didn't know he'd been sold out.

There could be people waiting in the room or the staircases. Or the hostel operator would make a call and tell whoever was tracking him that he was in for the night. When Spike hit the second floor, he glanced toward his room. Just past his room, there was a guy standing casually near the stairwell beyond Spike's room. When he saw Spike, he immediately started talking quietly. Spike recognized him from Jimmy's research. It was Vladimir Zmokinivich with his close-cropped gray hair, athletic stance, and cold blue eyes. He was using advanced tactical communication equipment. When Spike turned in the opposite direction, he knew he was trapped if he continued. The opposite staircase was covered because Zmokinivich didn't pursue him as he turned in the wrong direction. Spike decided to make a run for it down the center staircase and take his chances with the people in the lobby. He turned quickly after about three paces toward the opposite staircase and headed for the lobby stairs.

Spike made it to the lobby stairs before Zmokinivich reacted. Now he was speaking more loudly, and Spike heard "Kuluary," which meant lobby. Spike drew his Berretta and kept it along his thigh. No reason to create panic if he didn't need to shoot anyone. He took the stairs three at a time and ran through the lobby looking for targets but with his weapon low. He noticed the hostel operator was on a telephone and was tempted to shoot the fucker for turning on him.

Spike thought if they had the end staircases covered, they would be able to cut him off no matter which way he turned in front of the hostel. That left one choice. He ran across the street and launched himself over the railing and into the canal. Even before he hit the water, he could smell that is was not a clean waterway. The canal was about a hundred feet wide with a footbridge just west of where he'd gone in. The water flowed east, and the foot bridge would be a good place to shoot from, so Spike swam east underwater for about ninety seconds. From playing in his pool with the kids, he knew he could go about a hundred feet in sixty seconds. He figured with adrenaline flowing, he could probably make it almost to the other side and down river about seventy-five feet. That would get him past the east end of the hostel.

In the ninety seconds he was underwater, Spike thought about the plastic bags that Shauntel always packed with and thanked his lucky stars again that she was his wife. At least his money, IDs and electronics would be dry. Plus, he would have dry socks, underwear, and T-shirts, but he'd need to find clothes. The backpack was providing some drag, but it wasn't heavy, so it probably wasn't filling up with water. Spike surfaced as quietly as he could, took two large breaths, and saw a set of stairs leading out of the canal on the south side, away from the hostel and hostiles. As he began to go under, he heard splashes nearby and realized he wasn't clear of the enemy yet.

This would be a sixty-second swim. More time to think. Spike wondered what they knew that made them shoot at him and realized it was probably Igor who had blown his cover. Igor was working with an arms dealer who was certainly connected to the Mafiya. Fedderov had connections with Russian organized crime. The protection detail likely knew about the RPG-22s earlier in the day and decided to use the fast-vertical climb to defeat the effectiveness of the weapon. But why would they assume the RPGs were meant for him? Spike was missing something, and he now had an extremely dangerous adversary who knew he was in Moscow. He surfaced about 130 feet down river, which left about four hundred feet to the junction with the river. This time, he didn't hear any bullets splashing, but he couldn't be sure he was clear, so he took five full breaths and went under again.

He decided on this leg of his swim that he would need some help, and he would call Volga. When he popped up, he was alone and so he rolled over to have a better view of the area behind him. He reasoned that if Zmokinivich was planning to kidnap and interrogate him, the FSB likely wasn't involved yet. The small force Spike was facing was not capable of covering the canal and river like the government could. He decided to exit from the south side of the canal to avoid floating under the last two bridges before the canal rejoined the main channel of the Moscow River. In his mind, he pictured Zmokinivich leaning over the bridge with his Makarov trained on Spike.

He shuddered at the thought as he found a ladder to get out of the canal. As soon as his chest was above water level, he grabbed the Berretta and switched the backpack to the front of his body to give him a flat surface to field strip the weapon. Using one of the T-shirts from the backpack, he dried the parts. He removed all seventeen rounds from the magazine and dried them. He assembled the weapon and chambered a bullet. He loaded all three magazines, put one in the weapon, and put the other two in his left coat pocket. Beginning to feel the effects of the fifty-five-degree water and fifty-degree air temperature, Spike got to the top of the ladder and peered over the concrete wall. He didn't see any pedestrians, but a few vehicles were passing by at normal speeds. He waited for them to clear and got over the wall and onto the sidewalk.

He was dripping wet, but his upper body had dried some as he worked on the pistol. He needed to find clothes, so he headed a block away from the canal and then south toward what appeared to be a commercial area. As he was walking, he stayed alert to the vehicles passing. In the dark, it was hard to tell that he was wearing wet clothes. His shoes were leather and heavy and squeaking as he walked. He saw a restaurant up ahead and waited about ten feet from the entrance. After nearly an hour of shivering on the sidewalk, finally a man close to his height but probably forty pounds heavier walked out with a young boy around fourteen years old. As they headed toward them, Spike said, "Izvini menya. Mogu ya kupit' tvoy pidzhak?" which meant, "Pardon me, may I buy your jacket?"

The young boy laughed, but then looked closer and noticed that Spike was wet. The man, who was thinner than he first appeared, smiled and said, "Sixty thousand rubles. Da?"

Spike haggled and said, "For sixty thousand, I would like your shirt and pants too. How about one thousand euro and you include your shoes?"

The guy was considering it and asked if they should go to his car to change. Spike agreed, and they walked around the block to his vehicle. It was a new BMW. Spike was surprised because the guy didn't act like he would have a seventy-thousand-dollar vehicle. The guy opened the car door, removed his black leather jacket and light blue button-down oxford. He had a white T-shirt underneath it with dark hair sticking out of the V-neck collar. He sat down, kicked off his loafers, which looked like nice, soft Italian leather, and undid his belt. His waist was clearly larger than Spike's, so Spike said he would give him an extra hundred euros for the belt. The guy just smiled, removed his pants, pulled his legs into the car, and closed the door. He started the BMW and lowered the window. The kid had been giggling in the passenger seat since they arrived at the vehicle. Spike peeled off eleven hundred euro from one of his plastic bags. The guy handed him the pants, grabbed the cash, and quickly closed the window and drove away, nearly running over Spike's feet with the rear wheel.

Spike went into the front yard of what looked like an eight-unit apartment and hid between a large bush and the building. He stripped naked, pulled on a pair of underwear, a T-shirt and then the Russian's clothes. The shoes were a little wide but about close to the right size. That was his biggest concern, because the belt would hold the pants up. Spike pulled an extra pair of socks on, and the shoes became closer to the correct fit. He could run if needed. He slid the pistol with the silencer into his trousers at the small of his back. The difficulty of drawing quickly with the length added by the silencer made him pack the charcoal blazer into the backpack. The pants were dark blue; the shoes and belt were a light brown. Spike left the rest of his wet clothes behind the bush, but he packed his shoes and belt.

Spike opened the packaging for one of his smartphones. He found a Holiday Inn about a kilometer away and walked to it. He used his Oleksander Barabash credit card and passport to check in for four nights. He had kept the identity out of play until this point, so he doubted it would be a problem to use it now. When he got to his room on the third floor, he stripped down, laid the clothes on the bed, and jumped into the shower. He stood under the warm water for about ten minutes, then soaped up and rinsed his body. He noticed some blood flowing down the drain but wasn't sure where it was from until he shampooed his hair. The shampoo was stinging the top, back of his head. He rinsed the shampoo, turned off the water, and used some toilet paper to isolate the location of the wound. He thought about infection from the polluted water. He used the hand mirror to examine the wound. It was straight, and he realized it was probably from when Zmokinivich and his thugs were firing into the water at him. He hadn't felt it because he was operating on full adrenaline. He used toilet paper as if it were a shaving nick to stop the bleeding. He realized the infection was the least of his worries, a highly trained assassin was looking for him with bad intent.

Spike needed information more than anything. He dressed, put his pistol in his belt, took his backpack, and went to the lobby to take a taxi to central Moscow. He sat down across Red Square from Lenin's Tomb at the Bosco Café with a croissant roll and a bottle of orange juice. He sent a text to Blust simply saying, "Help, F's team found me. I escaped without harm."

It was about 3 p.m. in Sheboygan, and Blust answered immediately. "We thought so. FSB also noticed that they were hunting someone. F told them to mind their own business. That's good, FSB would be a tougher opponent. Do you want Volga to bring you in?"

"No, but my plan is shot."

"We have a team in place. They could use a hand. Like you did with SS Gomez."

Blust was referring to the al-Takfiri rendition. Staff Sergeant Gomez was heavily featured in the after-action report but probably not known to anyone monitoring the texts. That told Spike that they wanted to talk to Fedderov, not kill him. Having a team around him would reduce his risk in Russia but increase the pain when he returned home. The thing was, without them, he might not return home. Spike texted back, "How good is the team?"

"Great, the Padre is with them." Meaning Father/Trooper Tim.

"Unofficial?"

"Half and half."

That meant there were CIA Operations team members involved. Spike answered, "Okay, connect me."

"Same guy, same place, as soon as he can get there."

"Out." Spike immediately removed the SIM card. He finished all but a half inch of his orange juice and dropped the SIM card into the liquid. He put the cap on and dropped it in the trash on the way out of the seating area. He was curious about his car, so he walked near the parking lot. The Vesta was gone. Igor had screwed him, or Igor was interrogated and gave him up. Either way, Spike was lucky he had been careful with his tradecraft wearing the gaiter the entire time he was engaged with Igor. Pandemics were convenient for keeping your identity hidden.

Spike walked back north toward the center of Red Square and saw Volga walking briskly toward Lenin's Tomb. Spike headed him off about thirty feet from the mausoleum. They said nothing as they walked a circuitous route toward the shopping area. They got into an older Lada, and Volga said, "Close call?"

"Closer than I knew. Turns out, I took a glancing bullet to the scalp. Didn't even know until I took a shower. I had a nice swim in the canal."

"We'll get you some antibiotics at the safe house. The team is there. You know Tim. He and Ray Jones from Ops are running the show. They have a plan, but you will need to help them with some of the details."

CHAPTER 32

Moscow

The first thing Spike noticed when he met the team was that he was getting old. Father Tim and Spike were the only people in the room over thirty-five years old. The safe house was a fourth floor flat about three kilometers north of Central Moscow. The entire floor was theirs with four bedrooms and three full bathrooms. The dining area had become the operations center with a large map in the middle of the table. There were six chairs, and five were occupied by hard-bodied operators. It was obvious who was in charge, so Spike nodded at Ray Jones, the team leader, who nodded back but didn't seem too thrilled to see Spike.

Jones was thick in the shoulders but slim at the waist with thick thighs like a power lifter. He had ten years in Operations but was recently promoted to lead a team. After graduating from Boston College, where he was a varsity wrestler, Jones was recruited into the CIA in a direct-action paramilitary position. His role was similar to Spike's CIA role except he didn't embed with military units. He was the triggerman with a team that broke down doors and went after terrorists and other enemies of the US. This operation would definitely be the highest profile affair he had ever led. Spike realized that his presence was probably a threat to Jones.

The team members were all wearing jeans and T-shirts exposing extremely fit young bodies. Because they were operating in Russia, it was not surprising that they were all white. Spike was introduced to the team and provided short backgrounds. He didn't let on that he had the Ukrainian identity. They had already been briefed on his background, and they seemed intent on getting his input on their plan. The plan was simple: grab Fedderov as he left the speech the following afternoon. They knew for certain his entrance and exit point. They had watched another important speaker with heavy security enter and exit earlier today through the same area Spike had expected. They had a thick dossier of the security team and their tactics.

As they laid out the plan, Spike became concerned that they were thinking Moscow was like Peshawar or Baghdad. The plan was solid until they were faced with moving Fedderov from Central Moscow to an airfield to get him out of the country.

The team was solid. They had Jones plus two experienced operators who had been army and navy special operations officers. The army guy, Billy Jackson, had attended West Point was fully trained as a sniper, a medic and a helicopter pilot. The Navy guy, Sam Capuano, had graduated from Annapolis and led SEALs in nearly one hundred operations before joining the CIA operations teams. They were well-trained, smart, and ready to move. They had experience planning operations and executing with their teams. But, from Spike's perspective, they were young. They had no experience in Russia, and they didn't understand the consequences of fucking this up. Neither of them had any failures under their belt, which meant they might not understand how it felt to report back when things didn't work as expected.

They also had Father Tim and two additional contractors. Spike trusted Father Tim's pedigree and his commitment. Will McDaniel was larger than the rest, probably six foot three and 250 pounds. He was all muscle but seemed gentle and easygoing. Physically, he was impressive, but that wasn't important. The key was the ability to fit into his role. He was a former army ranger and then an NYPD street cop. His knowledge of urban situations might help. The other contractor was a diminutive person, almost a foot shorter than McDaniel. His name was Lance Marcus, and his sinewy build and clear focus were obvious. He had been a SEAL team sniper and appeared to be built to run a marathon. McDaniel and Marcus didn't have experience planning or leading operations, but they had both been involved in a lot of different operating environments. Spike thought they would be effective if their roles were well defined.

The plan called for McDaniel and Jones to be the ground muscle who would take Fedderov from the street. Marcus would be set up to cover the extraction. Jackson would drive the van, and Capuano would ride along with him to control Fedderov once he was taken from the parking lot. Before Spike joined the effort, the plan was that Father Tim would cover the security team that would be waiting with the vehicles. Adding Spike gave them two people who could neutralize those bodyguards.

There were three huge problems with the operation that Spike immediately pointed out. Following what was sure to be a gunfight in Central Moscow, moving Fedderov to the airfield twenty-five kilometers away with FSB and normal police intervention would be nearly impossible. Once at the airfield, the Russians would never just let them fly out of the country. Spike pictured MIGs shooting down a Gulfstream and the Russian pilot smiling and saying, "A kill's a kill." Third, they hadn't accounted for Zmokinivich. The team said they had Zmokinivich covered; he was just another member of the security detail. They would smoke him if he interfered. Spike let them think that because he knew that the bigger problems were getting to the airfield and out of Russian airspace.

Father Tim agreed that their odds of getting out of the country with this plan were well below 30 percent.

Spike said, "We need to convince him that he wants to join us, not kidnap him in the middle of Moscow. The best chance to do that is through deception, not brute force. Let's think about this some more. How could we fool him into joining us without his security becoming alarmed? Financial gain is the most important thing to this guy. What do we have to offer?"

Nobody answered. Father Tim grimaced as if he'd said the same thing in earlier planning sessions. Finally, Jones said, "We've considered similar ideas, but what can we offer? We don't buy oil, military hardware, or chemicals from these assholes."

"Just because we are Americans doesn't mean he knows were Americans. Granted, none of us could get away with pretending to be Chinese or Syrian, but Sovol is trying to get more contracts to acquire oil and natural gas in other European and even South American markets. Why not convince him we can get him access to that?"

"We don't know enough about oil contracts to fool him."

"MI-6 has an agent attending the conference who is an expert in oil and gas. She could likely help us to make contact with Fedderov and put us in touch with people who could be in a position to lease access to their oil or gas fields to Fedderov."

"We don't have authority to bring in another country," Jones said, looking pissed. Spike was beginning to think Jones had a death wish.

Spike looked over at Father Tim and said, "Call Blust, he can coordinate and get permission." Judging by the body language in the room, Spike could tell Jones was the outlier. Tension was suddenly relieved.

Spike looked around the room and said, "Okay, let's make sure we share our intelligence. Did you watch Fedderov and his security today? Anything stand out?"

Jones reengaged, "The security team is very well trained. For some reason, they were especially alert today. He used two limos and two SUVs when he went to the Kremlin. Normally for that trip, he would have just used one limo with a driver and two bodyguards. He had twelve people around him all day. His helicopter took off like it was leaving a war zone. When he arrived at his mansion outside Moscow, he had a whole extra set of security people already in place."

"How long have you been watching his security protocols? And has it ever been this intense?"

Jones shook his head and said, "Over three weeks, and not even close. He went from a fairly relaxed stance except during transport to this high alert level just today."

"What do you think precipitated this?"

"According to chatter the CIA picked up, some terrorist bought some RPGs. Apparently when weapons get distributed from the Mafiya, the FSB knows immediately. They give a heads up to all the oligarchs' security teams. The biggest fear is internal terrorism, and RPGs in the hands of rebels is one of their big fears."

"Seriously? That was me. I bought a car, three RPG-22s, and this." He pulled out his silenced weapon and placed it on the table. "I didn't keep the RPGs and car for long. They were stolen from a random parking lot near Saint Basil's. Fedderov's security chased me from my hostel. I had to jump into the canal to get away."

"So, they have the RPGs back, maybe they will relax," Jones said.

"Maybe, but I'm just not sure why it was Fedderov's team and not the FSB coming after me. The FSB would have got me; they have helicopters and enough forces to trap a guy in the canal. I was lucky. I was grazed by a bullet." Spike leaned forward and showed them the wound. As if on cue, Volga went and got a medical bag.

"Why would they shoot to kill? Do you think they know you're former CIA?"

"They must. At first, I think the plan was to capture and interrogate me. But when I bolted, they began firing at me. I saw Vladimir Zmokinivich."

Jones perked up. "I was going to ask you before, how did you know about him?"

"We're just sharing intel, not sources."

Father Tim interrupted, "Blust said it's okay to call her, but Spike and I need to be the intermediaries. Since we aren't official, we can be denied a lot easier than the rest of you."

Spike stood up. "She's at the Four Seasons, let's go. Can Volga drive?"

"Volga?" Father Tim asked.

"Sure, first, let me clean up that cut."

Spike sat back down and leaned forward. Volga cleaned the wound, squirted liquid skin in the cut, and gave him a shot of antibiotics. Spike said, "Thanks, let's go."

Spike put the black leather jacket on and put his gun in the small of his back. For the first time since he arrived in Moscow, he left without his backpack. When they left, Spike put the SIM card into the phone and sent a text to Saundra, the Brit he'd met at the airport. She told him to meet her at a bar about a block from the Four Seasons. Volga dropped them a block north of the bar, the Mumiy Troll. She was sitting along the back wall at a table when they entered. The place was crowded, and a band was playing loudly. Spike slid in next to her and Father Tim took one of the seats with his back to the crowd and door. Clearly, he was uncomfortable with that position. Spike told Saundra about the idea but said they didn't have the right connections to make it work. She smiled and said, "I do, and I have a private appointment with Fedderov before his speech. I spoke with Tim Blust earlier, and we worked out a plan."

"Fantastic. Tell me."

"He won't have time to meet with anyone in Moscow tomorrow. He isn't comfortable here, so you'll need to head up to Saint Petersburg. I will set an appointment for Thursday with two North Sea drillers who have been looking to sell and retire. Fedderov will know that they are in the market to sell their interests since it is true. I will need to escort them to make it realistic as if I'm brokering the deal. We will meet in his office surrounded by security. He loves to party, especially when he makes deals, so we'll invite him for drinks and dinner at a villa Blust found on the Gulf of Finland. We'll hope for Thursday night, but it could be Friday or Saturday. He will travel by helicopter with at least three bodyguards. You guys just need to neutralize the bodyguards and your helicopter pilot can fly him to Estonia. We will be met there by an agency jet to get you home."

Spike knew that Estonia was a NATO and European Union member and had a growing economy until COVID-19 and MARV slowed the world down. Estonia had been occupied by the Soviet Union at the end of World War Two until the Soviet Empire collapsed in 1991. The Estonians were concerned about the impact of an aggressive Russian neighbor, and the country was a willing participant in helping Western powers against the Russians. During the Soviet days, the Russification of Estonia caused resentment that hadn't gone away.

Spike nodded. "What happens to Fedderov?"

"It will be a joint interrogation. If he's cooperative, we might even sell him back to President Solokov if he wants him. We have proof of Fedderov's biological warfare, but to release that information to the world could cause World War Three, so some delicate diplomatic work will need to be done."

Spike asked, "Where did you get MARV samples?"

Saundra smiled. "Vladimir Zmokinivich had traveled to the Middle East and several oil and gas industry hotspots around the world. He was bringing MARV to be released. We noted his travel and correlated it to MARV outbreaks."

"When you say we…"

"MI-6 has been working with the CIA and especially Tim Blust for the past month on this. Mossad and DGSE helped too."

Spike was surprised. British, American, Israeli, and French intelligence working together against a Russian adversary. Blust's ability to build teams was clear in business, but this was even more impressive.

"So how did you get the MARV?"

"The CIA followed Zmokinivich in Houston and saw him place a dispersing unit near the docks where the oil riggers head out to the Gulf. We got the unit, but he slipped away and left via Mexico. He knew we were on his trail, and he hasn't left Russia since."

The spread of MARV seemingly haphazardly through oil communities now made sense. It was no wonder Guls had such a headache trying to track how the virus had spread. Biological warfare by a major power, whether state sponsored or not, was too sensitive to become public knowledge.

"If we get a chance, do you want to talk with Zmokinivich?"

"No, he needs to die."

CHAPTER 33

Moscow – Saint Petersburg

Volga picked up Spike and Father Tim in front of the Mumiy Troll. They headed straight back to the safe house where Volga dropped them off. The rest of the team was already asleep when they entered the flat, so Spike and Father Tim went straight to sleep.

At 7 a.m., Spike got up and stumbled into the kitchen to get coffee. Jones, Jackson, Capuano, McDaniel, Marcus, and Father Tim were eating at the operations table. All the maps had been destroyed. The safe house looked ready to be abandoned with luggage lined up near the door. They had a twelve-passenger Mercedes van to make the eight-hour drive to Saint Petersburg. Their visas all allowed them passage, but Spike would need to use his Ukrainian passport if they were stopped. He didn't want to share that identity with the group.

Spike asked, "Everybody know the plans?"

Father Tim spoke first, "Yes in broad strokes, but we need to see the terrain to build out the details. We need to be on the road in thirty minutes."

Spike decided another shower was the best use of his time. He grabbed his backpack and cleaned up. His head hurt a little, but he was feeling very fortunate that he hadn't been badly wounded. He put on the blue pants that were too large in the waist. His own shoes were dry enough to wear, so he tossed the light brown loafers and belt. He wanted his own heavy black shoes. He could get some clothes in Saint Petersburg. Spike was out of the bathroom in ten minutes, ready to go with his backpack and leather jacket. The charcoal sport coat was ruined by the nasty water in the canal.

As the team was wiping down the flat, Spike sat at the table with his coffee and some leftover bacon and toast. Sam Capuano was having another cup of coffee and asked, "Spike, when you were in Operations, did you ever wonder whether a mission was right?"

"Funny, as I got more experience, I began to question things more. How long have you been doing this?" Spike opened a fresh can of Copenhagen Long Cut and put in a fresh dip.

"I was part of twelve missions with the CIA before I left the navy two years ago. Since then, probably thirty to thirty-five missions."

Spike smiled. "You are way ahead of me, Sam. Right and wrong get blurred in your job. You can't expect to fight with Queensbury Rules when your opponent brings a hammer into the ring. America's enemies aren't concerned about fairness, ethics, or anyone else's life. Take this guy, Fedderov. He launched a global pandemic so he could make a few extra billion. For what? His opulent lifestyle isn't going to improve. He just wants to be richer for the sake of being richer."

"Well, I will admit, this one is pretty cut and dried. But, remember, we will probably have to kill his bodyguards and helicopter pilot."

"We won't kill them unless they try to kill us. And they might have to die. I've always rationalized that part. I'm not saying this is the only way to look at it, but these people know they've thrown in with a bad guy. They were hired to protect someone who pays them a lot of money for their loyalty. We'll see how they react when they realize they don't stand a chance. They may be smart enough to surrender. I think that is part of the reason why I'm here. I speak their language, and I will give them a chance to surrender."

"What about Vladimir Zmokinivich? We have him listed as a sanctioned kill."

"He deployed biological weapons against civilian populations in several nations. He would be considered a war criminal or terrorist even by the United Nations, but he'll just die, because nobody wants to drag this onto the world stage."

"I've seen civilians and non-combatants die because of our actions. Nobody likes it, but sometimes that collateral damage—a stupid euphemism—

keeps me awake at night. In my heart and my mind, I believe we are doing what's right, but sometimes the outcomes aren't perfect."

"Yep. I agree. Just remember, you don't have to do this work forever. When I realized that, I quit." Spike was speaking in a low voice and very intensely. He saw a warrior in pain.

Capuano said, "Easy for you, Stanford MBA, varied background with a cover that seemed to make sense."

Spike laughed. "Does anyone keep secrets anymore? You're right, I was lucky in that way. And I have a very supportive wife and family."

"I'm probably three months from divorce. My kids hardly know me."

"I thought the same thing. Look, Sam, we need to get our game faces on before our teammates hear what we're talking about. I'd love to help you figure this out. Do you still live in San Diego?"

"Yeah, I didn't want to move the family when Langley came calling."

"I did the same thing in Vegas. Look, when this is over, we'll talk. And there is no doubt about this mission—it's righteous."

"All right." Capuano got up, grabbed the dishes, and went into the kitchen.

Before Spike could get up, Jones and Father Tim came at sat at the table. Father Tim asked, "Everything good?" He sounded like a priest again.

"Yeah, good to go," Spike said.

Jones leaned forward. "Sam has had a tough time with the moral clarity of our role. You both have more experience than me. Do I need to do anything?"

"I doubt it," Spike said. He wasn't sure if Jones was sincerely concerned about his guy or looking for a reason to burn Capuano, so he picked a less controversial subject to explain the intensity of their discussion. "When I was CIA, I didn't live near Langley. My family felt isolated. He lives in San Diego and has a similar problem."

Jones relaxed, leaned back, and said loudly, "Let's roll, fellas."

Everybody finished their tasks; Father Tim went to take a leak, mumbling about getting old. Spike took his coffee cup into the kitchen. Sam was alone finishing the dishes. Spike leaned over and whispered, "I told them we talked about our wives being separated from the rest of the Langley support system. Nothing else."

Sam said quietly, "Thanks, I don't need the extra oversight."

They loaded up the van, hit the road before eight. The young guys were all listening to music with headphones attached to their phones. Father Tim slept in the front passenger seat while Jones drove. They stopped for gas and to get some food near a large national park in the rustic region between Moscow and Saint Petersburg. Spike hadn't noticed in the van that the topography had become hilly and beautiful. There was almost no conversation in the van, and nobody wandered far from the van when they stopped. Spike was the only one who spoke Russian, so he did all the talking. He prepaid for the gas and bought a case of water, a dozen rolls, two pounds of cheese, butter, and sliced ham. For dessert, he bought a box of chocolates and a bag of apples. They loaded into the van and headed north. They hit the outskirts of Saint Petersburg just before 3 p.m., and it took them another ninety minutes to get to the villa on the Gulf of Finland, which is the furthest east part of Baltic Sea. Jones told the group that Blust had a business interest in the firm that owned the villa. The firm had already stocked the place with food, liquor, and had a catering company on standby for Thursday through Saturday nights. The Fedderov visit wasn't scheduled, and if it didn't work, they would need to figure out a different plan.

The villa was fabulous. Set on eight acres, it had four hundred feet of frontage on the Gulf of Finland. The limestone block driveway from the main gate to the house was about seven hundred feet. The brick wall that surrounding the property was eight feet high and two feet thick and lined with large apple and pear trees. A grove of birch trees covered the area between the gate and the home. There was about a two-hundred-by-two-hundred-foot clearing for the helipad made of limestone blocks. The grounds were neatly trimmed, with tall shrubs in front of the mansion. Large granite fountains flanked the grand entrance that included a six-by-twenty-foot granite platform, which tapered down five steps to the forecourt level.

The twelve-year-old red brick villa featured beautiful fixtures and granite, marble, and walnut flooring. Spike realized that most of the high-end construction products had come from Maurer. Blust was clearly connected to this project. The main level had about ten thousand square feet, including a fifteen-hundred-square-foot owners' suite and three guest rooms, a library, a twenty-seat dining room, a large game room and bar with huge televisions spaced between dead caribou, elk, and moose heads. The second floor had eight suites all with their own bathroom and a theater. All in, twelve bedrooms, fifteen bathrooms, and twenty thousand square feet.

The lower level had a large exercise room with six treadmills facing a large television in the front of the room, four separate dressing rooms with showers, a large bar area that walked out to an Olympic-sized pool and hot tub with a twelve-hundred-square-foot pool house including a sauna and steam room. Two tennis courts were behind the ten-car garage that looked like a barn and had luxurious maids' quarters on the second floor.

The garage had a lower level as well, and it was equipped with a shooting range and a locker room. Conveniently, the company had delivered two Barrett M82 fifty-caliber sniper rifles, seven M4 carbines, and eight SIG Sauer M18s. These weapons came from a base in Germany and were still in their original packaging. Each of the weapons had silencers, three extra magazines, and gun cleaning equipment. The CIA had provided a total of ten thousand rounds. In each operator's locker stall, there were black and camouflaged combat uniforms, body armor, night vision and communications equipment, and web belts stocked with two flash-bang grenades, a Taser, a black combat knife, and pockets for extra magazines. There was also a box of smoke bombs, extra flash bangs, two sniper blinds, and four Stinger shoulder launched missiles. The trained snipers were thrilled to see their native weapon and the blinds. Jackson and Marcus were concerned that they would need to fire an unfamiliar weapon. There was a model replicating the exterior of the home and grounds on a table in a three-hundred-square-foot conference room. There was also a communications and safe room with a wall of video monitors connected to cameras covering the interior and exterior of the entire property.

The shoreline was rocky and about fifteen feet below the level of the pool. There was a pronounced slope between the pool and the water but no retaining wall or stairs. Next to a small boathouse was the private dock that extended about forty feet into the Gulf of Finland. Two boats, a twenty-five-foot Boston Whaler and a twenty-foot pontoon boat, were both about five years old and sitting on lifts on either side of the dock.

The team was starting to gel. After another half hour of getting a feel for the surroundings and examining the layout of the home, Jones and Father Tim gathered everyone for a meal. They prepared pasta with sausages, a chicken Caesar salad, and most of them drank American beer.

After the meal, they met in the basement of the garage to clean and assemble the weapons and load the magazines. They each test shot the weapons they had claimed. These were trained operators, so they thoroughly tested each of the magazines and sighted the weapons efficiently. Since the shooting range only had three lanes, they took turns and adjusted the equipment to meet their needs.

Spike asked Jones and Father Tim, "How are we going to scrub this place when we're done?"

Father Tim smiled, and said, "I think Blust and Director Oliva want them to know we did it. Who are they going to complain to? This guy could have started World War Three; the Russians aren't going to have many options when we provide the evidence of what he's done."

Jones said, "Hell, we should take his money as reparations."

Spike laughed. "I'm sure Oliva is working on that."

The team gathered around the model. The refrigerator in the garage basement was stocked exclusively with American beer, including a case of Spotted Cow. Other than Father Tim, nobody had heard of it. They gathered around the model and began thinking about the mission and how they could stop the bodyguards from committing suicide by fighting back. Earlier, Jackson and Marcus were checking on the angles and best hiding places.

Jackson said, "As soon as we have a clear shot at Zmokinivich, Lance or I will blow his head off his shoulders with a fifty cal. That will give them pause."

Jones replied, "These guys are all Spetsnaz-trained bad asses. They probably aren't as skilled as our team, but they will immediately triangulate toward the sniper."

"They will have handguns, and our shot will be from at least one hundred yards. They won't be able to hit us."

"If they start firing, they won't stop, which means we'll have to take them out," Spike said. "The bigger issue is that Fedderov might jump straight back onto the helicopter and head for the hills. We could take out the helicopter with either the missiles or the fifty-caliber Barretts, but we want him alive."

Pointing at the model, Father Tim said, "I think we wait for them to get about thirty feet from the heliport and sixty feet from the house. Zmokinivich always stays on Fedderov's left side, so it will be pretty easy to predict how they will deploy. They will likely leave the pilot and one of the bodyguards with the bird. It would be helpful to know how many are coming when they take off. Can we get eyes on the helicopter in Saint Petersburg?"

Jones said, "Yeah, we can get a spotter. Most places I've been, we would have a drone, but the Air Force already made it clear that they won't overfly Russia with a drone. The Russians would probably trade Fedderov for one of the new total stealth drones, and the Air Force is always worried a technical problem would take them down and the reverse engineering would remove our tactical advantage. Pussies." He looked at Spike, and said, "Oh, sorry."

"Ray, you can't hurt my feelings. I happen to agree with your assessment." Spike laughed and so did everyone but Father Tim.

He said, "I'll never understand your obsession with picking on each other's services. You Yanks are a strange breed."

Spike said, "Look, Father, don't bother trying to figure us out, but let's keep going on your plan. The bait—Saundra and her clients who want to sell their oil rights—should be in sight to keep up the appearance of a friendly visit. How do you see that working if bullets start flying?"

"I think it would be most disarming and natural if Saundra comes out alone. That's why we got eight pistols. She can take care of herself. Another concern is if Fedderov brings one or two of his executives. We can't massacre civilians. Bodyguards are one thing, but I think we try to keep the pilot and any ancillary executives out of the line of fire. They won't be armed. We know that the executives are usually a few steps behind Fedderov or on his right side. We really need to know who's coming before they get here. The helicopter can hold up to ten passengers plus the pilot and Zmokinivich, who usually acts as the co-pilot/navigator when he's with Fedderov on the helicopter. So, a max of twelve people, probably all men. The most likely is four to six bodyguards plus Zmokinivich, pilot, Fedderov and say two execs."

Jones added, "The pilot will most likely stay with the chopper. First wildcard is whether one or two of the bodyguards also stay back. When they hit the target zone, Jackson will shoot Zmokinivich from distance first without warning. As soon as the shot is fired, Spike announces in Russian that they are surrounded and should lie on the ground. That will be the moment of truth. The bodyguards will either go for their guns or surrender. If they go for their guns, the priority is the bodyguards covering Fedderov, then the bodyguards by the chopper. Spike and Capuano will be closest to Fedderov's party. Zip tie hands and feet and bag the heads of all survivors, take Fedderov to the chopper. Tim and I will secure the pilot and survivors near the chopper."

Father Tim yawned. It was almost 10 p.m., and the team had at least all day tomorrow and Thursday to plan. Father Tim said, "Sounds great, we can work on the rest of the details tomorrow and do a dry run in the evening. We should probably use the tunnel between these buildings during the day starting Thursday. Fedderov may be paranoid enough to check this place out ahead of time. For now, we're safe, because he hasn't been invited."

McDaniel said, "Wait, there's a tunnel? Where?"

"Actually two tunnels. One goes to the communications room, which can also serve as a safe room. In the house, it starts behind a false wall in the wine cellar. The other one leads out of here to an escape hatch behind the garage. I'll give you a tour tomorrow. We also need to cover the entrance from the garage with a false wall. The plans filed with the government didn't include this space. During the operation, one of us should probably be down here." Father Tim yawned again. "I'm going to get some sleep."

Jones said, "We have a lot of familiarizing to do. Sam and Will, test the boats tomorrow. Billy and Lance, figure out the best places to set up. Spike, Father Tim, and I will figure out the communications equipment, security system, and get weather for the next ninety-six hours. At noon, we can meet here and figure out if we need to tweak the plan. Breakfast is at seven."

The all started to get up. Spike nodded to Jones, and he stayed back as the others filed out. Jones went over to the refrigerator and asked, "Can I get you a beer?"

"Yeah, sure. I think your plan is solid. Do you mind if I give you some advice?"

Jones laughed. "I don't mind. Actually, I was going to ask for your input."

"Look, it's your operation. I'm going to do as I'm told, and I don't want any question who is in charge. That doesn't work. One commander. The only thing I would do a little different is ask for more input. Father Tim and I have enough experience to know that we need one leader, don't worry about your authority being questioned. But these guys might have some good ideas. Especially Jackson and Capuano, since they've also led teams in takedown operations."

Jones sighed. "You're right about both Jackson and Capuano. They both wait until there is a plan in place to make improvements. I think it is their training to take orders, but they're both really good at tactics, and they like to think for a while before they make recommendations. That's why I gave them the basic plan tonight. Tomorrow is the most important day. We'll be able to measure distances and timing. At noon, I'll make it clear to Tim, Will, and Lance that I need their input. Billy and Sam already know."

"They've all been through debriefings given their military experience. To prod them along, maybe ask about missions they've done in the past."

"Thanks, Spike. I have a question for you. I heard you were imbedded with military teams to get intelligence quickly from a mission. Are you comfortable if you need to be a shooter?"

"Yes, I'm comfortable, but I'm the least qualified. We shouldn't count on me to double tap a guy from twenty feet."

"You and Tim should spend some time shooting tomorrow. The seminary probably didn't have a range."

Spike said, "He should probably be down here during the operation anyway."

"I was curious about his comment about that. The CIA will be active in the Operations Center watching this live. We don't need to waste a shooter watching in the safe room. They can tie into our comms from Langley and see everything Tim could see to direct us. Do you think he doesn't know that? Or is there some other reason he doesn't want to be in the fight?" Jones asked.

"Want me to ask him? He was the priest who did my mom's last rites and funeral. I think he'd come clean."

"Sure."

"One other thing. You guys have been watching Fedderov for three weeks. Why do you think they recruited me so hard for this mission? I was trying to do something on my own anyway, but Blust pushed hard, even made a veiled threat to my family. He seems like a pretty straight shooter. Why bother with me?"

Jones was nodding. "Your language skills and being relatively unknown to the FSB were a big part. And your ingenuity."

"Ingenuity? I don't think that was in my record."

"I'm not sure, but the rumor I heard is that Oliva was tracking you to be the director of operations. She wasn't happy when you decided to move on. But knowing it was a possibility, she asked Blust to give you a place to land before you even knew you were leaving. They have been watching you ever since. That's the rumor anyway."

Spike looked perplexed. "So, do they think I would return or become another Blust? 'Cuz that ain't happening. It is too much fun living, and I care a lot about our country, but I already did the sacrifice thing."

Jones laughed. "Yeah, I'm not read in on how they are going to fuck up your life. I just know that they wanted you here, and I think it has something to do with Vladimir Zmokinivich. He's a smart guy, and the president signed off on eliminating him regardless of the rest of the mission. There's more to it than him infiltrating our country and releasing biological warfare."

"Okay, I'm going to speculate here a bit. Don't stop me until I puke it all out...okay?"

"Okay, but remember, I'm a true believer in the US of A."

Spike nodded. "Me too. Here's my speculation: Vlad is only on loan from Solokov. Maybe Vlad is a message, and Fedderov is leverage. And if that's the case, this isn't just some oligarch going off the rails. This is the Russian Federation's President Solokov attacking the US and several other oil producing nations. That's World War Three. And they want us to capture, not kill, Fedderov. That leads me to believe they are looking to blackmail Solokov to knock it off and quit trying to rebuild the Soviet Union. Part of the message to Solokov is killing his Spetsnaz goon Vladimir Zmokinivich."

Jones laughed again. "See, that's why they wanted you to be the DO. You may be right, but this is way above my pay grade, as you military guys like to say."

Now Spike laughed. He'd gone to the Air Force Academy at the very end of the Cold War. Everyone had focused on Islamic terrorism for most of his military and CIA career. The whole time the US was distracted by that, Russia and China grew stronger. They were still the real international adversaries. The jihadists were a threat, and a lot of them needed to die because of the way they had hijacked Islam. The jihadists wanted to ruin the modern world. But Russia and China didn't want to ruin the world; they wanted to rule the world.

Spike said, "Well, let's crush this mission so I can go home, okay, Ray?"

"Yeah, I'm good with that. I do have one question left. When you came into the safe house, you obliterated my plan. What was your impression of me and the team?"

"I figured you had a death wish. The plan was impossible—we would have all died. I thought the team was being way too passive, and that is a big part of why I wanted to talk with you now."

Jones laughed. "At Director Oliva's direction, we were testing you. We weren't really going to try to have a gunfight in central Moscow. She figured that if you went along with it, you would slip away, and we wouldn't hear from you again."

"You know, that is exactly why I wouldn't have made a good DO. The constant manipulations and mind games aren't for me. But I do love the action. Even when I was swimming away from a hail of gunfire in a polluted canal, I was pumped. This shit is addicting, and honestly, it's fun. But a millimeter better aim"—Spike lowered his head and pointed at his scalp—"and I'd be floating in a watery grave right now."

"It's crazy. But you're right; it's addicting."

Spike got up, grabbed another Spotted Cow, and headed to his second-floor bedroom.

CHAPTER 34

Saint Petersburg
The next day

Everyone but Father Tim got up before six to get in a workout. Spike hadn't worked out properly for almost a week, but he had been very active, so he didn't notice any degradation in his fitness. He ran about five miles with Marcus and Jackson. They were younger, but he kept up without any problem. Marcus looked like he could run forever, and he didn't even break a sweat running six-and-a-half-minute miles. When they got back to the garage, he took the same route again. Spike was doing pushups when Marcus showed up in the garage about twenty-five minutes later with sweat dripping off his entire body.

Spike asked, "Feel better?"

Marcus smiled and said, "That's my normal routine. Faster for the second half. I don't lift or do any strength work. As a sniper, it is all about breathing and heart rate. It's my secret sauce." He headed straight down to the gun range and shot two magazines in rapid succession with the Sig. The grouping was the size of a silver dollar at thirty feet. Then he ran through a magazine on the M4 using three round bursts. The grouping was smaller than the silver dollar. Since the range wasn't very long, he just shot three rounds with the Barrett. The hole was exactly the size of the fifty-caliber round after three shots.

They all met in the kitchen at seven for breakfast. The morning was spent in preparation with measurements being applied to the model, sniper hides being scouted, and the boats being tested. Spike and Father Tim checked the weather and did some shooting, and Spike was surprised that he scored better than Father Tim with the Sig. Father Tim was significantly better with the M4. The time together gave Spike a chance to find out about why Tim thought someone needed to be in the communications room during the operation.

As they were reloading their magazines for another round with the Sig, Spike said, "Father Tim, I think it would be redundant to have someone monitoring the security cameras from down here during the operation. The Ops Room in Langley will be connected to our comms and have full access to the security cameras. What's the benefit of having someone down here?"

"I don't know. Blust told me we should have someone in here on site. I have a history with Vladimir Zmokinivich, but I don't think that was the point. Maybe he thought he would see me, and that was his reasoning. Or maybe he wanted to keep Jones down here. His reputation is to shoot first and keep shooting. I better check with him before we meet at noon."

"Good idea. Please let Blust know that I think we need everyone above ground to improve our chances."

Father Tim nodded. They finished loading their fourth magazine, slammed one into the pistol and began shooting. The distance was twenty-one feet, and both had incredibly good groupings about the size of a beer can. No strays, and they decided that was enough shooting for now.

Tim headed into the communications room and shut the door. Spike wasn't welcome, so he went down to the dock and watched Capuano in the whaler and McDaniel in the pontoon testing the top speed. Capuano could have run circles around McDaniel. When he spotted Spike, Capuano slowed and swung by the dock to pick him up.

When Spike was aboard, Capuano brought the boat back out into the Gulf. As the weather report had said, the water was calm with just one to two-foot swells. Out in the main Baltic, it would be a little rougher, but for the next few days, it looked calm.

"Do you have charts?" Spike asked.

"One set on each boat, from Saint Petersburg all the way to Kattegat."

"What is the top speed and range of this thing?"

"I looked over the manuals. Top speed is forty-five knots, about fifty miles per hour. At that speed, we could go a little over two hundred miles. At thirty miles per hour, we can go about three hundred and fifty miles. Based on the capacity of the helicopter, we shouldn't need this boat. It's risky, we would be in Russian waters at top speed for about two hours. If we slow down when we are out of Russian waters, we could probably make about two hundred and seventy-five miles."

"If we end up being stuck with this mode of transportation, we'll need the Stingers," Spike said. "Any reason we would want to use the pontoon?"

"No, speed, range, and profile make it a poor choice for leaving."

"How about during the operation, could we use it to change angles for one of the snipers?"

"The water level is below the area where we would be firing. I asked McDaniel to look around for just that. He can tell us more, but I don't think it will work. If McDaniel thinks there's a chance, Marcus can check it out."

"Thanks, Sam. I better get back; Father Tim was checking in with Blust."

Capuano slammed the throttles forward, and the whaler accelerated quickly. Spike was lucky he was holding on. He looked over at Sam and yelled, "Wow, almost lost me there." Sam just shrugged.

When they got to the dock, Sam asked Spike to tie the boat to the dock. As they were stepping off the dock, McDaniel pulled up and tied the pontoon to the end of the dock. The boats were both running well, and neither needed any maintenance.

When Will caught up to Sam and Spike, he asked if he should top off the tanks. Sam said, "There are three big red gas tanks on wheels in the boathouse. Make sure it's normal gas, not diesel, should be labeled."

"I'm on it."

By noon, everyone was ready to talk. Ray Jones brought a plate of sandwiches and a pot of chili into the conference room. He said, "If you didn't eat, grab something. We'll start in five minutes."

They all needed to eat, so it took more like fifteen minutes, but there weren't any big deadlines. Everybody had water or sports drinks, choosing hydration over beer or Coke. As they gathered around the conference table, Jones started asking questions that forced the operators to help plan. Spike was impressed with his leadership style. He was forceful, but Jones was drawing the operators into the plan asking how they could get it better. Eventually, the team built consensus, and several new improvements were put into the plan. The team built on improvements, and they were all certain they could finish the operation in ninety seconds after Zmokinivich was decapitated. If the bodyguards began to fire, the snipers, Capuano and Jones, would take them out. Father Tim, McDaniel, and Spike would secure the survivors and get Fedderov to the helicopter. The survivors would be locked up in the garage and sedated to keep them from communicating with Russian authorities for at least two hours as the team got to Estonia and then into the air to their final destinations. The boat backup plan was put in place, but they all hoped that would be an unnecessary contingency. The helicopter could make it to the airfield in an hour versus three hours in the whaler.

Father Tim explained Blust's concern about the communications center was related to the risk of the connection failing. Blust agreed that the chance of that was less important than having an extra person in the mix. Everyone seemed satisfied. Spike wasn't sure. He made a mental note to follow up with Father Tim.

Spike asked whether Fedderov used advance teams to secure places before he arrived. Nobody had thought about that, but they knew he had done it in foreign countries. Depending on his level of paranoia, it was a possibility the team should consider. They would have to count on eyes in Saint Petersburg to keep track of the security teams to give them advanced notice. It would take at least an hour to get there by car, so they would have a little time to get into place and set up.

They finished the planning session at three. They would reconvene in three hours to make last minute changes and practice the operation. Spike went into the communications room and connected his phone to secure Wi-Fi to check his email drafts. The draft from Shauntel was short and to the point. Blust says RJ can be too aggressive; goal is minimal bloodshed. Spike immediately deleted her draft and typed: Correction, goal is zero of our blood shed.

Spike thought back to his own time in the field. Some guy sitting on Lake Michigan in Sheboygan, Wisconsin, should not be dictating anything to the on-site warriors. Just like in business, the people closest to the action should make tactical decisions. The best leaders set the objective and get out of the way, especially when you have capable team in place. Spike had enough experience to judge the team, and this one was good. Four former Special Forces operators, a ranger and New York City cop, two ten-year CIA veterans. All of them were in excellent physical shape except for Father Tim. For his age, Spike was in good shape, but he wouldn't be able to keep up with the rest if they needed to hike all day. The plan was to use the level of force required. The most dangerous adversary would die at the outset. From there, it was up to the Russians to decide how many more would die. If four bodyguards drew, four would die. The snipers were the advantage, and hopefully, the former Spetsnaz would recognize their tactical disadvantage and surrender.

The walkthrough went as expected. Everyone made minor adjustments for timing. The biggest questions remained location of the bodyguards and whether they went for their weapons. They had discussed the idea of an advance team coming in early to secure the location, but they didn't practice for that scenario. After the walkthrough, they ran the operation three times at real speed under both scenarios—bodyguards surrender or don't surrender. Small adjustments were made each time, and the result was a sixty-second operation for the surrender scenario. Don't surrender, it was ninety-five seconds. Thirty-five seconds for four lives.

They headed into the conference room for a debriefing. They named Surrender as Scenario One, Don't Surrender, Scenario Two. Spike brought up a third scenario in the case that Fedderov sent an advance team. He was starting to be a pest about Scenario Three, and Father Tim said, "Let's attack Three if it comes. It will add a lot of bloody uncertainty, but I think it is safe to say they won't surrender if they use an advance team. It will add two to four targets."

Spike said, "Okay, but everyone needs to think about how we can adapt if it happens."

Jones was responsible for the operation, and he didn't want to delve deeper as a group. "Okay, Scenario Three is unlikely, but Lance and Billy, think through how we could handle it from the sniper perspective. The rest of us will follow your lead if it comes to that."

Billy and Lance glanced at each other and nodded. They went through scenarios one and two again on the model. Everyone knew their tasks and targets. They would have throat mikes and ear buds, so they would be connected throughout. The plan was simple; after killing Zmokinivich, Jackson would take out one of the bodyguards near Fedderov, and Marcus would take out the other. McDaniel and Father Tim would take out the two bodyguards nearest the helicopter. If needed, Capuano and Jones would take out any additional bodyguards near Fedderov. No shot would be less than 90 percent certain, most much closer to 100 percent. The hardest shot would be for Jackson to take a bodyguard about one second after taking out Zmokinivich, but based on the expected angle, it made the most sense. The difficulty would be based where the executives were in relation to the bodyguards.

They all had a couple beers to decompress and told stories about other similar operations. Most of the stories ended with only bad guys down. Spike made a comment about how gamblers only told the story of when they hit an inside straight and won big. Nobody talks about when they left a card game down a thousand dollars. He was careful not to push too hard because, in his experience, a lot of operators were superstitious. Nobody varied to the less successful missions, and none of them bragged about their own part in the mission. It was always about how the team did it. Spike had another Spotted Cow and kept listening. They broke up the party at about ten and headed back to the mansion through the tunnel. On the way, Jackson asked Spike if he liked playing pool. Spike put a pinch of Copenhagen Long Cut into his mouth and said, "I'm not very good, but I like to play."

They went up to the main level game room, and Jackson racked the balls for a game of eight ball. He told Spike he could break. Spike chalked his cue stick and smiled. "You didn't really want to play pool, did you?"

"Not important, but I would like to discuss something."

"Okay, I'll shoot anyway." Spike broke and put the three ball into the corner pocket.

"Here's the deal: I think the odds are pretty good they'll send an advance team, maybe four guys. If I were them, I would have two or three roving the grounds as the chopper comes in. That will move Marcus and me out to a longer shot but not very far. We talked about it during the morning because we need to plan for Scenario Three, which we termed 'Worst Case Scenario.' After I kill Zmokinivich, I'll be targeted by the Rovers. If they are smart, they'll have at least one on the top of the villa or the garage. They will have AK74s, and they'll hose down my position if they see my muzzle flash. Marcus will be covering me for that issue, so he won't be able to take out the bodyguard next to Fedderov." Spike lined up the six ball in the side pocket, made it, which left an easy shot to put the one ball in the corner.

Spike was nodding. "So, you need me, Sam, and Ray to hit the bodyguards near Fedderov." He lined up a bank shot for the five ball but missed.

"Exactly. The thing is, Ray and Sam will be able to get one or two each, but if the Russians don't leave any bodyguards at the helicopter, we'll need to hit four bodyguards, two more rovers on the ground, and somehow get the rover on top of the house or garage. The bodyguards around Fedderov will have Makarov pistols, not a threat to me or Marcus. The rovers will have rifles, a much bigger threat. And the guy with the high ground will be in the best tactical position of all." As he talked, Billy knocked in two balls. When he finished, he surveyed the table planning the rest of his shots.

"Did you talk to Sam about this?"

Before he answered, Billy made a difficult shot that clinched the win. He just needed to make four easy shots before finishing Spike off with the eight ball. Then he continued, "Briefly, but Ray shut the conversation down—he's fairly certain we won't have to worry about this. He thinks Fedderov is over-confident in Saint Petersburg. He's probably right; he has a lot more information than we do. But earlier this week, Fedderov or, more likely, Zmokinivich put an unexpected security team in place in the Moscow mansion. They are paranoid, so I think it is likely they will send an advance team." Billy lined up the next shot and said, "You probably shouldn't have let me start shooting."

"Yeah, whatever. Draw up the plan, get with Sam and Lance to be sure you all know what you're going to do. If we get word a team is coming, we won't have much time to communicate the plan to everyone because you'll need to get to your hides quickly. And we'll need to clean up the mess of seven guys here for the past two days. At breakfast, I'll get them to humor me and move all our gear and garbage into the garage basement." Billy had cleared everything but the eight ball.

"I hope this party is on Friday or Saturday, but from what I know about Fedderov, he likes to celebrate when he makes a big deal, and that's going to happen tomorrow." He lined up the eight ball and finished the game.

"Billy, if we don't draw him out here, the complexity of the mission will increase tenfold. Getting him out of Saint Petersburg alive will be nearly impossible. Let's hope this deal is big enough to make him want to party. Nice game."

"I bet I won an average of a hundred dollars a week when I was at West Point. I used to con people into higher stakes. Makes me feel a little dirty when I think of it," Billy admitted.

"So, you were a pool shark. I'm not surprised. I used to do the same thing with chess until I went to Moscow my Second Class year. Then it was my turn to get swindled. The experience taught me that there is always someone else out there who's better. That's why I look at operations with a pessimistic view. My nagging questions have saved some lives, but it's never popular during the planning phase."

"Let's hope we have Scenario Three covered. I trust Sam. Lance is a shooting machine. I admit, he's better than me, but we agreed that I need to be the one to take out Zmokinivich because it is a sanctioned kill, and I have cover as a CIA employee. He won't have the same level of legal assistance in the investigation later. Congress will want to know what happened if this operation gets exposed. They love to hear war stories and then leak to the press."

"I've never had the pleasure of testifying, but the oversight was starting to get intense after Abu Ghraib. Many of my ops were investigated, but I was able to stay out of the limelight. The oversight and leaking were part of the reason I got out. I loved the missions, but it isn't really worth going to prison. Truth be told, I needed to get out for my family life, but the inconsistent political direction was a pain in the ass."

Billy smiled. "I've stayed single for that reason more than any other. I'm a believer. There is good and evil. We're good. Stuff gets a little gray sometimes, but we're serving the American ideal."

Spike grimaced. "That's why they like academy grads. We study the morality of war and that these missions are part of long-term undeclared wars. The Russians, the Chinese, the Islamists all want to stop the US from being the king of the hill for different reasons. The CIA takes advantage of our clearly defined patriotism and moral compass because we let them."

"Somebody has to do these things, and I love it. This job combines pool and chess. Like eight-ball, angles are incredibly important. Like chess, predicting how the opponent will react and planning several moves in advance wins the game. It is physically and mentally challenging. I don't know what else I would want to do."

Spike laughed. "I did this work until I couldn't do it and keep my family. And then I fell into a great job and an idyllic life in my hometown. I only came back for this one operation because I was uniquely qualified to help, and I'm a believer, too."

They fist bumped and headed up to their rooms. As they separated at the top of the stairs, Spike said, "Make sure Capuano and Marcus know your plan. You could join us in the garage at 5:30; we're going to run."

"I'll be there."

CHAPTER 35

Saint Petersburg
The next day

Jackson brought Marcus and Capuano up to speed during the stretch. He told them to think about it during the run and meet in the conference room after breakfast. Lance did the double run again. Spike, Billy, and Sam went to the gym in the villa's basement for a strength workout. Spike cut it short to swim a mile in the pool before breakfast.

At breakfast, Spike made sure everyone knew they needed to move to the basement of the garage. Everyone saw the logic, so Jones made it into an order and assigned tasks to clean up the villa. It needed to look like it did when they arrived. They also needed to put the wall in place in the garage so the basement was hidden. Spike and Father Tim were assigned that task, and they recruited Will to help because he was as strong as the two of them combined.

The meeting in Saint Petersburg with Fedderov was scheduled for 10 a.m. At eleven, Father Tim and Ray were in the communications room. Blust called to brief them; today was the day. Fedderov's plan was to land around 9 p.m. Sunset would be at 9:23, and he wanted to be on the patio to watch it. Apparently, it was the reason he wanted to come. Otherwise, they could have celebrated in Saint Petersburg. Blust said he was glad he had built the villa on the Gulf of Finland.

A CIA team was watching headquarters and Fedderov's home to track the security team. Nothing seemed unusual. They would be able to tell them who was on the helicopter ahead of time. Fedderov had accepted the invitation in front of his financial guy, his chief operating officer, and Zmokinivich. Fedderov implied that they were all joining him.

The team gathered to work through any details after lunch. Saundra had arrived a few minutes earlier with the two oilmen. The three of them went into the villa and moved into their rooms. The oilmen were in the dark that an operation was going to happen. Saundra had excused herself and joined the team in the conference room. At 2:30, a call came through. Zmokinivich and three bodyguards had left headquarters and were heading west. If they were coming to the villa, they would be here in an hour.

Jones said, "Fuck. This is going to be difficult."

Jackson got very serious very fast. "I got this boss." Jackson told them the entire plan, with Capuano and Marcus chiming in with details. The plan was solid, and as soon as Jackson finished his briefing, he and Marcus left with their gear. Saundra's role was backup, but that may need to change, so she took her silenced SIG Sauer in her briefcase and headed back to the villa.

Saundra would need to meet the advance security team and make sure they were comfortable. There was a significantly less capable security room in the villa basement that the security team would be shown. It had cameras at the gate, in front of the villa, in the entrance, and at the dock. If one of the bodyguards manned the security room, Father Tim would need to disable the cameras from time to time during the day so they would abandon the room. Otherwise, one of the operators would need to be wasted taking that bodyguard out at the onset of the operation. Tactically, having a three AK-74s roving the grounds would be smarter than two plus a guy in the security room.

They waited and were thrilled when it was 4 p.m. and the advance team hadn't arrived. Maybe they had some other mission. At 4:45, a black Mercedes SUV pulled up to the gate. The Sovol advance team called Saundra from the gate. She acted appropriately surprised and said the caterers wouldn't be there for another three hours.

Zmokinivich explained, "This is advance security team. Boris Fedderov is powerful man; we protect him. Assistance and food would be unnecessary."

Saundra said, "Oh, thank goodness. I would hate to disappoint Mr. Fedderov."

From this point forward, the plan was to have zero direct communication between the main house and the operational team. Father Tim and Ray would monitor the movements and conversations from the safe room. The house had listening devices throughout, but cameras were very well hidden. They would switch off all devices that weren't connected to the villa's security room as the team ran through with countermeasure devices to search for electronic surveillance. From Vladimir's point of view, it would look like a rudimentary system. Ray Jones was hoping he would switch it off altogether and not staff the security room in the villa.

McDaniel, Capuano, and Spike quizzed each other on the operation. Finally, they found a cribbage board and played for an hour. Ray came out of the communications room and told them what the advance team was doing. There were four of them including Zmokinivich. They inspected the villa first. They used electronic surveillance detection and eventually disabled the cameras in the security room. All four entered the garage and inspected the upper level maids' quarters. As they left the garage, it appeared like Zmokinivich gave instructions, and then he returned to the villa. The three bodyguards walked the grounds, spending nearly thirty minutes on the rear of the home toward the Gulf. Then they began roaming about the front of the home. Jackson and Marcus were on the other side of the wall of the estate when the bodyguards walked around. The bodyguards inspected the trees closely. One of them got into the SUV and parked on the villa side of the gate and entered the gatehouse. The other two wandered around for a few minutes and headed back into the villa.

It was about 7:30, and the catering van would be showing up soon. They were serving Mediterranean food, and the four women staff members were actually from Mossad. They would be unarmed when they entered, but they would be dangerous if needed.

Zmokinivich was with the oilmen and Saundra in the game room. The oil guys were celebrating already and had had two martinis each. Saundra was nursing a white wine while Zmokinivich drank water. Two bodyguards were instructed to monitor the caterers in the kitchen and, at 8 p.m., secure the helipad. Father Tim and Jones passed along the plan to the team and would help Jackson and Marcus into position while monitoring each advance team member. Now that Zmokinivich was on site and only carrying a Makarov nine-millimeter, they expected that he would come out of the front of the villa as the helicopter approached. Saundra would encourage him to meet the helicopter with her.

The team expected the roving bodyguards to set up in a triangle around the heliport with AK-74s. The big question was whether one of them would take the high ground of the second-floor windows in the maid's quarters over the garage. If so, that would need to be Jackson's second shot. All of those split-second tactical decisions would be made through team-work and communications.

The catering van showed up, and the bodyguard at the gate inspected their vehicle before moving his vehicle to allow them in. He followed them to the garage near the side entrance to the kitchen. The four women began carrying the food into the villa. None of the bodyguards offered to help, so they each made two trips to carry the trays of food to the kitchen. The Mossad agents took a careful inventory of all the weapons at their disposal—knives, pans, and large vases. They used an oven to keep the lamb and moussaka warm while preparing the sauces and salads. The bodyguards watched the food prep and ate some of the lamb and pitas with cucumber sauce.

Sitting in the safe room under the garage, Father Tim mumbled, "The Mossad agents could have drugged them. Damn."

Ray Jones laughed. "Might have looked a little suspicious, don't you think? Plus, drugs make people harder to predict. We know what they'll do, we just don't know where they'll be."

Spike, McDaniel, and Capuano were eating leftover pasta and sausage in the conference room. Due to the shadows along the house, Spike, Jones, and Capuano were dressed in black. McDaniel would be in the grove of apple and pear trees along the east edge of the grounds, so he was dressed in camouflage. Father Tim also wore camouflage as he would be positioned about thirty feet south of McDaniel. They all wore body armor and had throat mikes and ear buds. They would monitor where the bodyguards deployed while waiting to get word of who boarded the helicopter at the Sovol office.

Since it was still light outside, the snipers had used the caterers as a diver-sion to get into their positions. If Father Tim and Jones hadn't been directing them to their positions, they never would have seen them moving on the se-curity cameras. Once Marcus and Jackson were in place and immobile, they were invisible. Marcus set up just east of the garage to cover Jackson and be in place to cover the helipad. Jackson set up in the birch trees about three hundred feet in front of the villa.

The bodyguards came out of the kitchen service entrance directly to the rear hatch of the SUV. They each armed themselves with an AK-74 with two extra magazines. They also had handguns, but the combat rifles were the threat. The team was relieved that all three stayed on ground level. They wandered around a little, but mostly stayed in small designated areas. The helicopter would arrive in fifty-five minutes, and they seemed bored with their task already. The team designated each member of the advance team with a code. Zmokinivich was designated Romeo One. The bodyguard closest to the house was stationed in front of the garage and designated Romeo Two. Three hundred feet south of Romeo Two was Romeo Three at the edge of the birch grove. Romeo Four was about one hundred feet from the grand entrance to the villa. Each of the three were about 150 feet from the center of the helipad. Jackson was about two hundred feet due east of Romeo Three, and Marcus was about fifty feet northeast of Romeo Two. Both had clear shots at all three of the roving bodyguards.

The helicopter at Sovol took off at 8:30 with Fedderov, four bodyguards, two executives and the pilot on board. The CIA watchers didn't notice anything out of the ordinary from other times they had watched Fedderov over the past couple months. Zmokinivich must have given the all clear signal. If they headed directly to the villa, they should arrive at 8:50.

The team in the basement deployed to their designated locations except for Jones. He stayed to monitor the locations of the rovers to help Father Tim and Will McDaniel get into position. They needed to move about four hundred feet from the garage along the east side of the property to be within seventy-five feet of the helipad. Armed with M4s, they would be in a perfect position if the bodyguards decided to fight. Spike and Capuano would have a shorter distance and better cover to get into position in front of the villa behind the four-foot hedge and the fountain between the grand entrance on the garage side. Jones joined Spike and Capuano about ten minutes before the helicopter was due. Their role would be to neutralize the bodyguards with Fedderov and then secure the survivors. Since everyone expected the Romeo team to return fire, it was unlikely that the bodyguards would surrender. The bodyguards' weapons wouldn't be silenced, so Spike was thinking they would need to leave quickly if they got a lot of shots off.

The operators' chatter was mostly about covering Jackson after he took the kill shot on Zmokinivich. Romeo Two, Three, and Four would all turn to fire at Jackson if they spotted him. Jackson would have Romeo Four lined up before Zmokinivich hit the ground. Marcus would need to take Romeo Two and Three. Both were placing the probability of hitting their targets above 95 percent. That left four bodyguards for the other five operators.

The CIA Operations Center was tracking the helicopter. They announced a two-minute ETA as the operators heard the thump-thump of the rotors. The helicopter came in slow and landed smoothly. The engines were killed, and the doors opened. The pilot lingered in the cockpit while two bodyguards emerged from the rear passenger compartment. The two executives exited next followed by Fedderov and two more bodyguards. As Fedderov, two bodyguards, and two executives began moving toward the main entrance, the door opened.

The operators designated the bodyguard walking next to Fedderov as Papa One. The executives were Echo One and Two. The trailing bodyguard was designated Papa Two. Fedderov was Tango. Papa Three and Papa Four were staying with the helicopter. Fedderov's party was moving slowly toward the front door as Fedderov appeared to be turning back to tell the executives a joke. Like most underlings, they laughed loudly at the boss's joke. The front door opened on cue, and Saundra came out first, followed by Zmokinivich. Zmokinivich seemed to look to the left, where Spike, Jones, and Capuano were lined up.

Jones whispered, "Smoke him," as Zmokinivich started reaching for his weapon. Like every operation, this was not how it was supposed to go; Fedderov was short of where they wanted him to be when the action started. Getting Fedderov back to the helicopter seemed possible when Zmokinivich's head exploded. Romeo Four went down a second later. Romeo Two went down at the same time as Romeo Four. The bodyguards all drew their weapons, and before they could find a target, all four were hit with headshots. The communication was crisp.

Jackson, "Romeo One down."

Marcus, "Romeo Two down."

Jackson, "Romeo Four down."

Father Tim, "Papa Four down."

Marcus, "No shot at Romeo Three."

Father Tim, "Pursuing Romeo Three."

Spike, "Papa One down."

McDaniel, "Papa Three down."

Capuano, "Papa Two down."

That just left one threat. Romeo Three saw the muzzle flash from Jackson's shot at Romeo Four. He immediately ran toward Jackson's position while unloading his first thirty-round magazine. The shots were loud, and all the operators looked toward his position. As Romeo Three moved due west, the helicopter prevented Marcus from making the shot. Father Tim ran from his cover toward Romeo Three, firing his M4 on fully automatic. He heard, "McDaniel hit," and a second later, "Pilot down."

Tim knew he had hit Romeo Three several times, and the bodyguard went down, "Romeo Three hit."

He wasn't sure he'd killed Romeo Three due to the body armor the Russians were wearing. Tim dropped down to one knee and dropped his first magazine and put the second into his weapon and recharged it. He changed his angle of approach by moving deeper into the birch grove. As he came up to Romeo Three, Father Tim noticed the AK-74 was about four feet away and out of reach of the enemy, who was on his back writhing in pain. Romeo Three had his Makarov in his left hand and was trying to steady his aim toward Tim. From ten feet away, Father Tim shot him twice in the forehead. "Romeo Three down."

Father Tim ran as fast as he could to Jackson's position. He had been hit in the head and was dead. "Jackson KIA."

Father Tim performed last rites even though Jackson was a Baptist. Father Tim dropped his head when he realized he should have concentrated his fire on Romeo Three. He took out Papa Four first, but he should have known the AK-74 was much more dangerous and that Marcus's angle was impaired. He'd already killed Papa Four when Marcus asked for assistance, but Tim was close enough to see the angles. He looked back toward the helicopter, because he realized he'd heard a loud report from an unsilenced weapon and Marcus's report that McDaniel was hit as he was running after Romeo Three.

Marcus was in the woods where McDaniel had been. McDaniel had killed Papa Three at the same time Tim had killed Papa Four and the reports that Papa One and Papa Two were down. That only left the pilot and three unarmed executives. As Tim jogged back toward McDaniel's position, he saw Papa One and Papa Two were down, and Spike, Jones, and Capuano had black bags over the prisoners' heads and had bound their hands with zip ties.

Father Tim heard Spike say, "Tango, Echo One, Echo Two secure." He looked up to the grand entrance and saw Saundra's face and white blazer splattered with Zmokinivich's blood and brains and the two British oilmen standing next to her, clearly agitatedly, asking her what was going on.

Father Tim approached Marcus, who was trying in vain to administer CPR to McDaniel. He glanced to his left and saw the pilot on the ground with most of his head missing. Marcus had shot him with the M82, and Father Tim realized that the pilot had been armed and must have got a shot off at McDaniel. Marcus had his hand over McDaniel's throat. Blood was oozing through his fingers, and bubbles appeared as he breathed into McDaniel's mouth. Then, Marcus moved to apply chest compressions, and Father Tim knew it wasn't going to help. He put his hand on Marcus's shoulder and said, "Stop."

Then Father Tim said, "McDaniel KIA."

Marcus sat back on his heels and said, "Shit, the pilot..." His voice trailed off.

Father Tim said, "We need to keep moving. Debrief later. Go get the fireworks in the cabinet next to the workbench. Start lighting them off like crazy. It might give us cover for the AK-74 gunfire."

"Did Romeo Three get Jackson?"

"Affirmative. Jones and I will move the bodies into the helicopter."

Jones answered, "Tim, we don't have a pilot."

"We'll have to take the boat." Father Tim grimaced as he realized his decision to shoot Papa Four instead of going after Romeo Three immediately jeopardized their chances of getting out of this alive.

Jones said, "Marcus, fireworks. Spike and Saundra, secure Echo One and Echo Two in maids' quarters, then take Tango to the boat. Capuano, get the Stingers and slickers and fire up the boat. Tim, help Marcus, then escort the oilmen down to the boat. I'll get Jackson to the boat; then Tim and I can come back to get McDaniel. Go! Go! Go!"

CHAPTER 36

Saint Petersburg-Estonia

Ninety seconds later, the fireworks were flying. Nice professional fireworks shot out of a mortar tube. In the dusk, they weren't that impressive, but they were visible and may have provided some coverage for the gunfire. If it weren't for the two lost operators, Lance Marcus would have enjoyed the display. Instead, he was watching the show through teared eyes.

With the activity still happening all around them, Saundra and Spike approached Fedderov. As he lifted him to his feet, Spike said in Russian, "Boris Fedderov, you killed my mother."

Fedderov responded, "Casualty of war, Eastman."

Spike was surprised Fedderov knew who he was. He kneed him in the nuts, lifting Fedderov's feet off the ground. Fedderov went down to his knees, coughing underneath the black hood. Spike grabbed him by the back of his Italian silk suit coat and got him back on his feet. As they started to march him down to the boat, Spike said, "If we don't make it out of Russian waters, you'll suffer drowning in your own blood. That's the best retribution I can give my mother. If we do make it out of Russian waters, we'll torture you for years."

"You know Andrei will never allow that. And your politicians won't allow it either."

"Solokov will disavow you and hope we kill you. Any other Mafiya stooge can run Sovol. You are expendable. Our politicians will never know about this, you idiot."

"Solokov cannot allow me to talk, not with what I know."

Spike thought back to his interrogations of captured Islamists and said, "I suggest you start telling me."

"I will only talk to Oliva or Middleton."

Secretary of State Jonas Middleton was a blueblood from Boston who was always trying to bring Russia out of their dictatorial government and weak economic situation. The Russians thought he was an ally. Middleton figured if he could help Russia create a middle class, they would be a more stable nuclear power and build a democratic republic. Some politicians thought they could solve all problems with democracy. Spike thought they were idiots. Change centuries old cultures by trying to make them more like the United States. Total bullshit.

"Maybe Director Oliva will have a word with you; she actually likes torture. She's a dinosaur that way. It's good to be on her side."

"I only talk to them."

"You can keep saying that, but it will not make it true, asshole."

They arrived at the boat, and Capuano put a lifejacket on Fedderov and secured him to the starboard railing near the rear of the whaler. Spike removed the bag from Fedderov's head and duct taped his mouth with a four-inch piece and then wrapped duct tape from his mouth around the back of his head four times. Mostly for the pain of removing it, he did the same thing to his eyes and then put the bag back on. During the entire time, Saundra just followed along on the opposite side of Fedderov. The sun was down, and they wanted to have the cover of darkness to move out, but speed was more important at this point. While they didn't see anyone observing them, it was unlikely that they would simply leave without being noticed.

Spike asked Capuano, "Do you have any rope?"

"Yeah, there's a fifty-foot line and a hundred-foot line in the side pocket on the port side."

"Don't go all nautical on me—just point."

Capuano pointed at the side pocket on the other side of the boat and, despite the tense situation, laughed out loud and said, "Over there, flyboy."

Both of their smiles disappeared as Jones stepped onto the deck with Jackson in a fireman's carry. Capuano and Spike took him and gently placed him on the floor on the port side. They put a blanket over him, and Spike asked if he could help with McDaniel.

"Yeah, c'mon. It's gonna take some muscle; he was a big fella, and Father Tim is little." Jones grimaced.

Spike nodded and said to Saundra, "Get the oilmen on the boat; we're going to want to leave as quickly as possible. And you look like a mass murderer; clean up and lose the blazer." He turned to Capuano. "Sam, get her a slicker."

As Spike, Jones, and Father Tim slowly moved McDaniel toward the dock, Marcus gathered up the best weapons, both M82s, Romeo Two's AK-74, and McDaniel's M4, and brought them down to the dock. Marcus ran back up to the lower level of the garage and got twenty-five extra rounds for the M82s and five hundred rounds for the M4s. In his SEAL mind, more firepower is better. Good thinking.

Everyone boarded the Whaler, and Capuano fired it up.

The left the dock at about 9:40, and it was almost dark. The sunset had been beautiful, but nobody noticed. Capuano kept the speed down around thirty knots to avoid drawing attention. With the sun down and the wind over the water, the temperature dropped to around forty-five degrees, and everyone put on slickers. They slowed and looked like tourists as they passed Peterhof Palace, gawking and taking selfies with their cell phones. The other tourists in boats didn't pay much attention to them which was the idea. After they passed, Capuano brought the Whaler back up to thirty knots and moved further from shore increasing speed until they were running at fifty knots about a mile and a half from shore.

By ten o'clock, they were beginning to feel safe, and that's when Jones asked if anyone had fired a Stinger before. They were all surprised when both oilmen raised their hands.

Jones looked at them and said, "Huh?"

These guys were probably sixty-five years old but looked to be in relatively good shape. They'd both been drinking, but adrenaline was a big sobering factor. One of them replied, "We helped the CIA once before, in Afghanistan. We taught the mujahedeen to shoot down Russian helicopters with Stingers.

That's how we became friends. I'm Butch; he's Sundance. At least, that was what we told the holy warriors."

"Okay, Butch, we'll stick with that. You get two each." Jones pointed at the Stingers on the floor next to where Capuano was standing driving the boat. "Go get them ready. You might get a chance to shoot down your own Russian helicopters."

Jones looked at Marcus, who was sitting next to him. Like most elite Special Forces operators, he was resting, maybe even sleeping. Jones leaned over and nudged him with his elbow. Marcus opened his left eye and said, "What do you need?"

"Go get the Barretts ready. We are probably better off giving you two of them than letting the rest of us try to hit anything with them," Jones said.

"Yeah, but I've fired Stingers recently, and I think I should give the old duffers some pointers before I do anything else. That will be our best shot if we get visitors."

"Do both at once."

"Aye-aye." Marcus picked up the two M82s and headed toward the bow.

Spike watched him explaining some of the nuances of the more updated Stingers to Butch and Sundance. They were nodding and paying close attention to his instruction. Spike thought, *I'm counting on those three to stop the Russian Navy or Coast Guard if I'm heading home. Whiskey Tango Foxtrot!*

It was getting darker with some clouds covering the waning moon. Dark is better. Spike was wondering if the carnage at the villa had been discovered. He was sitting next to Father Tim and asked him what the plan was for cleaning up.

Father Tim said, "Blust had that covered with some contractors who would dispose of the bodies and clean up with the help of the Mossad catering staff as best as they could under the dark of night. The plan was to drop the Sovol executives off in a Saint Petersburg park in the middle of the night unconscious. When they wake up in the morning, they will likely go directly to Solokov or realize that they are expendable and get out of the country. Either way, by midday, someone would figure it out, and the FSB will tear the villa apart."

They kept waiting to be accosted by the Russians, but as they hit the border of Estonia at about 11:40, they were relieved. Another fifty miles, and they would hit their rendezvous point. Russia would consider them targets anywhere on the Baltic if they knew what the team had done, so they didn't feel totally out of danger.

Spike leaned over and asked Father Tim, "Headed back to the parish now?"

"Yeah, it's where I belong. This mission is for good, but helping my flock is much more fulfilling. I hate losing teammates the most. And I could have been better. In fact, I used to be better."

"Copy that, Father."

Tim said, "Aren't you going to ask me about the whole 'thou shalt not kill' thing?"

"I wouldn't dream of it. I'm more Old Testament than New. The morality of good versus evil overrides the big ten."

"The Catechism isn't as clear on that as you seem to be. Wait, you call the Ten Commandments the 'big ten'?"

Spike smiled. "Yeah, I think it sings better. Plus, you knew what I meant, so it must resonate."

"I'll still have to seek absolution. Not a lot of Catholic priests want to hear this confession."

"Most confessions are probably boring. I think it would be an honor, and you should go to a bishop, at least. Might give you a lighter penance. How many Hail Mary's would you give me for this deal?"

Father Tim laughed. "Probably five plus some community service and a large donation."

"You think Blust is pissed at me?"

"Probably, but given the outcome, all will be forgiven."

They both leaned back and rested. Spike was startled awake by the deceleration of the boat as they approached land. He was headed home with just a scratch in his scalp.

EPILOGUE

Joint Base Andrews, Maryland
The next day

Spike was seated alone for the past hour in a small four-person conference room in the CIA's hangar at Joint Base Andrews in Prince Georges County, Maryland. Father Tim and Lance had been directed to a different conference room when they arrived. Spike was happy that they had coffee and water on the table when he arrived. They brought him a box lunch after five minutes with an egg and bacon sandwich. He'd done some pushups and ab crunches after stretching. It was a good morning so far, but the isolation made Spike think he was being prepped for an interrogation versus a friendly debriefing.

After the rendezvous with a recovery team on the coast of Estonia, the team was whisked by two helicopters to a small airfield where the surviving members of the team split up. Sam Capuano, Ray Jones, Saundra, and Fedderov left almost immediately on a small unmarked private jet. Will McDaniel and Billy Jackson were taken by the recovery team back to the States through Ramstein Air Base in Germany. A larger executive jet landed a few minutes later.

The jet had room for eight passengers, but only five got on. Father Tim, Spike, Lance Marcus, and the two oilmen boarded the plane. There was a twenty-five-year-old staff sergeant crewmember acting as a flight attendant making sure they knew where the water, soft drinks, and beer were. He said, once in flight, they could get up and get their own stuff, but he'd be glad to get them something to get started. All five asked for two beers to get started. Lance and Spike asked for a bottle of water, too. The jet taxied and took off just as the five were seated. Two and a half hours and almost two cases of beer later, the plane landed at Royal Air Force Lakenheath, a US Air Force fighter base in Sussex, England.

Spike connected to the base's Wi-Fi and checked the draft email. The draft Shauntel had left was simple encouragement but no new information. Spike deleted it and typed, *On my way. F knows who I am. Harden in place. No need to go anywhere. Should be home in the afternoon.*

The plane refueled and left the oilmen with a team of MI-6 and CIA agents.

As the plane took off, Spike, Lance, and Father Tim stretched out to take a nap over the Atlantic. They were only told that the destination was Andrews, and they would arrive at 0430 local.

The door to the conference room opened, and Spike looked up to see CIA Director Elizabeth Oliva and Tim Blust entering. Blust looked exhausted, wearing khakis, a button-down blue shirt, and a leather jacket. Oliva looked refreshed dressed in black pants, a light blue silk blouse, and a dark gray blazer; Spike remembered that she always looked good on camera. Even when she was working through a scandal, she kept a cool, professional air. Reporters called her unflappable, her opponents called her cold and uncaring, and people in the company said she was tough but fair. Spike stood to meet them, and Oliva said, "Sit, you've done some things we need to discuss."

Her attempt at intimidating him didn't work, but it did make him curious. He smiled and said, "Thanks for seeing me so quickly. I really wasn't expecting you."

She wasn't going to be friendly. "Two things we need to understand. First, how did you know it was Fedderov? Second, your speculation with Ray Jones about Vladimir Zmokinivich seemed pretty specific. Was it just speculation?"

"Director Oliva, am I friend or foe? What I'm really asking is whether there is any chance that my freedom is at risk?"

"You're a friend, but it is dangerous to have private citizens going to a foreign country, acquiring firepower, and plotting to kill a powerful citizen of that foreign country. You know too much, and only some of that is due to us telling you things. You are going to spend the next few minutes talking to me and Tim, and then you, Tim, and Father Flynn are going to get on a jet to Milwaukee. You'll be home by noon. There is only one thing you can do to change that. If you lie to me, you're going to get interrogated for the next month."

"That's fair, but I would rather take the fifth on the first question."

"Not an option. Let's start there. How did you know it was Fedderov?"

"It was easy; he was the only person in the world who benefitted significantly by hurting the oil and gas industry and also had the means to alter the Russian vaccine and had labs that could create the biological weapon."

"So, you were willing to go to Russia and kill him based on circumstantial evidence?"

"I had some help." Spike put a pinch of tobacco in his mouth.

"Do I have a leak?" Oliva asked.

"Not that I know of."

"So, it was a hack?"

"I'd rather not say. But I might be able to arrange a discussion with someone who could help you close some of your infosec gaps."

"We have ways to find out without your cooperation."

"Tim threatened me, too. I don't like that. I'd rather work on this with you, but I'm not going to do that unless you help me."

Director Oliva sighed. Spike could tell his direct approach was wearing on her. She liked to do things with less clarity. She was starting to get tired of talking to Spike, so he needed to press on. Spike looked her in the eyes and said, "Promise me that my family and friends will not be harmed. You don't have to write anything down; I actually trust you and believe you are committed to the interests of our country and our citizens. Will you promise me in front of Tim that you won't come after us later?"

Oliva looked at Blust. He smiled and shrugged his shoulders. Blust said, "I told you he's smart and can read people better than anyone I've ever met."

Oliva shook her head. She said, "Yes, I promise you that I won't allow you or your family to become targets of our silly oversight committees. I promise you that the CIA won't pursue any charges."

"You missed friends. Steve Gulstone has been on my mind."

"Okay, friends, too."

"That's all I needed. We hacked into your systems and learned Fedderov was the culprit."

"Gulstone didn't do that. Who did?"

"That detail is below your paygrade. Just some kid I know, but I need to convince him to show your guys the way he did it. Again, let's do this together. He's a patriot, but the young people in this country trust the government even less than I do."

"Okay, I trust you, too. And I think I know who it is, but I will let you do this your way. And the speculation about Vladimir Zmokinivich? How did you know he was a plant from Solokov?"

"I didn't, but I assumed that if he was a kill, he was more important than just a Sovol security person."

"You were right, but that wasn't in any files. Tim and I knew. We'd run into him before, but it was somewhat complicated to find out how connected he was to President Solokov. We can't burn that source."

"Fedderov knew my name and that my mom died from MARV. Do you think I'm in danger?"

"I don't think they have resources to hit you in Wisconsin. But if Solokov is behind this, my confidence will go down significantly that you and your family will be safe."

"I know I don't have a need to know, but I'm curious. Would Solokov endorse an operation this risky?"

"I'm not sure. When we learn more from Boris Fedderov, I'll loop you in through Tim."

"Fedderov told me that he'll only talk to you or Middleton."

"Middleton is too naïve to be involved."

"That leaves you."

"He'll be primed for me while I travel to see him. I'm looking forward to hearing why he thought he could attack America and not pay a price."

"Good luck." Spike smiled.

Director Oliva smiled for the first time. She nodded and said, "I'm glad you helped us. Go home. We'll work through Tim on the details, okay?"

"Yes. It was nice to see you."

Without responding, she stood and left Blust and Spike alone in the conference room.